DV8
2375 Wilshire Boulevard
Los Angeles, CA 91523

National Center for Missing & Exploited Children
Charles B. Wang International Children's Building
699 Prince St.
Alexandria, VA 22314

May 9, 2016

To Who It Might Concern:

As per your request, enclosed are all relevant transcripts of recorded meetings, phone calls, email correspondence, raw video footage, edited-for-broadcast video footage, and confessional interviews used in the production (from development up until the glitch) of the reality television show *Waste of Space*. We apologize for the admittedly substandard quality of the transcripts; since you insisted on a rushed—some would say unreasonable—deadline, the task to type them up fell to an untrained intern who seems to have inserted personal commentary and conjecture in certain places. A more objective compilation is forthcoming.

We hope these documents will help you guys with your investigation, though we would be remiss if we did not insist yet again that we officially disavow any responsibility for the incident currently under investigation. Waivers were signed. Parents were informed, or so we thought.

This isn't on us.

Sincerely,
Chazz Young
CEO, DV8 Productions

AUTHOR'S NOTE

UNTRAINED INTERN HERE.

Shortly after my boss wrote the above letter, he instructed me to go down to the post office and mail it, along with the thick packet of documents that accompanied it. On the way, I was to ask his personal courier, Boris, to deliver to the office enough recreational drugs to "stop the heart of an elephant," as the DV8 team was "super stressed." Then it was suggested that, in honor of the people who were giving our company so much trouble, I stop by an Edible Arrangements store to buy a symbolic bouquet of "fruits with sticks up their asses."

I did none of those things. The packet was not mailed. Fruit was not purchased, sarcastically or otherwise. I spoke to Boris, but about a different matter altogether. Drugs were acquired—but only for me, and only in the form of caffeine. The decision to become a whistleblower is not an easy one, and faced with the daunting task of tearing into that packet of documents and learning things I could not unlearn, I needed a pot of freshly brewed courage.

The account that follows is my attempt to ascertain what really happened in January and February of the year 2016—not what was reported in the news, not what was claimed afterward in the statements from all parties involved. The evidence I will present is composed of the files found in the aforementioned packet, plus several additional records unearthed over the course of my investigation (some of which were obtained through measures that were not, I admit, strictly legal). All documents are presented in their original states and are labeled with as much information as I could discern.

The full body of evidence calls to mind a jigsaw puzzle at a yard sale—some pieces are missing, some are bent out of shape, and some don't make sense unless one can see the full picture. The truth may be out there, but I doubt anyone will ever be able to irrefutably prove what it is. All I can hope for is that my version is the closest.

Full disclaimer: Because I personally knew and/or met most of the witnesses, and as I was watching and listening from behind the scenes throughout many of the events described herein, it's inevitable that some of my own judgments and criticisms will leak into this report. But I'll do my best to keep my perspective to a minimum and to interpret the events in an unbiased manner. To that end, I will refrain from telling this story from my point of view, as it is not meant to be a tell-all. From this point forth I'll let the evidence speak for itself.

I am not the story here. I, like each of you, was only a helpless witness.

* * * *

WASTE
OF
SPACE

GINA DAMICO

Houghton Mifflin Harcourt
Boston   New York

www.hmhco.com

Text set in Minion Pro

Library of Congress Cataloging-in-Publication Data is available.

ISBN 978-0-544-63316-2

Manufactured in the United States of America

DOC 10 9 8 7 6 5 4 3 2 1

4500658673

When I accepted an internship at DV8, I knew it wasn't going to lead to a Pulitzer. The network isn't what you'd call "prestigious" or "groundbreaking" or "staffed by literate individuals," but the road to a degree in journalism is fraught with despair, douchebags, and dead ends, and I was aware of and prepared for that. In today's competitive job market (especially in an allegedly dying profession), I was ecstatic to land any internship at all. I vowed to throw myself into the inane, unending errands. I'd cheerfully fire off meaningless tweets, retweets, and "impactful hashtags." I'd withstand indignities and humiliations galore, and after all that, I'd be on my way with six college credits and nary a look back at the eight months of hell I'd had to endure, all in the name of my education.

But then came *Waste of Space*.

And a different type of education presented itself.

—An Intern
July 11, 2016

PART
ONE
PRE-PRODUCTION

DEVELOPMENT

THE YEAR IS 2016.

Things aren't looking good for the future of space exploration. Things aren't looking good for the state of reality programming, either. It is at this intersection of earnestness and stupidity that the idea for *Waste of Space* is born.

Naturally, it involves teenagers.

And so it comes to pass that in the midst of a rare Los Angeles thunderstorm, a dozen shadowy figures meet in the small hours of the morning at a secret and nefarious location: the Denny's off Wilshire Boulevard. They take up two tables, eight urns of coffee, and five carafes of orange juice. The astrophysicists wittily order Moons Over My Hammy. The television executives order nothing.

The following meeting ensues.

Item: Transcript of audio recording
Source: Development meeting
Date: January 4, 2016

[Note: Due to the difficulty in identifying multiple voices,

most speakers have been labeled with their organizations rather than as individuals; this format will be employed in several instances throughout this report.]

DV8: You're okay with us recording this, right?

NASAW: We don't know what "this" is yet.

Waiter: [*off-mike*] Who ordered extra hash browns?

[*thirty seconds of unintelligible chatter, rustling, sound of plates being placed on table and silverware clanging*]

DV8: All right. Now that you've got your breakfasts—

NASAW: Aren't you going to eat?

DV8: We don't have time to eat.

NASAW: Not even a bagel?

DV8: Especially not a bagel, Paleo doesn't—forget it. Back to the matter at hand: our proposal. Chazz?

[*sound of a throat clearing, then a chair scraping across the floor as Chazz Young, CEO of DV8, stands up to address the group*]

Chazz: Ladies and gentlemen of science, I hate to break it to you, but astrophysics isn't cool anymore. Sure, people embrace technology when it allows them to post photos of epic bacon-wrapped food items, but drag them into a planetarium and you'll end up with desperate scratch marks on the walls. Funds have been cut, the man on the moon is several decades in the rearview mirror, and the youth of America continue to respond to the vast and impossibly boundless possibilities of outer space with an emphatic yawn.

NASAW: What about *Cosmic Crusades*? *Cosmic Crusades* is cool.

Chazz: Science fiction is cool. Science is not.

NASAW: But—

Chazz: Example: two different panels at Comic Con, one with the cast of a space-movie franchise and one with genuine astronauts. Which do you think will be better attended?

NASAW: [*unintelligible grumbling*]

Chazz: Exactly. Likewise, we admit, people have grown bored with the repetitive nature of reality television. They can only watch so many bar fighters, spurned lovers, table flippers, bug eaters, bad singers, and cat hoarders before it all seems like stuff they've already seen before. The world is clamoring for something new! Otherwise they'll have to turn off their devices and go read a book, and we simply can't have that.

NASAW: Books aren't bad!

Chazz: Books are the worst.

NASAW: [*unintelligible grumbling*]

Chazz: So. *You* need to drum up interest in the space program, and *we* need more eyes on more screens. Luckily, we've come up with a solution that we feel will be mutually beneficial to both of us.

NASAW: And that is?

Chazz: We want to take a bunch of teenagers and shoot them into space.

[*choking noises*]

Chazz: And put it on television.

NASAW: That's—er—not possible.

Chazz: Why not?

NASAW: Aside from reasons that should be apparent to anyone with a functioning brainstem, it's a logistical nightmare. They'd need to undergo months of training and health assessments. You'd need a ship big enough to accommodate a cast, crew, equipment—

Chazz: Oh, we'll be faking it. The whole thing will be shot on a soundstage. You really think *The Real Housewives of Atlantis* was filmed at the bottom of the ocean? Please. Those women were so full of silicone they would have floated straight to the surface.

NASAW: But we thought this would be a purely educational endeavor. Didn't you say you were from PBS?

Chazz: Yes! We lied. We're from DV8.

NASAW: DV . . . 8?

Chazz: It's a cable television network with several blocks of programming across multiple platforms, including streaming services, our own website, and every social media outlet there is. We'd like to cram all of them full of this.

[*sound of coffee urns shakily hitting the rims of coffee mugs*]

Chazz: Which is why we need you! Our first choice was obviously NASA, but they not-so-politely declined. So the low-rent version of NASA it is!

NASAW: I beg your pardon. We are the National Association for the Study of Astronomy and Weightlessness. We are not some piddling little administration—

Chazz: Which is *exactly* why we'd like you to be consultants. We'll take care of the casting, the production, everything on that end. You, meanwhile, design a convincing spaceplane—

NASAW: [*overlapping*] Spaceship.

Chazz: —you tell us what all the rumbles and beeps and boops are supposed to sound like, and we'll bring in the best special-effects team money can buy.

NASAW: But won't this seem like one big joke? With all due respect to your special effects, not even the major Hollywood movies can get it a hundred percent right. It's going to look silly.

Chazz: People believe what they want to believe. Remember *America's Next Top Murderer*? Viewers thought that victims were *actually* being picked off by a serial killer. The network had to start airing a disclaimer before each episode, saying, "No one's really dying, you morons."

NASAW: Are you serious?

Chazz: Well, I'm paraphrasing.

NASAW: I'm sorry, I'm having a hard time wrapping my head around this. It just doesn't seem necessary. We've got a bunch of new initiatives in the works—

Chazz: *Snore. Yawn. Coma.* Let's be real. Space is passé, and everyone knows it. But you still need a new generation to carry on that galaxy research gobbledygook, or your life's work will be nothing more than a sham, right? [*hearty laughter*] So let's get them excited. Let's take a bunch of young, gullible, energetic, absurdly good-looking teenagers, stuff them into a spaceplane—

NASAW: [*overlapping*] Spaceship.

Chazz: —give them some bullshit training, and tell them they'll be the first ones ever to set foot on Jupiter!

NASAW: You can't set foot on Jupiter. Jupiter is a gas giant.

Chazz: *You're* a gas giant! [*sound of high-fiving*] That's what they'll say. That's what the kids will say. Comedy gold like that.

NASAW: But—

Chazz: Point is, this'll get the youth of America high on space again. Audiences will watch those beautiful idiots floating out there in zero G and want to be *just like them.* They'll buy spacesuits. They'll buy that astronaut ice cream that tastes and looks and feels like Styrofoam. The merchandising possibilities alone are astronomical. Pun intended! [*sound of more high-fives*]

NASAW: Now, you listen here. I've raised teenagers, and if there's one thing I can tell you about them, it's that they do nothing but talk. All day long. On the phone, on the computer, to themselves. How do you expect to get a group of high-schoolers in on a secret like this and not blab thirty seconds later about how lame and fake it is?

Chazz: Easy. We tell them it's real.

[*pause*]

NASAW: You want to trick a group of kids into thinking that they're *actually* being launched into space?

Chazz: Yes.

NASAW: You want them to think that they're *actually* being torn away from their friends and family for months, undertaking a dangerous mission from which they *actually* might not return?

Chazz: Yes. Drama.

NASAW: But isn't that cruel?

Chazz: "Cruel" is such a subjective word . . .

NASAW: Not in this case! The entire proposition is morally questionable! I'm sorry, but we—we can't sign on to do something like this.

Chazz: Fine. Continue your recruiting efforts in the same way you have been. How's that going for you?

[*silence*]

Chazz: Envision with us, for a moment: Plucky kids. Touching backstories. Plaintive piano music. They first set foot in the spaceplane. Their eyes light up. Our intrepit explorers are—

NASAW: Intrepid.

Chazz: Huh?

NASAW: The word you're attempting to use is "intrepid."

Chazz: Pretty sure it's intrepit. Anyway, the mission commences. Lifelong friendships are formed. Bitter fights erupt. Maybe a slap or two. A slap in zero gravity—that's never been done before! [*sound of a pen scribbling in a notebook*] Every eye in America will tune in to check on their new cosmic sweethearts. We'll edit it down to a half hour each week, plus a live segment tacked on at the end of the show so the cast can wave to their furiously jealous friends in real time. We'll air it online, too. Live stream, 24/7. Shove it into viewers' faces until they can't help but get swept up by it. And before you know it, their impressionable young minds will be putty in your hands. They'll sign up in droves to join the *Cosmic Crusades*!

NASAW: That is a fictional movie featuring fictional space heroes.

Chazz: All the more reason to bolster their ranks! Point is, once this show airs, you'll have an entire generation of walking, talking, floating space zombies begging to be a part of it, ready to do your bidding.

[*sound of chairs scraping*]

Chazz: We'll give you some privacy to discuss.

[*rustling*]

NASAW #1: Has it really come to this?

NASAW #2: The worst part is, they're right. We've tried so hard, reached out as much as we can, but we still haven't connected with the voice of today's youth. These . . . *people*, horrible as they are, *do* have the kids' attention.

NASAW #3: It pisses me off! Sitting here across from these plastic, vapid nincompoops, having to listen to this claptrap. We're scientists, for Galileo's sake! People should be looking to *us* as golden gods of knowledge, worshiping *us* for our big brains and thick glasses! Why can't anyone see that?

NASAW #4: I don't know. But something has to be done. Something drastic.

[*commotion*]

Chazz: All right, time's up. What do you say, nerds?

[*long pause*]

NASAW: [*dejected*] When do we get started?

Chazz: Casting begins next week!

CASTING

DESPITE THE ASSUMED GLAMOUR OF IT ALL, THE LOGISTICS OF organizing a nationwide audition are tedious, daunting, and involve more screaming fits than one might think. Hundreds of phone calls, emails, contracts, and location deposits go into the organization of the *Waste of Space* Star Search (pun intended!), and within one breakneck week, all necessary casting and administrative personnel are marshaled and five lucky shopping malls across America are chosen as casting locations.

Thousands of teenagers show up. Each is photographed, given an applicant number, and paraded before a panel of network representatives. Those deemed attractive enough are admitted through to the interview phase, where casting directors interrogate them on the spot.

Not a single interview is recorded. DV8's casting procedures are unconventional at best and impulsive at worst; this is by design, as will be described in the pages ahead. But this particular lack of content may be for the best. Many applicants are desperate, depressed, lonely, and/or starving for attention, the sorts of

17

kids for whom the opportunity to be shot into space would be an improvement to their lives rather than a calamity. The fact that their audition interviews will never see the light of day will be, for many of the applicants in the years to come, a blessing in disguise.

Besides, the evidence that's left is, in some ways, far more enlightening.

———————————

The following is a small compendium of documents featuring the applicants that are eventually chosen as cast members on *Waste of Space*. Not all final cast members are represented in this selection, and not all documents are particularly relevant to the troubles that befall the show, but they are provided here to offer a bit of insight into the curious mindsets of those who would endeavor to audition for this particular reality program in the first place.

Item: Email
From: jamarkuscurbeam@gmail.com
To: a.evans@mit.edu
Date: December 18, 2015

Dear Mr. Evans,

You probably don't remember me, but we met last month at the "Leaders of Tomorrow" luncheon. I'm the one who lost out on the scholarship. No hard feelings, though! For the chair of the MIT Aerospace Engineering program to take note of my academic achievements and flight simulation skills and even go so far as to label me a "future astronaut"—that was reward enough. I am humbled and honored to have met you, and your vote of confidence means more to me than you can ever know.

Thank you again for your consideration. I hope our paths cross again one day—in space!

Item: Transcript of audio recording
Source: Chazz's cell phone voicemail
Date Recorded: January 14, 2016

Hey Uncle Turd,

It's me again. I know you think you can keep blowing me off, but guess what? Circumstances have changed. I think you'll want to pay attention to me this time.

But first, let's talk about how you declined to cast me last summer in *Pantsing with the Stars*—an egregious oversight, I think it's now clear. I wept for the unwatchable drivel that you doomed yourself to produce without my tour de force personality in the mix. I can only assume that your foul, idiotic casting directors were felled by the brain-altering effects of a chlamydia outbreak. How else to explain their insistence on my absence? My appeal is boundless. My charisma is unmatched. My pores are impeccable.

And my middle finger is extended in their direction.

But you've got a chance to make it up to me. I heard about your new show. I want in.

And this time, I think you want me in too. Would be a shame if that video of you and Mom were to end up in Dad's inbox.

Tell me when and where I should show up. Peace OUT.

Item: Post on *Cosmic Crusades* online forum

Username: LadyBalwayGalway
Posted: January 8, 2016

[*excerpt from page 3 of 5*]
. . . and if you freeze the frame at exactly eighty-three minutes and thirty-seven seconds, you can see that the gamma-ray missile that Fekawa Gooe sets up is NOT in fact aimed at the Intragalactic Senate, in fact it's cocked at an angle of 52.6 degrees, which would in fact point it directly at Lord Balway Galway, WHO, if you'll RECALL, stated during the Transnebula Peace Talks that his home planet of Gavinjia was sure to escape the conflict unscathed, so OBVIOUSLY the bombing mission was intended as a wake-up call to prove him wrong and send a TELEKINETIC message that . . .

Item: Online video
Username: the_entropy_within
Posted: January 10, 2016

[*IMAGE: hands strumming a mandolin while words are spoken over the tuneless chords*]
looking up at the sky /
and a thought floats by /
what if the galaxy /
is just a strawberry /
and all the stars we see /
are only flecks of seeds /
that get stuck in your teeth /
and increase carbon emissions /
and line the pockets of corporate America

Item: Social media account
Username: @BacardiParti

[collection of more than 2,000 photos, half of which are unprintable because they are blurry, the other half of which are unprintable because they feature underage nudity]

Informative as these documents are, there are two cast members in particular who warrant closer attention. They will emerge as the most crucial players in this chronicle for a variety of reasons, not the least of which is that they personally provide a substantial volume of information about what occurs during production— both of them by way of personal video diary entries, also known in reality television parlance as "confessionals." A small window into their pre-shooting mental states is provided in the following two documents.

(It's also worth pointing out that both cast members choose to express themselves in the form of dispatches to their parents— symbolically in one case, and literally in the other. This is nothing more than a coincidence, but as their body of work will come to show, the bond between children and their absent parents is a complicated one, to put it mildly.)

The first is a clip from Nico's personal GoPro video camera. Nico rarely captures himself in the frame of these videos; rather, he uses his words as a soundtrack for the often mundane images he is recording, which are mostly of wherever he happens to be at the time.

Item: Transcript of video recording
Source: Nico's camera
Battery charge: 100%
Date: January 16, 2016

[*IMAGE: Nondescript room. From the angle of the camera, it seems that Nico is seated at a large table at the center.*]

Nico: [*voiceover*] Hi Mom. Hi Dad.

Um.

I did something stupid.

[*The camera pans downward under the table, now pointing at his feet. They are rested on a skateboard, which he rolls back and forth.*]

I don't know why I did it. I don't know *how* I did it. A lot of systems had to come together to make it happen. My legs had to push me here, my mouth had to say things, my eyes had to make contact with other eyes, my brain had to formulate thoughts, my hamster-size soul had to blow up to ten times its size and pretend to be a lion. And I can honestly say I don't know how all those things worked in tandem to do what I did.

I auditioned for a reality show.

[*pause*]

Shit.

Saying it out loud makes me feel like throwing up.

[*Nico gets up from the chair. Camera pans to window and holds steady on people walking down the sidewalk—a couple, then a woman pushing a stroller, then two men smoking cigarettes.*]

It was like . . . like I couldn't help myself. I'd heard that they were holding auditions at the Queens Center mall, so

I told Diego that I was going there to see a movie with some friends—which he didn't buy, by the way. "What's wrong with movie theaters in the Bronx? Since when do you have friends in Queens? Why ride the subway for an hour for no reason? Are you out of your mind?"

All fair questions. Especially that last one.

But it was the weekend, and I pointed out that I can do whatever I want with my free time, and he washed his hands of me like he always does, so I went. Just to watch. Just to film the people in line. Figured they'd be an interesting crowd. When I got there, I saw the DV8 banner hanging across the entrance, and I thought, *obviously I would never audition, obviously that is something for the other ninety-nine percent of the teenage population to embarrass themselves with*, but when I went inside . . . I got in line.

Okay, in my defense:

You know how rough I've had it.

You know how miserable I've been.

(I know you don't *really* know. But let's pretend that you actually watch these videos. That for the past couple of years I have not been pouring the contents of my heart into a digital cache that I'd rather chuck under the B train than let anyone see. Let us pretend that the phrase "pathetic delusion" does not figure into any of this.

Because the thought of college feels like a five-ton block of concrete pressing on my back, and the thought of getting a job instead feels like the floor is rushing up to squish me against the ceiling. Like I'm trapped in a dungeon in a video game, with all these moving contraptions of torture trying to flatten me into a splat of pixels. Like no matter what I do, the future is going to crush me.

I wish you were still here. Diego's all right, but legal-guardian-slash-older-brother is not the same as parent. And I don't know why I thought that this show was the answer, but it was something different, a change, an honest-to-God *decision* in a haze of fuzzy, unknowable . . .)

[*Camera pans away from window and focuses on a pair of vending machines in the corner of the room.*]

Anyway. Back to the mall.

The line was so long, it wrapped all the way past the escalators and ended near Macy's. I thought, *obviously I'm not going to give them my name, obviously I'm not going to forge Diego's signature on the waiver, obviously I'm not going to stand in that ridiculous line—*

But the line moved fast, and before I could change my mind, my name was called. They brought me into a vacant store where they had set up screens to make little cubicles, like the kind they use in blood drives. There was a cameraman and an interviewer, a woman with a blouse that was cut so low I could see her bra.

(Sorry for that detail, Mom, but I couldn't *not* notice. It was staring me in the face, and I'm a sixteen-year-old boy.)

(Dad, it was bright turquoise with little rhinestones. You get what I'm saying.)

She asked me all sorts of awful questions, and I answered them. Told her my age, where I'm from, that I'm into skateboarding and shooting videos. To be honest, I don't remember most of what I said, because it all went by so fast, and she kept nodding, so I kept talking—and also, you know, the bra. All I remember is that her face lit up like Yankee Stadium when I told her you were dead, and after that, it all felt like a done deal. That's when the dread started, the feeling that this might actually happen. Like I'd stepped into a pool of sticky tar and it wasn't going to let me go.

I mean that literally. They wouldn't let me go.

They brought me into this break room, told me to wait, and closed the door.

[*Camera pans to door handle. Hand reaches out to jiggle it.*]

Locked.

They ducked their heads in about fifteen minutes ago and said that it shouldn't be much longer, that they'll be reaching a decision soon.

Shit. Shit shit.

I mean, even if I do get cast, it's not like I have no choice in the matter, right?

Obviously I can say no.

Obviously I'm not going to do it.

———————————

The final pre-taping document is another video, this time featuring cast member Titania. She is in a public restroom, aiming her phone camera at the mirror. She looks straight into the lens.

Item: Transcript of video recording
Source: Titania's cell phone
Date: January 17, 2016

Titania: Remember *Trackleton's Guide to the Big Outdoors*? Cute little picture book that you bought for three ninety-nine at the ranger's station. The pages were held together with a plastic coil. It had maps of Washington's hiking regions. And it followed Trackleton, that charming, bearded outdoorsman, as he went on adventures.

His catchphrase was "Keep moving. Keep exploring." Advice so good it became our family motto.

You read it every time we went camping, which added up to a lot of readings over the years. We used to snuggle into our sleeping bags, and you would read it aloud to us by the lantern light, little black specks of bugs giving a shadow puppet performance against the walls of our tent.

[*Titania's reflection smiles.*]

We loved that book. Patrick liked the colorful maps. Nathan liked to chew on the coil. Lily made up songs to go along with the words—remember how you used to tell her to sing quietly so the rest of us could still hear you read? As if that girl would ever stop singing.

[*Her smile fades.*]

I've been thinking a lot about that book lately. About Trackleton's cheery optimism and can-do attitude. I hadn't for years, not since it slipped out of Dad's pack during the hike through the Columbia River Gorge. But after our last trip—*the* trip—it all came rushing back to me. I can't get it out of my head. And I finally realized why.

It had only two rules: Keep moving. Keep exploring. Hard and fast, with no room for error. Don't overthink them, don't second-guess them, and everything will work out.

But life isn't like that at all. Keep moving, and maybe you'll succeed. Or not. Keep exploring, and maybe you'll be happy. Or not. Do both, and they could lead to the best possible outcome.

Or do both, and they could ruin everything.

Keep moving, keep exploring.

I'd always thought it was good advice. The best advice.
But I'm not so sure anymore.

The applicants are impressive enough to warrant this response from Chazz Young, the CEO of DV8, delivered via an all-staff conference call.

Item: Transcript of audio recording
Source: Chazz's cell phone
Date: January 18, 2016

Chazz Young: Hey guys! Chazz here.

So I'd like to bring the entire DV8 family up to speed on our new project. As mentioned at the companywide meeting last week, this project is going to be groundbreaking. It's going to break, like, every ground that's been put there since television started.

So over the past week we've been holding casting sessions in cities around the country, and—hang on a sec, before I go any further, we all need to give up some mad, *mad* props to the publicity department. Thanks to your commercials, press releases, and social media efforts, over *ten thousand* kids came out to audition! That's a lot of hormones to shoot into orbit!

So as usual, we're implementing the classic smash-and-grab casting technique our network has become famous for. Any of you out there who are new to the DV8 family, allow me to elaborate on our patented selection process. Back when we were a tiny fledgling network that didn't know any better, we dragged out the audition process for weeks. We left no stones unturned, no cell phones untapped. We were thoroughly exhaustive in our attempts to pinpoint what potential castmates might do to one another.

But let us recall the season-four finale of *Alaskan Sex Igloo*. We had thought, based on Saffron's tendency to fly off the handle and start stabbing things, that she would break one of the icicles off the ceiling and use it to stab Khaleesi. We spent all season leading up to it, right? With foreboding music? And tasteful close-ups of the icicles? And Saffron's confessional, where she talked about "getting her stab on"? It's *why* we *cast* her. But for all of our efforts, look what happened—she and Khaleesi *hugged* and *cried* and shared a *snow cone*. With *Jared*. Jared was the one who was supposed to be so lonely and ignored that he left the safety of the igloo to seek the loving embrace of a grizzly bear!

But the bears never came. And no one got stabbed.

From that point forward, we decided to take a more hands-off approach. Now, rather than have the whittled-down pool of applicants come in for a final round of casting, we simply go with our gut reactions and finalize the cast based on their original, uncut interviews. In fact, we whisk them directly out of the auditions as soon as their parents or guardians sign the waiver! (Reminder to all employees: any questions from the press that contain the word "kidnapping" should be forwarded straight to the PR department.) And so we are proud to announce that we have already chosen the final ten cast members—only one week after auditions!

We've still applied the standard network reality casting percentages: fifty percent male, fifty percent female; sixty percent white, thirty percent ethnic, ten percent undetermined; balanced dispersal of ages from fourteen to eighteen; plus the four Golden Tokens: gay, foreigner, disabled, and orphan. And as per usual, we'll be throwing all sorts of plot bombs and crazy situations at the poor bastards—*with* the new added twist of a live segment at the end of each episode.

Of course, we'll still leave some things up to chance. Fifteen percent of the editing will be done on the fly, based solely on the relationships and developments that we'll be monitoring closely over the course of each week. Who knows how it'll unfold? Who knows where it'll lead? Who knows what those hyperactive, questionably sane caricatures will throw at us?

I do: *Drama.*

A brief word about Chazz Young, CEO of DV8, walking innuendo, and overall trash barge of a human being.

The word that pops up most often when people attempt to describe Chazz is "exceedingly." He is exceedingly tanned. His teeth are exceedingly white. He is exceedingly self-centered, as evidenced by his initiative to move the human resources department to the basement of DV8 headquarters so his twin puggles could have their own corner office. He is exceedingly arrogant, treating everyone involved in his television productions—cast members, crew, staff, and, yes, interns—as insignificant specks who exist solely to make his star shine more brightly. And he is exceedingly cocky, given the fact that he unilaterally declared himself to be the best candidate for on-air talent. Plenty of talented hosts have presented themselves to DV8 over the years, and although a lucky few manage to grab a sliver of airtime now and then, it's Chazz's vinyl face that you're most likely to see whenever you tune in. Especially when it comes to something as high-profile as *Waste of Space*.

Which calls to mind another of Chazz's qualities: he is exceedingly lazy. He thought that *Waste of Space* was going to be a home run no matter what, and that all he had to do was plug in the numbers to a tried-and-true formula that hadn't failed him yet. But when someone as oblivious as Chazz Young stops seeing people as human beings, he might also stop noticing other details. Smaller details.

Important details.

Item: Transcript of audio recording
Source: Chazz's cell phone
Date: January 11, 2016

Chazz: You nerds there? Ready to get this conference-call party started?

NASAW: We're here.

Chazz: Great. So let's—[*doorbell rings in background*] oh, hang on a sec, everyone. Rock-climbing-wall delivery.

NASAW: You have your own rock-climbing wall?

Chazz: *Two* rock-climbing walls. LA's an earthquake town, it's important to always have a backup—listen, just talk amongst yourselves for a few minutes. I'll be right back.

[*beat*]

NASAW #1: I can't believe we agreed to this. [*sound of papers sifting*] These people are certifiable.

NASAW #2: And irresponsible.

NASAW #3: Don't forget soulless.

NASAW #4: [*sighing*] Well, there's nothing we can do about it now. We signed the papers. We're in this whether we like it or not.

NASAW #2: But look at these emails! They are *hurling* money at this thing. We've been trying to get this sort of funding from the government for years and received nothing—because apparently the money's all wrapped up in television! I called to double-check the budget because I figured it couldn't possibly be correct, but it *is*. The girl on the phone offered to throw in an extra million just because I asked how her day was going!

NASAW #4: How do they have so much money? They're a television network!

NASAW #2: Two words: Chazz Young. I did some research on this guy. Got rich off his daddy's trust fund, then used it to buy a struggling sports channel. He did an extensive overhaul, switched all its programming to trashy reality television, bumped up its online presence, and installed his own in-house production company to develop his own projects.

NASAW #4: What does that mean?

NASAW #2: It means that whenever a ridiculous idea pops into Chazz Young's mind, he has the unlimited budget and power to make it into a show, air it on television, and spread it all over the internet, just like that.

NASAW #3: Let me see those figures. [*sound of coffee being spit across the table*] Jesus Christ! We could buy a brand-new shuttle for that kind of money! Plus fuel!

NASAW #4: I say we round up the lot of these dolts and send *them* into space.

NASAW #2: And I quote: "We will spare no expense on the visuals. None whatsoever." They're teaming up with a company called ImmerseFX—it makes video games or virtual reality or theme park rides, I don't know what the heck it is—to handle the special effects. Which we're supposed to keep quiet about, by the way, since they're trying to pass this thing off as real.

NASAW #4: *Psfff.* Good luck.

NASAW #2: They've reserved the largest soundstage in the New Mexico desert, and they're handing it over to us, keys and all. "Build a spaceplane inside!" they said. "Bounce it up and down! Make as much noise as you want!" The effects people will be out there for a few days to build the thing based on our designs—then after that, it's up to us. All for the purpose of torturing these poor kids with ridiculous pre-written plot points—

NASAW #3: Pre-written? I thought this was a reality show.

NASAW #2: Ha! Reality, my ass. The only thing that's real is the team of video editors they've got on call, ready to craft it into whatever they need it to be, while we get to sit around with our thumbs up our posteriors, shaking a tin can with a bunch of spoiled little fame whores sealed inside.

NASAW #4: But there's a host onboard with them, right? Some form of adult supervision?

NASAW #2: Nope! [*slightly hysterical laughter*] The network people aren't even going to be on set! They said they'd, quote, "rather be shot into the sun than spend three months in that shithole of a desert," so they'll be monitoring everything via live feeds, safe and cool in their air-conditioned offices in Los Angeles, and sending us their instructions. Instructions that, I might add, would be hilarious if they weren't so blisteringly idiotic.

NASAW #4: [*papers sifting*] "Week number one: Asteroid Attack. Will require impacts against the walls of the spaceplane. Week number two: Spinning Out of Control. Will require a rotating video animation to be displayed in the spaceplane's window."

NASAW #2: And there'll be more where that came from! The cameras onboard the ship will record six hours at a time, upload the video files to the main server we'll have on-site, then automatically wipe the memory cards and begin recording again. It's a process that can sustain itself indefinitely without any manual upkeep, which frees up even more time for them to dream up even more foolishness. And then there's the list—the twenty-three-point list!—of consultants who are only a phone call away should we wish to contact them. Industrial Light and Magic, Pixar, a charter helicopter company, the Jim Henson workshop—

NASAW #3: Are you kidding me? Puppets? Do they want aliens?

NASAW #2: They might! They might want aliens!

NASAW #1: Enough. [*sound of a coffee mug pounding the table*] There is a clear path through all this.

NASAW #2: Yeah, right through to the unemployment office. Better get in line.

NASAW #1: You're looking at this from the wrong angle. What we have here, ladies and gentlemen, is an opportunity. A golden opportunity.

[*pause*]

NASAW #2: What are you proposing?

[*sound of coffee being poured*]

NASAW #1: We make their spaceship.

[*sip*]

NASAW #1: We make their show.

[*sip*]

NASAW #1: And then we make history.

PROMOTION

WITH PRE-PRODUCTION WELL UNDER WAY, DV8 SPRINTS HEAD-long into its promotional efforts. Whereas other networks might have planted seeds months in advance, building up a buzz over the course of half a year, DV8 chooses to blitzkrieg the media with a loud, obnoxious in-your-face campaign, bombarding the airwaves with ads and sending an exasperating number of press releases to anyone unlucky enough to have landed in DV8's directory of contacts. A small sample of one such press release is below; there is no need to reprint the full document, for reasons that are plainly evident:

Item: Press release
From: DV8 Productions
To: TMZ
Date: January 20, 2016

HEY TMZ:
WANNA KNOW WHAT IT'S LIKE TO GO TO SPACE?
FIND OUT ON JANUARY 28, ONLY ON DV8!

SPACE SPACE SPACE! SPAAAAAAAAAAAAAAAAAACE!
SPAAAAAAAAAAAAAAAAAAAAA . . .

[*continues for 1576 more characters*]

Ads are slapped onto the surfaces of every public transportation station and vehicle in America. Catch a glimpse at a passing bus in any major city in January 2016, and without a doubt you'd see Chazz Young's face beaming back at you, along with the words: WHAT IF THIS BUS WAS A SPACEPLANE? FIND OUT AT 10 PM EASTERN/7 PM PACIFIC ON JANUARY 28, ONLY ON DV8!

But in person, the man of the hour wisely limits his screen time, choosing to teasingly build an air of mystique around the specifics of the project. Chazz makes his sole promotional appearance on DV8's own late-night talk show, visiting the perennially raunchy Perky Paisley (catchphrase: "My eyes are up here!") to spread the word and, as many sources later claimed, her legs.

Item: Transcript of video recording
Source: *The Perky Paisley Show*
Date: January 21, 2016

[*Chazz emerges from behind a curtain to thunderous applause. He crosses to Perky's desk and takes a seat on the guest couch, a bright red velvet sofa shaped like a pair of lips.*]
 Perky: Welcome, Chazz!
 Chazz: Thanks, Perk. Are those new hair extensions?
 Perky: You bet. Are those newly frosted tips?
 Chazz: I'll frost *your* tips!

Several minutes of heavy flirting later, they discuss the show.

Perky: So what's this new project I'm hearing about? Something space?

Chazz: Yeah. Something *super* space. Ten intrepit explorers, all smokin' hot and in the prime of their lives, risking their futures and dreams and shit for the once-in-a-lifetime opportunity to hop into a rocket and fly to the outer reaches of the galaxy. It's gonna be epic.

Perky: Wow. What a show!

Chazz: It's so much more than a show, Perky. DV8, long at the forefront of cutting-edge reality experiences, has once again innovated the format beyond anything that's been tried before. *Waste of Space* is going to be brought to you in *real time*. We're talking live feeds, streaming 24/7 on DV8.com. And every Thursday episode will end with a *live* segment, coming directly from the spaceplane itself!

[*applause*]

Perky: And is this a competition? Will the participants be vying for a cash prize or a scholarship or something? Are there going to be challenges or games for them to play? Are they going to be eliminated?

Chazz: [*chuckling*] Patience, Perky. I can't give away all my secrets.

Perky: Oh, Chazz, you're so bad. [*giggles*] So the cast members—

Chazz: Please, Perky, let's not refer to them as cast members. Pioneers such as these deserve a far more dignified title.

Perky: Such as?

Chazz: Spacetronauts.

Perky: Fantastic. And I hear this is all being done in conjunction with a space agency, right? Are the Spacetronauts gonna, like, do science while they're up there? Experiments?

Chazz: Yeah. [*saucily raises an eyebrow*] On each other.

[*Crowd hoots and hollers.*]

Perky: I like what I'm hearing! Care to elaborate?

Chazz: All I can say is that we're locking ten angst-ridden teenagers in an area no bigger than a small apartment for an extended period of time. You do the math.

Perky: Chaaaaazz. Are you implying that this will be the first-ever broadcast of hooking up in zero gravity?

Chazz: [*winks at camera*] You'll have to tune in to find out.

Meanwhile, the middle of the New Mexican desert is witnessing an altogether different type of erection.

As DV8's promotional efforts reach a deafening, fevered pitch, NASAW constructs the *Waste of Space* ship, quietly toiling away inside a cavernous workspace. The size of an aircraft hangar, Soundstage G-96 is made of solid steel, is equipped with its own WiFi signal, and, unlike other facilities of its kind, has only one point of entry, making it virtually soundproof.

ImmerseFX makes the eleven-hour drive to the soundstage from Los Angeles and begins construction on the ship, transforming NASAW's conceptual designs into a glistening reality. Visual and physical effects are assembled, and motion simulation mechanics are rigged. Once the basic shell of the ship is up and the controls are tested, ImmerseFX heads back to Los Angeles, leaving the final stage of construction in NASAW's hands.

The chosen Spacetronauts, on the other hand, are enjoying a life of luxury in their fabulous hotel suites . . . which they aren't allowed to leave. Security guards posted outside each room make sure of that. This weeklong solitary confinement gives them time to sort through a bevy of complex emotions, including excitement, apprehension, and scads of self-justification. Here are more accounts from Nico and Titania, which again parallel each other—one feels trapped, while the other is paralyzed by choice:

Item: Transcript of video recording
Source: Nico's camera
Battery charge: 91%
Date: January 20, 2016

[*IMAGE: A dressing room. The camera is pointed at a large mirror bordered by bright light bulbs. Nico's reflection is haphazardly captured in the bottom corner of the frame, along with the wooden director's-style chair he is sitting in, but he is not making direct eye contact with the lens.*]

Nico: Hi Mom. Hi Dad.

I'm doing it.

They cast me. I'm going to be on the show.

It's been . . . a blur. When the producer told me, I freaked out because—well, I didn't *really* want to do it. I didn't think I'd get picked; how does "painfully shy skater kid" scream "compelling television"? So I called Diego, hoping he could get me out of it. I figured if I told him what I did—forged his signature—he'd be mad and tell me to come home and how dare I and all that, and . . . and he *did* say all that, but then we got into a fight about how if I'm going to make my own terrible decisions like an adult would, maybe I should have to live with the terrible consequences like an adult would, so . . . I don't know how it all happened, but by the end I basically called his bluff and said screw you, I'm going to do it. And I hung up and haven't talked to him since.

He sounded so fed up. Like I do this all the time or something, and this was the last straw. Doesn't he know how big that audition was for me, meeting those casting directors? Doesn't he know that sometimes just talking to a teacher or a bus driver or, like, a *girl* takes more courage than I can manage to scrape up in a day? How I had to scale a Mount Everest of terror to even get here?

I guess he doesn't know.

After the audition they put me into a windowless van, drove me straight from the mall to JFK, and flew me out to freaking Los Angeles. I've been in a fancy hotel for a week, soaking in my fancy personal hot tub and wearing a fancy robe—since all I have is the clothes I wore to the mall plus a few new packages of socks and underwear they gave me. I guess we're going to wear jumpsuits or something on the ship. Bet they'll be hideous.

But mostly I've been looking out my window at the beach. It's so bright. Sunny. The Pacific Ocean is . . . I never thought I'd see something like that. Little blue crystals stretching out for miles, for—ever.

How can that be the same substance that makes up the East River?

About an hour ago the producers picked me up and drove me—in a windowless van again—to the DV8 studios, and now I'm waiting in this green room, getting ready to be interviewed. Can you hear that?

[*There are muffled voices in the background.*]

I think some of the other kids are in the rooms next to me. We're not supposed to meet until the first day of shooting, tomorrow, so we have to be isolated, but I can still hear them. There's a girl yelling at a producer about needing more hair spray. And there's a guy who I think is snorting like a pig—

[*There is a knock at the door. The camera pans away from the mirror to a pair of headsetted DV8 employees peeking into the doorway.*]

DV8 #1: Are you all right in here? Need anything?

Nico: Um—

DV8 #1: Speak up, please.

Nico: Uh, water, maybe?

DV8 #1: No can do, buddy. Dehydration ups the drama.

Nico: Oh.

DV8 #1: You're on in five. Try to stop sweating, it'll mess with the lights.

[*They leave.*]

Nico: [*under his breath*] How do you command yourself to stop sweating?

[*DV8 #2 reappears in the doorway with a bottle of water in hand and tosses it to Nico.*]

DV8 #2: Here. Don't tell anyone.

Nico: Thanks.

[*DV8 #2 leaves. To open the water bottle, Nico sets down the camera; it is now pointed at the door.*]

[*He takes an audible gulp of water, then a deep breath.*]

Guys. I'm terrified.

[*another gulp*]

But you know what the weird thing is? I'm also kind of . . . excited?

I don't know. It's the same spazoid feeling that drove me to the mall in the first place. Like something inside is hitting the override button, some little voice urging me to do something spontaneous and stupid.

I know, this all sounds like bullshit.

I'm just—

I'm tired of trying to find my place in the world. Maybe from hundreds of miles above the planet I can look down and figure out where I should look next.

In the green room down the hall, Titania records the following video on her phone.

Item: Transcript of video recording
Source: Titania's cell phone
Date: January 20, 2016

[*Titania is also sitting in front of a mirror and aiming the phone's camera at it; unlike Nico, she is looking directly into the shot.*]

Titania: You want me to explain the canoe? I'll explain the canoe.

I know it was hard for you to understand why it held so much meaning for me. Why I had to chop down that tree and carve a boat out of it, because, honestly, who does that?

After our last trip—*the* trip—I needed something big in my life. Everything had become so small, so shrunken—all concentrated and compressed into the size of a particle, like the Big Bang in reverse. The Big Shrink. I'd get up in the morning, and when I stretched out my arms, it felt like my fists were banging into an invisible barrier, a bubble around my bed.

It was suffocating. I couldn't breathe.

Enter: the tree. Hacking at its core, breathing the dust of it, wood splintering into my fingers, bending and shaping a force of nature to my will—the bubble finally got bigger. I had dominion over something. My world had expanded again. I'd kept moving, kept exploring.

And now—

[*There is a knock at the door, along with a producer saying, "Titania? It's time."*]

[*Titania gives the camera a small smile.*]

Now it's about to expand even more.

On January 21, 2016, the world gets its first look at the cast members of *Waste of Space* in a special twelve-minute promo that airs during DV8's Thursday-night prime-time lineup. Though the airtime is limited to roughly one minute per cast member, their first impressions speak volumes, making #WasteOfSpace the number one trending topic and launching infinite online buzz the following day.

Reprinted here is the full transcript of the spot, plus all onscreen captions. Physical descriptions are provided where appropriate.

[A note about format from this point forth: The transcripts of scenes that were officially broadcast on television will be denoted by camera icons and clearly defined borders spanning the duration of each clip. This is for the purpose of making on-air content more easily identifiable—and to provide a distinctive contrast to the discarded footage. As the body of evidence will come to show, there are many discrepancies between what made it onto the airwaves and the unaired, raw footage that never saw the light of day.]

■◄ ··············· **ON-AIR** ····················

Item: Transcript of video package
Source: *Waste of Space* Promo #1
Date: January 21, 2016

Chazz Young: [*in voiceover, during the rolling credits of the preceding show,* So You Think You Can Pole Dance] What uuuup, DV8 nation? Chazz Young here, getting ready to take you into another hour of *Forever 21 Fitting Room Surveillance Camera Idol,* but first—a totally bitchin' sneak peek at the cast of our groundbreaking new reality show, *Waste of Space*! I recently got the chance to chat with the incoming Spacetronauts, and they did *not* disappoint. Our ten intrepid explorers dished about their upcoming mission in these exclusive interviews you won't see anywhere else! So let's meet the hottest, sexiest new heroes of the universe—and be sure to tune in to the premiere next Thursday night as we launch them into space! It's *literally* gonna be out of this world!

[*CUT TO: Stock footage of things in space: planets, stars, comets, the moon landing, a still photo of a UFO*]

Chazz: [*voiceover*] Two hundred miles above the Earth . . .
Ten strangers . . .
One spaceplane . . .
INFINITE ADVENTURES!

[*CUT TO: Stock video of a swirling wormhole, out of which emerges a series of shots of Chazz and his interviewees standing against a backdrop digitally altered to look like the night sky*]

[*Note: All onscreen captions <u>underlined</u>*]

[*CUT TO: Bottle-bronzed girl with black bird's-nest hair, heavy mascara, and purple lipstick*]

<u>**Bacardi**</u>
<u>**The Party Girl**</u>

Bacardi: Wooooooo!

Chazz: Well aren't you a bundle of—

Bacardi: WoooooOOOOOOO!

Chazz: *Love* your energy! And—oh yes, *very* nice twerking skills. Do you take off your top like that all the time?

Bacardi: *All* the time. [*slurring words*] See my bra? It's got, like, space and shit on it.

Chazz: It does! Are they real constellations?

Bacardi: Who the hell knows?

Chazz: Certainly not me!

[*They high-five.*]

Chazz: So what are you, ethnically speaking?

Bacardi: One hundred percent party animal, bitch! Woooooo!

Chazz: Woooo! [*laughs*] No, but you look very exotic. Are you Italian? Latina? Pacific Islander?

Bacardi: They asked the same thing at my audition, and you know what I said? I said, "Put me on your show and I can be whatever you want me to be."

Chazz: Great answer. And do you have any daddy issues?

Bacardi: Tons!

Chazz: *Perfect.* So if you could bring only one item with you into outer space, what would it be?

Bacardi: Uh . . . my space bra!

Chazz: Hot!

Bacardi: [*directly addressing the camera*] And I've got more where that came from, America. [*moves hand down torso*] Betcha can't wait to see my black hole . . .

[*CUT TO: Husky redheaded boy in denim overalls caked with dirt*]

Snout
The Hick

Chazz: So you're from—

Snout: Coon Rapids, Iowa!

Chazz: Tight! So tell me, if you could steal the yacht of any celebrity, who would— Wait. I'm sorry. *What* is that smell?

Snout: Which smell, sir? You'll have to be more specific. Are you asking about the smell coming from my shoes? Or the one coming from my pants?

Chazz: I don't—

Snout: My hat? Because it's a funny story about the hat. Seems ole Colonel Bacon managed to wriggle out of his pen and get himself tangled up in an onion patch, and—well, here's a bit of trivia here for ya, sir: they don't make diarrhea medication for pigs.

Chazz: They don't?

Snout: [*sighs*] Not like they used to.

Chazz: [*tries to leave shot, is nudged back by producers*]

Okay. Gross. So if you could bring only one item with you into outer space, what would you bring?

Snout: Oh, sir. I'm not going anywhere without Colonel Bacon.

Chazz: And Colonel Bacon is . . .

Snout: My pig! [*bends down to pick up a pig the size of a border collie, straightens up, and hugs it to his chest*] Been rearing him since he was just a shoat!

Chazz: And he goes wherever you go?

Snout: Shoot, we've never even left Iowa until I came to audition for this here show! There's a great big world out there, and we wanna see it!

Chazz: That's the spirit.

Snout: Also, my tractor was abducted by aliens once. And I've got some *pretty* pressing follow-up questions.

[*CUT TO: Petite girl with hands folded, looking worried but keeping calm*]

Kaoru
The Foreigner

[*NOTE: Kaoru speaks only in Japanese. Subtitles are never displayed in the* Waste of Space *broadcasts, so an English translation is provided here, notated with {brackets}.*]

Chazz: What kind of music do you listen to?

Kaoru: {I am confused about what is happening.}

Chazz: I haven't heard of them! They must be huge overseas.

Kaoru: {Is this a television show?}

Chazz: Why, thank you! I *have* recently joined a CrossFit! Thank God for kettlebells, right?

Kaoru: {I see a lot of space things. Are you sending me into space?}

Chazz: Totally!

Kaoru: {Please do not send me into space.}

Chazz: Right on, girl! *Domo arigato!*

[*CUT TO: Well-built boy who looks like an action figure and smiles like a model*]

Jamarkus
The Black Gay Astronaut

Chazz: Well, you're just a diversity jackpot, aren't you?

Jamarkus: Excuse me?

Chazz: First, let's chat about your academic background. You're a smart one, I hear!

Jamarkus: Thanks! I am the captain of my school's Math Team. And its Science Squad. I was a finalist for the National Aeronautic Scholarship. And I've already been accepted to MIT, though I'm still trying to figure out a way to pay the tuition.

Chazz: So you know things about space?

Jamarkus: I sure do. And I can't wait to get up there! It's a dream come true!

Chazz: So *Jamarkus knows things about space.* It'll be nice for your fellow planemates to have a resident expert they can trust up there. Sometimes textbooks and training and "airtight scientific principles" might turn out to be vastly different from what you'll find in the field. I hope our viewers remember that too. Keep an open mind, America! Space can be unpredictable! Right, buddy?

Jamarkus: Uh, yeah. Right.

Chazz: So, you're gay, too? Are you sassy? Gonna be bringing a lot of sass?

Jamarkus: I wouldn't call myself a sassy person, no—

Chazz: Gonna be telling it like it is?

Jamarkus: This is bordering on offensive—

Chazz: *There's* the sass!

Jamarkus: I wasn't—

Chazz: But space, huh? Isn't it the best?

Jamarkus: Space *is* the best.

Chazz: Aaaand a big smile into the camera!

[*Jamarkus smiles into the camera. A sparkling twinkle is digitally superimposed over his teeth.*]

[*CUT TO: Frizzy-haired girl wearing a patchwork vest and pleated pants*]

Louise
The Nerd

Chazz: Pleated pants, huh? That's a choice that you made?

Louise: What?

Chazz: So! If you could bring only one item with you into outer space, what would you bring?

Louise: My FTL jump drive.

Chazz: And what is that?

Louise: It's a device that allows for faster-than-light interstellar travel. So far all I've been able to do with it is lightly toast English muffins, but I'm confident that a breakthrough is right around the corner.

Chazz: [*looking disgusted*] Jump drive? Is that from a movie or something? [*more disgusted*] A nerd movie?

Louise: Um . . . [*looking squirrelly*] . . . no.

Chazz: Phew! Then what kind of movies *do* you like?

Louise: Oh, I guess I've always had a soft spot for *The Fast and the Furious.*

Chazz: *Really?* That's my favorite!

Louise: It's just so . . .

Chazz: I can't even . . .

Louise: And I'm just like . . .

Chazz: Right? *Right?*

Louise: Exactly. Exactly.

Chazz: Can I just tell you how refreshing this is? So many of the applicants to this show were like, *Interstellar Battle* this, and *Galactic Bullshit* that. There was this one girl who stalked the audition team to multiple cities, dressing up in different *Cosmic Crusades* costumes! Can you believe that?

Louise: No way!

Chazz: Where would a teenager get the money and time off from school for that?

Louise: Maybe she's homeschooled. And maybe she wants it really, really bad. So bad she'd be willing to lie about her favorite movie to get in, if that's what she thought the network wanted to hear.

Chazz: Thank *you,* at least, for being honest.

Louise: You're welcome!

[*CUT TO: Boy with a pierced lip in ripped jeans and a T-shirt, having difficulty making eye contact*]

Nico
The Orphan

Chazz: So, Nico! Where are you from?

Nico: New York.

Chazz: Oh. Right, but where are you *originally* from?

Nico: The Bronx.

Chazz: [*impatiently*] And your parents came to the Bronx from . . .

Nico: Ecuador.

Chazz: *There* it is! I'm so sorry, by the way, about their passing.

Nico: [*to the floor*] Thanks.

Chazz: What was that?

Nico: I said thanks.

Chazz: You're going to have to speak up if you want to be heard over your fellow planemates. Lots of larger-than-life personalities onboard. One-word answers aren't going to cut it.

Nico: Okay.

[*Chazz waits for him to say more, then makes a noise of impatience.*]

Chazz: So what's the one item you'd like to bring to space?

Nico: My video camera.

Chazz: Bro, seriously? With all the opportunities for expressing yourself onboard—the confessional camera, the live broadcasts, conversations with your fellow planemates?

Nico: Yes.

Chazz: Yes, because . . .

Nico: I like having it.

Chazz: That's not a real answer. Come on, speak up! Why would you possibly need to bring your own camera?

Nico: I imagine there'll be extensive litigation at some point—

Chazz: [*interrupting nervously*] Whoa, whoa, whoa. What are you doing?

51

Nico: You told me to talk more.

Chazz: [*with a hollow laugh*] You know what? The limelight isn't for everyone. You be as shy as you want, bro.

Nico: [*looking back at the ground*] Okay.

[*CUT TO: Girl with large plastic-framed glasses, a headband, a fedora over the headband, and headphones over the fedora*]

Hibiscus
The Musician

Chazz: And what are *you* doing? Hey, can you hear me? I've started talking.

Hibiscus: Oh, sorry. [*takes off headphones*]

Chazz: What are you listening to?

Hibiscus: You've never heard of them.

Chazz: All right. What's that in your hand? What are you drinking?

Hibiscus: [*sips from a terracotta mug*] Artisanal mud tea.

Chazz: What's mud tea?

Hibiscus: It's silt from the bottom of a top-secret bog in Manitoba, Canada. Steeped in water from that very same bog.

Chazz: What does it taste like?

Hibiscus: Socialism.

Chazz: Great. So if you could bring only one thing into space, what would it be?

Hibiscus: My mandolin. Oh, and plenty of locally sourced mushrooms.

Chazz: For eating, or for . . . recreational use?

Hibiscus: Both. And a third thing that's illegal in forty states, according to The Man.

Chazz: And which man is that?

Hibiscus: [*with a snort*] You wouldn't understand.

[*CUT TO: Befuddled-looking boy in a Pretzel Shed employee uniform*]

Matt
The Disabled Hero

Chazz: So, I don't want to be insensitive here. In fact, I want to be as sensitive as humanly possible. I know it must be difficult to discuss your disability with a complete stranger—and with *all* of *America*—but I've always found that honesty is the best way to heal. So, if you're comfortable, please: share with us.

Matt: Share what now?

Chazz: Your devastating injury.

Matt: Um. Are you talking about my finger? [*He holds up his right hand; his middle finger ends in a stump below the first joint*] It got caught in my stroller when I was a baby—I'm sorry, were you expecting someone else? [*He tries to leave, is blocked by a security guard.*] I think there's been a mistake—

Chazz: No mistake! Get back here—carefully, no rush, don't hurt yourself. Now. As painful as it may be, can you find the courage to tell us more about your daily hardships?

Matt: I . . . don't really have any.

Chazz: I know it's hard to talk about. But try.

Matt: Uh—I can't flip anyone off?

Chazz: Tragic. Tragic.

Matt: Listen, I don't know why I'm here. I was on break from my job at the mall, and I was waiting for my burrito in the food court, and when they called my order number, these two shadowy figures took my food and held it hostage until I agreed to come with them—

Chazz: Oh, I'm *so* sorry about that. Those were our friendly casting directors—guys, where's this brave young man's burrito? [*gestures offscreen*] Here we go! [*presents him with a burrito*] I hope hunger doesn't aggravate your disability?

Matt: [*takes bite*] What disability?

Chazz: Your . . . finger stump.

Matt: Oh, I wouldn't call it a disa—

Chazz: No, it counts! [*at camera, insistent*] It totally counts!

Matt: Counts toward what?

Chazz: So! If you could bring only one item with you—

Matt: [*overlapping*] With me where?

Chazz: —what would it be?

Matt: [*shrugging and chewing*] Mmm. Probably this burrito.

Chazz: Tight! And last but not least, why do you want to go to space?

Matt: *Space?*

[*CUT TO: Pointy-jawed boy with impeccably groomed eyebrows, a permanent sneer, and eyes that were made for rolling*]

Clayton
The Rich Kid

Chazz: So if you were a smartphone app, what kind of smartphone app would you be?

Clayton: I'm not doing this.

Chazz: Doing what?

Clayton: This interview. It's stupid. The show hasn't premiered yet.

Chazz: But we're interviewing all the Spacetronauts. If you're going to be on the show, you have to give an interview.

Clayton: Are you this bossy in the bedroom, Chazz? Or should I just ask my mom—

Chazz: So! Why do you want to go into space?

Clayton: Because I can. *Uncle.*

Chazz: [*talking over him*] Ha! No, no, no. It's because . . . [*reading from offscreen cue card*] because you're a well-rounded, deserving individual who has received no special treatment and has not violated any eligibility clauses prohibiting the casting of family members of individuals who are employed in any capacity at this network.

Clayton: That's right. [*waves at camera*] Hi, Mom.

Chazz: So! Are you looking forward to meeting your fellow Spacetronauts?

Clayton: Not really. They're only going to get in my way.

Chazz: That's not very sociable.

Clayton: Who gives a flying [*beep*]? I'm not here to make friends.

Chazz: You won't have much of a choice, all cooped up in a tiny spaceplane.

Clayton: Then I'll just have to make some enemies, won't I?

Chazz: That's right. That's exactly right. [*smiles maniacally*] So! If you could bring only one item with you into outer space, what would you bring?

Clayton: It's a secret.

Chazz: Well . . . can you tell us what you might do with it?

Clayton: I've heard a rumor that in space, no one can hear you scream. [*smirks at the camera*] I'd like to disprove that.

[*CUT TO: Girl with bleached hair about three inches long on top and buzz cut on the sides, wearing a cargo-pocketed canvas dress over cargo-pocketed pants*]

Titania
The Tomboy

Chazz: What do you like to do for fun?

Titania: Build things.

Chazz: Like what?

Titania: Tables. Bookcases. Last summer I carved a ten-foot canoe out of a cedar log.

Chazz: Wow! What'd you do with it?

Titania: Tried to canoe.

Chazz: Tried? What happened, did your boat spring a leak?

Titania: No, the boat was fine. Border Patrol was less forgiving.

Chazz: Ha! Have we got a fugitive on our hands? [*to an offscreen producer*] Wait, do we? [*after most likely being given the signal to keep talking*] So why do you want to go into space? Let me guess: you want to fill all those pockets with space rocks!

Titania: There are literally hundreds of reasons that make more sense than that.

Chazz: Name them!

Titania: To expand human knowledge. To search for something greater than ourselves. To experience absolute silence.

Chazz: So that's why you want to go to space? To explore?

Titania: Yes.

[*more to herself*]

I have to keep exploring.

[*CUT TO: Stock video of swirling wormhole*]

Chazz: [*voiceover*] DV8's revolutionary new series will SUUUUCK . . . YOOOOOU . . . INNNNN. Tune in each week for an exhilarating new episode, followed by a LIVE segment at the end of each show! PLUS, be sure to check out DV8.com for a twenty-four-hour LIVE feed of the cast, LIVE onboard the spaceplane! Don't miss a single second as the world stays glued to the screen, millions of viewers across the globe all asking one question:

WHO

WILL

GET

WASTED?

OFF–AIR

PART TWO

PRODUCTION

THE PREMIERE EPISODE OF *WASTE OF SPACE* IS SCHEDULED FOR Thursday, January 28; the launch is set to be broadcast live on both DV8 and DV8's website. One would think that the conspicuous absence of any other relevant parties—such as the national news outlets or, say, NASA—would tip off audiences that what they are watching is not real, but the list of daft notions that Americans have happily entertained includes, but is not limited to: sharknados, dinocrocs, piranhacondas, and palatable fat-free cheese. By the time *Waste of Space* came along, the concept of starfaring teenagers took no stretch of the imagination.

The night before the launch, the Spacetronauts are told that DV8 producers will arrive at 5:30 a.m. to pick them up, confiscate their phones, and drive them to the launch site. The ungodly hour is by design. It's DV8's hope that with such an early start, the kids will be more likely to roll out of bed and into the producers' waiting hands and less likely to wait, fidget, glare at the hideous art displayed in their respective hotel rooms, wallow in self-doubt, second-guess their decision, and drop out of the show at the last minute.

Some do sleep until they have to leave. But others get up early, taking advantage of the last opportunity to privately document their feelings before their connection to the outside world is severed.

Item: Post on *Cosmic Crusades* online forum
Username: LadyBalwayGalway
Date: January 28, 2016

[excerpt from page 4 of 4]

... and so it is with a heavy heart that I bid you *rega kegof*, my fellow Aurekalians. I go now into the depths of an adventure so profound and so pure that whilst I am in the midst of it, I shan't have time to dispatch any missives to you, my loyal squadron. But! Rest assured that my days and nights will be filled with the noblest of planetary pursuits— and rest assured, should I be blessed with the good fortune to chance upon the Lord Balway Galway, I'll deliver the message of support that we so laboriously crafted during last week's Federal Summit Group Text. I look forward to our future rendezvous on Kafaldhia, and to sharing tales of my thrilling exploits and daring escapes should I survive this perilous journey.

Watch me on DV8 tonight at 10 p.m. Eastern/7 p.m. Pacific!

Item: Transcript of video recording
Source: Nico's camera
Battery charge: 100%
Date: January 28, 2016

[*The camera is sitting on the hotel room bed, aimed at a Nike backpack personalized with the word "Nico."*]

Hi Mom. Hi Dad.

It's really happening.

It's really happening it's really happening.

Like the new bag? The DV8 people gave it to me yesterday, told me to fill it with my one personal item, plus the socks and underwear they gave me. I asked how many days I should pack for. They said, "A lifetime of fun!"

They also told me that my one personal item couldn't be this camera, but one of them stuck up for me—the nice one who gave me the bottled water—and said I should be able to, if it's my one and only choice. So they checked it out and finally gave their approval because it's one of the cheaper models that doesn't have a WiFi connection.

I don't know why that would matter. I don't think there are too many WiFi hotspots beyond the troposphere. And it's not like I can charge it onboard. As soon as I unplug it from this wall, the countdown begins. It'll only last for as long as the battery holds out.

They said they'll put my skateboard in safekeeping, that I can pick it up when I get back.

From space.

[*He takes a deep breath.*]

I got up in the middle of the night and threw up. I did it again this morning.

My nerves are fried.

I can't believe I did this. Am doing this.

I called Diego last night. It was awkward. He said, are you sure you want to do this? I said I wasn't. I asked, do you think I should do this? He said he didn't know. We made zero progress. We came to zero conclusions. He said good luck, and I said goodbye.

[*Nico picks up the camera. The shot is wobbly.*]

God, look how shaky my hands are. Talking about it is making me more nervous.

I have to stop. I'll do another one of these once I'm . . . there.

I wish you were here. A producer told me that the g-forces I'm going to experience during takeoff will be the strongest pull I've ever felt, but I can think of a stronger one.

Item: Transcript of audio recording
Source: 911 call log
Date: January 28, 2016

911 Operator: 911, what is your emergency?

Matt: Yeah, hi. Um, I think I've been kidnapped by a television network.

911 Operator: Can you repeat that, sir?

Matt: They're going to shoot me into space, I think? Without my consent? And I'm not a "sir," I'm only sixteen—

911 Operator: And you said you're on television?

Matt: Not yet. Tonight, maybe? They won't tell me anything. They haven't let me leave this hotel room for days! I'm on a high floor and I can see the ocean and it's scenic and beautiful but I can't appreciate it right now because I'm a little preoccupied about being *forced into aeronautic labor*—

911 Operator: Kid, prank-calling 911 is a federal offense.

Matt: No, wait! Please don't hang—

[*end of call*]

Item: Transcript of video recording
Source: Titania's cell phone
Date: January 28, 2016

So why space? What with our family's pursuits always being so nature- and Trackleton- and earth-centric and all. Closest I've ever gotten were those little plastic glow-in-the-dark stars on my bedroom ceiling. So why this show?

Because there's no sound in space.

No screaming. No beeping.

According to the laws of astrophysics, everyone has to shut the hell up.

Item: Social media post
Username: @BacardiParti
Date: January 28, 2016

[*selfie of Bacardi with both tongue and middle finger extended*]

Caption: KISS MY ASTRONAUT, BITCHAZ!

———————————————

At 5:30 a.m., ten windowless vans pull into the hotel parking lot. The kids are led down to the lobby, one by one, and loaded into their transports.

They won't see the sun again until they're hurtling toward it at eighteen thousand miles per hour.

EPISODE #1

Item: Transcript of video broadcast
Source: *Waste of Space,* **Episode #1**
Date aired: January 28, 2016

ON–AIR

[*START OF ACT ONE*]

[*A spotlight points at an empty stage. An image shimmers into being: Chazz Young, dressed in a sequined black tuxedo.*]

Chazz: Good evening, America.

Once every few centuries or so, a generation gets the chance to do something big. Something meaningful. Something that will have a profound impact on the universe as we know it. Our parents, grandparents, great-grandparents—all worthless losers, with nothing to show for their miserable lives but the Great Depression and something called the cotton gin. Great job there. You can't drink cotton, morons.

And so for decades we've been waiting. Waiting for our chance. Waiting for the stars to align and for God to point down his wrinkly old-man finger and bestow upon us a new beacon of hope. For years we've toiled in utter misery, with no reprieve from the drudgery of everyday life except for our phones and the emojis that deliver us pizza. Our lives have become empty. Until now.

It's time, world. Time to break free of the shackles of mediocre entertainment. Time to rise up from the gravity that holds us here on Earth. Time to shatter the limits of what humanity is capable of and see how many orbits it takes for a person to mentally snap and start beating their fellow planemates with a fire extinguisher.

It's time . . . to blast off.

[*Chazz smiles into the camera for a good seven seconds.*]

Time to blast off.

[*five more seconds*]

Cut to the goddamn—

[*CUT TO: A swirling black hole*]

The thing is, live television is difficult even for major networks to pull off flawlessly; for a channel such as DV8, whose editors primarily specialize in taped broadcasts, the hour is an unmitigated disaster. Dropped feeds, uncensored swearing, frozen frames, cuts to static—seemingly every error that could befall a live broadcast befalls the *Waste of Space* premiere. It doesn't help matters that the film crew on the other side of the cameras consists solely of the team of NASAW scientists; despite their many advanced degrees, not one of them knows how to do a proper sound check.

But the show is live, and it's too late to fix anything, so the broadcast bumbles along unabated.

Chazz: [*in voiceover, killing time while the glitch is ironed out*] And, uh . . . for all you fashionistas out there, here's a fun fact: while in space, our brave young heroes will be clad in high-performance uniforms custom-designed by internationally renowned fashion designer Alexander Wang! Traveling every aeronautical mile in aeronautical style!

The premiere episode is an hourlong special with limited commercial interruption, breaking at the twenty- and forty-minute marks. (Note: In television parlance, each chunk of show between commercials is called an act; they are labeled as such from here on out.) But, as so often occurs in reality television, much of that hour is filler. The first ten minutes is a rehash of the promo that aired a week prior, followed by a cursory meet-cute as the Spacetronauts are shepherded into a staging room and introduced to one another for the first time. There are snotty asides from some of the more alpha kids, and eye-contact avoidance from the quieter ones. Stationary cameras, operated remotely by DV8, perform obligatory zoom-ins on any salacious glances exchanged.

The NASAW scientists, all wearing identical white lab coats, introduce themselves to the kids and give a speech about the importance of the upcoming mission—none of which is audible, as the scientists' microphones do not seem to be connected. Before long, Chazz interrupts.

Chazz: It seems that the Einsteins over at NASAW are having some minor sound problems, so I'll take it from here. Kids, can you hear me?

[*CUT TO: A wide shot of the cast, standing and looking into the camera. They appear to be varied degrees of anxious and excited. Jamarkus gives the camera a thumbs-up while Matt looks from side to side, as if searching for an exit.*]

Chazz: [*voiceover*] Spacetronauts: Welcome to *Waste of Space!*

[*The kids cheer and clap. Smiles all around, mostly. Their custom Alexander Wang uniforms are simultaneously futuristic and androgynous; although the designs differ slightly in order to complement each cast member's body type, all are the color and texture of hammered silver.*]

Chazz: [*voiceover*] Your one-of-a-kind, out-of-this-world adventure is about to begin. Over the next few weeks, you will encounter a multitude of physical, mental, and emotional challenges. You will be subjected to the psychological rigors of complete isolation hundreds of miles above the planet. You will be separated from your friends and loved ones, with no one to talk to but the other Spacetronauts, the confessional camera, and occasionally, during the live broadcasts, me. You will not have access to computers, phones, music, video games, television, or any other forms of entertainment or communication. You will be forced to endure the quirks, habits, and grating personalities of your fellow planemates. You will be watched, listened to, and scrutinized by all of America in real time.

And you have only one mission: endure it all for as long as you can.

That's it. No voting. No judging. No alliances. No immunity. All you have to do is last longer than everyone else.

[*General commotion as the kids look at one another, sizing up the competition*]

The rules couldn't be simpler. The pressure couldn't be greater. And the stakes couldn't be higher. Because I've got one more surprise for you all.

Whoever can stick it out the longest will win . . . A MILLION SPACE DOLLARS!

[*There is a raucous cheer as the Spacetronauts go nuts, their reactions ranging from "Oh God!" and "Good gravy!" to "What's the space-dollar-to-American-dollar conversion rate?"*]

But for now, it's time to get suited up! Don't go anywhere, America—the launch is minutes away!

[*MUSIC CUE: "The Final Countdown" by Europe*]

[*END OF ACT ONE; CUT TO COMMERCIAL*]

OFF–AIR

It's no wonder that problems arise straightaway. In the weeks leading up to the premiere, communication between DV8 and NASAW has been spotty at best. DV8 furnishes NASAW with a single phone line; that, plus email, are the only modes of communication that the two parties use to discuss the demands of production. Most of the emails are answered by anonymous DV8 minions, but every so often Chazz Young steps in to handle larger issues.

Item: Transcript of audio recording
Source: Chazz's cell phone
Date: January 20, 2016—8 days prior to launch

Chazz: Chazz here.

NASAW: Yeah, hi. I've got some questions about your previous email.

Chazz: *Now* what?

NASAW: I don't appreciate that tone. This is only the second time we've called to ask for clarification, even though your emails are rife with spelling errors, logistical impossibilities, crude emojis—

Chazz: I hear a lot of complaining and not a lot of questions . . .

NASAW: It says here that you'd like the ship to have "a bunch more buttons and gizmos and levers and shit." Now, ImmerseFX already installed plenty, but there are still blank spaces everywhere, so it seems that it has fallen to us to fill those in with more. What would you like their functions to be?

Chazz: Oh, they don't need to function. We'll make it abundantly clear which instruments the kids should interact with and when. The rest are for decoration.

NASAW: You're okay with someone flipping a switch that does absolutely nothing?

Chazz: Make it honk. Or let out a gush of air. Harmless crap like that.

NASAW: I would once again like to point out that this is a television show that's going to be aired in front of millions of people. You are aware of that, correct?

[*muffled noises as Chazz puts his hand over the mouthpiece and shouts away from the phone*]

Chazz: Khloe! Kourtney! That's not what the Roomba is for! [*to NASAW*] Sorry, my puggles are horny as hell. You were saying?

NASAW: [*after a shocked silence*] Remind us again why those special-effects wizards you sent didn't bother to stick around so they could build and control all this themselves?

Chazz: Because we need to create some distance there. Today's viewers are goddamn know-it-alls—they'll be researching and nosing around and crying wolf on the internet if they get even a whiff of fakery. The less evidence that ImmerseFX is involved—and the more that *you* are—the better.

NASAW: But useless levers and buttons will give off more than a whiff of fakery—

Chazz: Don't get your pocket protectors in a twist, all right? We've got it covered. And if any of the Spacetronauts start to have their own doubts—let's just say reinforcements are in place to make them believe.

NASAW: Very well. *Where* would you like the useless levers and buttons?

Chazz: All over. Every inch of the spaceplane. Everywhere the kids look. Keep 'em guessing as to what they do.

NASAW: Which is nothing.

Chazz: Correct. Ooh, and make a control panel. I think I saw that on *Cosmic Crusades*. Like, a big dashboard with *lots* of buttons on it. And a cup holder. They'll be impressed by a cup holder.

NASAW: Fine. Moving on. We received nine video cameras today and several small microphones, but no instructions on where to place them.

Chazz: I'll email you the schematics. Shouldn't be too hard—plug 'em in, point, shoot, etcetera. Maybe put all your mental energies into making *those* work.

NASAW: But—

Chazz: And make sure there's plenty of storage space in the kitchen. We got a *great* deal on a bulk order of surplus Soviet-era space food. Borscht in a tube! Classic.

NASAW: Food from the Soviet space program? That can't possibly still be edible.

Chazz: You know what they say: you have to break a few space eggs if you want to make a space omelet.

NASAW: You know, you can't just put the word "space" in front of everything and act like it makes sense.

Chazz: Watch me!

NASAW: [*after taking a deep breath*] So aside from the filming equipment, nothing on this ship needs to be functional?

Chazz: Nothing but the toilet. And even that can go on the fritz once in a while. Drama.

NASAW: You know, we *could* make things. We've got half a dozen Ph.D.s over here, a combined eighty-seven years of robotics research, fieldwork in electromagnetism, quantum—

Chazz: Yeah, and I've got about two more minutes before I have to leave for my seaweed wrap. Have your precious Ph.D.s quantum up some glue guns and get crafting, Captain Magnets.

NASAW: [*after an audible grumble*] On to the most pressing issue. You've stipulated that you want the kids to be "floating around in zero gravity and bumping into things and shit." Now, I'm sorry to have to be the one to tell you this, but we cannot actually replicate the effects of weightlessness here on Earth.

Chazz: Dude, what? You are the National Association for the Study of Astronomy and Weightlessness! This is why we hired you! How can you not know how to do that?

NASAW: Well, because of physics.

Chazz: I don't want to hear excuses! Figure out how to punt those kids into the air, Potato Battery!

NASAW: Here's what I propose. Instead of punting the kids into the air, why don't we tell the world that we've invented a brand-new form of simulated gravity? That DV8 was the very first entity to pioneer it, and it's being tested out for the very first time on these innocent, helpless children.

Chazz: Ooh. And if something goes *horribly wrong*, they'll all be flung out into space!

NASAW: Sure.

Chazz: That could work. Really ups the tension.

NASAW: Glad that's settled. Now—

Chazz: Seaweed time. Later hater!

[*end of call*]

After the commercial break, viewers are treated to an extensive introduction to the spaceship. A computer-animated image of the ship fills the screen, then spins around and is shown from numerous angles. Named the *Laika,* "after one of the most influential cosmonauts in space exploration history," the ship looks like an amalgamation of existing shuttles, spacecraft designs from fantasy and sci-fi movie franchises, and, curiously, a Dyson vacuum cleaner. Whatever it's supposed to be, it is white, clean, shiny, and emblazoned in several places with the American flag.

◼◀ · · · · · · · · · · · · · ·   **ON–AIR**   · · · · · · · · · · · · · ·

Item: Transcript of video broadcast

[*continued*]

   [*START OF ACT TWO*]

   Chazz: [*voiceover*] So! Here's how this'll work, America. The Spacetronauts are currently getting suited up and loaded into a custom-designed shuttle, courtesy of the good folks at Southwest Airlines. [*An on-air graphic flashes across the bottom of the screen, urging viewers to book their low-airfare vacations today using the discount code SPACE.*] The shuttle will blast into the air at seventeen thousand five hundred miles an hour until it hooks up with the *Laika*'s airlock. Once the pressure has equalized, the Spacetronauts will step out of the airlock and into the *Laika*, getting their first look at the most trendsetting, luxurious accommodations ever to hit Earth's orbit.

[*CUT TO: Schematics of ship*]

LAIKA:
THE SPACEPLANE!

SHIP AREAS:

A: AIRLOCK
B: FLIGHT DECK
C: IKEA LÜNAR LOUNGE
D: SPA
E: BATHROOM
F: CONFESSIONAL CLOSET
G: BEDROOM
H: KITCHEN

CAMERA LOCATIONS:

1: AIRLOCK
2: FLIGHT DECK
3: IKEA LÜNAR LOUNGE
4: IKEA LÜNAR LOUNGE
5: SPA
6: BATHROOM
7: CONFESSIONAL CLOSET
8: BEDROOM
9: KITCHEN

NASAW

Chazz: [*voiceover*] Our state-of-the-art, revolutionary spaceplane is made up of six separate areas, each more swag than the last. Let's explore them, shall we?

[*CUT TO: Montage of sweeping panoramic shots of the* Laika *interior*]

First up is the IKEA Lünar Lounge, complete with this season's hottest home furnishings, a pool table, and plenty of board games and playing cards for those rainy meteor-shower days. [*Several shots are held at length on the various furniture items, with an on-air graphic popping up at the bottom of the screen reminding viewers to visit the company's website for more styles and colors.*]

There's also a bar, fully stocked with—sorry, kids, plain old water! Dozens of bottles (glass, with swing-top rubber stoppers, available online and in stores, product name: Slom) will supply our crew with enough fresh drinking water to last the length of their mission.

And then there's the flight deck!

[*CUT TO: A raised platform sitting two steps above the lounge area. At its center are two swivel chairs facing a broad control panel covered with blinking lights, levers, and switches.*]

Our crew will use this control panel to press all the buttons and switches that'll keep them alive or flying through space or . . . whatever it is they'll be doing up there. Evasive maneuvers? *Maybe.* As you can see, the flight *deck* is also *decked* out with a massive triple-pane, super-durable plastic Windows Window, through which our intrepit explorers can gaze into an awe-inspiring view of Earth, the stars, comets, and UFOs, probably. Thanks to Microsoft for its generous donation!

[*Close-up on the Windows Window. A superimposed Microsoft logo appears.*]

On to the kitchen! Fully stocked with IKEA dinnerware, a rechargeable hot plate, and plenty of freeze-dried and dehydrated rations. That's right, America—they'll be eating like real astronauts up there! And thanks to our friends at Soupernova Soups, our Spacetronauts have been provided with a plentiful supply of Meteor Chowder! Soupernova Soups: a nebula of flavor in every bite.

[*CUT TO: Copious drawers of food—packages of ramen noodles, chalklike disks of unidentifiable origin, stacked cans of chowder, and toothpaste-like tubes covered in Russian writing*]

Of all the areas, the bedroom is the coziest—*and* sexiest. Seven beds, ten kids . . . *you* do the math!

[*CUT TO: A tiny bedroom. Three sets of bunk beds surround a California King mattress in the center, all of them crammed in so tightly they are almost touching.*]

The bathroom includes one shower, three sinks, and one toilet. Gonna get crowded up in this piece!

[*CUT TO: The bathroom, which looks like that of a prison. Although the toilet mercifully has a stall door, the shower curtain is practically transparent. The sole decoration: one cracked seashell arbitrarily tossed between two of the sinks.*]

We know one room that's going to get a lot of use: the spa! Provided by Heavenly Hot Tubs, this handcrafted sauna-grade-cedar interior and twenty-five-jet tub will melt away the explorers' troubles—*or* pump them full of rejuvenation. With its specially designed viewing glass, their fellow Spacetronauts won't miss a second of the action—and neither will we!

[*Three walls of the spa are lined with a rich, reddish wood;*

the fourth is made of glass and serves as the back wall of the Lünar Lounge bar, with the transparent hot tub raised and strategically placed against said window.]

And last but never, *ever* least: the Confessional Closet. Our fearless adventurers will be feeling plenty of inner feelings and thoughts and opinions and shit. Can't keep them all bottled up, can they? That's what this soundproof booth is for, available for the unloading of emotions at any time, day or night.

[*CUT TO: A rectangular room the size of a cupboard, with a camera on one end and a little leather stool on the other. The walls are paneled with soundproof wooden tiles. A blown-up photo of the Milky Way serves as the background.*]

[*CUT TO: More sweeping panoramas of the ship*]

Chazz: But here's the best part, America. The *Laika* is equipped with nine high-definition cameras whose ranges cover nearly every inch of the spaceplane. Highly sensitive microphones are embedded in the walls and in the ceiling. Every minute of every day in every room will be documented. Every conversation. Every fight. Every . . . kiss? There's nowhere to hide, and we'll be bringing it all to you live online, 24/7!

Of course, this also means there's no bulky production crew for the Spacetronauts to maneuver around. No one for them to turn to if things go wrong. Not a shred of adult supervision. These kids will be onboard the *Laika,* from start to finish, *in total isolation.*

It'll be up to them to decide how to use it.

The broadcast cuts to a live shot of the staging room, where the sleek, uniform-clad bodies of the Spacetronauts are being bundled into puffy, ugly white spacesuits, fishbowl helmets and all. It is difficult to tell who is who under all that plastic—a problem that the folks in DV8's control booth are acutely aware of, as sporadic, desperate name-tag graphics keep popping up onscreen to label the fluffy marshmallow beings. The only distinguishable one is Snout's pet pig, Colonel Bacon, in his own specially fitted suit, his curly tail sticking out from a hole on his rump.

Over the suiting-up footage, Chazz dispenses more instructions.

Chazz: [*voiceover*] Looking good, Spacetronauts! Now, we don't expect you to automatically know how to fly a spaceplane, so NASAW will be remotely controlling the ship from down here on Earth. But that's not to say that you won't encounter tests of your endurance and resourcefulness, so be prepared for anything! Danger! Disasters! Enemies! Crisises!

[*One of the NASAW scientists pauses in securing a spacesuit to look up and mouth "Crises."*]

Chazz: [*voiceover*] I'll give you further instructions in a bit. For now, it's time to board the shuttle!

After everyone is suited up, they waddle comically into the next phase of their journey. A stationary camera captures the action as the scientists buckle the Spacetronauts (and Colonel Bacon) into their seats on the shuttle, which is obviously, unmistakably, the cabin of a passenger aircraft. The Nike backpacks are stowed in the overhead storage bins. One of the cast members attempts to push the flight-attendant call button and is quickly scolded by a scientist. Once it has been established that all seatbacks and tray tables are in their upright and locked positions, the scientists flash thumbs-up at the kids, which they return.

With that, the NASAW scientists deliver some unintelligible goodbyes and good lucks, leave the shot, and close the cabin door.

Chazz: [*voiceover*] This is it, you guys. We'll see you off through the launch, then take a quick commercial break while you complete your journey. It will take eight and a half minutes for the shuttle to reach orbit altitude and dock with the *Laika*, so we'll reestablish contact with you then. Can I get a thumbs-up?

[*more thumbs-up all around*]

Chazz: [*voiceover*] Godspeed, Spacetronauts! Catch you on the other side!

Robot Voice: T MINUS TWENTY SECONDS. NINETEEN. EIGHTEEN . . .

As the countdown commences, questions abound.

What are the Spacetronauts thinking as those numbers tick away? What frenzied, terrified, psyched, confused thoughts are invisibly ricocheting off the walls of that Boeing 737? What emotions are simmering to a boil beneath the glassy glare of those ten fishbowl helmets? Is regret one of them? How much do they know about the trueness or falseness of this thing they've signed their lives away for?

And what's going to happen next?

As the countdown reaches zero, none of that matters anymore.

With a deafening burst of acoustic energy, the full frame shudders, sending the limbs of the ten besuited travelers akimbo.

The vibrations intensify.

There is a deep, sonorous boom.

The lights flicker.

The scene cuts to an exterior shot of a nighttime rocket launch; ImmerseFX's considerable visual-effects budget is in full regalia as a fireball blooms beneath the ship, chasing the darkness away. The glorified-vacuum-cleaner ship ascends—slow and jarring at first, then smoother, faster, higher,

.

                              light

                    a point of

              nothing but

         until it becomes

     and fading

   then shrinking

 beginning to arch,

rising gracefully,

[*END OF ACT TWO; CUT TO COMMERCIAL*]

・・・・・・・・・・・・・・・ **OFF-AIR** ・・・・・・・・・・・・・・・・・・

America holds its breath.

As NASAW holds its tongue.

Item: Transcript of video recording
Source: Dashboard camera, DV8 Company Van

Date: January 22, 2016—6 days prior to launch

[IMAGE: A large steel wall with a door set into it—the soundstage. One of the NASAW scientists opens the door to greet Chazz Young's personal courier, Boris, who is seen getting out of his purple windowless van.]

Boris: I got a delivery for . . .

NASAW: *[hurriedly getting up]* Yep! I'll take it.

Boris: You guys sure do use a lot of Styrofoam.

NASAW: *[signing for the package]* Yeah, well, that there's a perfect metaphor for this entire operation. All fluff, no substance.

Boris: Lots of black fabric, too.

NASAW: To blanket the exterior of the ship, eliminating any rogue sources of light and muffling any external sounds.

Boris: And the duct tape?

NASAW: *[chuckling]* We'd have no space program at all without duct tape, my friend.

Boris: But what about this other stuff? The boxes marked "Fragile"—

NASAW: *[stops laughing]* Are none of your business.

Boris: I don't mean to step out of bounds, buddy. I know my place. Pick up supplies from your L.A. headquarters and bring 'em out here. Why this isn't something that FedEx could do, I have no idea—

NASAW: The materials are sensitive. They can't be trusted with commercial delivery services.

Boris: I'll say. Some of these boxes, they sort of—it sometimes seems like they *hum*—

NASAW: It doesn't matter what they are. Or what they "seem" to do. Unload them and leave.

Boris: Listen, pal, this place ain't exactly a stone's throw away. If I gotta drive eleven hours to get out here every few days, I'd like to know that the contents in my van aren't gonna give me radioactive poisoning or nothing—

NASAW: Unload them. And leave.

◼◀ · · · · · · · · · · · · · ON-AIR · · · · · · · · · · · · · · · · ·

Item: Transcript of video broadcast
[*continued*]

[*START OF ACT THREE*]

Chazz: [*in the studio*] Welcome back, America. I'm now receiving word that the shuttle has reached an altitude of two hundred miles above sea level and is about to dock with the *Laika*. Shuttle, can you give us an update?

Robot Voice: CONTACT AND CAPTURE. SHUTTLE IS DOCKED.

[*There are offscreen noises of celebration and applause from the DV8 crew. Chazz breaks out into a huge smile.*]

Chazz: Spacetronauts, can you hear me? It's now safe to unbuckle your seat belts, remove your spacesuits, and move into the airlock!

While the Spacetronauts shed their suits offscreen, Chazz explains that new advances in "astronomically scientific research" will allow the Spacetronauts to move about the ship without being subjected to the weightlessness of outer space. How this is being accomplished is illustrated with a graphic:

As if that thoroughly explains that, Chazz moves on to the big reveal.

Chazz: All right, the Spacetronauts have left the shuttle, sealed the outer airlock door, and are awaiting our signal. We are a go for Camera One!

Source: Camera #1—Airlock

[*The cast members are clumped together in a room no bigger than a single-car garage. Some look nauseated; some dizzy. Their formerly lustrous uniforms have taken on a rumpled appearance. All of them seem glad to be out of the shuttle and are looking around the airlock with tangible anticipation.*]

Chazz: [*voiceover*] And . . . enter!

[*Jamarkus pushes a button. There is a whooshing noise. Nozzles set into the wall of the airlock emit a spray of vapor, like a fog machine. After thirty seconds, a large green light flashes and the door to the* Laika *opens.*]

The Spacetronauts pour into the lounge. Immediately the Windows Window arrests their attention, stopping them in their tracks as they wordlessly gape at the stunning view of the stars and the tremendous blue marble of Earth below.

There is a brief, beautiful moment of pure awe.

Even Chazz shuts up, seeming to recognize this encounter for what it is: one of hushed reverence. He gives it to them, sinking into the grandeur for *just* the right amount of time, no doubt calculated down to the millisecond.

Source: Camera #3—Lünar Lounge

Chazz: [*voiceover*] Abso*lut*ely unbe*liev*able.

So listen up, Spacetronauts: there are a few more super-crucial orders of business we need to address before I leave you to your adventures. Take a look at the control panel in front of you. In addition to the very cool buttons and levers and switches and shit, you'll also find a ratings dial, plus a DV8 network indicator—that means we're watching every move you make!

But as cool as these instruments are, it's imperative that *you not touch any of them without permission.* Everyone got that? Ask the onboard computer first, then proceed once your request is granted. As the mission progresses, you will be faced with several grueling challenges, each with its own specific solution; using the wrong button to overcome them could be a dire and costly mistake. These instruments are the keys to your success—don't waste them. Got it?

There is one exception to this rule. At the center of the control panel, you'll find a big red I QUIT™ button. [*An on-air graphic pops up at the bottom of the screen, informing viewers that they can order their very own I QUIT™ buttons from Staples.com.*] If you've finally had enough, if you've eaten your last morsel of space food, if your bunkmate has kicked you in the face for the last time, if you just can't take it anymore, if you want nothing more than to get the ever-loving hell off that ship—just press the button. The inner airlock door will open, you'll step inside, the door will close behind you, and you'll wait for the NASAW shuttle to come pick you up and bring you back to Earth like the loser that you are. The most important thing to remember is that this is an *irreversible function*—once you press that button, you're gone. You're off the show, with no chance of winning the million space dollars. Got it?

[*The Spacetronauts nod their assent.*]

Chazz: Which leaves only one thing left to do: in your first test of cooperation and teamwork, you must collectively elect a leader—

Clayton: I call leader!

[*Pushing others out of the way, Clayton strides to the front of the pack, as if his coronation is a foregone conclusion. But behind him, Jamarkus's hand has shot straight up, followed by Louise's. Ostensibly intimidated by the older boys, Louise lowers hers. Clayton scowls at Jamarkus.*]

Titania: [*to Jamarkus and Clayton*] Tell us why you want to be leader, I guess.

Clayton: What? Why?

Titania: Because this is an election, not a power grab. Plead your cases.

Clayton: [*glaring at her*] My case is that I called it.

Titania: [*to Jamarkus*] And you?

Jamarkus: [*opening his arms in a wide, friendly gesture*] Fellow Spacetronauts, my name is Jamarkus. I'm an Eagle Scout and a National Aeronautic Scholarship finalist. I have over a thousand hours of flight-simulation training, and I am prepared to ensure your safety at all costs. It would be an honor and a privilege to lead such a remarkable group of courageous trailblazers.

[*The group eagerly nods its assent; Jamarkus has clearly won. Clayton fumes and is about to say something when Chazz cuts him off.*]

Chazz: [*voiceover*] Now that that's settled, you are free to move about the spaceplane! To celebrate your conquest, please enjoy a round of sparkling apple cider, compliments of our friends at Martinelli's.

Leaving Clayton behind to sputter in disgrace, the rest of the cast is off to squeal over the posh furnishings (an onscreen graphic reminds viewers which retailer has provided them—as if the catalog prominently displayed on the coffee table isn't reminder enough). Some of them splay across the plush sofa, while others pour refreshments into funky polka-dotted glasses under whimsically modern lighting. Gradually they split off into groups of twos and threes and begin to converse.

Source: Camera #4—Lünar Lounge

[*Jamarkus rushes around the room, eagerly taking everything in, while Hibiscus assesses the décor with disdain.*]

Hibiscus: Surely they jest. All this budget, and they couldn't spring for a single authentic item not easily assembled with an Allen wrench?

Jamarkus: But how mind-blowing is this? We're in space!

Hibiscus: Yeah, onboard a ship that was probably constructed in a Chinese sweatshop.

Jamarkus: But in space! [*extending his hand*] Nice to meet you. I'm Jamarkus.

Hibiscus: [*ignoring his hand*] Hi, Jamarkus. This is Svalsta, the coffee table. This is Älvsbyn, the chandelier. And Slom, the water bottle. Cookie-cutter, eye-candied, no-personality abominations purchased by deplorable, unimaginative, vapid, materialistic sheeple.

Bacardi: Omigod, Svalsta, the coffee table! [*She barrels into the living room area, drink in hand.*] Älvsbyn, the chandelier! Fjälkinge, the shelving unit! Slom bottles! OOOH! [*She rushes over to a hot-pink inflatable seat made with faux fur.*] A puffy Püffi chair!

Hibiscus: Case in point.

Bacardi: Hi, I'm Bacardi! Who are you?

Hibiscus: Hibiscus.

Bacardi: Eye Piss Kiss?

Hibiscus: Hibiscus.

[*Bacardi tries to walk over to Hibiscus but trips over her own feet, sending a splash of cider to the floor.*]

Bacardi: [*delighted*] I made a mess!

Hibiscus: You *are* a mess.

Bacardi: Kiss my astronaut!

[*She slaps her own rear. Clayton, sensing an impending catfight, approaches—but Jamarkus heads him off.*]

Jamarkus: Hello! I hope we can put that ugly election behind us. I'd like to be friends!

Clayton: [*ignoring his hand*] Not if I can help it.

Jamarkus: Sorry?

Clayton: I'm not here to make friends. I'll be throwing you under a bus the first chance I get.

Hibiscus: Hey look, a walking cliché!

Clayton: [*rounding on her*] Hey look, a homeless person! Ever heard of deodorant?

Hibiscus: Deodorant is a capitalist construct designed to squash the inalienable rights of Mother Nature.

Clayton: We're gonna be locked in this flying soup can breathing the same air for weeks, maybe months. Did it not occur to you that the rest of us might not want to sample the festering fruits of what Mother Nature, in all her bacterial glory, can unleash upon the numerous pits and valleys of your disgusting body?

Hibiscus: Sorry, but it's my personal philosophy never to take seriously the opinions of people who pluck their eyebrows.

Clayton: It's called proper grooming, you derelict—

Snout: [*as he and Colonel Bacon approach*] Howdy, friends!

Jamarkus: Howdy, brother!

Clayton: [*rounding on Snout*] No. No. We are officially dispensing with the howdys until someone explains to me what in heaven and hell's name this fat, revolting *thing* is doing here.

Snout: [*extending his hand*] The name's Snout.

Clayton: [*ignoring his hand*] Not you. Well . . . yes, you. But also *that*.

Snout: Who, Colonel Bacon?

Jamarkus: *I* think he's cute!

Hibiscus: And I appreciate your commitment to sustainable farming.

Snout: Thanks, High Biscuits!

Hibiscus: Hibiscus.

[*Colonel Bacon takes a whiff of Hibiscus, snorts, and runs away. Snout chases after him.*]

Clayton: [*to Hibiscus*] Do you see what I'm saying? An actual *pig* is disgusted by you.

Hibiscus: *You're* the pig, one-percenter!

Jamarkus: [*pulling her away*] I have an idea: let's get you some delicious apple juice! Do you like apples?

Hibiscus: I like the tragically minuscule fraction of our apple crops that aren't riddled with pesticides.

[*Jamarkus escorts Hibiscus away, leaving Bacardi and Clayton alone.*]

Bacardi: She seems fun.

[*Clayton, clearly about to dispense a rude reply, instead takes note of the way Bacardi is sitting on the puffy Püffi chair and the manner in which it enhances her cleavage. He leans in as they sip from their flutes.*]

Clayton: Not as fun as you. Where are you from?

Bacardi: Brooklyn, baby! You?

Clayton: Los Angeles.

Bacardi: That's interesting.

Clayton: Know what else is interesting? Once my trust fund kicks in, I'll have a net worth of over ten million dollars.

Bacardi: That's funny, because I can tie a cherry stem into a knot with my tongue.

Clayton: Cool, cool.

[*They assess each other.*]

Clayton: So . . . we're probably gonna bang, right?

Bacardi: [*answer obscured by sound of champagne flute hitting her teeth as she vigorously nods*]

Source: Camera #2—Flight Deck

Matt: Oh God. I'm not dreaming this, am I? We're really in space?

Louise: [*smiling maniacally, eyes darting back and forth between the control panel and the Windows Window*] Affirmative!

Matt: Holy crap. [*He puts his hands out, as if to balance himself.*] The ship is moving. We're rocking from side to side—can you feel that? Holy crap.

Kaoru: {Do they expect us to believe that we are in space?} [*gestures at the Windows Window*] {This is clearly a computer screen.}

Matt: Oh jeez, I'm sorry. You don't speak English? You must be more terrified than I am.

Kaoru: {I am fairly certain we are on a film set of some kind.}

Matt: How are you so calm right now? Look at all these controls! How are we supposed to know how to use them?

Kaoru: {Are these props meant to impress us?}

Matt: Ooh, a cup holder!

Kaoru: {None of these buttons are functional.} [*poking at a joystick on the control panel*] {This joystick does nothing.}

Louise: [*batting Kaoru's hand away*] Stop it! Chazz said not to touch anything! [*squinting at one of the control panel's gauges*] The DV8 network indicator is lit. Guess that means they're watching. [*eagerly nodding toward window*] But I bet not as closely as our new cosmic neighbors. Wherever they're hiding.

Matt: Oh God.

Louise: Don't worry. I bet they're good guys. And if they're bad guys, I'll protect us. I brought something that can get us out of here in no time. What personal item did you bring?

Matt: I didn't get a chance to pack, so I . . . I grabbed the TV remote control from my hotel room.

Louise: Oh. Well, worst-case scenario, that could certainly be used as a projectile. Might distract a Wingobian for a few seconds before it vaporizes you.

Matt: Oh God. [*breathing heavily*] This is all a huge mistake. I'm not supposed to be here. I have to get off this ship!

[*He lunges for the I QUIT™ button, but Louise bats his hand away.*]

Louise: Are you out of your tree? We just got here!

Matt: But I want to leave!

Louise: [*quieter*] Hey, now. [*She gently places her hand on his.*] Give it a chance, okay? This is an amazing thing we're doing. Don't end it before it's begun.

Matt: [*hesitates, then backs away from the flight deck*] Okay. I'll give it a chance.

Louise: Good. Because I suspect we've drifted into quadrant J8043, where the z-coordinate for dark matter is counteracted by the q-coordinate for black hole probability, which, because Mercury is in retrograde, is currently holding somewhere around 5.2 quintips—

Matt: What's a quintip?

Louise: [*shaking her head*] Poor Earthling. You've got a lot to learn.

Source: Camera #3—Lünar Lounge

[*Nico stands by himself at the bar, sipping apple cider. Titania sidles up to him.*]

Titania: So what are you in for?

[*Blushing, Nico promptly gets tongue-tied and looks at the floor. Titania watches him, patient. After a few seconds, he looks up and stammers a reply.*]

Nico: Token orphan. Bonus points for being ethnic. You?

Titania: Token Portlandian, I guess? Bonus points for the criminal record.

Nico: Ah.

Titania: They sure know how to pick 'em, huh?

[*They survey the others.*]

Titania: This is going to be one dumpster fire of a show.

[*Nico nods.*]

Titania: Look on the bright side, though. Some lucky therapists out there are going to make a fortune on these nutballs.

Nico: Good thing you seem normal.

Titania: Good thing seeming is believing.

[*They survey each other.*]

Titania: I'm Titania.

Nico: Nico.

[*They clink glasses.*]

By this time, the full hour has elapsed. After a few parting shots of the *Laika* grandly soaring over the Earth, Chazz returns to wrap things up.

[*CUT TO: Chazz, in the spotlight, as credits roll across the bottom of the screen*]

Chazz: That's all we have time for, America. On behalf of myself and the team at DV8, we want to thank you for watching tonight's broadcast—all 307 million of you, my sources estimate! From here on out, I'll be handing over the reins to the Spacetronauts, popping in only to say hello during the live portion at the end of every episode. Be sure to tune in same time next week as our fearless Spacetronauts settle into their new life onboard the ship. Who will get along? Who will become mortal enemies? Who will be the first to clog *the one and only toilet*?

But in the meantime—can't get enough of *Waste of Space*? Head over to DV8.com to watch the live stream onboard the *Laika* for all the laughs, danger, fights, and action you can't get anywhere else!

Until next week—Catchphrase forever!

[*Due to improper timing, Chazz unwittingly has about ten more seconds of live television to kill, so the camera keeps rolling.*]

Chazz: [*to producer*] What kind of a catchphrase is that?

DV8 Producer: [*off-mike*] Yeah, our bad. That was a placeholder from an earlier draft of the script. The writers were supposed to come up with something cool and memorable, but I guess they never did.

Chazz: Goddammit, what am I paying you people for—

[*MUSIC CUE: "Intergalactic" by the Beastie Boys*]

[*END OF EPISODE*]

◼◀ · · · · · · · · · · · · · · · **OFF–AIR** · · · · · · · · · · · · · · ·

ONLINE

CHAZZ'S ESTIMATE OF 307 MILLION VIEWERS IS ABSURD (FOR comparison, the Super Bowl, usually the most watched television program of the year in the United States, gets an average of 100 million), but what's more absurd is that he isn't wrong in terms of its groundbreaking impact. Around 20 million people across America tune in that night, television and online combined, making the premiere episode of *Waste of Space* one of the most watched pilots in recent memory.

What's more, a substantial number of those eyeballs migrate to the 24/7 online feed immediately following the broadcast. All through the night and into early the next morning, America continues to wolf down every second of its new spacy sweethearts, with nine camera feeds displayed in a three-by-three grid on both DV8.com and the DV8 app—an intergalactic Orwellian Brady Brunch taking up residence on countless computer and phone screens across America.

And the cast doesn't disappoint. Once Chazz signs off and the Spacetronauts are left alone for the first time, things go as one might expect things to go when ten teenagers are randomly thrust into close proximity with one another: messily.

Item: Transcript of video recording—24/7 online feed
Source: Camera #6—Bathroom
Date: January 28, 2016

Clayton: Your pig took a shit in my shoe!

Snout: Oh, I'm mighty sorry, sir. He does that sometimes. Still broken up about our abducted tractor, I reckon. Hey, if you happen to see it floating around out there in space, let me—

Clayton: These shoes were given to me by the Prince of Monaco. I will *end* you!

Bacardi: [*words slurring*] Oh fun, are we yelling? YELLING!

Clayton: The pig shit in my shoe!

Bacardi: Ohnosorry, that was me.

Clayton: What the—are you drunk?

Bacardi: Maaaaybe.

Clayton: How are you drunk?

Bacardi: I raided the minibar in my hotel room and smuggled some little bottles of vodka onboard. Don't tell anyone shhhh. [*takes a swig*]

Clayton: Where did you hide them?

Bacardi: [*side-eye*] I'd rather not say.

Source: Camera #7—Confessional Closet

Kaoru: {I thought this was the bathroom. I have made an error.

I think I am supposed to look into the camera and deliver my emotion.

My emotion is that I am displeased.

I visited Los Angeles to compete in a judo tournament, and I got separated from my team while we were touring a local mall. I asked an adult for assistance, and the adult put me into a van and locked me in a hotel room. Now I am not sure where I am. It appears to be an interactive real-life video game of some kind. But I would prefer to be practicing my grip drills, not poking at inoperative buttons.

I do not feel well. I normally eat nutritious foods, which the American diet is not. It is worse inside this fraudulent spaceship. I looked in the kitchen, but there is little hope there; the food is barely food. If the boredom does not kill me, the dehydrated macaroni and cheese will.

My peers are strange. They are also delusional if they think that we are really in space. The girl with the large breasts is ostentatious and bold. The boy and his pig smell bad but mean well. The girl with the almost-white shaved hair is troubled but smart—maybe smarter than our elected leader. The skater boy seems shy but nice, and so does the girl with glasses, when she is not in her own world, talking to herself. The rich boy makes me uncomfortable. The hipster girl is dumb. The boy with no finger is confused.

And I? Am displeased.}

Source: Camera #2—Flight Deck

[*Hibiscus is nibbling at a mushroom with a singular focus. She offers some to Matt, who refuses, looking predictably terrified. Titania is watching from the flight deck while Louise is kneeling on the swivel seat next to her, facing the Windows Window.*]

Louise: If my calculations are correct, we should be passing by the axiom-gamma-releasing station right about . . . now.

Titania: Is that a good thing?

Louise: [*unable to contain her joy*] It's not a bad thing!

Titania: You sound like you know what you're talking about.

[*The smile falls off Louise's face.*]

Louise: [*quietly*] Are you making fun of me?

Titania: No. Why?

Louise: You sounded sarcastic.

Titania: I get that a lot. It's just how my voice sounds.

[*Louise still looks unsure.*]

Titania: I swear, I wasn't mocking you.

Louise: Sorry. I thought—I've heard about girls like you—

Titania: Girls like me?

Louise: Yeah. The klepdugs.

Titania: The what now?

Louise: The ones who smoke and drink and do drugs and other illegal things.

Titania: With all due respect—[*points at Hibiscus*] she's the one who is doing drugs *at this very moment.*

Louise: Yeah, but you—your shaved head. Your tough body language. You seem like a real . . . [*lowers her voice, as if she's unaccustomed to swearing*] badass.

Titania: I'm not, though.

[*Louise knits her brow.*]

Titania: Is this the first time you've interacted with such a . . . diverse group of people, Louise?

Louise: In person, yeah. Most of my friends are online.

Titania: This might sound hypocritical, considering the setting we currently find ourselves in—but in the real world, people don't fall so easily into the categories that a show like this assigns them to.

Louise: I do. I'm a nerd, and nerds are like catnip to

klepdugs. Or so I've been led to believe. I was just being preemptive.

Titania: I won't clobber you. Promise.

[*Titania gets up to leave, giving Louise a friendly wink. Louise watches her go, then whispers to herself.*]

Louise: Further research is required.

Source: Camera #6—Bathroom

[*The back legs of Colonel Bacon are kicking wildly, as he has become lodged between the wall and the toilet*]

Snout: Oh, cripes. [*calling out to group*] Little help?

Source: Camera #8—Bedroom

[*Nico has staked an early claim on a top bunk. He is lying on the bed and talking into his GoPro camera.*]

Hi Mom. Hi Dad.

I AM IN SPACE.

I can't charge the battery, and I don't know how long it's going to last, so I'm trying not to use it much. But I'll do what I can.

They put us in spacesuits. Then the shuttle shook so hard it felt like my brain was going to spurt out of my ears. Then there was a pull of gravity, and then—

Then it stopped. First bummer of the galaxy so far: no weightlessness. They said they've come up with new technologies that'll keep us from floating. Which takes away most of the fun, in my opinion.

Not that I'd be having gobs of fun anyway. I'm too scared to do much of anything. Or talk to anyone. Or, like, breathe.

But whatever.

This is still amazing.

The rest of the cast, though—major train wreck. Plane crash. Iceberg collision. *Hindenburg* explosion. These kids are insane—

[*There is a clearing of a throat. Nico turns around to find Clayton leaning in the bedroom doorway.*]

Clayton: Whatcha got there?

Nico: Oh, my—it's a camera. Thing.

Clayton: You brought a camera to a TV show?

Nico: Just for, like, personal video diaries and stuff.

[*There is a piggish squeal from the bathroom, followed by a "Never mind, I got him!" Clayton takes no notice of the commotion, but rather keeps his eyes locked on Nico and takes a step closer.*]

Clayton: So do you think *I'm* insane?

Nico: What?

Clayton: I heard what you said. Train wreck, etcetera. [*walking all the way into the room, keeping his eye on Nico*] You're one of the quiet ones, huh? Playing everything close to the vest?

Nico: Um—

Clayton: Not a fan of that, I gotta say. I like to know where people stand. What they're thinking.

[*Clayton drops his Nike bag onto the floor. It lands with a heavy thud. Nico stares at it.*]

Clayton: Wondering what's in my bag?

Nico: Uh . . . a little.

Clayton: [*clucking his tongue*] It isn't wise to pry into my affairs like that.

[*There is another shriek in the hallway. Bacardi appears in the doorway, her face flushed.*]

Bacardi: Clayton, there you are!

[*Clayton's sneer transforms into a debonair smile, Nico all but forgotten.*]

Clayton: Hey, babe.

Bacardi: [*realizing where she is*] Ooh, the bedroom. I call the big bed!

With a squeal, Bacardi tackles Clayton onto the king-size mattress. The rest of the cast hears the commotion in the bedroom and has a simultaneous panicked realization that it's time for a cutthroat game of Musical Chairs: Bedroom Edition. They rush in to claim the remaining spots, with Titania and Kaoru scoring the other two top bunks, and Jamarkus, Matt, and Snout getting the bottoms. Louise and Hibiscus are the last to arrive, consequently becoming the losers who must share the big bed with Clayton and Bacardi. Grumbling, they gingerly place their pillows on either side of the couple, who are already canoodling in the center.

Jamarkus: So, while we're all gathered here—why don't we go around the room and talk about our things?

Snout: Our . . . things?

Jamarkus: Our hobbies! Our passions! The things we do that aren't school, homework, sleep, texting, eating, or breathing! My thing is space stuff. And flight simulators. Bacardi, what about you?

[*Bacardi drags her lips off Clayton's.*]

Bacardi: My thing's internet. I bet I have more likes and shares and followers than all you combined!

Louise: [*sarcastically*] There's a worthy accomplishment.

Bacardi: Shutup, geek squad. I got eyes and ears and body parts in all digital corners of everywhere. I got so many hookups I could be a goddamn spy. [*pointing at Camera #8*] Youhear that, CIA?

Snout: My thing is farming!

Louise: My thing is *Cosmic Crusades*.

Matt: I don't have a thing. Pretzels, maybe? I work at a pretzel store—

Hibiscus: [*shouting at her bedmates*] You know what my thing is? Personal space. Something I am *woefully* lacking right now.

[*She tugs on the blanket, pulling most of it to her side of the big bed. Undaunted, Clayton and Bacardi go back to snuggling.*]

Jamarkus: Titania, what about you?

Titania: I make stuff out of wood.

Snout: Really?

Titania: Yep.

Matt: That's so cool. Like what?

Titania: Tables. Chairs. A secret hidden doorway.

Louise: No way! I've always wanted one of those.

Titania: So did my little sister. I put one in the back of her closet—it blended right in with the wall panels. The only way you'd know it was there was if you knocked on it and could tell that there was a hollow patch. It led to a tunnel to the attic.

Jamarkus: Very impressive. What else have you made?

Titania: Last summer I carved a canoe out of a tree.

Snout: Good gravy. A functional canoe?

Titania: Depends on the function. Did it float? Yes. Did it get me to where I wanted to go? No.

Nico: Where did you want to go?

[*As it's the first time Nico's spoken in front of the whole group, Titania looks directly at him.*]

Titania: Away.

Nico: Anywhere specific?

Titania: Nope. Just away.

From there, the evening peters out. Despite a few fights erupting over bathroom procedures—some want to shower, some take too long to brush their teeth, some just want to poop in peace—the night draws to an uneventful close.

At 11:00 p.m. Pacific time, the robot voice announces "BEDTIME IMMINENT." Five minutes later, there are a series of strident beeps, followed by a not-so-soothing "LIGHTS OUT." Online viewers watch as the bathroom, spa, kitchen, and airlock camera feeds go dark, except for a strip of green emergency lights along the floor. As for the rest: the bedroom camera, number 8, is outfitted with night vision; the Lünar Lounge cameras—numbers 2, 3, and 4—are mostly dark, with a bit of ambient light spilling in from the Windows Window; and the Confessional Closet stays fully lit, camera 7 ready to capture any spewing of emotions, night or day.

That first night, it gets a visitor at around three a.m.

Source: Camera #7—Confessional Closet

Titania: Well, I've kept moving. I've kept exploring. About as far as a person can, I guess.

I—

[*She looks down and pinches a bit of her pewter sleeve*

between her fingers. When she looks back up at the camera, her expression is vulnerable.]

I came in here wanting to talk directly to my parents, but now that this camera's staring back at me, that seems kind of stupid and contrived, and not very . . . confidential. What with the whole country listening in and all.

[*She stops fiddling with her sleeve and wipes her hands on her pants.*]

I can't believe I'm really here. On this show. In space. [*She smirks.*] Allegedly.

When I think about all the thousands—hundreds of thousands; millions, maybe—of choices I've made that led up to me being here at this very moment, it's . . . the sheer volume is crushing. And if I'd chosen differently for any one of them, I probably wouldn't be here at all . . .

[*She trails off.*]

You know how you see your biggest choices more clearly than the rest? Like with high-definition detail? They say hindsight is twenty-twenty, but I think it's sharper than that. It's like looking under an electron freaking microscope. Every fiber, every molecule, every atom. At that level of scrutiny, you don't ask yourself the big questions anymore. You don't wonder what would have happened if you'd said no instead of yes. You ask yourself what would have happened if you'd said yes a millisecond later. Would that have made a difference? If you'd moved a centimeter to the right or a sixteenth of an inch to the left, would the outcome be the same?

Such little things.

[*She blows out a puff of air and laughs at herself.*]

I blame quantum mechanics. That whole separate branch of physics that needed to be discovered when scientists realized that if you shrink your focus down to the smallest possible planes of existence, the basic laws of science fall apart and break down and don't apply anymore. Like the tiniest things in our universe are looking back up at us, telling us they're not going to play by our rules, and giving us the finger—

[*The door opens.*]

Nico: Oh crap. Sorry. I didn't realize anyone was in here.

Titania: It's okay. I'm just rambling on about . . . physics. Or something.

Nico: [*rubbing his eyes*] I couldn't sleep.

Titania: Me neither.

Nico: Okay. Sorry to bother you.

Titania: Wait. Stay.

[*Titania moves to sit on the floor, with her back against the side wall, feet against the wheels of the leather stool. After a moment's hesitation, Nico sits down on the floor, his back against the other side wall. From the camera's perspective, they are both in profile, facing each other.*]

Nico: Now what?

Titania: You came to the Confessional Closet. Confess something. All of America is listening.

[*Nico looks at the camera, then quickly looks away.*]

Titania: Sorry. You don't have to.

Nico: No, I will. At some point. I just—I'm not great with . . .

Titania: Talking?

Nico: Yeah. I mean, I don't even know how to talk to *you* yet. How am I supposed to talk to all of America?

Titania: Fair enough.

[*pause*]

Titania: We could waste America's time instead.

[*Nico raises his eyebrows.*]

Titania: Ninety-nine bottles of Slom on the wall, ninety-nine bottles of Slom—

[*Nico joins in.*]

Both: Take one down, pass it around, ninety-eight bottles of Slom on the wall . . .

[*It takes fifteen minutes for them to get to zero, after which Nico gets up and leaves the room, but not before the camera catches half a second of a smile.*]

[*Titania sits there lost in thought, not saying anything, swaying with the hypnotic motions of the ship. About ten minutes later, the door bursts open.*]

Clayton: [*surprised to see her*] Oh.

Titania: Hi.

Clayton: Get out.

Titania: Excuse me?

Clayton: Get out, bitch.

[*He pulls her up by the elbows and forcibly removes her from the room.*]

Titania: Hey! What the—

[*Clayton shuts the door and locks it.*]

Clayton: Uncle Chazz, we need to talk. This casting is absolute bullsh—

[*Titania is not going down without a fight. She bangs on the door a few times, then gives a muffled shout of "Asshole!" and leaves.*]

Clayton: [*pointing at the door*] This is exactly my point. These animals seem to be under the impression that they have as much of a right to be here as I do, which: Are you kidding me? Don't get me wrong—Drunky McBoobs is a nice piece of ass, but everyone else? What were you *thinking*? I thought this party was going to be *turnt*. I thought this ship was going to be full of people like *me*. Like *us*. Instead I get a mob of gold-digging losers more deserving of McDonald's uniforms than spacesuits. Do you have any idea what being seen with these people is going to do to my reputation? And to lose out on being leader to a pansy-ass Boy Scout? It's *libel* and it's *slander* and if you don't switch it up soon, I swear to God I'll sue the sparkly leather *pants* off your network—

OFF-AIR

With that, the 24/7 online feed cuts out.

For good.

RECEPTION

Item: Online article
Source: ViralLoad
Date: January 29, 2016

DV8 has done the impossible.

People said it would never work. They said it would fall flat on its face. What else could we expect from DV8—the ratty, loud, obnoxious little brother of televisiondom? What magical blend of factors could possibly come together to create something that people would want not only to watch but to devour? How else could one hour of television, followed by twelve hours of online content, spawn thousands of virtual words, hundreds of news segments, half a dozen dedicated podcasts, and a slew of new blogs and recaps, including by yours truly?

DV8 has tapped into something big.

The kids are perfectly cast. The spaceship is beautifully designed, well laid out, and provides infinite potential for titillating sight and sound bites. I mean, hello! HOT TUBS IN SPACE!!

And can we talk about the launch? The seemingly

low-budget air that pervaded the first half hour, with neither a hint of glitz nor glamour (aside from those *to-die-for* Alexander Wang ensembles)? The bad audio and the dead air: so preciously retro. Just a bunch of interstellar voyagers stuffed into spacesuits and flung out into the troposphere. NBD. Business as usual. Another day at the space office.

But then when they get to the ship—opulence! Trendiness! Gratuitous product placement!

And Clayton. DV8 has its hands full with that one! Insiders say that Clayton has been nipping at his uncle's heels for a while now, trying to carve out a slice of fame for himself. So what took so long for Chazz to cast him? Why now?

Regardless of the circumstances, he's jumped out to an early lead as villain of the season. In fact, his confessional outburst has led some to say that the online feed was cut off on purpose and not, as DV8 has since stated, because of technical difficulties. Then again, perhaps the blackout was planned all along. Maximum ratings can be achieved only if the footage is aired once—no one's going to tune in to the weekly broadcasts if half the world has seen and leaked the live feed already. So the theories are already pouring in that Chazz yanked the online coverage just as America was reaching its galactic climax. Always leave them wanting more . . .

To which I say: bring it on. I'm perfectly happy to gulp down whatever DV8 chooses to feed me each week. In this humble reviewer's opinion, reality is boring; abridged reality is not. As long as it's as compelling and watchable as the launch, wild space horses couldn't drag me away.

So I tip my hat to you, DV8.

Despite the shuttered online feeds, America's obsession with the show doesn't diminish; if anything, the scarcity of footage causes the phenomenon to balloon far more rapidly than even Chazz must have predicted.

Advertising dollars pour in. Everyone wants a piece of the space pie, especially those with opportune brand names: Orbit gum, Mars chocolate, and StarKist tuna all sign on as sponsors. Sales of Moon Boots soar. Consumers flock to IKEA, hoping to turn their homes into galactic/Swedish habitats. Bacon sales spike. KISS MY ASTRONAUT and CATCHPHRASE FOREVER T-shirts spring up everywhere. Stellar Acne Cream promises to pay DV8 ten thousand dollars every time someone says "Stellar!" onscreen.

Of course, not all press is positive. While many viewers believe—or choose to believe—that the ship really is in space, others question its veracity from the start. The most booming voice of dissent is the whistle-blowing website Fakefinders, offering a scathing take on the premiere episode within hours of its broadcast.

Item: Transcript of video recording
Source: Fakefinders
Date: January 29, 2016

[*A person in a Bigfoot mask faces the camera. His or her voice is distorted.*]

Bigfoot: *Waste of Space*, how do we fake thee? Let us count the ways:

1) Those spacesuits were not real. They are film-grade A7L white EVA suits. You can rent them from any decent costume shop in Hollywood.

2) That shuttle was an airplane cabin, perhaps modified to operate as a centrifuge to give the occupants a sense that they were traveling at high velocity.

3) Antigravity has not been invented yet.

4) All the wood onboard the ship—the sauna, the soundproof panels, the furniture—would never be allowed in space. Wood burns.

5) Chazz Young conveniently neglected to tell us anything

about the filtration systems onboard the ship—or what happens to all the human waste that's bound to be created with a crew that size.

6) And how did the ship get up there in the first place? If the cast had to use a shuttle to get there and dock with it, the ship must have been placed in orbit well beforehand. I didn't hear anything about a floating mansion being launched into space. Did anyone?

Need we go on?

Wake up, America.

Regardless of the naysayers, the show dominates the news cycles. Chazz Young suddenly becomes the hottest ticket in town. Though he is invited to appear on all the major talk shows, he sticks exclusively to Perky Paisley, for obvious reasons.

📹 · · · · · · · · · · · · · **ON–AIR** · · · · · · · · · · · · · · · · ·

Item: Transcript of video recording
Source: *The Perky Paisley Show*
Date: January 29, 2016

Perky: Can I feel your muscles?

Chazz: Go for it.

[*He flexes his bicep. Perky happily squeezes it. The crowd goes wild.*]

Perky: [*giggling*] I know that has nothing to do with the show. I just couldn't help myself.

Chazz: Few women can.

Perky: So! On to the matter at hand. Needless to say, last night's premiere has turned *Waste of Space* into a ginormous, monster Godzilla hit. It's all anyone can talk about!

Chazz: [*laughing*] Can you blame them?

Perky: No! I know I'm hooked! What's going to happen next?

Chazz: Sorry, Perky. [*with a coy grin at the camera*] I'm not at liberty to discuss.

Perky: You're soooo mean! How can you give us such television gold and then snatch it away?

Chazz: Oh, you know me. I like to tease.

Perky: But I was promised twenty-four-hour online access!

Chazz: I know, I know.

Perky: Be honest. What happened with the online feed?

Chazz: [*adopting an air of discomfort*] That's a bit of a sore subject, Perky. As you know, we've devoted the most cutting-edge resources to the production of this show. But no matter how many contingencies we plan for back on Earth, interstellar travel is unpredictable. Space things are bound to go space awry, and we just have to roll with the space punches.

Perky: You're so brave.

Chazz: Thank you.

Perky: But does this change mean anything in terms of the show's long-term plan?

Chazz: The way I look at it, this snag is a good thing. Now, every second counts. You'll be getting a full week's worth of action distilled into a half hour of pure, concentrated, spacy goodness.

Perky: Of course, that leaves a lot of room for editing.

Chazz: Perky, you have my solemn vow: what you see in the weekly episodes will remain as faithful as we can be to what is happening onboard the ship. No spin. No clever editing.

Everything exactly as it unfolds. Besides, it's not like we erase the rest of it—maybe when this is all over, we'll air a clip show of never-before-seen footage!

Perky: Sounds like a plan to me! So is there anything else you can tell us? Come on, give us a tease!

Chazz: What you saw in the pilot? A mere appetizer, America. A tiny taste of what's to come. You have no idea what we've got in store for these kids. Just think of what we'll be able to show you on the next episode, with a week's worth of footage under our belts!

Perky: We can't wait!

Chazz: I know.

Perky: Until next time . . . My eyes are up here!

■◀ • • • • • • • • • • • • • • **OFF-AIR** • • • • • • • • • • • • • • • • • •

_____

Over the course of the next week, the hype builds. DV8's editors get cranking. Viewing parties are organized.

And when Thursday night rolls around, America overwhelmingly tunes in.

EPISODE #2

Item: Transcript of video broadcast
Source: *Waste of Space*, Episode #2
Date aired: February 4, 2016

[*START OF ACT ONE*]

[*IMAGE: Morning. The Spacetronauts are gently roused from their slumber with another round of beeping, a "LIGHTS ON" announcement, and the sudden illumination of every light on the ship. Half of them pile into the bathroom to launch the shower/toilet/sink fight anew, while the others shuffle into the kitchen and pick helplessly through the drawers of food, perhaps expecting the contents to hop out and cook themselves.*]

Source: Camera #9—Kitchen

Snout: Let's see what's in the ole larder! [*He picks up a few items and reads the labels.*] Oat Meal Product, Dehydrated Potato Butter, Condensed Pizza. Hoo boy, this isn't looking good. [*He moves on to the toothpaste tubes.*] Heck, this stuff isn't even in English!

Bacardi: [*examining the tubes*] Goulash. Borscht.

Snout: Powdered Eggs. [*He rips open a packet.*] Let's see what I can do with this.

[*He pulls a pan out of the cabinet, turns on the hot plate, and gets cooking.*]

This setup is followed by a goofy montage of the kids trying to choke down the food they've been given. While it quickly becomes evident that Snout's omelets are the only edible provisions onboard the ship (along with the occasional foray into mystery-meat Meteor Chowder territory), DV8 can't help but play a series of clips wherein the alternatives are explored. Some of them are akin to the microwavable frozen dinners one finds in the Sadness Aisle of the grocery store, while some look legitimately like scientifically engineered space food, and not in a good way. The more horrifying among the packets are dense bricks emblazoned with such unsettling labels as GLUTINOUS GRAVY and DAIRY PRODUCT. Jamarkus warily removes a slab from the packaging and crumbles it over his Macaroni and Curd Sustenance. Bacardi chomps down on another, creating a noise like a cleaving glacier and sending fragments across the floor. Kaoru looks very, very sad.

After the culinary hijinks have been exhausted, the earlier scene picks up where it left off.

[*Each cast member is given an omelet, and Snout is given several thankful pats on the back. As the dining area in the kitchen is too small to accommodate the full crew, they eat together in the Lünar Lounge.*]

Source: Camera #3—Lünar Lounge

Hibiscus: [*picking at her omelet with disdain*] Wasn't there a vegan option?

Bacardi: Gahd. [*takes a swig of something*] Even *I* think you're the most annoying one here, Eye Piss Kiss.

Hibiscus: Hibiscus.

Bacardi: Whatever. Go back to your yoga.

[*Hibiscus glares at her, then launches into a headstand.*]

Titania: [*inspecting a wall of switches*] What do you think all these instruments do? Should we futz with them?

Jamarkus: No way. You heard Chazz—we shouldn't touch anything unless we are explicitly instructed to.

Louise: But we're explorers! We have to make things happen!

Titania: Exactly. They can't cram ten of us into a ship full of tempting buttons and expect us not to press them. [*She reaches out to flip a switch.*]

Jamarkus: Wait!

[*Titania hesitates, but Louise jumps in front of her and flips it anyway. Nothing happens.*]

Louise: [*crestfallen*] It didn't do anything.

Jamarkus: That you *know* of. What if it sent out a signal? What if it turned off our guidance system?

Titania: I feel like there'd be some indication that—

Matt: Guys? [*pointing at the control panel*] This red light is blinking. Was it doing that before?

Jamarkus: [*hurrying to join him*] Oh no.

Matt: What's happening?

[*A repeated beeping noise sounds. The disembodied robot voice announces, "ASTEROID ATTACK."*]

Titania: I think it's an asteroid attack.

Louise: Yay!

Snout: Oh no!

Colonel Bacon: [*squeal*]

Jamarkus: Everyone grab hold of something!

Bacardi: Should we duck?

Titania: [*her hands over her ears*] Can someone please turn off the beeping?

Jamarkus: Prepare for impact!

[*A series of crashes assaults the ship. Dents appear in the walls. Small pieces of plastic break off the control panel and skitter across the floor. The Windows Window displays jagged rocks hissing by, trailing wisps of steam. Hibiscus falls out of her headstand. Snout hugs Colonel Bacon. Bacardi vomits in the corner, though it's unclear whether this is related to the unfolding situation.*]

Titania: [*hands still over her ears*] I mean it! Stop the beeping!

Matt: Oh God. What's happening?

Kaoru: {It sounds like someone is throwing rocks at us.}

Clayton: [*emerging from the bedroom*] How much longer is this going to—ow! [*A piece of the ship strikes him in the forehead. He puts a hand to his head, then shouts directly into Camera #3*] What the bleeding hell—

Source: Camera #4—Lünar Lounge

Hibiscus: It's futile to resist the pulsations of our natural environs. Stop trying to impose your human supremacy on . . .

Everyone else: SHUT UP!

Clayton: [*bleeding from the head*] Where's the first aid—[*He trips over Colonel Bacon.*] Godammit! Get this stupid pig out of my way!

Snout: So sorry, I—

Clayton: Don't be sorry! Be less useless!

Bacardi: I found a fire esssstingisher, does that help?

Clayton: Do you see any fires? Then no.

Matt: Oh God, we're gonna die. I quit. I quit!

[*He lunges for the I QUIT™ button, but Louise yet again stands in his way.*]

Louise: No! That's for real emergencies!

Matt: What would you call this?

Louise: A setback! That button is the sort of thing that should be saved for something really terrible, like—

Matt: An asteroid attack?

Louise: You honestly want your time up here to end so soon?

Matt: If the alternative is certain death, then it's kind of a no-brainer, isn't it?

Louise: I don't see it that way.

Matt: What if an asteroid breaks through? What are we supposed to do then?

Clayton: We could use the pig to plug up the hole.

Snout: Hey! Colonel Bacon is not a plug!

Colonel Bacon: [*squeal*]

Hibiscus: [*produces her mandolin and strums a tuneless melody*] The pig is not a plug / big religion is a drug . . .

Everyone else: SHUT UP!

Jamarkus: Everyone remain calm! I got this!

[*Jamarkus rushes to the control panel.*]

Jamarkus: *Laika*, permission to fire?

Robot Voice: PERMISSION GRANTED.

[*Jamarkus grabs the joystick. In the Windows Window, a target sight appears. Jamarkus drags the cursor until it's hovering over an asteroid, then pulls the trigger, then repeats. The asteroids explode one by one, disintegrating into smaller,* harmless debris. Within a minute the field is clear, the ship stops vibrating, the blinking lights go dark, and the beeping ceases. The cast members cautiously get to their feet.

Thus begins a confessional montage.]

Source: Camera #7—Confessional Closet

[*Snippets of private interviews are played back-to-back in rapid succession.*]

Nico: So. Asteroid attack.

Jamarkus: I was scared, to be sure—but fortunately, I was able to fend off the projectiles, steer us to safety, and triumph over adversity. I couldn't have done it without the support of my loyal crew.

Clayton: What a goddamn jackass.

Titania: [*head in hands*] Please stop the beeping. The constant beeping. At bedtime. In the morning. During emergencies. I cannot take it. It's like little pings of torture stabbing at my nerves, pecking away at them like—like—

Matt: Oh God. I guess we flew through a field of galactic debris or something. And, uh—crap, for a minute there, it really did feel like we were in trouble. But we're not, right? I mean, we're on TV. They wouldn't let us get killed by moon rocks on TV.

Kaoru: {The asteroid attack has only served to further upset my already distressed stomach. Please give us some real food.}

Bacardi: [*wiping off her mouth and looking at her hand*] Ugh. I definitely don't remember eating that.

Louise: It's unlikely that the rubble we encountered was from the asteroid belt between Mars and Jupiter, as that would mean we've traveled one hundred and thirty-four million miles in just seven days. So I suspect that this was either a rogue patch of remnants from a planetary collision or possibly wreckage

from an unidentified destroyed spacecraft. Or maybe . . .
[*quieter, to herself*] maybe Lord Balway Galway is testing us . . .

Hibiscus: [*still playing her mandolin*] Battered by an
asteroid / seven million unemployed—

Snout: The colonel's doing all right. He got spooked, for sure,
but I think he's back to normal now. Ain't that right, buddy?

[*Colonel Bacon squeals. Snout sighs.*]

This is harder than I thought it would be. And not just the
space stuff—the people, too. I've done my darnedest to relate
to the others, but what a tough bunch of corn to shuck! So
complicated. Always saying the opposite of what they mean,
and being ugly to each other for no reason, and fighting when
we should be putting our heads together to figure this out. I
just don't know what's gonna happen.

[*Another squeal issues from off-camera.*]

Colonel Bacon, no! Not the tripod!

Disaster or not, the asteroid attack produces one positive outcome: cast members begin to open up to one another, testing the
waters with the unlikely companions they must now rely upon for
support. Some accomplish this via heartfelt conversations; others,
via toys.

Source: Camera #4—Lünar Lounge

[*Matt inspects the board games contained within the
Fjälkinge shelving unit.*]

Matt: Anyone up for a game of Hungry Hungry Hippos?

Jamarkus: Yessss! I call Homer Hippo!

[*Matt and Jamarkus sit down to play. Louise joins them. Nico
looks up from the couch, where he is paging through the IKEA
catalog.*]

Jamarkus: Hey, buddy! You in? It's real good training for hand-eye coordination—which we'll all need to brush up on if there are any more attacks coming our way!

Nico: No, thanks.

Jamarkus: Suit yourself. Kaoru, wanna play?

[*He mimes the gameplay to Kaoru, who has been looking wistfully out the Windows Window. She joins them with a sigh.*]

Kaoru: [*pointing at the box*] {This says it is for children five through nine. Can we play something more age-appropriate?}

Jamarkus: That's right, make the hippo eat the marbles! Annnnd . . . go!

[*The players furiously pump the levers, plastic clacking at a feverish pace. As soon as Jamarkus nabs the last marble, he grabs the whole game and jumps to his feet.*]

Jamarkus: CRUSHED IT!

[*He throws it to the floor as if spiking a football. The plastic shatters, sending shards and marbles flying across the lounge. Homer Hippo knocks a complicated-looking circuit board off the wall.*]

Jamarkus: Oops! Sorry, guys. Got carried away there, didn't I? I can get kind of competitive.

Matt: Should we be concerned about that?

[*He points at the circuit board, now lying face-down on the floor. No emergency beeping is sounding. There are no exposed wires, because the circuit board had not been connected to anything. It appears to have been held in place with shiny strips of sticky fabric.*]

Jamarkus: Nope! [*He rushes to pick up the circuit board, sticking it back onto the wall.*] Not to worry. Look, good as new!

Matt: Was that duct tape?

Jamarkus: [*chuckles*] Common misconception. It's highly conductive adhesive. Developed by the Soviet space program back in 1968.

Louise: Oh yeah . . . I think I heard about that! They used it onboard their Soyuz spacecraft, right?

Jamarkus: [*after staring at her for a moment*] Right! It's a modern marvel!

[*The circuit board falls to the floor again. Louise adopts a confused, hurt expression as she hurries to put it back in place, while Kaoru looks at Camera #4 and mouths the Japanese word for "deceit."*]

Source: Camera #8—Bedroom

[*Colonel Bacon is alone in the bedroom, sitting proudly on the king-size bed. Bacardi enters.*]

Bacardi: Heylook! A pig inna blanket!

[*She dissolves into hysterical laughter. Snout rushes in.*]

Snout: Cripes, I'm sorry. Colonel Bacon, get off that bed!

Bacardi: Nah, it's okay. [*She sits on the bed and pets Colonel Bacon.*] I guess he is kinda cute. Here, piggy, piggy.

Snout: Aw, see? He likes you!

Bacardi: Yeah, I guess he does!

Snout: Oh—oh dear. Colonel Bacon, stop that.

Bacardi: Why? He's a better kisser than most of my boyfriends.

Snout: You know, he's still very much a piglet at heart, so maybe you shouldn't tug so hard on his—

Bacardi: *Here, piggy, piggy!*

Snout: Oh my. Oh my. [*looks helplessly into camera*]

Source: Camera #9—Kitchen

[*Nico and Titania are seated at the table, attempting to eat a* package of astronaut ice cream. They have split the sponge-like brick into pieces and are crunching it between their teeth and wincing.]

Titania: I rule this inedible.

Nico: Seconded.

Titania: [chewing it anyway] So where are you from?

Nico: You mean currently? Or originally?

Titania: I mean however you want to answer.

Nico: You don't care where I was born?

Titania: Should I?

Nico: Most white people are curious.

Titania: Because most white people like to be able to tick off the box and congratulate themselves on making a Diverse Friend.

Nico: That is . . . exactly right. How did you know that?

Titania: Because I just congratulated myself on making a Diverse Friend.

[Nico snickers.]

Nico: Maybe I'm just really suntanned.

Titania: Uh-huh.

Nico: Or maybe I'm an alien.

Titania: If we land on another planet, we'll all be aliens.

Nico: True. [brushing ice cream crumbs off his hands] I'm Ecuadorian. My parents moved to New York when I was two, hoping to find better opportunities. [quieter] And much later is when we all found out what a fun little mistake that all was.

Titania: How . . .

[Nico shakes his head quickly, firmly.]

Titania: Okay.

[The ensuing silence is palpable. Titania begins to fidget; she clearly wants to break the silence but doesn't want to push him.

Nico's face, meanwhile, is screwed up in the eternal shy-guy internal argument: shut up while he's ahead or attempt more conversation? Everything is then made ten times worse as Bacardi, flailing down the hall, ducks her head into the kitchen and lets out a guffaw.]

Bacardi: Well, isn't this sickeningly adorable—an ice cream date. Bet America is shipping you two so hard right now.

Nico: Huh?

Bacardi: Y'know, rooting for you to bump nasties. Get a room, lovebirds!

[She prances off.]

Nico: *[dazed]* We *do* have a room.

Titania: *[with a flustered yet cleansing breath]* Anyway. Your turn.

Nico: Hmm?

Titania: I asked you a question. You can ask me one, if you want.

Nico: Oh. Okay. *[grasping]* What's . . . your favorite color?

Titania: *[starts to laugh at him, but catches herself and smiles politely]* Blue.

Nico: Why blue?

Titania: I find it calming. Safe. Quiet. What's yours?

Nico: I don't know. Clear.

Titania: *Clear?* Clear is not a color.

Nico: Technically, it's all the colors.

Titania: You're thinking of white.

Nico: No, white is white. Clear is all the colors at once.

Titania: You're not very good at questions. Or colors, for that matter.

Nico: In my defense, I've gotten about ten hours of sleep over the past few days. This place is majorly screwing with my head.

[*Titania looks around the lamentable kitchen.*]
Titania: I think it's supposed to.
[*MUSIC CUE: "Crazy" by Gnarls Barkley*]
[*END OF ACT ONE; CUT TO COMMERCIAL*]

◼◀ · · · · · · · · · · · · · · · · **OFF–AIR** · · · · · · · · · · · · · · · · · ·

_____

The second episode of *Waste of Space* gives the impression that it's nonstop action onboard the ship and that aside from a few hiccups, the crew has pulled together under the stellar leadership of Jamarkus to triumph over all the adversity that's being thrown at them.

But offscreen, things aren't going well. The jump cut during the asteroid attack is one telling example of DV8 editing out what they didn't want the audience to hear. Clayton's full statement into camera number 3 was:

"What the bleeding hell, Uncle Chazz? I was promised there'd be no physical danger! You want me to sue you for this too?"

Chazz's solemn vow to accurately capture the happenings onboard the ship is, of course, a spicy stick of baloney. Airing only twenty-two minutes out of a full week leaves 10,058 minutes on the cutting-room floor—and the lack of an online feed means that aside from what is carefully handpicked to be broadcast in the weekly episodes, the raw, unedited footage shot onboard the *Laika* is seen by no one.

Luckily, DV8's internal data-security protocols are so flimsy that even a disgruntled former employee can gain access to them. Here's the unseen second half of the previous conversation:

Item: Transcript of video recording—RAW, UNAIRED FOOTAGE
Source: Camera #9—Kitchen
Date: January 30, 2016

[*Clayton enters the kitchen. Noticing that Nico and Titania have torn into the astronaut ice cream, he grins.*]

Clayton: Let me see that.

[*Nico hands him a piece of the ice cream. Clayton pulls out a lighter and holds the flame up to it.*]

Clayton: *Psf.* Doesn't even explode.

Titania: They let you bring a lighter?

Clayton: They let me bring a lot of things. [*He puts the lighter away and crumbles some ice cream onto the table.*] This stuff wasn't actually sent into space, did you know that? It was too gross even for the astronauts, so they let the myth persist and sold it in museum gift shops instead.

Titania: How do you know that?

Clayton: My parents rented out the Air and Space Museum for my seventh birthday, and that's what the museum director told me after I stole the packets out of all the other kids' gift bags. I think he was trying to trick me into giving them back, but I flushed them all down the toilet anyway.

Titania: At least you took the high road.

Clayton: [*turning to Titania*] Oooh, is it time to pass judgment? Awesome. My turn. So what happened back there with the asteroid attack? You really fell apart.

Titania: Did I.

Clayton: Don't like beeping, huh? Why not? Flashing back to your robot childhood? [*He jabs Nico with his elbow, laughing. Nico does not laugh.*]

Titania: I dislike annoying things and choose not to put up with them. Allow me to demonstrate. [*She gets up and leaves the room.*]

Clayton: Whatever, bitch.

Nico: Hey.

Clayton: What?

Nico: [*backing down*] Nothing.

[*Clayton grabs Nico in a headlock.*]

Clayton: Cheer up, emo kid. I know you've said, like, three words since we got here, so you've probably gotten, like, three seconds of screen time. But there's still plenty of opportunity to make a strong impression. You won't be the breakout star, obvs, but you might want to come up with a way to stand out, if you want to be remembered. But no flushing other people's stuff down the toilet! That's gonna be my thing!

Nico: [*muttering into Clayton's arm*] If only you could get the same outcome by being a decent human being.

Clayton: I know, right? Oh well. [*He lets go of Nico, grabs the ice cream off the counter, and runs out of the room. Seconds later there is a sound of a toilet flushing, followed by cheering.*]

These juicy morsels of content, however, are rare. That first week, the majority of the footage shot onboard the *Laika* is of unwatchable tedium. Apparently even a futuristic spaceship can get real old, real fast.

**Item: Transcript of video recording—RAW, UNAIRED
FOOTAGE**
Source: Multiple cameras
Date: February 2, 2016

[*Seven of the ten Spacetronauts are in the Lünar Lounge,
lounging, as the ship gently rocks, causing runaway marbles from
the Hungry Hungry Hippos game to skitter back and forth across
the floor. Kaoru and Titania are sitting on the swivel chairs at the
control panel, swiveling listlessly. Jamarkus, Matt, Snout, and
Hibiscus are sitting on the floor, each playing their own game of
solitaire. Bacardi is passed out on the puffy Püffi chair. Louise
is sitting on her bunk with the sheets pulled over her head like
a ghost, a flashlight dancing within her tented form. Nico is
showering. Clayton is skinny-dipping in the hot tub, his naked body
prominently visible through the window behind the bar.*]

Hibiscus: He's mooning us.

Jamarkus: Ignore him. He only wants attention.

[*They go back to their cards. An hour goes by before anyone
speaks again.*]

So the day before the second episode airs, Chazz makes a phone
call.

Item: Transcript of audio recording
Source: Chazz's cell phone
Date: February 3, 2016

Chazz: They're not *doing* anything!

NASAW: That's not our fault. We built the ship, we suited
them up, we pretended to launch them into space. We held

up our end of the bargain. Anything beyond that is out of our control.

Chazz: No one's talking! And none of them have hit the I QUIT™ button! After the thrill of the asteroid attack, everything went stale. It's like watching a middle school dance, with everyone off in their own corners! The only action is in the bedroom with Clayton and Bacardi, and we can't even air that due to underage indecency laws!

NASAW: Yeah. Pity, that.

Chazz: *They're not making good television.* They're sitting around being lethargic! They're looking out the window! They're using the confessional room to sing goddamn drinking songs! They're—

NASAW: Being teenagers?

Chazz: Yes! What the hell?

NASAW: What did you expect to happen? Was your plan to simply throw millions of dollars of special effects at them and hope for the best? Did you expect a 168-hour week to fill itself with content? Because you're right—watching ten strangers sit around doing nothing *is* excruciatingly boring, no matter what age they are or where in spacetime they're flying—

Chazz: You have to do something. Spring a gas leak. Set a fire.

NASAW: We're not going to set a group of children on fire. [*muttering*] Never thought I'd have to say *that* out loud—

Chazz: Well, we have to do something. Throw the next Instigating Plot Point at them.

NASAW: Already? The schedule says the gyrostatic system failure isn't supposed to happen until next week—

Chazz: But they're being boring *now!*

NASAW: These plot points were supposed to last us for another two months. You want us to start burning through the schedule on a daily basis?

Chazz: Screw the schedule! We need to *ramp things up!* Otherwise none of them are going to quit, no one's going to get eliminated, and watchability is going to plummet!

NASAW: But—

Chazz: Do it!

📹 · · · · · · · · · · · · · · · **ON-AIR** · · · · · · · · · · · · · · · · · ·

Item: Transcript of video broadcast

[*continued*]

[*START OF ACT TWO*]

[*After another commercial break, instead of more footage from the ship, DV8 plays . . . filler. Man-on-the-street interviews with viewers, plus an extensive overview of how swiftly the show has caught on and a clip of Chazz's appearance on* The Perky Paisley Show. *Then some social media coverage, featuring posts submitted by viewers whose opinions apparently warrant the nation's full attention. Then there's an exclusive interview with the cast of the upcoming* Cosmic Crusades *movie, followed by an exclusive trailer for the upcoming* Cosmic Crusades *movie. Then, finally, it's back to the matter at hand.*]

Source: Camera #6—Bathroom

[*Titania and Snout are squeezed together in front of the mirror, both brushing their teeth. Matt is showering.*]

Titania: [*spitting into the sink*] I don't know why we're bothering with this. Our food is practically toothpaste itself.

[*As if on cue, Snout's stomach growls.*]

Snout: Wish we had some real grub.

Titania: Me too. Seems a shame to have such a good omelet chef and no real eggs.

Snout: If we had eggs, I'd screw that up somehow too. Drop 'em all. [*He looks at her.*] You think I'm dumb, huh?

Titania: [*frowns*] No, I don't.

Snout: Everyone thinks I'm dumb. And I bet they're mad at me because I eat the most because I'm the biggest.

Titania: I don't think that's the case.

Snout: But how do you know? I see the way they look at me. Like I'm nothin'. Like I'm less a person than they are because my town don't got a stoplight.

Titania: Hey. [*catches his eye*] I don't think you're less than.

Snout: [*squeezing his tummy*] Yeah. More like more than.

Titania: I don't think you're dumb, either.

Snout: Yeah, but—but I don't know about any of this space stuff. I haven't seen any of the world.

[*Music swells.*]

Titania: There are plenty of ways to be dumb, Snout. But there are also plenty of ways to be smart.

[*Matt lets out a screech from the shower. Titania and Snout turn toward him, but the scene cuts away.*]

Source: Camera #2—Flight Deck

[*The Spacetronauts are lounging. Louise and Bacardi are apart from the rest, sitting at the control panel. Louise is looking out the Windows Window. Bacardi is drinking "water" out of a Slom bottle.*]

Louise: Space is so beautiful, isn't it?

Bacardi: Yurra sweet kid. How old are you?

Louise: Fourteen.

Bacardi: You the youngest one here?

Louise: I think so. But what I lack in age I more than make up for in space knowledge.

Bacardi: Oh yeah?

Louise: Oh yeah. Did you know that the scene in *Cosmic Crusades* when the Jjesibian Nebula collapses due to intergalactic transdimensional space tornadoes *could* theoretically happen?

Bacardi: [*hiccups*] I didnot know that.

Louise: And that long ago a secret race of lizard people crashed to Earth, and they've spent the last several millennia building the pyramids and establishing clandestine governmental agencies and causing global warming with weather machines, all in an effort to open up wormholes that'll send them back to their home planet?

Bacardi: [*attention wandering*] Really.

Louise: *And* that the technology for travel between multiverses is well within our power, and that if one were so inclined, one could use everyday household goods to construct one's own FTL drive?

Bacardi: FTL?

Louise: Faster than light. It's the quickest way to get from one end of the universe to the other. The technology is there. We just need to figure out how to unlock it.

Bacardi: *I* unlocked the hotel mini fridge! [*burps*] You know, Louise, we're notso different, you and I.

[*Bacardi sloppily brushes her hand down Louise's face. Louise dodges away, miffed.*]

Louise: I find that hard to believe.

[*A dripping-wet Matt comes running into the lounge from the bathroom, holding a towel around his waist.*]

Matt: Um, guys? Something's wrong!

Clayton: It's called shrinkage, kid.

Matt: No, no, it's—come look!

Source: Camera #6—Bathroom

[*They all pile into the bathroom, where Titania and Snout are staring into the shower stall.*]

Matt: Look at the soap!

[*A bar of soap is sliding in circles along the bottom of the shower—by itself.*]

Louise: We're spinning.

Jamarkus: Dear God, no. [*shouting*] To your battle stations!

Bacardi: We have battle stations?

Source: Camera #4—Lünar Lounge

[*The kids run back into the lounge. The instant they get there, the room bucks beneath their feet. Everyone crashes to the floor and rolls violently across it along with the furniture, some Slom bottles, and the Hungry Hungry Hippo marbles, everything and everyone smooshing into a pile of limbs and shrieks against the legs of the pool table—except for the inflatable puffy Püffi chair, which cheerfully bounces about the room like a balloon.*]

Snout: [*gripping the tail of Colonel Bacon, who looks petrified*] What's going on?

Jamarkus: We've lost attitude control!

Bacardi: Speak for yourself, *my* attitude is flawless.

Jamarkus: No, attitude as in spatial balance—as in flight dynamics! The orientation actuators! The gyrostatic system!

Matt: In English, please!

Jamarkus: The thing that controls our balance has switched off. We've lost all equilibrium, and we're spinning uncontrollably. Look!

[*He points at the Windows Window. Outside, the stars blur by in streaks. Intermittently the blue ball of Earth appears, pinballing wildly across the view.*]

Matt: That's it! [*He staggers to his feet.*] Screw the million dollars, I'm done!

[*He lurches across the lounge to the flight deck and pounds his fist on the I QUIT™ button—but it does not oblige.*]

Matt: It won't push! It's stuck!

Hibiscus: What do you mean, it's stuck?

Matt: Something's wedged between it and the control panel! [*He inspects the button.*] It's a marble!

Clayton: Those goddamn marbles. You *had* to feed the hippos—

Matt: [*struggling to free the marble*] It's really jammed in there! I can't get it out! [*He takes another look at the reeling Windows Window.*] Oh God. I'm gonna be sick.

Hibiscus: Me too.

Kaoru: {Me too.}

[*A shared vomiting session commences.*]

Jamarkus: Wait! I know what to do! *Laika*, permission to pull stabilization lever?

Robot Voice: PERMISSION GRANTED.

[*Jamarkus pulls the lever, and the ship instantly begins to level out. The return to digestive normalcy, however, is not as speedy, as the sustained gagging noises demonstrate.*]

[*CUT TO: Chazz, in the studio.*]

Chazz: How about *that*, America?

Don't worry about our space pals—they all made a full recovery. But right now it's time for what you've all been waiting for: our *live* check-in! We're going to take a quick break, and when we come back, we've got a HUGE surprise for you all—and for our Spacetronauts. Don't go anywhere!

[*MUSIC CUE: "Down with the Sickness" by Disturbed*]

[*END OF ACT TWO; CUT TO COMMERCIAL*]

🎥◀ ················· OFF-AIR ····················

Chazz is the very model of a confident pitchman. But if hawk-eyed viewers look a little closer, they may notice the faint sheen of sweat creeping across his brow. Because he knows something no one else does. Something that wouldn't have been a problem if he had put more effort into casting. Something that leads to more frantic, anxious phone calls.

Item: Transcript of audio recording
Source: Chazz's cell phone
Date: February 3, 2016

Chazz: Well, that was a major misfire.

NASAW: How so? You succeeded in emptying the stomachs of every kid onboard. Isn't that a success, in your deranged book?

Chazz: It would be—*if* the I QUIT™ button had worked! What are the odds of that goddamn marble getting stuck in there?

NASAW: Pretty good, if it was crammed in on purpose.

Chazz: Wait—what? Are you saying someone sabotaged it?

NASAW: It's not outside the realm of possibility.

Chazz: Did you see something? If you saw something, say something!

NASAW: It's not my job to watch these kids twenty-four hours a day. If anything happened, someone in your control room should have spotted it. Of course, the kids know where the cameras are. It'd be easy for them to block the angle of—

Chazz: Whatever. This is bad, is what I'm getting at.

NASAW: Why? Can't you still send someone to pick up the quitters? The button doesn't work anyway.

Chazz: But we need the illusion that the button *does* work. If it doesn't, none of them will even try to quit!

NASAW: May *I* quit?

Chazz: No! What are we going to do now? We were planning to use the live segment this week to trash-talk the losers—what are we going to do if there are no losers?

NASAW: I think we're all losers at this point.

Chazz: Dude, *work with me here*. We're going live on the air in less than twenty-four hours, and no one's been eliminated yet! We need to figure something out!

NASAW: But—

Chazz: Wait a minute. I have an idea.

NASAW: Does it involve the Cosmic Crusaders? Because as I've already explained to you on a baffling number of occasions, the Cosmic Crusaders cannot help us, because they are not real.

Chazz: No, no, something else. Don't go anywhere, I'm putting you on hold.

[*"Payphone" by Maroon 5 blasts for a minute and thirty-seven seconds.*]

Chazz: Back. Are you still there?

NASAW: I'm in the middle of a desert. There's nowhere to go.

Chazz: I just emailed you a list of new builds. Please have them ready to go by tomorrow night.

NASAW: *Wait.* Stay on the line while I read them, in case I have any questions.

Chazz: Ugh, fine. [*away from phone*] Khloe, don't you dare. I'm not scrubbing poop out of Kourtney's ears again.

NASAW: [*reading from the email*] "A large, functional robotic arm"?

Chazz: That's right.

NASAW: Are you serious? [*muttering*] That's going to put us way behind schedule.

Chazz: What schedule? The only schedule you're on is the one *we* give you.

NASAW: But how do you expect us to install something like that without the kids hearing us?

Chazz: Hey, you're the scientists. You figure it out.

[*There is a weary sigh on NASAW's end.*]

NASAW: If you ask me, you're heading down a real slippery slope here.

Chazz: I don't recall asking you.

NASAW: I'm serious, Chazz. Pivoting your concept like this on such short notice—it's a recipe for disaster. The more you mess with the plan, the more dangerous everything becomes. Someone could get hurt.

Chazz: Of course they could. That's what makes it so thrilling.

NASAW: I—what?

Chazz: You know, you dorks could stand to be more like the real NASA. They were masters of marketing, did you know that? Back in the days of the space race, when garnering a positive public opinion was all that mattered, they developed a little saying that we here at DV8 have taken to heart—and I think you should do the same.

NASAW: And that is?

Chazz: Better dead than look bad.

[*end of call*]

Item: Transcript of video recording—RAW, UNAIRED FOOTAGE
Source: Camera #4—Lünar Lounge
Date: February 3, 2016

[*It is nighttime. Stars lazily drift by the Windows Window, its meager output the only source of light in the room.*]

Source: Camera #8—Bedroom

[*All the Spacetronauts are in bed.*]

Source: Camera #1—Airlock

[*Several shadowy figures bring a large, unwieldy piece of equipment into the airlock, set it on the floor, and get to work.*]

[*An hour passes.*]

Source: Camera #8—Bedroom

[*Someone stirs, throws off the blanket, and gets out of bed.*]

Source: Camera #4—Lünar Lounge

[*Titania walks into the lounge and stands in front of the airlock, frowning, as the noises behind it persist. She knocks quietly on the door. The noises pause, then continue.*]

[*Nico enters the lounge and walks to her side.*]

Titania: [*whispering*] You heard it too?

Nico: Yeah. I couldn't sleep anyway.

[*They stare at the airlock.*]

Nico: What do you think it is?

Titania: I don't know. Wanna wait to see if anything happens?

Nico: Sure.

[*They sit on the frizzy purple rug in front of the airlock. Nico picks at the rug's fibers before visibly screwing up his courage.*]

Nico: Can I ask you something personal?

Titania: Maybe.

Nico: What's with the scar on your stomach?

[*Titania stiffens.*]

Titania: Excuse me?

Nico: The scar—

Titania: How did you see that?

Nico: [*courage fading*] I—I'm sorry. I didn't mean to. You were changing into your pajamas last night, and I accidentally—I wasn't *watching*—

Titania: All right, all right. Relax.

[*pause*]

Nico: I'm sorry. Forget I said anything.

Titania: No, it's okay. It's a . . . puncture wound.

Nico: Oh.

Titania: I was in an accident.

Nico: What kind of accident?

Titania: The kind I don't want to talk about.

Nico: Okay. Is it the same reason you hate the beeping?

[*She nods.*]

Nico: Okay.

[*Nico taps his fingers on his knee.*]

Nico: If it makes you feel any better, I have a regrettable puncture wound too.

[*He points at his pierced lip. Titania smirks.*]

Titania: Why'd you get it?

Nico: Seemed like a good idea at the time.

Titania: And now?

Nico: Now I have to keep the ring in so my face doesn't spurt like a water gun.

[*Titania stares at him—then snorts.*]

Titania: You made a joke.

Nico: You almost laughed.

Titania: Almost. [*She forces her mouth into a straight line, then lets her shoulders slump.*] We are officially the sad sacks of the show, aren't we.

Nico: Afraid so.

Titania: What do you think America thinks of us?

Nico: I don't know. I hope we're the wry, sarcastic ones the audience most relates to. I'd rather that than get lumped in with the nutballs.

Titania: You're not a nutball?

[*pause*]

Nico: Honestly, I don't have the first effing clue who I am.

Titania: Meh. No one does.

[*The noises behind the airlock stop. Nico and Titania wait for more, but none come.*]

Titania: [*softly*] Nico? Do you think we're really in space?

[*He looks at her with wide eyes, as if surprised by the insinuation that they might not be. Then, mulling it over, he frowns.*]

Nico: I don't know. I hope so. But I don't know.

[*More waiting. More quiet.*]

Titania: Guess the show's over.

[*They stand up and walk back into the bedroom together.*]

Source: Camera #1—Airlock

[*The large piece of equipment is gone. The shadowy figures have left.*]

Source: Camera #4—Lünar Lounge

[*The next morning, the kids wake up and groggily head into the lounge, none the wiser.*]

······ ▪◀ ······· ON–AIR ······················

Item: Transcript of video broadcast

[*continued*]

[*START OF ACT THREE*]

[*IMAGE: Chazz, in the studio*]

Chazz: Welcome back, America. It's time for that big surprise I promised!

But first, a small confession. Those of you out there who either visited DV8's website or used DV8's app at any point over the past week were given a pop-up survey asking you to vote for your favorite cast member—but what we *didn't* tell you is that the results of that vote will have real-life consequences. That's right: the least-liked cast member will be eliminated from the show—live, on-air, tonight! [*to someone offscreen*] How are we doing on that satellite feed?

[*He presumably gets a thumbs-up, as he gives a thumbs-up back.*]

All right, I'm being told we're good to go! Spacetronauts, hello!

Source: Camera #4—Lünar Lounge

[*The cast is gathered in front of the camera as if it's elementary school picture day. Their discomfort is evident, except for Jamarkus and Louise.*]

Jamarkus: Hi, Chazz!

Louise: Greetings, Earth!

Chazz: Looking good, intrepid explorers! Now, I know you can't see us, but we can see you—so why don't you give all of America a big wave?

[*The cast gives all of America a tepid wave, except for Jamarkus and Louise, who pump their hands vigorously.*]

Chazz: Bitchin'! How's it going up there?

Louise: Amazing!

Jamarkus: Stellar!

[*A graphic accompanied by the words "Brought to you by Stellar Acne Cream!" flashes across the bottom of the screen.*]

Hibiscus: Still queasy from the loss of equilibrium.

Matt: And it's super dry in here from all the recirculated air. Our skin is chapped, and I got a nosebleed—

Chazz: That's wonderful! All of us back on Earth are so proud of you, and we can't wait to see what adventures you get up to next. But we've got one little piece of business to take care of first. The audience has spoken, and I'm afraid you're going to lose one of your planemates tonight.

Matt: . . . Lose them? What do you mean?

[*Music swells.*]

Chazz: The next name that I call will be the cast member with the fewest number of votes.

Snout: Votes? What votes?

[*The cast members exchange nervous glances. The music builds to a frenzied climax.*]

Chazz: And that name is . . .

[*The music drops out.*]

Hibiscus. Hibiscus, *you* are a waste of space.

Hibiscus: [*frowning*] What?

143

[*The ship's alarm sounds, filling the air with strident, inescapable beeping. The airlock door opens to reveal a twitchy robotic arm unfolding itself from the wall and clumsily extending all the way into the Lünar Lounge. Its claw clamps around Hibiscus's waist, then hauls her, kicking and screaming, into the airlock. The door closes with a pneumatic swish, sealing her inside. A few more seconds of her pounding on the door, and then—WHOOOSH.*]

[*CUT TO: Exterior shot of a spacesuited person being expelled from the* Laika, *bubble helmet gleaming in the glow of the sun, spinning uncontrollably, limbs flailing*]

[*CUT TO: Interior shot of the* Laika, *the remaining Spacetronauts frozen in a stunned silence.*]

[*CUT TO: Chazz, in the studio, beaming.*]

Chazz: So long, Hibiscus! Your fedora can't save you now! [*He laughs heartily as the credits roll.*] Well, that wraps it up for tonight. Tune in next week for another thrilling episode of *Waste of Space*—and until then, be sure to log on to DV8.com or the DV8 app to vote, or your favorite cast member might be ejected next! Catchphrase forever!

[*MUSIC CUE: "Blank Space" by Taylor Swift*]

[*END OF EPISODE*]

OFF–AIR

ACCLAIM

Item: Online article
Source: ViralLoad
Date: February 5, 2016

It's official. DV8 has officially lost its mind.

And we are *loving every second of it.*

Major network executives, I hope you're paying attention. Drop your lattes and study each frame of what they're doing over on *Waste of Space.* THIS is compelling television. THIS is the future of entertainment as we know it.

You want ratings?

Shoot a sixteen-year-old girl out of an airlock.

DV8 has redefined the meaning of unpredictable television. What in the hell is Chazz Young going to do to those poor space kids next?

Let's be honest—technical glitches aside, what we saw in the premiere episode wasn't anything new. Sure, blasting a bunch of teenagers into space on live television hadn't been done before, but the rest of it oozed with reality clichés. The hyperbole. The predictable, stereotypical casting. The tour of the poshly furnished living quarters and its conspicuous product placement. Chazz Young's freshly frosted tips.

But this week we got a glimpse of something new. Something spine-tingling.

Uncertainty.

Those kids have *no idea* what's going to happen next.

And neither, we're guessing, does DV8.

Most reality-show cast members are savvy viewers themselves; none of them walk onto sets as innocent bystanders. They know they're going to be manipulated by producers into predetermined plotlines. They know they're going to be edited to pieces. But at the end of the day, they know they're going to leave the set alive.

Yet with one swift swipe of a robotic arm, DV8 has taken away that certainty. What in the name of obligatory hot tubs is going on here? Are Chazz Young and the folks at the renegade network making everything up as they go along?

We're guessing they are. And it's BRILLIANT.

These kids don't know what to expect. They're *literally* flying blind. They are scared and confused and isolated in a sealed tin can hundreds of miles from home.

That is raw emotion up there.

It is heartbreaking and poignant and singular and extraordinary.

Episode #2 reduces the internet to a pile of smoking embers.

DV8.com crashes for more than an hour. #WasteOfSpace remains the number-one trending topic for *three straight days*. The Enormous Robotic Arm explodes into memes, GIFs, and its own handle (@EnrmsRoboticArm). And Bacardi's prediction comes true—America ships Nico and Titania hard, in the form of fan fiction, fan art, and the writing of a petition to allow them to get married onboard the International Space Station.

But once again, the show gets its fair share of detractors.

Item: Transcript of video recording
Source: Fakefinders
Date: February 5, 2016

Bigfoot: Oh, *Waste of Space.* Where do we begin?

With the fact that Hibiscus couldn't possibly have been shoved into a spacesuit against her will? Or that even if she'd done so willingly, such a thing would have been impossible to accomplish in the span of three seconds?

Or that there's *no way a multimillion-dollar corporation would eject a teenager into the grievous vacuum of space?*

Wake. Up. America.

The multimillion-dollar corporation does not eject a teenager into the grievous vacuum of space, of course.

Item: Transcript of video recording
Source: Dashboard camera, DV8 Company Van

Date: February 4, 2016

[*IMAGE: Nighttime. The exterior steel wall of the soundstage is lit by a pair of headlights. Boris, Chazz's personal courier, exits the soundstage door with the limp body of a teenage girl thrown over his shoulder. He walks out of the frame. The image then shudders as his cargo is deposited roughly into the back of the windowless van.*

Eleven hours of driving follow.]

But America falls for the ruse anyway, especially once Hibiscus makes an appearance—albeit an odd one—on Perky Paisley's show the following evening.

Item: Transcript of video broadcast
Source: *The Perky Paisley Show*
Date: February 5, 2016

▶ • • • • • • • • • • • • • ▶ `ON-AIR` • • • • • • • • • • • • •

Perky: So spill, girl. Tell us everything about life onboard the *Laika.*

[*Hibiscus is sitting, unstable, on the lip couch, her eyes focusing and unfocusing as she absent-mindedly strums her mandolin. Her typical angry demeanor is conspicuously absent.*]

Hibiscus: Utterly transcendent /
and beautifully resplendent /
flying to the moon /
with a Fjälkinge shelving un . . . it.

Perky: That's nice. Did you bang anyone?

[*Hibiscus's hands limply fall from the strings of the mandolin, her dreamy gaze drifting to the rafters.*]

Hibiscus: Only the drum of freedom, sister.

[*Perky, exasperated, looks offstage for help from her producer.*]

Perky: Okay, well—tell us about the elimination. What happened after you were grabbed by the Enormous Robotic Arm?

[*A cheer erupts at the mention of the Enormous Robotic Arm. The commotion seems to jar Hibiscus into a state of meditative concentration. She hugs the mandolin to her chest, closes her eyes, and speaks in a stream-of-consciousness manner.*]

Hibiscus: I was dragged into the airlock and after the door sealed behind me I heard a soft whispery hiss of air and the room went dark. Because if you think about it really think about it the walls had been built up around us to protect us from the vacuum of space but now it was the space that was inside *me*. It was so . . . so . . .

Perky: Don't say meta.

Hibiscus: . . . meta . . .

[*Perky rubs her temples.*]

Perky: Then what happened?

Hibiscus: I don't know. I guess I was put into a spacesuit and shot out of the airlock, but I can't remember any of that. [*tunelessly strumming the mandolin again*] I must have drifted off under the awesome majestic majesty of it all because I woke up in a hospital bed here in Los Angeles /

miraculous /

incredulous /

emerging from a chrysalis.

[*Perky stares at her.*]

Perky: Well, there it is, folks, straight from the space cadet's mouth. And don't forget—every week, I'll be chatting with the eliminated cast member from *Waste of Space*, so keep tuning in to your girl Perky. Until next time . . . My eyes are up here!

◼◀ • • • • • • • • • • • • • **OFF-AIR** • • • • • • • • • • • • • • • •

This bizarre interview leads some to wonder whether Hibiscus has been forcibly drugged (a muddy prospect, given her own established interest in mind-altering substances) or bribed by Chazz Young's deep pockets (a more plausible option, given the social media posting she writes soon thereafter about having signed with DV8's record label).

Or, most come to agree, some combination of the two.

But no one onboard the *Laika* shares in her breeziness. Hibiscus's computer-animated body, lifelessly floating through the vacuum of space and across the screens of America, may not be real—but the rest of the cast's terror is, judging by the footage shot immediately after the elimination.

Item: Transcript of video recording—RAW, UNAIRED FOOTAGE
Source: Camera #4—Lünar Lounge
Date: February 4, 2016

[*Cast members are yelling over the beeping alarm.*]
Nico: What just happened?

Snout: A robot reached in and threw her off the ship!

Bacardi: It did, right? [*grasping at his shirt*] It wasn't just me whosaw that?

Matt: Oh God. Oh God.

Titania: *Turn off the beeping.*

Jamarkus: Everyone remain calm. There must be some sort of fail-safe built into the system—

Louise: Exactly! Maybe the ship's artificial intelligence recognizes and eliminates any factors that may compromise our mission, and Hibiscus was identified as a potential threat!

Matt: [*pacing back and forth*] Oh God.

Snout: [*pointing at the Windows Window*] There she goes!

[*A spinning spacesuited figure drifts into view, across the window, then out again.*]

Matt: Is a shuttle going to pick her up? Or are they going to let her die out there? I don't see a shuttle!

[*They all strain to look out the window—except for Kaoru, who hangs back, arms crossed.*]

Kaoru: {I see they did not bother to computer-animate a shuttle.}

It should be noted that by this point in the show's run, there appears to be a wide range of skepticism among the cast members. Some, like Kaoru and Titania, seem extremely doubtful that they are in space, while others, like Snout and Bacardi, don't seem to have any suspicion at all. The rest fall somewhere in the middle, as shown by Nico's video recording from around this time.

Item: Transcript of video recording
Source: Nico's camera

Battery charge: 75%
Date: February 5, 2016

[*The image is dark; only audio can be heard. Nico is whispering.*]

Hi Mom. Hi Dad.

Can't sleep. Again.

[*muffled sounds of rustling bedsheets, then stillness*]

Do you hear that? Sounds like voices.

Outside the ship.

[*Seven seconds pass.*]

They're gone now. I thought I heard—I don't know. Never mind.

Sorry for the radio silence, but I've been afraid to record anything. Clayton was so mean about it the first time. And, well . . . things are getting tense up here. I'd say this experience has been a roller coaster, but that does a disservice to roller coasters. I don't know of any roller coasters that have long stretches of boredom punctuated by the most terrifying moments of your life.

I don't know. Here we are, trapped up here in this claustrophobic keg, at the mercy of television producers who can do whatever they want to us . . .

[*Five seconds pass.*]

I'm just . . .

I'm starting to wonder.

I wonder why nothing happened when Jamarkus threw the hippo at the wall and that important-looking piece broke off. Louise put it back with duct tape, but shouldn't something bad have happened? An alarm beeping, or the lights going out, or—I don't know, *something*?

I wonder why the flame on Clayton's lighter looked so normal. I remember reading once that fire is supposed to look different in space—like, it's bluer, and it burns in a tight little ball because lack of gravity lets it burn in all directions at the same time. I know we've got artificial gravity onboard the ship, but would that affect how fire behaves? Because that fire behaved exactly the same way it would on Earth. And it wasn't blue.

I wonder why I hear voices at night.

I still wonder about the scar on Titania's belly. I saw it again when she was changing her shirt last night—I mean, I wasn't perving. I swear. We're all just so crammed in here, I've seen a lot of things I didn't mean to see.

Anyway.

It's this warped pink blot just under her ribs. Like the scar left over after a gunshot, but a little bigger. What could leave a scar like that?

Who *is* she?

[*Eleven seconds pass.*]

[*There is the sound of rustling bedsheets, then footsteps.*]

Item: Transcript of video recording—RAW, UNAIRED FOOTAGE
Source: Camera #7—Confessional Closet
Date: Febuary 5, 2016

[*Titania has been in here for a while. She keeps rubbing her eyes. A long time passes before she speaks.*]

Titania: I had a bad dream.

Not, like, a nightmare. Just a dream about Lily singing her weird made-up songs.

Those songs drove me crazy. *She* drove me crazy. I mean, she was my little sister. My shadow. All those years she followed me around, copied me, begged me to hang out with her, dragged me into stuffed-animal tea parties I didn't want to attend. And all those years I screamed at her to leave me alone.

But that's what older sisters do. Older sisters get mad at that stuff—even though they secretly, deep down, love that they get their own little built-in fan club looking up to them all the time.

Figures that the one time she didn't want to follow me, I made her.

That I was the one who dragged her in.

Dragged her down.

[*The door opens. Titania looks up at Nico.*]

Titania: Hi.

Nico: Hi. May I?

[*Titania slides off the leather stool and sits on the floor. Nico sits across from her, both of them again in profile.*]

Nico: Can I ask you something? Did your parents really name you Titania?

[*She looks surprised—then, embarrassed.*]

Titania: No.

Nico: Why did you change it?

Titania: I didn't. Not officially, anyway. Just for this show.

Nico: What's your real name?

[*Titania squirms.*]

Nico: Can you at least tell me how you picked it? Because you don't strike me as a queen of the fairies.

Titania: Your school made you read *A Midsummer Night's Dream* too?

Nico: Doesn't everyone's?

Titania: Yeah. But it's not from that.

Nico: Then what?

[*She blows out a puff of air.*]

Titania: In fourth grade, for some history research project thing, our assignment was to look up an important event that happened on our birthdays, so that we would always remember it. My birthday is January 11. On that date in 1787, William Herschel discovered two moons of Uranus, which he named Oberon and Titania.

[*She examines her cuticles.*]

Titania: When I was filling out the audition form, it asked for date of birth, and—I don't know, I guess writing it down triggered that memory, and I just made a split-second decision. Crossed out my real name and gave myself a new one.

Nico: Didn't your parents notice when they signed the consent form?

Titania: My parents [*cracking her neck*] did not give their consent.

Nico: What?

Titania: I sort of . . . ran away. Again. The first time with the canoe didn't work. I'd say this attempt stuck better.

[*Nico's mouth hangs open. Titania puts her hands out, her face apologetic.*]

Titania: I'm sorry—I know it must piss you off to hear that.

Nico: What?

Titania: That I voluntarily walked out on a mint-condition set of not-dead parents, while yours . . .

[*She trails off. Nico considers this, then shakes his head.*]

Nico: No. I know we don't know each other *that* well, but I think I know by now that you're a decent enough person to not "walk out" on your parents without a damn good reason.

[*Titania looks down.*]

Titania: Thank you.

[*pause*]

Titania: Look, I *want* to tell you. I do. But something about putting the worst day of your life into words, and saying them out loud, and on camera—it's—I can't.

Nico: I know. I can't either. It's terrifying.

[*Another pause as Nico seemingly mulls over exactly how terrifying it is, and exactly how much courage he'd need to muster up to surmount it. Finally he squeezes his eyes shut and blurts:*]

Nico: A fire.

Titania: What?

[*He takes a deep breath, then nervously blows on his hands.*]

Nico: My parents died in a fire. Our apartment building burned down.

[*Titania has gone white.*]

Nico: I wasn't there when it happened. [*His agitation dissipates as he settles into the memory.*] I was at the skate park. I heard sirens and saw the fire trucks go by, but I didn't run home until my neighbor saw me and told me what was happening.

What surprised me the most was that the flames were—they were big, but they weren't *huge.* I'd never seen a fire in real life before, but it just—it seemed *manageable,* you know? Like anyone could run in there and scoop up everyone inside, no problem.

[*He swallows.*]

And not to say anything bad against the firefighters—they were doing everything they were supposed to do, spraying the water, getting lots of people out. They were great. But there was this back staircase, right? And none of them seemed to be using it, no one seemed to know it was there. I knew, though, because I used to use it to sneak out at night when I couldn't sleep. And I thought—I mean, the flames didn't look that big. How hard would it have been to run up there and get Mom and Dad out, if they were still alive? We lived on the fifth floor of a six-story building. That's a lot of stairs, and those firefighters were beefed-up guys with a lot of equipment. It would have been a lot easier for a skinny, fast kid to dart up there instead.

[*He stops.*]

Titania: But you didn't go.

Nico: No. I got scared. I hesitated, as usual. And they died. And—look, I know they probably would have anyway. I get that. But I saw my chance and I didn't take it. I'll never know what would have happened if I did.

Titania: You might have died too.

Nico: Maybe. Maybe not. I just—

[*He runs his hands through his hair.*]

Nico: A staggeringly overwhelming percentage of my life has been dictated by fear. Fear of talking to people, fear of speaking up, fear of taking action. I don't know why. But it's always been there, blinding me like a stoplight. And most times, it's little stuff. Not raising my hand at school, not asking a girl out. But this was the one time it mattered. Really mattered. And I just stood there.

And I did nothing.

[*Though the camera is not at an angle that could confirm it, it seems that Titania adjusts the position of her feet— presumably to touch them to Nico's.*]

Source: Camera #2—Flight Deck

[*The room is dim, the only light that of the Windows Window.*]

157

[*Suddenly the room gets brighter. A chime sounds.*]

[*It stays that way for ten seconds, then goes dark again.*]

Source: Camera #7—Confessional Closet

Titania: But you weren't scared to come on this show. That's something.

Nico: I don't know. The longer we're here, the more I feel like I made a mistake. My life is back there. My *future* is back there. My parents gave up everything to come to this country— and then, what, I just cut and run? Just like that? It's the total opposite of what they would have wanted me to do.

[*After a moment of silence, Nico exhales roughly.*]

Nico: Anyway, that's it. My big sob story.

Titania: [*quietly*] Thank you for telling me. I've always hated when people say that it's "brave" to open up and talk about stuff like that, but . . . that *was* brave.

Nico: It wasn't.

Titania: Yes, it was. I honestly don't know how you just did that. I wish I could.

Nico: If I can, you can. It actually felt kind of good.

Titania: Yeah?

Nico: Yeah. And whatever it is, I won't judge. Promise.

[*There is an expectant, uncomfortable lull. Titania opens her mouth, closes it. This repeats several times as the urge to divulge something profound surges, then subsides. Finally she gives her head a firm shake.*]

Titania: No. I can't.

Nico: But—

[*Titania stands abruptly.*]

Titania: Leave it, Nico. We're done.

Nico: Wait—

Titania: [snarling] *Stop.*

[*Nico is taken aback. He says nothing, just watches as she slams the door on her way out. He stays seated on the floor, his knees folded to his chest, head down. After about ten minutes he gets up and leaves the room.*]

Source: Camera #2—Flight Deck

[*Nico peeks in, then walks into the lounge once he sees Titania sitting on one of the swivel chairs on the flight deck, watching the stars fly past the Windows Window.*]

Nico: Hey. Are you okay?

Titania: Yeah.

[*Nico takes the other seat. They swivel for a while without speaking, until Titania decidedly turns away from the Windows Window.*]

Titania: I can't look at that thing anymore. It pisses me off.

Nico: [*swiveling in solidarity until he, too, is facing the bar*] Then behold the cleansing waters of the hot tub, shimmering boldly in the moonlight.

[*Titania lets out a snort.*]

Nico: I'm sorry. I didn't mean to push you.

Titania: Don't worry, that wasn't even *close* to real pushing. [*She rubs her eyes. When she speaks next, her voice is bitter.*] I should know; it's what I do. Needle and prod until I get my way. It's gotten me into more trouble than you can imagine.

[*She snorts again, this time at herself.*]

Titania: And here I thought this was my chance to escape. Go somewhere new. Keep moving, keep exploring—that's the family motto. But this—[*She gestures to the empty room.*] this is more of a dead end than an escape.

Nico: You don't think we're really in space.

Titania: At first I did. I wanted to. But that's becoming less and less likely. You can only keep lying to yourself for so long—

Nico: Before common sense kicks in.

Titania: Right.

[*They fall silent. Titania pulls her feet up on the stool and puts her head down on her knees, while Nico swivels around to look out the Windows Window.*]

[*Once again, the room slightly brightens.*]

Nico: Oh my God. [*tapping Titania's elbow*] Look.

[*Titania raises her head and follows his gaze.*]

Titania: What the . . .

[*They watch the Windows Window for a few more seconds. Their faces morph from shock to confusion to despair. Only when the last trace of hope fades from their expressions do a pair of bittersweet smiles creep in. Hushed, dry laughter fills the air.*]

Nico: Wow.

Titania: Well, there it is.

Nico: Should we tell the others?

Titania: Nah. Not yet. Let them keep believing what they want to believe. This can be our little secret.

[*They both get up and dazedly make their way back into the bedroom, shaking their heads as the room darkens once again. The screen displays nothing but stars now, with no trace of the error message.*]

EPISODE #3

■📹 ·············· **ON-AIR** ·······················

Item: Transcript of video broadcast
Source: *Waste of Space*, Episode #3
Date aired: February 11, 2016

[*START OF ACT ONE*]

[*Serving as a reminder of the previous week's episode, a confessional montage illustrates the Spacetronauts' reactions to Hibiscus's departure. Clever editing strikes all the right dramatic notes while at the same time eschewing the acutely real fear that they experienced.*]

Source: Camera #7—Confessional Closet

Matt: I'm like, what happened? The ship plucked her up and spit her out the door!

Snout: Poor thing never saw it coming.

Bacardi: [*sits down and stares off into space for a few seconds, then recognizes the camera*] Oh! Sorry, I thought this was the bathroom. [*looks down*] Oops.

Nico: This changes everything. You can't help but think, who's next? How safe are we up here, really?

Snout: Can't believe she's gone. Real nice girl.

Colonel Bacon: [*squeal*]

Snout: That's right, buddy. She *was* a kind soul. We're all gonna miss her something fierce.

Clayton: DING-DONG! THE HIPPIE'S DEAD!

Louise: [*looking smug*] Guess she didn't have what it takes.

Bacardi: Before she left, Eye Piss Kiss told me, "Bacardi, if anything ever happens to me, I want you to have my stash of mushrooms." So I did 'em all, in her honor. [*blinking dreamily*] Now I can smell music!

Jamarkus: I think it would be best to treat this as a learning experience and move forward, ever stronger, as a unified team.

Bacardi: [*sniffing*] Beyoncé?

Of course, it's not all tense introspection and halfhearted eulogies. Once the Spacetronauts learn what's at stake, the campaigning begins. They realize they'll need to crank up the charm to convince the viewers to keep them around—and they'll have to throw others under the bus to thin out the competition.

[*The confessional montage continues.*]

Louise: Look, I'm not saying that my fellow shipmates are dingbats—just that they're dingbats when it comes to space stuff. I mean, what if the ship falls into the hands of an alien intelligence—one that's far, far more advanced than we? When it comes down to a battle of wits between us and a highly evolved Gavinjian genius, do we really want someone like Snout at the helm?

Bacardi: D'you want gossip? I gots—goss—got gossip.

Jamarkus: I am a tad concerned about the cleanliness of

this ship. I've been trying to keep things tidy and hygienic, but there's only so much one man can do about hair clogging up the shower drain. I would never speak ill of my beloved space brethren, but where I come from, girls with long, unruly hair and a careless attitude and little consideration for others and a questionable grasp on sobriety would never be considered for a mission as important as this. Our drainpipes deserve better!

Bacardi: Justa put the record straight, Snout's the one who clogged the toilet. *I* only made it worse.

Clayton: Jamarkus is so full of shit. I can see it right there on his face, with his empty smile and clueless eyes. He doesn't deserve to be leader. I do. But you already know that, don't you, America? You're not feeble-minded automatons like the rest of the imbeciles up here. You're smart. *You* know who to keep around. *You* know who deserves to be here.

Bacardi: Kaoru is a computer. [*She cups her hand over her mouth and speaks in a stage whisper.*] *That's why she speaks computer.*

Snout: This sure is a sturdy ship. With all the beatings it's been taking, it's a testament to the hardworking craftsmen and craftswomen of America that it's still in one piece. And to the brave troops serving our country overseas, too. I'd like to tip my hat to each one of them. So would Colonel Bacon!

Colonel Bacon: [*squeal*]

Nico: There's something about Clayton. He's really vicious. So pushy and greedy and wants to be the first to do everything and won't let anyone get in his way. I think he might be dangerous.

Bacardi: Louise is doing something secret. I seen her alone in the bedroom, under her blanket with a flashlight and a screwdriver. Where'd she get a screwdriver? [*pouting*] I'd like a screwdriver.

Matt: Vote me out. Please. I want to get off this ship!

Titania: Let me stay. Please. I don't want to go back. I *can't* go back.

Kaoru: {I do not know how the lucky ones are chosen to be removed from this place, but I hope that I will be granted the privilege soon. I do not wish to be fondled by the robot arm, but if that is the only way out, I will endure it.}

Bacardi: Clayton is a jerk.

Snout: [*humming the national anthem*]

Bacardi: Matt is a communist.

Louise: I'm the only one who can save us.

Bacardi: Colonel Bacon is a breakfast.

Clayton: You have no idea what's at stake here.

Bacardi: Nico and Titania are tooootally doing it. They're always together, talking private talks, and youknow what? I saw them banging on the pool table. Balls everywhere! ALL KINDS OF BALLS. Black balls, blue balls—oh wait. No. That was the time I got banned for life from the ChuckECheeseballpit. [*hand cupped around mouth again*] But I still bet they're tooootally doing it!

Nico: I guess I want to stick around, though. I really could use the money.

Titania: Please don't vote me out.

Clayton: Don't you *dare* vote me out.

Louise: I will literally kill myself if you vote me out.

Bacardi: [*sniffing*] Kanye?

But what happens in the Confessional Closet stays in the Confessional Closet. To one another's faces, the cast members remain strategically silent. They know how to keep things close to the vest. They know how to play the game.

Source: Camera #5—Spa

[*Bacardi and Clayton are making out in one corner of the hot tub while Louise longingly (and creepily) watches them from another. Titania stands a few feet away, not partaking of the hot tub at all. Arms crossed, she inspects the cedar planks lining the walls, which have become bumpy and misshapen.*]

Bacardi: [*coming up for air from Clayton's lips, then sighing dreamily*] This is nice.

Clayton: It *would* be nice, if that freaknugget over there weren't staring at us.

Louise: Um, I can hear you.

Bacardi: [*grabbing his chin and pulling it toward hers*] Don't look at her. Look at me. I have boobs.

[*She points them directly at Camera #5.*]

Clayton: [*grinning*] I gotta say, your fame-whore game is *on point*. Bet you're getting shitloads of screen time.

Bacardi: You think so? [*She hiccups.*] Yay!

Clayton: So what do you want out of all this? Your own show? Endorsement deals?

Bacardi: I told you, I wanna join the CIA.

[*Clayton bursts out laughing.*]

Clayton: What, Cocktail Imbibers of America?

Bacardi: [*giving him a teasing push*] No, the real one! The CIA needs internet people! [*very seriously*] They have a *lot* of internets.

Clayton: Right. And if that doesn't work out?

Bacardi: I dunno. Isn't Chazz your uncle or something? Maybe he can give us a show together!

Clayton: [*looking slightly disgusted*] Yeah, I don't know about that. I'm gonna be pretty busy when we get back. I've got big plans for my time here. People are going to want to talk to me. Important people. [*He is lost in thought for a moment, then snaps out of it and winks at her.*] But hey, for an ass like yours? Hit me up once we're back home and maybe—*maybe*—I'll grant you a second or two of my precious, invaluable time.

Bacardi: Thanks!

[*She goes back to licking his face. Nico enters, spots Titania, and joins her.*]

Nico: What's wrong? Don't want to take a dip in the human petri dish?

Titania: I thought about it. Ultimately decided that now was not the time to invite a bacterial infection into my life.

Nico: Is there even a medical team on call if we get sick or hurt?

Titania: I don't know. Punch me in the face and we'll find out.

What the audience doesn't know, and what DV8 attempts to disguise with filler and cleverly added commercial time, is that the kids barely produce anything watchable this week. Again. Whereas nothing happened in Week 1 because everyone was still too new and reserved, Week 2's tedium comes because they're all too freaked out. Once they realize how much is at stake—that they could be kicked off the show against their will, or, slightly worse, killed—a new mood settles through the ship. A tense, introspective mood that's mighty boring to watch.

So once again, Chazz Young throws a panic bomb at them.

[*A high-pitched screech fills the room, water splashing as everyone scrambles to cover their ears.*]

Titania: Great. More beeping.

[*The bubbles begin to modulate, cutting in and out in a rhythmic, pulsing pattern. Nico and Titania rush to the pool's edge and peer in.*]

Nico: What's happening?

Louise: [*mouth agape as she watches the bubbles*] Are they . . . is that a pattern? [*She ogles the water's surface, her mouth moving as she counts out a rhythm.*] Maybe it's a code!

Clayton: Yeah. It says you suck.

Bacardi: SICK BURN! [*She attempts to high-five him, miscalculates, and tumbles under the surface of the water like a drunken seal.*]

Louise: I bet it's a communication from an alien intelligence! Come on!

[*She flops across the hot tub and gets out, splashing everyone in the process. Nico and Titania watch her go, while Clayton and Bacardi go back to making out.*]

Source: Camera #4—Lünar Lounge

[*Jamarkus, Matt, Kaoru, and Snout are playing Operation. Kaoru removes the Spare Ribs. Colonel Bacon seems offended. Louise storms in, dripping wet.*]

Louise: You guys! Aliens are trying to communicate with us through the hot tub!

[*Everyone looks at the hot-tub window, against which Clayton and Bacardi are pressed at an angle the FCC deems worthy of pixelation.*]

Kaoru: {Ew.}

Snout: Colonel Bacon, don't look. [*He covers the pig's eyes and shouts at the pool.*] Come on now! He's just a baby!

Louise: No, no—the bubbles! They're pulsing in a distinctive rhythm, like it's a code or something!

Jamarkus: To the hot tub!

[*Everyone follows him except for Kaoru, who turns her attention back to the game, removes the funny bone, and gives Camera #4 an ironic look.*]

Source: Camera #5—Spa

[*Clayton and Bacardi don't even look up as their shipmates pile into the room.*]

Titania: Come to sample the human soup?

Louise: [*jumping back into the water*] Come on, you can hear it better when you're in here!

Matt: Surely we don't need to submerge ourselves to—

Jamarkus: Everyone in! [*He removes his clothing with all the speed of a seasoned stripper and flings himself into the water. Matt, Snout, and Colonel Bacon follow.*]

Clayton: [*finally breaking from Bacardi's face*] Is it orgy time? [*growing increasingly intrigued as he watches the others hop into the water*] It's orgy time!

Louise: *No.* We're trying to figure out what the bubbles are saying.

Jamarkus: [*listening to the water*] I think . . . my God, I think it's Morse code!

Louise: Do you know Morse code?

Jamarkus: I do!

Clayton: Of course you do.

Snout: Is it aliens? Ask them what they did with my tractor!

Jamarkus: It says—hang on—[*Screwing up his face, he listens.*] "Pulsing, surging, bubbly bliss—nothing's more serene than this."

[*Louise gasps.*]

Louise: By the moons of Dinatorq . . . [*shouting at the ceiling*] Lord Balway Galway! *I'll* be your bubbly bliss!

Snout: Wait, wait, wait. So it *did* mean something?

Jamarkus: Afraid so, my friend.

[*He looks meaningfully into Camera #5 as music swells.*] It's a message.

[*MUSIC CUE: "E.T." by Katy Perry, featuring Kanye West*]

[*END OF ACT ONE; CUT TO COMMERCIAL*]

OFF-AIR

Item: Transcript of video recording—RAW, UNAIRED FOOTAGE
Source: Camera #5—Spa
Date: February 5, 2016

Titania: Or a hot tub jingle.

Louise: But who's it from?

Titania: Probably the hot tub company.

Louise: And what do they want?

Titania: To sell more hot tubs.

Jamarkus: [*to Titania*] Hey, hey, hey—that sort of doubt and second-guessing is detrimental to our mission. True scientific breakthroughs always come from keeping an open mind and allowing creative thinking to expand, no matter how radical or unexplainable things may be.

Louise: Yeah! [*to Titania*] What do *you* know anyway? *You're* not a professional space expert like Jamarkus and me—

Jamarkus: Well, hey now, you're not—

Louise: And *we* think that it's real. What more proof do you need?

[*Titania opens her mouth to reply, but looks at Nico, who shakes his head, barely suppressing a smile.*]

Titania: You know what? I don't. [*She and Nico start to leave.*] Enjoy your speech bubbles.

Nico: Maybe they come from the Planet Jacuzzi!

[*Dissolving into laughter, they push each other toward the door. Nico tries to pull it open, but the handle slips from his grasp.*]

Nico: Whoa. Who locked the door?

Titania: It's not locked, just stuck. The humidity is warping the wood. [*She grips the handle and gives it a good tug, popping the door open with a cringe-inducing screech that startles everyone, with messy results.*]

Colonel Bacon: [*distressed squeal*]

Snout: Oh, cripes. Fire in the hole, everyone out!

[*The spa is hastily abandoned. Most of the cast members end up in the bathroom to shower, but Titania and Nico steal away to the Confessional Closet instead, still laughing.*]

Source: Camera #7—Confessional Closet

[*They sit on the floor, across from each other.*]

Nico: Because humidity is totally a thing that's allowed on a spaceship. It's not like water droplets would harm the instruments or anything.

Titania: Wood is great too. Not a fire hazard at all.

[*Their giddiness soon fades.*]

Titania: I'm only laughing because I'm so disappointed I want to cry.

Nico: Me too. Should have known it was too good to be true.

Titania: I guess that's on us, right? It's not like this is the first time a network media conglomerate has tricked a bunch of sad, desperate kids into appearing on TV. It's just the first time they did it with the empty promise of outer space—

[*Beeping fills the air once again, along with the announcement of "HOT-TUB CHLORINATION COMMENCING." Titania automatically puts her hands over her ears and waits for it to pass, her eyes squeezed tight. When it stops, she heaves a quivering sigh.*]

Nico: You okay?

Titania: Yeah.

Nico: Why . . .

[*He trails off; there's no need for him to ask out loud. She rubs one foot against the other.*]

Nico: It's just—I've told you so much. Don't you trust me?

[*Her eyes soften.*]

Titania: Yeah. I guess I do.

[*She swallows.*]

Titania: It's because it reminds me of the hospital, after the accident. The machines beeping. The monitors.

[*She rubs the spot near her scar as she speaks.*]

Titania: Want to know why my favorite color is blue? Because it was the only calming thing about that hospital room. Blue floor—not sky blue, not navy blue, not ocean blue—but this gorgeously saturated *blue* blue. The *definition* of blue. The walls and the ceiling too. Blue above, blue below. I'd lose myself in blue for hours trying to ignore the beeping. Drenching myself with it. Drowning in the blue, to drown out the noise.

Nico: [*quietly*] Did it work?

Titania: Never for as long as I needed it to.

[*They fall silent again. Titania wipes an eye with her wrist and clears her throat.*]

Titania: Anyway. [*Her eyes dart back and forth as she tries to figure out how to shift the focus away from her.*] Who do you live with now that your parents are gone?

[*Nico, grateful for the change of subject, lets out a breath.*]

Nico: My older brother. He's seven years older than me, so he'd already moved out and gotten a job by the time the fire happened. I went to stay with him afterward, and he became my legal guardian.

Titania: Do you get along with him?

Nico: Get along? Yeah. But that's about it.

Titania: What do you mean?

Nico: He resents me. Me being there, intruding on his life.

Titania: Even though—

Nico: Even though it's not my fault, yeah. I mean, it's not like he tried to get out of it. He took me in right away. But I know he's sick of me. He got a taste of adult life, being out on his own, and then here I came, a needy pile of responsibility he never asked for. All that freedom, gone in a second. No warning, no time to prepare. Bam—you're a parent now. Deal with it.

And he's been great—never complained, never got directly mad at me. And I know he's hurting too. He misses Mom and Dad, although we never talk about that stuff because—I don't know, because we're boys and boys don't talk about emotions, all that macho junk. But I can see the bitterness underneath sometimes. Like, he'll say things, normal things, but you can tell there's a hidden meaning behind them. Like when he's on the phone with his girlfriend. "Nico needs new sneakers for gym." But really: *"Could have saved that money to take you out* to dinner." "Still haven't gotten that promotion." *"Because I had to leave work early to go take my stupid non-kid to the dentist."*

It's easier now that I'm older—I can do more stuff on my own. But I know he wants to move in with his girlfriend, maybe get married—and he can't do that while I'm around. Or he doesn't feel like he can.

He's probably having a blast right now. I mean, I'm sure he misses me—I miss him—but I don't think he's crying about it or anything.

[*Nico bites at his nail.*]

I shouldn't complain. I had a happy childhood, considering. There are lots of worse ways it could have gone.

Titania: There always are.

Nico: But still.

Titania: But still.

[*pause*]

Titania: My parents hate me.

Nico: Every kid thinks that.

Titania: Yeah, but mine really do.

Nico: I'm sure that's not—

Titania: I'm sorry if it makes you uncomfortable. No one likes to think that two people who loved them so hard for seventeen years can suddenly stop, just like that. But it can happen. It did to me.

Nico: But not out of the blue, right? There had to be a reason.

Titania: There was.

[*Titania appears to be on the verge of saying something big. But she gives her head a small shake.*]

Titania: I could no longer look them in the eye, and they no longer wanted me to.

It's worth noting that although Nico and Titania have many conversations throughout the rest of their time on the ship, and although the chats would be much adored by fans of their budding relationship, DV8 doesn't air a single frame—not after the two of them come to the realization that the show is bogus. The risk of them exposing the fraud is too great.

From this point on, Nico and Titania have a tremendous amount of power. DV8 knows it. And DV8 fears it.

◼️◀ · · · · · · · · · · · · · · **ON-AIR** · · · · · · · · · · · · · · · ·

Item: Transcript of video broadcast

[*continued*]

  [*START OF ACT TWO*]

  [*IMAGE: Chazz in the studio. He has a stack of index cards in his hand and a swoop to his hair that can only be described as "sail-like."*]

  Chazz: Welcome back, space fans! This week's elimination is coming right up—but first, let's take a few minutes to get to know our breakout star of the week. That's right, I'm talking about America's newest sweetheart: Enormous Robotic Arm!

  [*For five full minutes DV8 plays a montage of clips featuring Enormous Robotic Arm—snippets of late-night show monologues, screenshots of memes, the countless parodies that have sprung up online—in another barefaced attempt to replace the entertaining content that the Spacetronauts have so rudely declined to provide, what with their meaningful conversations and incriminating discoveries and all.*]

Eventually the episode cuts back to the ship—just in time for the Instigating Plot Point of the Week.]

Source: Camera #4—Lünar Lounge

[*It appears to be late morning. Most of the Spacetronauts are eating eggs in the lounge.*]

Nico: Damn. For powdered eggs, these are delicious, Snout.

Snout: Thanks!

Nico: You're a good cook.

Snout: Aw, nah. I just know how to rustle up some grub in a hurry. Reckon it came naturally to me, growing up on a farm. Eggs for breakfast, eggs for lunch. Sometimes I have egg dreams!

Nico: You have a chicken farm?

Snout: Chickens, pigs, corn, potatoes, a few other vegetables. Some raspberry patches.

Nico: Wow. I've never even seen a farm.

Snout: You a city boy?

Nico: Yeah, I live in the Bronx. New York. With my brother. [*reddening*] It's a weird situation.

Snout: Aw, I'm sorry, buddy. That sounds rough.

Nico: It's not ideal. But I can't complain.

Snout: Hey, everyone's got their own manure to scoop. I always got food in my belly and a bunch of animal buddies, but my daddy's getting old, and soon it'll be up to me to take over the farm. And we're having a rough go of things these days, what with the economy and all. We've had to cut back on expenses, and it's getting harder and harder to squeeze out a profit. I don't know what I'm gonna do. [*He frowns and swirls his fork through his eggs, then gives Nico a grin.*] But hey—at least at home I don't have to eat powdered eggs!

Nico: [*smiling back*] At least there's that.

Bacardi: Hey look! [*pointing out the Windows Window*] There's something out there!

[*Everyone in the room adopts a skeptical look, except for Nico and Titania, who exchange wary glances.*]

Clayton: Like, a flying vodka bottle, or . . .

Bacardi: No, for *real*. I swear I saw something!

Clayton: The only thing you've seen for the majority of this excursion is the inside of a toilet seat—

Snout: Wait, I see it too!

[*Everyone watches the Windows Window as one by one, the stars wink out. Passing by is something dark, massive, and invisible—until a glint of black metal shines in the reflection of the sun.*]

Snout: What is that?

Kaoru: {An animation.}

Matt: Maybe it's the shuttle they sent to pick up Hibiscus?

Snout: No way. All these days later?

Jamarkus: That's no shuttle. [*He stands in a dramatic fashion. Music swells.*] That's something . . . else.

Matt: Maybe it's someone trying to contact us!

Jamarkus: [*his face darkening*] Or destroy us.

Clayton: And beat me to it? How dare they.

Jamarkus: Everyone remain calm. I know what to do. [*He takes a seat at the control panel.*] I'll fire a signal flare. If what we saw is nothing—then no harm, no foul. If a dark and sinister enemy really is out there, they'll know we're friendly because we didn't shoot directly at them.

Clayton: Or they'll shoot at us anyway because they don't adhere to your random set of moral rules.

Jamarkus: I say it's worth a shot. *Laika,* permission to fire flare?

Robot Voice: PERMISSION GRANTED.

[*Jamarkus presses a complicated combination of buttons on the panel. A streak of light fires across the Windows Window.*]

Matt: Now what?

Jamarkus: Now we wait.

Snout: Well, this is a fine kettle of fish.

[*Kaoru recognizes the word "fish" and brightens.*]

Kaoru: [*in English*] Fine kettle? Of fish?

Snout: Yes, ma'am. We're in a real mess up here.

[*Realizing there is no fish, Kaoru deflates.*]

[*MUSIC CUE: "Grenade" by Bruno Mars*]

[*END OF ACT TWO; CUT TO COMMERCIAL*]

OFF-AIR

But that's not quite where the action ends. When Jamarkus fires the flare, all the anxiety that's been building since Hibiscus's elimination finally bubbles over.

Item: Transcript of video recording—RAW, UNAIRED FOOTAGE
Source: Camera #2—Flight Deck
Date: February 8, 2016

Matt: But I can't take any more waiting!

Bacardi: They're gonna kill anotherone of us!

Clayton: What are you talking about, you lunatics?

Everything is part of the show. Nobody's dead! This is all part of their plan!

Snout: Then what happened to High Biscuits?

Bacardi: Eye Piss Kiss.

Titania: Hibiscus.

Clayton: She's *fine.* I'll bet you a cool five thou she's back home, happily snorting a handful of mushrooms right now.

Snout: But—

Clayton: No buts! They're not going to let us die on national television!

Matt: But how do you know?

Jamarkus: Because he's one of them.

[*They all turn to look at Jamarkus.*]

Clayton: Excuse me?

Jamarkus: [*to Clayton*] None of the rest of us are so confident that we're safe, because we, unlike you, are completely in the dark. None of us have a "cool five thou" to bet against you, because we, unlike you, are not rich. And none of us have ever uttered the words "Uncle Chazz," because we, unlike you, are not related to him.

[*Heads swivel back toward Clayton.*]

Clayton: I hope you're not implying what I think you're implying, Captain America. I had to bite, scratch, and claw my way here like the rest of you.

Jamarkus: Then tell us about your audition, Clayton. Where was it?

Clayton: At a . . . studio.

Jamarkus: Oh? Not a mall? I believe the rest of us auditioned at malls, correct?

[*Everyone nods.*]

Clayton: Oh, you mean the *first* audition. Yeah, that was at a mall.

Jamarkus: I see. So your *second* audition was at a studio.

Clayton: Yeah.

Jamarkus: Quick show of hands—how many of you got a second audition?

[*No hands go up.*]

Jamarkus: Interesting.

Clayton: Look, you got something to say to me, you can come over here and say it to my face.

Jamarkus: No, thank you. I can smell the nepotism from here.

Bacardi: [*whispering to Titania*] Nepo-what?

Titania: [*whispering back*] It means he got picked for the show because he's Chazz Young's nephew.

Bacardi: [*gasp-burp*]

Clayton: You know what? Yes. I'm on this show because I got special treatment. You know why? *Because I'm special.* Do you know how much these sneakers cost? More than you spend on clothes in a year. Wanna guess who gave me this watch? Her name starts with Angelina and ends with Jolie. *And no longer Pitt.* My parents have given so much money to the Smithsonian that they're naming their next wing after us. The fact that for the last twelve days I've even been breathing the same air as the rest of you human trash barges would be laughable if it weren't so vile. You! [*He points at Louise.*] Where'd you get those pants?

Louise: Kmart.

Clayton: Gross. You! [*points at Snout*] What do your parents do for a living?

Snout: They're farmers.

Clayton: Disgusting. Who knows what sort of peasant diseases are burrowing into my lungs as we speak? As soon as I get home, I'm spending a week in my hyperbaric chamber and scrubbing away every last skin cell that came in contact with you bottom feeders. *I'm* the only one who truly deserves to be here. *I* deserve to be the first human being to achieve interstellar travel. *I* deserve to be the sole winner of this acid trip of a game show. And if you think for one second I'm going to let any of you cheat me out of it . . . believe me when I say I have ways of stopping you.

[*An uncomfortable silence takes hold, broken only when Bacardi points out the Windows Window.*]

Bacardi: The thing's not there anymore.

[*another beat*]

Nico: Maybe it was a trick of the light.

Louise: [*eyes bright and hopeful*] Or maybe it was Lord Balway Galway!

Titania: [*peering out the window*] Whatever it was, it's gone now.

Clayton: Well, if it comes back—

[*He reaches behind his back and pulls out a shiny chrome-plated handgun.*]

Clayton: I'll be ready for it.

[*Everyone stops, frozen in horrified stances. Clayton storms out of the room.*]

Bacardi: [*gasp-burp*]

———————————————

Item: Transcript of audio recording
Source: Chazz's cell phone
Date: February 8, 2016

DV8 #1: Chazz, Clayton is becoming a big problem.

DV8 #2: What are we going to do about him? He's ruining the integrity of the show!

Chazz: I know, but I'm up shit creek when it comes to Clayton. He sort of has something on me that I'd rather not be made public. So I have to keep him happy.

DV8 #1: He doesn't look happy! He looks as though he's going to bring the whole thing crashing down at any moment!

DV8 #2: How did he get a gun onboard in the first place?

Chazz: I didn't bother to check his bag because I didn't think he'd do anything to jeopardize his shot on the show! You guys don't know what it's been like—this manipulative little cretin's been on me for *years*. Major inferiority complex. Three older brothers—NFL quarterback, decorated Marine, and CEO of a startup valued at $50 million—and, you know, me. The kid is *obsessed* with being famous for something. Anything. Doesn't care what it is, as long as he comes in first.

DV8 #1: But he's not going to come in first.

Chazz: He doesn't know that.

DV8 #2: What *does* he know? How much did you tell him about the reality of the project? Does he think he's in space?

Chazz: He does. As far as I know.

DV8 #1: But he *also* believes that he can be rescued by Unky Chazz, that Unky Chazz will never let anything happen to him. And if he believes that, the rest of the crew will believe it too.

DV8 #2: They just witnessed one of their own being flung out of the ship. Fear and paranoia is at an all-time high. But the more this brat shoots off his mouth, the quicker we're going to lose that fear!

DV8 #1: And before you know it, all tension and conflict and watchability is sucked out of the ship faster than it would be in the vacuum of real space!

Chazz: Dudes! You're not telling me anything I don't already know! You think I *wanted* to cast him? You think I *want* to defend him? It's playing right into his hands—obviously he knew he could get away with the gun because he knew I'd protect him. Trust me—he's way smarter than any of us are giving him credit for. You don't think he's got other schemes in the works here? You don't think this is all going *exactly* the way he planned it? Of course it is! But we can't do anything about it!

[*pause*]

DV8 #1: We had a thought.

DV8 #2: We could eliminate him next, regardless of the vote results.

Chazz: Absolutely not. Think of what he'll tell the media!

DV8 #2: But he could shoot someone!

Chazz: Ha. We should *be* so lucky.

[*shocked pause*]

Chazz: Unless—

DV8 #1: Yes? We're open to anything.

Chazz: Unless we double down on the elimination and play it up as a triumph. He's been playing the villain angle, right? He knows that fights and drama always get the most airtime, so he just keeps giving the audience what he thinks it wants—and he's right! He hasn't even come close to losing the vote! But if we lie and tell him that the vote was overwhelming, that he's the least-liked, most-hated reality-show contestant in history, maybe he'll see that as a win?

DV8 #2: I don't know, Chazz. Someone as shallow and needy as Clayton wouldn't react kindly to learning that he's lost a nationwide popularity contest. Not unless he gets something out of it.

Chazz: Like his own spinoff.

DV8 #1: Um. Seriously?

Chazz: Look, I despise the kid more than anyone, but *he's* what our audience is buzzing about. Villains and bullies are the ones who get all the attention. People love him.

DV8 #1: Love to *hate* him.

Chazz: Same thing.

DV8 #1: So what are you suggesting?

Chazz: We eliminate him. He'll be pissed, but not after I offer him his own show, which he'll definitely take. He'll get what he always wanted, and it'll be another ratings slam dunk for us. Win-win.

DV8 #1: That . . . could work. At least this way, no one gets hurt.

DV8 #2: In *theory.* You really think it's a good idea to spring elimination on a mentally unstable teenager and hope for the best?

Chazz: Yep. Drama.

DV8 #1: But—

Chazz: Sorry, I got another call coming in. Later hater.

DV8 #2: Chazz? Chazz!

[*end of call*]

Item: Transcript of video recording—RAW, UNAIRED FOOTAGE
Source: Camera #7—Confessional Closet
Date: February 8, 2016

Jamarkus: So I'm thinking what we saw pass by was

some sort of quantum abnormality, perhaps a rogue black hole . . .

[*Jamarkus trails off. He makes sure the door is locked. Then, as quietly as possible, he slips one of the soundproof panels off the wall, reaches into a hidden compartment, pulls out a bulky satellite phone, and dials. The voice on the other end is loud enough to be picked up by the Confessional Closet's microphones.*]

Chazz: What are you doing? I told you never to call me on that phone unless it was an absolute emergency!

Jamarkus: This *is* an emergency! Your psychotic nephew has a gun!

Chazz: I understand your concern, Jamarkus, I do. But trust me when I say that we're doing everything we can to fix it.

Jamarkus: You better be. Otherwise the deal's off. No amount of money is worth getting shot at!

Chazz: Of course not, of course not. [*laying it on thick*] Hey, *real* strong work on that dark and sinister enemy stuff, by the way.

Jamarkus: [*anger fading*] Really? I'm not sure they bought it—

Chazz: Oh, they did, they did. You're doing an *incredible* job. I knew it the second I saw your audition—I said, there's my ringer. He's the one who's going to sell this. Smart, good-looking, heroic, and a National Aeronautic Scholarship finalist? He's practically an astronaut already!

Jamarkus: [*muttering*] The gayness and blackness probably didn't hurt either.

Chazz: They sure didn't! It's like watching a master craftsman. Every time those kids suspect something, you're right there to subtly guide them back from the edge. Those evasive maneuvers on the asteroid attack? Perfection, Jamarkus. Perfection.

Jamarkus: Yeah?

Chazz: ImmerseFX said it was the best commercial they've ever aired. *Well* worth the millions of dollars they've sunk into this project. Think of the endorsement deals you'll get when this is all over! Bet you'll get a nice bonus from Heavenly Hot Tubs, too.

Jamarkus: I better. That slogan was the dumbest thing that ever came out of my mouth.

Chazz: The point is, you're doing great. And you're going to keep doing great. MIT will be lucky to have you.

Jamarkus: That isn't a done deal yet. Acceptance doesn't mean anything if I can't pay for it.

Chazz: Oh, you'll be able to pay for it. Just stay the course, my friend.

Jamarkus: How am I supposed to do that with a gun to my head?

Chazz: Again with the gun thing? What did I just say? *We're handling it.* In the meantime, do what you've been doing and keep everyone calm. They look up to you. They trust you. Make them feel safe.

Jamarkus: But—

Chazz: Goddammit, kid! All you have to do is spout a few empty promises and play a giant version of Space Invaders and act like our sponsors' products are the best thing ever to grace God's green earth while *we* eliminate everyone else until *you* emerge as the sole winner! We're literally handing you a million dollars! The least you can do is *do what I say!*

Jamarkus: [*shaken*] Okay. You're right. Sorry, Chazz.

Chazz: Whatever it takes to make them feel safe. *Whatever it takes.* And keep up those "Stellars" too.

Jamarkus: Right. Got it.

[*Jamarkus ends the call, puts the phone back into the wall, and replaces the soundproof panel. He swallows and takes a moment to compose himself. Affixing a winning smile on his face, he stands up and walks out of the room.*]

📹 · · · · · · · · · · · · · **ON–AIR** · · · · · · · · · · · · · · · ·

Item: Transcript of video broadcast

[*continued*]

[*START OF ACT THREE*]

[*IMAGE: Chazz, in the studio*]

Chazz: Hey, America! Time to check in with our friends live onboard the spaceplane. Hey, Spacetronauts!

Source: Camera #4—Lünar Lounge

[*wide, awkward shot of the cast, looking more demoralized than ever*]

Chazz: [*voiceover*] How's it going up there?

Louise: Okay.

Matt: Abysmal.

Jamarkus: Stellar!

[*A graphic accompanied by the words "Brought to you by Stellar Acne Cream!" flashes across the bottom of the screen.*]

Chazz: [*voiceover as the music begins to swell*] I'm afraid we don't have the element of surprise this time, so I'm sure this is the moment you've all been dreading. Regardless, one of you received the fewest number of votes this week, and will be leaving the spaceplane tonight.

[*Music climaxes.*]

And that person is . . .

[*Music drops out.*]

Clayton. Clayton, *you* are a waste of space.

Clayton: *What?*

[*Without missing a beat, Clayton draws his gun. Chaos breaks out on the ship. Some of the kids run for cover, while others remain frozen in fear. Most of them are screaming. Meanwhile, the airlock door has opened and the Enormous Robotic Arm has swung out into the Lünar Lounge.*

Its claw yawns open, moving in to grab Clayton.

Clayton cocks the gun and fires it.]

Jamarkus: Nooooo!

[*Jamarkus lunges at Clayton, knocking him off balance. The gun discharges again, punching a hole in the hot-tub window. Water starts gushing into the bar area, and as Clayton falls to the ground, Jamarkus unwittingly moves into the spot where Clayton just stood—causing the Enormous Robotic Arm to clamp around Jamarkus's waist instead.*]

Jamarkus: [*startled*] What? Wait. No!

[*The chaos escalates. The Spacetronauts are uncontrollably running and flailing about the cabin. Nico and Louise join Kaoru on the flight deck, followed by Titania, her hands clamped over her ears to muffle the beeping. The others try to pull Jamarkus out of the Enormous Robotic Arm's grasp, but it's no use. It yanks him out of their clutches and hauls him off into the airlock. With a pneumatic swish, the door seals him inside.*]

[*CUT TO: Chazz, in the studio. His face is ashen.*]

Chazz: I—I'm sorry about that, America. I'm not sure what happened. Rest assured that all of us here at DV8 will get to the bottom of this, and fast. Until then—sit tight. Catchphrase forever.

[*MUSIC CUE: "Oops! . . . I Did It Again" by Britney Spears*]

[*END OF EPISODE*]

OFF–AIR

OBSESSION

Item: Online article
Source: ViralLoad
Date: February 12, 2016
OMG
[*GIF of Oprah yelling*]
WTF
[*GIF of screaming goat*]
AND I'M JUST LIKE
[*GIF of panda falling out of tree*]

After the airing of Episode #3, America once again loses its collective mind. Speculation abounds, conspiracy theories emerge, and rumors are proliferated with reckless abandon, but no one learns the official (read: fictional) account of what happened onboard the *Laika* until *The Perky Paisley Show* airs the following night.

But it all has to be scripted out first. Exactly eleven hours after Episode #3 airs, a purple windowless van pulls into the ambulance bay of Cedars-Sinai Medical Center. The patient is admitted under a false name and given a luxury suite with a fabulous view of the Hollywood sign.

Item: Transcript of audio recording
Source: Chazz's cell phone
Date: February 12, 2016

Jamarkus: What the *hell*, Chazz?

Chazz: Calm down, Jamarkus. Let me explain. I'm recording this call, by the way—

Jamarkus: Why?

Chazz: I record all my calls. You never know when you'll need a little leverage. Where are you right now?

Jamarkus: You know exactly where I am! A hospital! As opposed to *on the television show that you promised I'd win.*

Chazz: Hey, *I'm* not the one who jumped into the gaping claw of the elimination robot! What the hell were you thinking?

Jamarkus: I was making them feel safe. *Like you told me to!*

Chazz: Yeah, well, I've got a lot of explaining to do to our sponsors now, and it's all your fault.

Jamarkus: Might want to save some explaining for the viewing public after I go on Perky's show . . . and tell her *everything.*

Chazz: Oh, I don't think you'll be doing that.

Jamarkus: Why not?

Chazz: You'll be appearing on Perky Paisley's show tonight, all right. But only as your Captain America act. You will smile and be charming and act humble and heroic and shit. You will not utter a peep about what you were recruited for. You will not rat on DV8. You will not sell out our sponsors. You will continue to peddle the story we have crafted for you, and then—and only then—will you get paid. And you *will* still get paid, Jamarkus. As long as you behave yourself.

[*pause*]

Jamarkus: I understand.

Chazz: Good. I knew you'd be reasonable.

Jamarkus: So . . . what should I say?

Chazz: We're drafting a narrative right now, should have it to you soon. Feel free to embellish if that's what you need to do to sell it. Trust me—once you get going, it's impossible to stop.

Jamarkus: And then what? You shoot me back to the *Laika* to save everyone?

Chazz: No, no. You've done enough.

Jamarkus: But—then how will I win the million dollars?

Chazz: Oh, the million dollars is off the table. That'll have to go to whoever wins. But if you do everything I say, we'll still throw something your way. Enough to cover a semester or two of tuition.

Jamarkus: But we had an agreement!

Chazz: Did you not hear anything I just said? You're going to be a national hero! You displayed calmness and took action in the face of a galactic disaster! What space agency wouldn't want you?

[*pause*]

Jamarkus: I—

Chazz: Go on Perky's show. Sell your story. Or you're not getting a dime of DV8's money. I'll personally drag your name through the mud, and you can kiss any hopes of a career as an astronaut goodbye.

[*end of call*]

Item: Transcript of video broadcast
Source: *The Perky Paisley Show*
Date: February 12, 2016

Perky: Welcome, Jamarkus!

Jamarkus: Hi, Perky. It's a pleasure to be here. [*smiles and winks at camera*]

Perky: Wow. You're even more impressive in person. [*puffing out her chest*] So don't keep us in the dark a second longer. What *happened* up there?

Jamarkus: You reeeeally want to know?

Perky: Yes! All we saw back here on Earth was Clayton about to be eliminated, and then he pulled something that looked like a gun, and it was cuckoo bananas and—and you have to tell us what happened! Don't make me beg!

Jamarkus: First off, I'd like to clear one thing up: Clayton did not have a real gun. DV8 never would have allowed something so dangerous onboard the ship. What you saw was a cleverly constructed prop Clayton made from duct tape and the aluminum packets of astronaut ice cream. He was just trying to scare everyone and incite a panic—and unfortunately, it worked.

Perky: Until you stepped in to save the day.

Jamarkus: I knew what I had to do, Perky. Unfortunately, it cost me a shot at the million dollars, but I'd never be able to live with myself if I let a little thing like money stop me from saving my friends.

[*The audience "awwws."*]

Jamarkus: And as far as I understand it, the ship is back to normal and everyone is safe.

Perky: I certainly hope you're being compensated for your valiant efforts.

Jamarkus: Yes, thank you for mentioning that—DV8 has

generously offered to pay a portion of my tuition to MIT's Aerospace Engineering program, into which I've already been accepted. With any luck, I'll be back in outer space before you know it!

Perky: [*fanning herself*] That's so . . . so impressive.

Jamarkus: Thank you, Perky.

Perky: Jamarkus, how old are you?

Jamarkus: I turn eighteen next week.

Perky: I see.

Jamarkus: You know I'm gay, right?

Perky: We'll see about that. [*blows a kiss to the audience*] And that's our show, everyone! Until next time . . . My eyes are up here!

◼◀ · · · · · · · · · · · · · **OFF–AIR** · · · · · · · · · · · · · · · ·

What *really* happened after Jamarkus was lugged into the airlock is, of course, never aired by DV8 at all.

Item: Transcript of video recording—RAW, UNAIRED FOOTAGE
Source: Camera #4—Lünar Lounge
Date: February 11, 2016

[*Note: Although the three camera angles in the Lünar Lounge cover the majority of the space, a number of blind spots still exist.*]

Louise: [*pounding on the airlock door*] Jamarkuuuus!

Titania: First things first. Is anyone hurt? [*No one speaks up.*] Good. Nico, grab the duct tape and seal up the hole in the hot tub before everything floods. Did anyone see where the other bullet went?

Matt: Up there.

[*He points to the ceiling. Titania climbs onto the pool table and squints up. Nico finishes sealing the leak in the hot-tub window and tosses Titania the roll. She tapes up the other hole, then rounds on Clayton, who is still on the floor, panting.*]

Titania: What the hell was that? What is the matter with you?

Clayton: [*standing, smirking*] Oh, relax. No one got hurt. Nothing happened.

Louise: But a lot of things could have happened! We could have depressurized or exploded or imploded or gotten flung into the outer reaches of the universe or any number of other things that can happen when a hole is punched in a ship!

Matt: I personally would rather *not* be flung into the outer reaches of the universe, if possible? I'd kind of like to get back to my home planet at the end of all this?

Bacardi: Or lessssgotothemoon! The moon has moonshine.

Clayton: [*raking his hands down his face*] Oh my God. *Wake up.* Can't you morons see what's going on here?

Bacardi: No. What?

Clayton: I really need to say it out loud, don't I. Fine. And I'll speak real slow so my words can softly and safely squish into those brains of yours without causing irreparable damage. You ready?

Titania: Clayton, don't—

Clayton: NONE . . . OF . . . THIS . . . IS . . . REAL.

[*pause*]

Louise: What do you mean?

Clayton: It's fake! All of it! This isn't a real spaceship. It's Styrofoam and particleboard all staple-gunned and hot-glued together in a veritable bacchanalia of bad crafting. Think about it—don't you find it strange that there is a specific button to solve each of the problems we've come up against? Just like in a video game?

Snout: Yeah, but—

Clayton: Asteroid attack—bam, there's a joystick-trigger weapon to blast them out of the sky. Loss of equilibrium? Bam—lever to restabilize the ship. Enemy sighting? Bam—shoot a flare at them.

Snout: But Jamarkus was the one who did all that stuff. How could he have known about all that?

Clayton: Yes, how *could* he have known? Let's all think critically for a moment and see if we can come up with an answer.

[*Their shoulders all slump at once in a collective epiphany.*]

Nico: Could Jamarkus have been a plant?

Titania: If he was, that means all those emergencies were scripted, and he knew they'd happen ahead of time.

Louise: [*lip trembling*] But he pushed the buttons.

Clayton: Yeah. But DV8 or NASAW or whoever's controlling what happens on this ship—*they're* the ones who execute the effects whenever a button is pushed.

Snout: Huh?

Clayton: Don't you know how movie sets work? When you see an actor push an elevator button, that elevator isn't functional. Crew members open the doors manually. Same thing is going on here. Someone out there is watching everything we do and pulling the strings as we do it. Lord knows *where* we really are, but I'll bet you dollars to cronuts it's somewhere on Earth, not hundreds of miles above it.

[*Titania pulls Clayton aside, out of earshot.*]

Titania: [*whispering*] Why are you doing this?

Clayton: [*whispering back*] I was perfectly willing to go along with this charade while I still had a chance of sticking around until the end, but what's the point now? If my uncle's going to eliminate me, why should I keep playing by his rules? Why keep pretending? For *their* sake? [*He makes a disgusted gesture toward the others.*]

Titania: Yes, for their sake. We should be keeping things as calm as possible. We don't know for sure if there are medics standing by, so if someone has a panic attack—

Clayton: You want to keep your head in the sand, go for it. But *I* think it's time to stir things up. Time for a wake-up call. For Christ's sake, *I shot a hole in the ship!* [*He points to the duct-taped spot on the ceiling.*] Ever heard of instantaneous decompression? If we were really in space, we would have been turned into freeze-dried space husks in a billionth of a second—

Snout: [*interrupting them*] But how can it be fake? We put on spacesuits! We blasted into the sky!

Clayton: [*turning back to face the others*] Then we should be in zero gravity. Why aren't we floating?

Louise: It's artificial gravity, dumb-dumb. Weren't you listening to the scientists?

Clayton: Oh yes, let's talk about these [*air-quoting*] "scientists." From NASAW, which is *not* the same as NASA. Who *were* those people? They sure as hell didn't shoot us into space, so what was their deal? Were they actors? Or are they still watching us, experimenting on us?

Louise: [*close to tears*] They were *not* actors! They were scientists! And of *course* we're in space—how else do you explain the stars? And what about the fully functional airlock? What about the asteroid attack, and the dark and sinister enemy?

Clayton: [*laughs*] You want a dark and sinister enemy? That's the one thing out of all of this that's real. And his name is Chazz Young. When I get back home, I'm going to *destroy* him.

Louise: You're lying. You're just doing this to piss everyone off, and even though it's working, *I* still know what I know. We're in space.

Clayton: We're on Earth!

[*Titania puts her fingers in her mouth and blows a whistle.*]

Titania: Everyone. Calm. Down.

[*Clayton studies her.*]

Clayton: Oh, okay. I see what's happening here. Now that Captain America's gone, you think you can be the new leader of this ship. Well, I've got news for you, sweetheart. [*He reaches behind his back again—then frowns. He does a quick scan of the floor.*] Where'd it go?

Matt: Where'd what go?

Clayton: The gun!

Snout: [*pointing at a spot offscreen*] You dropped it right there on the floor. Made a real loud clang, I coulda sworn.

Louise: I heard it.

Bacardi: Metoo.

Titania: [*to Clayton*] Wait. You don't have it?

Clayton: No! [*looking around the room*] Which one of you fuckers has it?

[*silence*]

Clayton: [*with a bitter laugh*] That's the way you want to play it? Fine by me. Let the goddamn games begin.

[*He storms out of the lounge, leaving everyone floored.*]

Nico: Guys, seriously, who took the gun?

[*silence*]

Nico: *Someone* must have taken it.

[*silence*]

Later that night, Titania and Nico meet up in the Confessional Closet again.

Item: Transcript of video recording—RAW, UNAIRED FOOTAGE
Source: Camera #7—Confessional Closet
Date: February 11, 2016

[*Titania is already inside and sitting on the floor, wide-awake, when Nico opens the door.*]

Titania: Hi. Here to endlessly speculate about who now has the power to shoot us as we sleep?

Nico: Hell no. If I don't think about something else, I'm gonna lose it.

[*Alarmed, Titania beckons him into the room. Nico sits down across from her and folds his hands over his knees. They are shaking.*]

Nico: I couldn't sleep. I mean, I can never sleep. But especially not now. All of us crammed into that room, trapped, and any one of them could . . .

Titania: Shh. Nico, look at me. Are you having trouble breathing?

[*Nico nods. Titania leans forward and puts her steady hands over his.*]

Titania: Then just listen to me. Close your eyes.

[*He does.*]

Titania: I'm going to tell you something that's going to help, but it's a dumb story. Don't laugh.

Nico: Okay.

Titania: When I was nine, our family dog died. My brothers and sister and I were absolutely wrecked. Cried for days. Totally inconsolable. Finally, after a week, my parents sat us all down and told us the truth: that Snuffy had gone on a magical journey to Planet Tailwag.

[*Even in his panic, Nico snickers.*]

Titania: I told you not to laugh!

Nico: [*flattening his smile*] Sorry.

Titania: At that age I must have known that what they were saying was a load of crap, but still—it was comforting to me. I just loved the idea of a planet full of dogs. Where there are streams to swim in and grass to roll around in and dirt to dig. Where they can do whatever they want, all the time.

[*She bites her lip.*]

For a long time after that, I became obsessed with the idea that when animals and people die, they don't go to heaven, or hell, or into a hole in the ground—they go to a real place somewhere else in the universe. Whenever I was afraid—like on our camping trips when we heard something rustling in the woods at night—I'd think about my afterplanet, and then things never seemed so bad or so scary. It was the only thing that comforted me after . . . what happened.

[*Nico opens his eyes. He is breathing more evenly. His hands have stopped shaking. But now Titania is lost in thought herself, her voice getting raspier as she continues.*]

It's not like I didn't know what I was doing. I knew I was deliberately disobeying my parents. We'd had such a nice time until then—one of the best camping trips ever. I didn't want to get into a fight about it, but they just made me so *mad*. I hated being told no. And to forbid me from going out and hiking on my own, when I'd done it so many times before? It didn't make any

sense to me. I thought they were being unreasonable. I mean—
I'd never hiked a trail as dangerous as the Notch before. But I
thought I could do it. I was sure of it.

So I disobeyed them.

And maybe if it had just been me, that would have been
excusable. Risking my own safety is bad, but it's—

[*She presses her fingers to her forehead.*]

I was angry. I wasn't thinking straight. I grabbed my pack
and hers too, and told her she was coming with me. She didn't
want to. But I made her. I told her we had to prove a point, that
we were old enough to make our own decisions, that we didn't
need Mommy and Daddy to tell us what to do anymore.

[*By this point she is punching each word out of her mouth
and through her welling tears with a great deal of effort, as if it
physically hurts to speak.*]

I slipped. The trail snaked alongside the edge of a tall bluff,
and I lost my balance. I reached out for something to grab
onto—and that something was Lily.

We fell.

The scar from the branch that I was impaled on—it looks
worse than it was. I was out of the hospital in a few days. But
Lily hit her head. Hard. And drifted into a coma.

It was her room, in the ICU, that I remember the most. All
that staring down at the floor that I did—avoiding eye contact
with my parents, the doctors, the nurses. That was the calming
blue. That's where the beeping was, the machines that were
keeping her body alive.

The beeping didn't stop, not on its own. It had to *be*
stopped. I wasn't there when they did it, wasn't asked to be part
of the decision.

So in my head, it's still beeping.

[*There is a long pause. Nico is staring at her, almost in tears himself. He swallows several times before whispering:*]

Nico: I'm so sorry, Titania.

[*She sniffs.*]

Titania: Not as sorry as I am.

The Clayton/gun issue remains very much unresolved, but Chazz seems to be of the opinion that time heals all wounds, judging by the way he imperviously and obliviously charges ahead with the next challenge without bothering to fix the previous one.

Item: Transcript of audio recording
Source: Chazz's cell phone
Date: February 15, 2016

Chazz: Hey, nerd! Got time for a brainstorming sesh?

NASAW: About the gun? Good, I'm glad you're willing to discuss—

Chazz: Nah, don't worry about that.

NASAW: I beg your pardon?

Chazz: It'll all work itself out in the end.

NASAW: That seems unlikely.

Chazz: And yet it's the plan I'm going with.

NASAW: I see. [*somewhat gleefully*] Then—are you scared that the kids have figured out they're not in space? Worried they're going to ruin the show?

Chazz: Nah, that's no big deal. We can hide all their skepticism with editing. As far as America is concerned, our beloved Spacetronauts still 100 percent believe they're 100 percent galactic.

NASAW: Oh. Then why are you calling?

Chazz: Got a fun little challenge for you. The Enormous Robotic Arm is still super popular, but we're running the risk of it growing stale. We need to punch it up next week. Any thoughts?

NASAW: No! We didn't want to use the damned thing in the first place!

Chazz: I'm thinking we could play a song while it grabs the screaming children. "Another One Bites the Dust," maybe?

NASAW: You *can* hear yourself, right? Or are you merely spouting words as fast as your mutated brain can form them?

Chazz: Then again, musical accompaniment doesn't quite carry with it enough of a sense of danger. There needs to be something more. Something hazardous.

NASAW: You already pelted them with asteroids, flung them around the ship, permitted a loaded gun onboard—

Chazz: Exactly, so we can't repeat ourselves. It needs to be something new. Something worse.

NASAW: It can't *get* much worse.

Chazz: [*gasps*] I just thought of something! Something that'll work both with our Instigating Plot Points this week *and* as a bonus for the elimination!

NASAW: What?

Chazz: A solar storm!

NASAW: How in the name of Copernicus do *you* know what a solar storm is?

Chazz: I saw it in a movie once. So how about this: a solar flare is ejected from the sun and travels toward the spaceplane. First we crank up the heat real high. Then we set a bunch of shit on fire—

NASAW: [*overlapping*] A solar flare would obliterate the ship altogether—

Chazz: Then, when they realize they have to outrun the solar wind—

NASAW: [*overlapping*] Solar winds travel at one million miles per hour. They're not something you can simply outrun—

Chazz: —they'll be told they have to get rid of some extra weight in order to escape, and we'll do a surprise double elimination! Like liposuction, but with human beings instead of fat! It's brilliant!

NASAW: It's ludicrous. None of that makes any sense, scientifically speaking.

Chazz: *You* don't make any sense, scientifically speaking.

NASAW: Yes I do!

Chazz: Besides, no one's gonna check up on whether or not it can really happen.

NASAW: Yes they will! The scientific community is going to rake us over the coals—more than they already have! It's illogical! The science is impossible!

Chazz: Do it anyway. I'll email the specifics within the hour.

NASAW: [*exhaling heavily*] This is—

Chazz: What?

NASAW: This is not what we signed on for.

Chazz: Listen, Baking Soda Volcano, you do what I tell you to do, okay? So long as I get what I want, I'll happily look the other way while you do whatever it is that you're doing out there.

[*pause*]

NASAW: Pardon me?

Chazz: I get it. Funding is hard to come by. No one cares about science anymore, wah wah wah. And here comes this television network, giving you a truckload of money, and you see an opportunity to skim a little off the top and use it to do some research on the side. No one blames you.

NASAW: I don't . . . we're not—

Chazz: It's fine. I'm cool with it. Just don't let it interfere with the show. And follow my instructions without complaint next time. Got it?

NASAW: Yes. [*swallows*] Got it.

Chazz: Stellar. Later hater!

[*end of call*]

EPISODE #4

.... ON-AIR ....

Item: Transcript of video broadcast
Source: *Waste of Space*, Episode #4
Date aired: February 18, 2016

[*START OF ACT ONE*]
Source: Camera #8—Bedroom
   [*It is morning. The lights have snapped on; the cast members in the frame are squinting or rubbing their eyes. Most have shed their blankets, their hair plastered to their foreheads with sweat. More bunk beds have been freed up due to the exits of Jamarkus and Hibiscus, but Bacardi and Louise are still forced to share the California King bed. Bacardi is draped over Louise.*]
   Louise: Hey, get off me!
   Bacardi: Teddybear.
   Louise: For the last time, I'm not your teddy bear! I'm a human girl!
   Clayton: Debatable.
   Matt: [*stretching*] At least each week it gets less cramped in here.

205

Snout: Soon there'll be enough space for Colonel Bacon to get his own bunk!

Clayton: I'd rather we got him his own spit.

[*Snout stares.*]

Clayton: For a roast.

[*Snout stares.*]

Clayton: To eat him.

Snout: Hey! That's not nice!

Clayton: Constricted living quarters, no room to run around—bet there's plenty of juicy, delicious fat on those bones by now—

Snout: Stop it! [*consoling Colonel Bacon*] Don't listen to him, little buddy. You're safe with me.

Titania: [*snorting*] No one is safe. Haven't you learned that yet?

Matt: What do you mean? After Jamarkus sent that signal flare, no one shot back at us.

Louise: That doesn't mean they're not still out there. I bet they're just biding their time. The dark and sinister enemy could be upon us at any moment.

~~**Titania:** [*to herself*] I'm more concerned with the enemy onboard this ship.~~

That last line is edited out of the broadcast; Titania's mouth isn't in view from the camera angle, so the audio is simply removed. But the others hear her say it, judging by the uncomfortable hush that follows and the way the visible cast members all look away or begin to fidget.

The loaded, concealed elephant in the room is tangible. Everyone wants to broach the topic because everyone wants the gun to be surrendered—but at the same time, no one wants to bring it up, because no one wants the thief to fly off the handle and start shooting.

Snout: [*doing his best to hurriedly change the subject*] And there's the next elimination to fret over too. Another fine kettle of fish!

Kaoru: [*sadly, in English*] No fish.

Bacardi: Who's on the chopping block this week?

Clayton: Well, none of you are very likable, so—

Louise: Oh, come on! You were already officially eliminated!

Clayton: [*with a chuckle*] I'll never be eliminated, darling.

Louise: But you're the least likable of all of us.

Clayton: What can I say? Go big or go home.

Louise: Then why don't you go home?

Clayton: Hey, now. That's the kind of hurtful talk that gets someone voted out. Without ever being reunited with Lord Balway Gal—

Louise: Don't you say his name! You are not worthy!

Clayton: Ooh! [*grinning and rubbing his hands together*] Why is everyone so cranky today?

Snout: I reckon it's the heat—I'm sweating like Colonel Bacon after a run round the slopfield! Why's it so darn hot in here?

Bacardi: I'm MELTING.

Matt: It does seem warmer than usual. Is there a thermostat on the control panel? Maybe we could adjust the temperature.

Clayton: Or we could take all our clothes off.

[*MUSIC CUE: "Blurred Lines" by Robin Thicke*]

[*END OF ACT ONE; CUT TO COMMERCIAL*]

The episode cuts to commercial, but, as always, there's more to the scene than what the audience sees.

Item: Transcript of video recording—RAW, UNAIRED FOOTAGE
Source: Camera #8—Bedroom
Date: February 15, 2016

Titania: I'd say climate control is the least of our problems.

Clayton: Hey everyone, pay attention to our fearless leader! She's making passive-aggressive comments under her breath, so this must be important!

Titania: No one else wants to bring this up? Fine.

[*She gets up from her bunk and faces Clayton.*]

Titania: I will ask you again: Did you take the gun?

Clayton: [*smiling ear to ear*] Nope.

Titania: [*to Snout*] Did you take the gun?

Snout: No, ma'am.

Titania: [*looking around the room*] Who has the gun?

Clayton: [*under his breath*] My money's on you.

Titania: Is it.

Clayton: You like to be in control. Don't deny it—we all see it in your eyes, that fiery desire to get that hot little pistol in your hands—

Nico: Hey, leave her alone—

Titania: [*rounding on him*] Don't fight my battles for me, Nico.

Nico: I . . . wasn't.

Clayton: [*getting fired up*] Yeah, Nico. You're the one who just sits back and observes. Always observing, never doing. Why start now?

Nico: I—

Clayton: If anyone deserves to be eliminated this week, it's you. You're using up valuable oxygen. So shut your mouth and go back to being a wallflower. It's what you're good at. [*to Titania*] Wouldn't you agree, Not-Captain?

[*Titania gives him the finger, then storms out of the bedroom.*]

Clayton: What crawled up *her* ass?

Source: Camera #7—Confessional Closet

[*Titania sits down in front of the camera, agitated.*]

Titania: This is bullshit, DV8. Why aren't you stopping this? Why aren't you doing anything about it? I didn't come all the way out here, lie to my family, and leave my entire life behind just to get gunned down by one of the many delusional sociopaths you've invited to your televised death match of insanity.

You need to let us out of here.

[*She waits.*]

Hello?

[*She smacks the camera.*]

IS ANYONE EVEN LISTENING?

[*There is a knock at the door.*]

Nico: [*muffled, from outside*] Titania, are you okay? Can I come in?

[*She hesitates, then unlocks the door. Nico peeks his head through the door.*]

Nico: Hey. What's going on?

Titania: I am so unbelievably pissed off, I can't even—[*She hisses air through her teeth.*] Last night, after our talk—I was lying awake in bed, feeling all these cathartic feelings from having finally said all that stuff out loud, but then . . . then my mind wandered to the gun, and I just started to get so mad. I came on this show to restart my life, not end it. This isn't fair.

Nico: I know.

Titania: Why aren't they stopping this? Where are the responsible adults? How is anyone letting this happen?

Nico: I don't know. But I do know one thing: they're not going to win. We won't let them.

[*Titania's face softens, her grimace fading as she allows herself to believe him.*]

Titania: Okay. You're right. We won't.

Nico: I'm sorry about back there. I didn't mean to—

Titania: No, *I'm* sorry. You were just trying to help. And don't listen to anything Clayton says about you. He's full of shit.

Nico: He wasn't wrong, though. I *am* pretty useless up here.

Titania: Not to me.

◼◀ • • • • • • • • • • • • • • `ON-AIR` • • • • • • • • • • • • • • •

Item: Transcript of video broadcast
[*continued*]
   [*START OF ACT TWO*]
Source: Camera #4—Lünar Lounge

   [*Clayton, Snout, Bacardi, and Louise are playing Clue. The rest are lounging in the lounge, joylessly eating bowls of Meteor Chowder.]*

Snout: I've got it! It was Toothless Sal in the auto garage with the tire iron!

Clayton: See, this is what I keep trying to tell you. None of those things are part of this game. You can't pull murderers and locations and weapons out of thin air.

Snout: Oh, I'm not making them up. Toothless Sal is Iowa's best-known criminal. Currently serving twenty-five to life!

Clayton: [*turns to Bacardi*] What about you?

Bacardi: Letssee . . . I think it was Colonel Mustard in the conservatory with the candlestick.

Clayton: And you're not just saying that because they all start with *C*, right? Because you didn't get confused again about what game we were playing and thought we were playing the Sesame Street Match the Letter Game?

Bacardi: Um—which answer will make you not flip the table?

[*Clayton flips the table.*]

Clayton: You people are impossible! How are you permitted to leave the house without wearing helmets?

Snout: Maybe it's time for something less controversial. Y'all want to play some Chutes and Ladders?

Matt: Why bother?

Snout: We gotta do something! I'm bored out of my mind here!

Clayton: How can you be bored out of something you don't have?

Snout: Hey, now—

Nico: Guys, don't. Fighting isn't going to get us anywhere.

Clayton: Oh, are we supposed to be "getting" somewhere? Far as I can tell, all we're supposed to be doing is waiting patiently for the next elimination.

Louise: We could take some readings from the atmospheric spectrometer. When the Flubsuvian Capsule—

Clayton: Zip it, sweetie. The grownups are talking.

Louise: But—

Clayton: We don't want to hear it. Your stardust-clogged brain may be festooned with the trappings of your fictional wonderland, but the rest of us are planted far more firmly in the realms of reality—

[*Suddenly a fireball erupts from the ceiling, blooms, and disappears—but not before catching the arm of the sofa on fire. Soup bowls plummet, splashing Meteor Chowder everywhere. Kaoru tries to dive to safety, hitting her head on the coffee table and landing on the floor in a heap. Snout grabs her under the armpits and drags her away from the blaze while Bacardi runs around the room collecting furnishings to save. Nico hugs the wall, frozen. Titania pulls the pin on the fire extinguisher and sprays it straight at the couch, but as soon as the last flame dies out, another fireball appears, this time aimed at the pool table. Seconds later, another consumes the Älvsbyn chandelier.*]

Bacardi: Nooo! Our only accent lamp!

Snout: [*struggling under Kaoru's limp weight*] Someone hit the sprinklers!

[*Louise lunges for the control panel, but yet another column of flame blocks her path. At this point it is clear to anyone watching at home that the fire effects are carefully choreographed pyrotechnics that are unlikely to hurt any of* the cast members or the structure of the ship, but this is not immediately obvious to those in the thick of it.]

Titania: Matt! The sprinklers!

[*Now the only one with a clear route to the control panel, Matt dives for the console, the sprinkler button squarely in his sight—and slips on a rogue Hungry Hungry Hippos marble. On his way to the floor, he heroically reaches out his hand and slams it down to push the button. Or rather, he could have pushed the button . . . if only he'd had a full finger.*]

Clayton: Goddammit, Stumpy! You've killed us all!

Titania: No, he hasn't. Everyone calm down.

[*She deftly weaves through the inferno, kicks Matt aside, and presses the button. Then presses it again.*]

Titania: [*panic rising in her voice*] It's not working.

Nico: [*picking up the fire extinguisher and trying to use it*] And this is empty.

Matt: What do we do?

[*There is a beat of pure panic.*]

Snout: I know!

[*Leaving Kaoru on the floor, he darts over to the hot-tub window and rips the tape from the bullet hole. Water shoots out.*]

Snout: Grab some pails!

[*The Spacetronauts retrieve ice containers from the bar and form a bucket brigade, filling them with water, passing them down the line, and pouring them onto the flames about the room. Before long, the fires are out. When all is said and done, a foot of water remains in the hot tub, while the rest of it has settled into an inch-deep flood throughout the Lünar Lounge and mixed with the spilled Meteor Chowder, creating a funky sludge in which Colonel Bacon begins to wallow.*]

Bacardi: [*holding up broken pieces of the shattered coffee table*] Svalsta! Noooo!

Snout: [*panting*] What . . . in tarnation . . . was that all about?

Kaoru: [*waking up*] {Do I smell barbeque?} [*She looks around, disappointed.*] {Oh.}

[*A reaction montage follows.*]

Source: Camera #7—Confessional Closet

Clayton: So you're setting us on fire now, huh? Classy move.

Titania: You have got to be kidding me.

Bacardi: Allthat furniture, ruined. Ruined!

Nico: I, uh—[*presses hands to eyes, hard*] I don't like fire.

Kaoru: {I missed most of what happened. I woke up to a floor full of soup.}

Snout: Colonel Bacon sure does love that Meteor Chowder. He slurped up every last drop!

Kaoru: {Lucky for us, because this ship is not airtight, the soupwater seeped out through the cracks in the floor.}

Matt: I really screwed up back there. I . . . I deserve to go this week.

Nico: This is so crazy.

Titania: This is so dangerous.

Louise: *This is so much fun!*

[*MUSIC CUE: "Set Fire to the Rain" by Adele*]

[*END OF ACT TWO; CUT TO COMMERCIAL*]

◀ · · · · · · · · · · · · · **OFF–AIR** · · · · · · · · · · · · · · ·

During the commercial break, NASAW places a highly irregular call to Chazz. The following is not a flashback—it occurs in real time, right after the airing of Act Two.

Item: Transcript of audio recording
Source: Chazz's cell phone
Date: February 18, 2016

NASAW: Hello, Chazz.

Chazz: Hey, Potato Battery! Real strong work with the fireballs. We barely had to edit the footage! The way you manipulated the timing for maximum drama was exquisite. You sure you nerds have never worked on a reality show before?

NASAW: No. And we did *not* feel good about setting fire to those poor kids.

Chazz: Oh, lighten up. It was brilliant television. Do you know how many Emmys we're gonna get for this? They'll have to invent a new category!

NASAW: You are the most delusional person I have ever encountered.

Chazz: Thanks!

NASAW: Good thing we no longer have to put up with you.

Chazz: Excuse me? Sorry, there was someone talking in my headset. So we are a go for tonight's elimination. You ready with the Enormous Robotic Arm?

NASAW: Yes, we're ready.

Chazz: Stellar.

NASAW: And we're sorry.

Chazz: For what?

NASAW: For what we're about to do.

Chazz: What are you talking about?

NASAW: Well, my empty-headed colleague, we've made a breakthrough. The one we've been waiting for. Now we don't need all this extra DV8 weight, so we've decided to get rid of it. Like liposuction, but with human beings instead of fat!

Chazz: What the—we're going back on live television in five seconds! What are you going to do?

NASAW: Later hater!

[*end of call*]

After the commercial, the desperation is plain on Chazz's face; it clashes so fiercely with his Botox that his eyeballs appear to be melting, or at least leaking a toxic substance. But he soldiers on anyway, flashing his teeth in a frantic approximation of a smile.

ON-AIR

Item: Transcript of video broadcast

[*continued*]

[*START OF ACT THREE*]

Chazz: [*in the studio*] Welcome back, space fans! This week, we're upping the ante yet again.

[*CUT TO: Footage from 1969 moon landing*]

Chazz: [*voiceover*] Not only will our broadcast be LIVE, but this week we'll be holding . . . a DOUBLE ELIMINATION!

[*CUT TO: Clip of a speeding asteroid from the 1998 Bruce Willis thriller* Armageddon]

Chazz: [*voiceover*] Are those enough surprises for you? No? Then how about one more? Hold on to your fedoras, because the best part is . . . the cast doesn't even know it yet!

[*CUT TO: Video of a cat falling off a couch*]

Chazz: [*voiceover*] Intrepit explorers, how's it going up there? Exciting week, huh?

Source: Camera #4—Lünar Lounge

Titania: Exciting? Is that what you'd call it?

Snout: Chazz, I gotta be honest with you. We're not doing so great.

Matt: This week has been awful!

Kaoru: {We caught on fire, and I hit my head.}

Bacardi: And the Svalsta coffee table is *ruined!*

Chazz: [*voiceover*] Are you sure things aren't . . . stellar?

[*A graphic accompanied by the words "Brought to you by Stellar Acne Cream!" flashes across the bottom of the screen.*]

Matt: No. Definitely not stellar.

[*A graphic accompanied by the words "Brought to you by Stellar Acne Cream!" flashes across the bottom of the screen.*]

Chazz: [*voiceover*] Well, I've got another surprise for you this evening—

[*Suddenly the* Laika's *power goes out. Emergency lighting comes on, illuminating the cast members in a sickly, faint glow. Some look panicked, while others look annoyed. They murmur cranky questions—"Again?" and "What now?"—for a few seconds until the lights come back on. They shoot irritable looks at the camera, waiting for Chazz's explanation.*]

[*CUT TO: Chazz in the studio, talking to an offscreen producer*]

Chazz: What did you do?

DV8 Producer: Nothing! We were waiting for your cue!

Chazz: Then what happened with the power?

DV8 Producer: I don't know! Quick, say something to them.

[*CUT TO: Lünar Lounge*]

Chazz: [*voiceover, in a cartoonish voice that he's clearly making up as he goes along*] WhoooOOOooa! Guys, hang on a sec, we're getting some craaaAAAzy readings over here in mission control. Looks like . . . uh . . . those SOLAR FLARES you experienced the other day were only the beginning! There's now a humongous SOLAR WIND headed your way, and you need to outrun it! In order to do that, you'll have to jettison some extra weight, so I'm sorry to inform you that TWO intrepit explorers will be leaving us tonight!

Matt: Wait. Two?

Chazz: [*voiceover*] This week's biggest wastes of space are . . .

[*MUSIC CUE: "Another One Bites the Dust" by Queen*]

Matt and Kaoru!

The airlock door opens. The Enormous Robotic Arm unfolds itself from the wall (you can almost hear the collective cries of adoration from across the country) and snatches up both Matt and Kaoru in its grasp. Even with twice as many flailing limbs, it drags them off into the airlock, same as before.

But this time, just before the airlock seals shut, Colonel Bacon makes a run for it.

And the door closes behind him.

Snout: Colonel Bacon! [*turning to camera*] Chazz! Do something!

[*CUT TO: Chazz, not bothering to hide his surprised, delighted smile*]

Chazz: Sorry, kid! Nothing we can do!

[*CUT TO: Lünar Lounge*]

Snout: Nothing . . . ?

Nico: I'm sorry, Snout.

Clayton: Me too. I was so looking forward to Pork Chop Night.

Titania: Hey, asshole. Give it a rest.

[*Clayton glares at her but says nothing more.*]

Snout: [*sniffling*] Poor little piggy.

Bacardi: Issokay, Snout. I bet he's going wee, wee, wee all the way home.

Snout: Yeah. [*brightening a little*] Yeah, I bet he is!

Titania: So is no one concerned about the two human beings who were just discarded, or . . .

Louise: They'll be all right. *I'm* more worried about—

BOOM

Except it's not really a boom. It's more of a SSHHWUUMMP or a FLLLLRRRX or a WWWWHHHHHSSSSK. The difficulty in defining it lies with the fact that it's not a noise anyone has ever heard before, and therefore the onomatopoeia doesn't exist to describe it.

Regardless, it sounds.

The noise is evidently deafening to the cast members; they clap their hands over their ears, squeeze their eyes shut, and scream. Two seconds later, the ship gives a violent lurch, sending them across the floor in a tangle of bodies and shrieks. For the next five seconds, the camera shakes so forcefully it is impossible to see what is happening through the blurred motion.

[*CUT TO: Chazz, in the studio*]

Chazz: What in the [*beeping*] [*beep*] is going on?

[*Furious, his attention veers offscreen, most likely aimed at a hapless producer who is expected to know what's happening. Then, remembering that he is live on national television:*]

Chazz: I mean—surprise! Hey Spacetronauts, what do you think of this?

[*CUT TO: Lünar Lounge*]

Bacardi: I donnlike it!

Nico: I'm bleeding!

Louise: Is this the work of the dark and sinister enemy?

The shaking continues for a few more seconds, then stops—
As every one of the Spacetronauts lifts off the floor.

Their faces are ashen, dumbfounded, awestruck as they eerily drift several inches up into the air, each captivated by the same invisible force. It's clear that this, whatever it is, is different from anything they've experienced onboard the ship up to this point. This is not some cheap trick. This is not a special effect. This is not make-believe.

[*CUT TO: Chazz in the studio, a frosted-tip deer in headlights*]

[*CUT TO: the Lünar Lounge*]

One more second of footage flashes onto the screen, that of the remaining six cast members levitating. Then another—

BOOM

SSSHHHWWUUUMMMP

FLLLLRRRRRRRRRRX

WWWWHHHHHHSSSSSSK

OFF–AIR

The power goes out.

And the signal is lost.

For good.

DAMAGE CONTROL

WHEN THE FOURTH EPISODE OF *WASTE OF SPACE* INAUSPI-
ciously cuts short, viewers are treated to about thirty seconds
of dead air, followed by a hastily cued-up rerun of DV8's sign
language competition show, *Top Deaf*. Meanwhile, the crew
back in the studio at DV8 are caught so off guard that the camera is left rolling, though the footage is—luckily for them—
unaired.

**Item: Transcript of video recording—RAW, UNAIRED
FOOTAGE
Source: In-studio camera, DV8
Date: February 18, 2016**

    Chazz: What do you mean, gone?
    DV8 Producer: I mean there's no more signal! NASAW cut
us off!
    Chazz: What are you talking about?
    DV8 Producer: The power went out, and the signal was
lost. We can't see anything. The screens are blank.
    Chazz: I STILL DON'T GET IT!
    DV8 Producer: The scientists did . . . something. That

double shwumpy noise—it knocked out the power, along with our communications. That may not have been intentional, but their failure to answer our attempts at communication *is*.

Chazz: What are you saying?

DV8 Producer: I'm saying the scientists have locked the doors, pulled the curtains, given us the finger, and claimed those six kids as their personal lab rats.

Chazz: [*raking his fingers through the sail of his hair*] Oh my God.

DV8 Producer: We still don't know how they did it—

Chazz: [*storming off the set*] I don't give a hot goddamn how they did it! I want it fixed! NOW!

Regrettably, there is no footage of the havoc Chazz then wreaks in the DV8 control room. Eyewitnesses claim that he burst in like something out of a slasher movie, screaming and stomping and pushing stacks of papers to the floor, demanding that the situation be fixed.

This is more or less what the DV8 crew tells Chazz at that point:

- The feed is gone. If the cameras are still recording, DV8 has no way of knowing it. They can no longer log on to the main server to see if files are being regularly uploaded. They have no way of knowing whether the ship or the people within it have come to any harm. All they are able to conclude is that the soundstage has not been reduced to a smoking crater, because they are still able to make contact with the satellite phone hidden in the Confessional Closet—though no one is answering, presumably because Jamarkus kept the ringer turned off.

- All communication with the NASAW scientists has been severed. The phone line is no longer operational. Emails are being returned with the message "Delivery to the following recipient failed permanently, domain name not found."

- NASAW's social media accounts have been deleted. Their website is still up, but the contact link produces an "Error 404: Page not found" notification.

The sudden dematerialization of NASAW strongly suggests some form of sabotage, but DV8 is more concerned with how to fix it than why it happened. They work feverishly through the night to reestablish contact—to no avail. Finally, desperate, a team of staff members hops in a car and begins the eleven-hour drive directly to the soundstage.

DV8 has one advantage, though: they're the only ones who know that they've been shut out. The viewing public remains under the impression that only the live satellite feed has been cut; they know nothing of the total radio silence, the unnervingly blank screens of the DV8 control room.

Luckily for DV8, they think that they have until the next episode airs (a full week later) to figure it out.

Unluckily for DV8, they haven't the first clue how to do so.

Even more unluckily, they are wrong about having a full week. DV8 couldn't have known it at the time, but *Waste of Space* proceeds to collapse in on itself far sooner than anyone could have predicted, coming to its wholly unpredictable conclusion nine full weeks earlier than its anticipated run—

And less than *twenty-four hours* after the signal goes dead.

The remainder of this report will provide a breakdown, hour by hour, of that final, harrowing day. This is where the evidence provided by Chazz Young ends and where my own evidence, obtained without permission, begins. Paradoxically, you'll find that my narrative interjections will be fewer and farther between, as I believe it's imperative for the content to speak for itself.

Because what DV8 doesn't know is this: the cameras on the ship *are* still recording. Still recording, and still uploading files to the main server.

After the Shwump, as the double-pseudo sound explosion comes to be called, all nine cameras spark back to life.

From here on out, nothing is aired. Nothing is edited.

But everything is recorded. And everything is evidence.

———————————

Ten seconds after the signal is cut, power is restored. Cameras blink on, one by one.

Item: Transcript of video recording—RAW, UNAIRED FOOTAGE

Source: Camera #1—Airlock

Date: February 18, 2016
Time: 10:23 p.m.

[*Both the outer and inner doors of the airlock are closed. The Enormous Robotic Arm is still clutching Matt and Kaoru, who continue to flail and fight to be released from its grip, while Colonel Bacon trots around the small space, squealing.*

After about five more seconds, the outer door of the airlock—the one that theoretically leads to the vacuum of space but in actuality leads to the soundstage—opens.

Colonel Bacon makes a run for it.

Two seconds later, a collective cry of surprise goes up among the scientists. The camera in the airlock is situated above the outer door and aimed inward, so nothing outside it can be seen—but it's clear that whatever's happening in the soundstage is nothing short of earthshattering. The NASAW scientists are shouting, screaming, and hurling so many instructions at one another—"It worked!" "Shut it down!" "It went through!"—that it's impossible to make out what the clamor is about.

Meanwhile, in walks Boris, unfazed, with a stun gun in his hand.]

Boris: [*yelling over his shoulder at someone on the outside*] I don't care how many world-changing discoveries you're making with your science crap, I got a job to do and I intend to do it! [*turning to the captives*] Hold still, kids.

[*He calmly electrocutes Matt and Kaoru. They go limp. The Enormous Robotic Arm lowers their lifeless bodies to the floor, and Boris drags them out one by one.*

Amid the scientists' persistent shouting, the outer airlock door closes.]

[*Titania is keyed up, talking faster than usual and fighting an unfightable smile.*]

Titania: Something happened.

Something . . . *warped.* We floated. And I felt, for the first time in a long time . . .

Hope?

[*Tears are welling up in her eyes. She brushes them away, awestruck as she makes a stammered attempt to describe what she's experiencing.*]

I don't know how to—it's like—okay, when I was maybe five years old or so—Lily was three, and the boys weren't born yet—we all took a trip to Dad's office one Saturday. There were some papers he forgot to grab before he left on Friday, and the plan was for all of us to go out to dinner in the city after he picked them up. So we went downtown, took the elevator up to his firm's office, and oohed and aahed over all the blueprints and scale models while Dad grabbed his stuff.

When it was time to leave, I made the executive decision that Lily and I were going to race my parents to the elevator—but I didn't tell them that. Instead, I grabbed Lily's hand and ran, pulling her toward the elevator bank, and when it got there, I shoved her in, pushed a button . . . and then watched as the doors closed. A five-year-old and a three-year-old, all alone inside.

The elevator whisked us off.

[*She pauses to catch her breath, brushing a clump of sweaty hair off her forehead.*]

The thrill wore away real fast. After a few seconds we were

huddled together in the corner, clinging to each other for dear life. Like we'd blasted off in a rocket ship, and all we had left was each other. Lily said "I'm scared" and I said "Me too." Then I said "I'll protect you," and she said—

[*Titania breaks off, then swallows and continues.*]

She said, "I know."

[*She swallows again.*]

When the doors opened, we found ourselves on the roof. It was dusk on a cloudy day, it had snowed the night before, and in the fading light, everything was blue. Electric, beautiful blue, washing over us, wrapping us in its glow. We instantly felt calm. The roof was so peaceful. And quiet. Incredibly quiet.

I reached out past the elevator door, scooped up a bit of snow, and dabbed it on the end of Lily's nose. She laughed.

Then the elevator door closed and we were on our way again. I don't remember how my parents found us—either we went back down to Dad's office or we met on another floor— but when they did, all remaining fear washed away. We were safe again. But—

[*She cocks her head.*]

But here's the weird thing. As we were walking to the car, when I told my parents that the elevator had taken us to the roof, they gave me the strangest look. And my dad said, and I'll never forget it:

"Sweetie, that elevator doesn't go to the roof."

To this day I don't know what happened. Maybe I blacked out. Maybe I got so scared, my imagination took over. Or maybe the only way I could protect the both of us was for me to make up a new reality.

Whatever it was, it worked. I don't know what was really on

the other side of that elevator, but I know it wasn't a dead end. It was a way to keep moving. Forward.

That's how I'm feeling now. Like a way forward has been opened.

Emily Dickinson says that hope is the thing with feathers.

But I think hope is the thing with a doorway.

When the cameras in the Lünar Lounge snap back on, the remaining cast members (minus Titania) are in one of those shell-shocked holding patterns that people fall into after a catastrophe, as if they're waiting for someone to tell them what to do—or for something worse to happen. Nico is consoling Snout on the couch, Louise is nervously looking out the Windows Window, and Clayton is woozily getting up off the floor.

Source: Camera #3—Lünar Lounge
Time: 10:24 p.m.

Louise: Hey, look—the little red camera lights turned back on. I think they're filming again.

Bacardi: [*popping up from the floor to wave*] Welcome back, America!

Clayton: Hate to break it to you, but America's stopped watching. [*He points to the control panel.*] Flatline. Has been since the second blast.

Note: Clayton is referring here to the DV8 network indicator, the one that signifies that the folks in the DV8 control room are at the helm; since they no longer are, the indicator is not on.

Snout: [*sniffling*] So . . . we're on our own? That's not good.

Louise: [*brightening*] Yes, it is! It's a golden opportunity! Now we can do whatever we want! We can explore the outer limits of the universe! We can go farther than any manned spacecraft ever has before, with no mission control to control us! We can track down Lord Balway Galway and assimilate into his alien civilization and maybe take a stab at the mysterious mating rituals of his home planet!

Nico: I think—

[*They all turn to him, as if surprised that he is speaking. Nico seems surprised, too, but also resigned—as if realizing that now that there are only six remaining people on the ship, there's no more room for him to hide.*]

Nico: I think we might be getting ahead of ourselves here. Shouldn't we talk about how we, um, floated?

Bacardi: Ohshit, that really happened?

Snout: Shoot, I thought I imagined it too!

Louise: I don't know what you're all so surprised about. Of course we were bound to experience weightlessness sooner or later.

Clayton: Seriously? *Seriously?*

Louise: What?

Clayton: I can*not* believe you're falling for this again.

Louise: Hey, you were the one who said that not floating meant we weren't in space. But now we *are* floating. So there.

Clayton: We're not floating *anymore.*

Bacardi: But we're still movingandbobbingandswaying—

Louise: Yeah. How do you explain that, Mr. Jerkface Know-It-All?

Clayton: [*steaming mad*] Because we are in a motion

simulator, same as every ride at every theme park in America! All they did was switch it off, drop us into free fall for a few seconds, then switch the damn thing back on again!

[*pause*]

Snout: I don't know, buddy. That sounds pretty far-fetched.

[*Clayton closes his eyes, takes a deep breath, and leaves the room.*]

Louise: Gukadia, maybe. The findings from the Interstellar Probing Squadron found evidence of gravitational sinks there. Or maybe we fell into a wormhole! Or! OR! *Maybe* we're caught in a tractor beam. The double shwumpy noise was when we got caught in it, then the shaking was when they reeled us in, then the weightlessness was them securing us inside their warship somewhere in the Jjesibian Nebula! *It makes perfect sense!*

[*They blink at her.*]

Nico: Look, the floating thing was extremely weird. But I think we should try to stay calm before we jump to any conclusions. If anything, we—

Bacardi: My ears hurt.

Nico: Huh?

Bacardi: [*working her jaw around*] My ears. Theypopped when we floated.

Snout: Mine did too.

Nico: [*looking around*] Did everyone's?

[*They all nod.*]

Louise: See? [*smirking*] Tractor beam.

No one has anything else to say to that. As if collectively realizing that nothing else is going to get solved that night, or perhaps out of exhaustion from the ordeal, they all start drifting into the bedroom. Clayton is already curled into himself in his bunk, his only movement that of pulling the blanket over his head when the rest enter. No one has to share a bed anymore, so the cast members each get into their own bunks and fall asleep.

Except for Nico, who goes off in search of Titania.

Source: Camera #7—Confessional Closet
Time: 10:31 p.m.

Nico: [*entering room and sitting on floor*] Are you okay? You disappeared.

Titania: I know, I'm sorry. [*She keeps smiling, then trying not to, then smiling again.*] I—after we floated, I . . . *felt* something. Almost spiritual? I can't explain it. But yeah, I'm okay. Are you?

Nico: As much as someone who just spontaneously levitated can be, I guess.

Titania: [*distracted*] Right.

Nico: It's like, here I am, I'm thinking one way, then something else happens, and then I start thinking five ways different from the first. I'm maybe eighty percent sure we're not in space, then it goes up to ninety-nine, but now with those wonky noises and the shaking and the floating—the percentage changes all over again. It's hard to know what to believe anymore.

Titania: [*still distracted*] Right.

Nico: What do *you* think is going on?

[*longish pause*]

Titania: I don't know.

[*Nico studies her.*]

Nico: Are you sure you're okay? Your face is doing some crazy things.

[*She blinks hard, snapping herself out of it. She gives him a grin.*]

Titania: I feel crazy. But good crazy.

[*Nico lets out a small laugh.*]

Titania: What?

Nico: This is what you wanted, isn't it? For us to keep exploring?

Titania: Yeah. I guess it is. [*She nods at the door.*] How's everyone doing out there?

Nico: Clayton is—I think he's losing it. Louise too. Snout and Bacardi . . . who knows what they're thinking. If they're thinking anything at all. And we can't trust anyone at DV8 either. Wonder what they'll say when they restore contact with us.

Titania: *If* they restore contact with us.

Nico: It's gotta be soon, right? Tomorrow. Or . . . or do you think we're really cut off?

Titania: You want my honest opinion?

Nico: Yes.

Titania: I think we're really cut off.

DV8 scrambles.

Chazz Young connives.

NASAW conspires.

America holds its breath.

And through it all, the cast members remain ignorant

protected

      isolated

           drifting deeper

               and deeper

                    into the depths of uncertainty.

PART THREE

THE LAST DAY

Item: Transcript of video recording
Source: Dashboard camera, DV8 Company Van
Date: February 19, 2016
Time: 3:28 a.m.

[*IMAGE: Night. Headlights illuminate a speeding ribbon of road. Camera picks up audio of conversation on speakerphone.*]

Boris: I don't know. Pancakes?

Annette: I made pancakes last week.

Boris: Oh, right. How about sausage?

Annette: Sausage gives you gas.

Boris: Look, I don't know why this always has to be such an in-depth discussion.

Annette: Because I want it to be something that you like! You come home so tired and spaced out from that awful overnight drive, the least I can do is give you a warm, delicious breakfast to—

Boris: AGGUGHH

Annette: Boris?

Boris: GUGUAAAH

Annette: Boris? What's wrong?

Boris: GGGAUUUUHHH

Annette: Honey, hold tight! I'll call for help!

[*Five seconds pass. The strangled noises cease.*]

[*Fainter voices emerge from the background.*]

Matt: Oh God. Is he dead?

Kaoru: {He is only unconscious.}

Matt: He has a pulse. I think he blacked out. [*exhales forcefully*] Holy crap. Are you a trained assassin or something?

Kaoru: {I have never delivered a chokehold to a stranger before. There is one for the bucket list.}

Matt: One second *I'm* unconscious, the next I wake up rattling around in the back of a windowless van, the next I look up and you're strangling the guy who stun-gunned us—

Kaoru: {It is a good thing the muscle spasms convulsing through his body caused his foot to stomp on the brake.}

Matt: What if he had crashed the car? We could have been killed!

Kaoru: {I am glad we are off that spaceship. We could have been killed.}

Matt: Where are we? It's too dark to— Hang on.

Kaoru: {Please do not get out of the car.}

[*Matt appears in the frame, illuminated by the headlights.*]

Matt: Oh God!

Kaoru: {Please get back in the car.}

Matt: [*looking around*] We're in a desert! How did we end up in a desert?

Kaoru: {We have been in a desert this whole time.}

[*Matt gets back into the car.*]

Matt: Where was he taking us? Did we crash-land here? Are we on Mars?

Kaoru: {Judging by how long it took them to transport us here in the first place and the fact that it is currently three thirty in the morning, I believe Los Angeles is roughly 500 miles due west.}

Matt: No, of course we're not on Mars. Mars has no air. Or windowless vans. I'm an idiot.

Kaoru: {We should keep going forward to California and find a responsible adult. But I do not know how to drive.}

Matt: Okay. Okay, I have an idea. I'll drive back in the direction we came from. Maybe we'll find someone who can help us there.

Kaoru: [*in English*] This is a fine kettle of fish.

Overnight and into the next morning, the public-relations arm of DV8 struggles to stay afloat in the resulting deluge of questions from the media. Even major networks—who, up until now, have remained distant and condescending when it comes to the maverick network gobbling up all their ratings—jump into the fray.

The PR team admirably evades the public's questions, giving vague and slightly provocative answers, as if they know something that the rest of the world doesn't and the media hoopla explosion is all part of their master plan—all while remaining as in the dark as Chazz and the rest of the DV8 team. But they're the ones who know how to put the best spin on the situation. By the time viewers wake up the next morning to consult their opinionators of choice, the verdict has already been rendered that the cutoff was a publicity stunt, that the signal loss is yet another cog in the clockwork masterpiece narrative that Chazz Young is so deftly crafting, and that both the Shwump and levitation trick have been engineered solely to entice the world to keep watching, watching, watching.

Item: Online article
Source: ViralLoad
Time: 7:39 a.m.

They've done it again!

DV8 continues to break ground on the most fascinating entertainment in years. Cutting their latest episode short—by *eight minutes!*—in the guise of losing the satellite feed is yet another notch in the epic, diamond-studded belt that is this show. I can't believe we have to wait a *whole week* to find out what's happening up there in space right now!!

I just have so many questions. What caused those two explodey noises right before the end of the episode? Were they explosions at all? Could they be retaliation for Jamarkus's attack on the "dark and sinister" enemy? Or is this a new threat?

AND DID MY EYES DECEIVE ME OR DID THOSE SPACETRONAUTS *FLOAT*?

Wherever this is going, it's amazing. So-called technical difficulties coupled with that trademark flying-by-the-seat-of-their-sequined-pants DV8 attitude makes for fascinating television. How much of this was planned? How much of it is master puppeteer Chazz Young gone mental at the controls, laughing maniacally as he pulls the strings? Does it even matter?

This reviewer doesn't think so. As long as DV8 continues

to blur the line between fantasy and reality, I'm going to keep watching.

Back at DV8 headquarters, things are getting sticky. By 8:00 a.m. Chazz Young still hasn't come into the office; paparazzi photos show him lounging by the pool at his mansion in the Hollywood Hills, his puggles floating by on an inflatable doghouse.

Item: Transcript of audio recording
Source: Chazz's cell phone
Time: 8:02 a.m.

    DV8: What's our current status, Chazz?

    Chazz: No change.

    DV8: I know you said we should wait this out, but I don't think that's going to work for much longer. You need to give us some direction here.

Chazz: Not yet. You guys are blowing this way out of proportion. Boris should be arriving with Matt and Kaoru soon—we'll find out from him what went down and go from there. I don't know why he isn't answering his phone, but—

DV8: Chazz, no. Whatever it was that happened, it's now clear that NASAW has gone on lockdown and is no longer willing to communicate with us. This has essentially turned into a hostage situation!

Chazz: Hostage situations make excellent television.

[*pause*]

DV8: Are you serious?

Chazz: All I'm saying is that it might behoove us to simply sit back and document this thing until it reaches its inevitable conclusion, then retrieve the footage and edit it into a movie. I've been wanting to break into the feature film biz for a while now. Maybe this is my chance! I mean—DV8's chance.

DV8: Chazz. Tell me you're not suggesting that we leave those kids to their own devices, at the mercy of those deranged scientists who are performing who knows what kind of sick experiments on them.

Chazz: Hey, whatever they're doing can't be any sicker than what we were doing. Those Instigating Plot Points were paying off like gangbusters until—

DV8: Until NASAW went off script and broke the laws of gravity! Don't you see the predicament this puts us in? We can't rescue them without breaking the illusion that they're in space—the media's breathing down our necks on that front, watching every move we make, and it's only going to get worse. But we also can't give NASAW free rein to do whatever they want to those kids!

Chazz: Why not?

[*pause*]

DV8: Here is what we propose. Our team is already on its way out to the soundstage. They demand to be let in, then they try to negotiate with NASAW.

Chazz: And if that doesn't work?

DV8: Then we get the police involved.

Chazz: No. No law enforcement. Unless . . .

DV8: Unless what?

Chazz: Nothing. Let me know how the team makes out. And don't you dare call the authorities—that's my call to make, and I'll make it only when necessary.

DV8: What are you going to be doing in the meantime?

Chazz: What I do best.

DV8: What is *that*?

[*end of call*]

———————————————

Morning comes to the *Laika*. When the lights turn on and the occupants of the bedroom are illuminated, Clayton is not among them—but no one takes much notice of this at first. Snout, Louise, and Titania head into the bathroom while Bacardi stays in bed and Nico talks to his camera.

Item: Transcript of video recording
Source: Nico's camera
Battery charge: 40%
Time: 8:30 a.m.

Hi Mom. Hi Dad.

I can't talk long. I'm at 40 percent, and if this is the only functioning camera left on this ship, it might be a good idea to conserve the battery in case anything horrible happens.

Which, given the events of last night, is entirely possible.

I don't know what's happening. But I'll say this: there's a purple blob on the LCD screen of this camera right now. It wasn't there yesterday. And it took me three tries to turn it on. I don't know of anything that could cause electronics to malfunction like that, but . . .

Anyway, I better go. I'm now at—

Whoa.

Now I'm at 41 percent.

How is *that* possible?

Item: Transcript of video recording—RAW, UNAIRED FOOTAGE
Source: Camera #8—Bedroom
Time: 8:34 a.m.

[*Frowning, Nico puts away his camera, gets up from his mattress, and assesses the room. Bacardi is the only one left, sprawled out across the big bed.*]

Nico: Hey. [*giving her a gentle nudge*] Bacardi. Time to wake up.

[*Bacardi doesn't move.*]

Nico: [*nudging her harder*] Bacardi? You okay?

[*Nothing.*]

Nico: [*mildly panicked now*] Hey, wake up! Bacardi! Can you hear me?

[*She makes a noise not unlike that of an injured elephant, then rolls over, opens her eyes, and looks at him.*]

Bacardi: Heythere, sexypants. [*tugs at her shirt*] Wanna see what's in my space bra?

Nico: No, stop. [*He stops her hand.*] You don't have to do that.

Bacardi: [*rubbing her eyes*] I know, I know. You got a thing with Titania going on.

Nico: What? No, I don't.

Bacardi: *Psfff.* Right.

[*She blinks each eye, one at a time.*]

Nico: Are you all right?

Bacardi: Yeah. Just a little fuzzy in the brainspace.

Nico: We all are. I don't think I slept. Kept thinking we were going to implode at any minute. .

Bacardi: Yeah. It's scary. [*reaches for a Slom bottle on the nightstand*] But nothing a liter of vodka can't fix—

Nico: [*pulling it out of her reach*] You think that maybe you've had enough?

Bacardi: Enough of what?

Nico: Like, every substance onboard this ship?

[*She mulls this over.*]

Bacardi: Nah.

Nico: Well, I don't want you to die.

Bacardi: *Psf.* I'm not gonna die. Maybe from starvation or from scientist attacks. But not from liquids.

Nico: The liquids aren't doing you any favors.

Bacardi: The liquids are the only things that can reliably make me happy.

Nico: That is . . . a very sad thing to say.

Bacardi: Yeah.

Nico: Is it true?

[*Bacardi hesitates. When she speaks, she sounds demonstrably more lucid.*]

Bacardi: Be honest, Nico. Do you think we're still on TV?

Nico: Not really.

[*She reaches for the bottle.*]

Nico: [*pulls it away again*] Bacardi—

Bacardi: Give it to me!

[*She yanks it out of his hand. She looks at it, then pours the rest out onto the mattress.*]

Bacardi: All gone.

Nico: Okay. Well, good. I'm . . . proud of you.

Bacardi: [*sarcastically*] Thanks.

Nico: Although this room stinks bad enough already, not sure we needed to add alcohol to the mix.

Bacardi: Have you ever even drunk vodka?

Nico: No.

Bacardi: It doesn't smell.

[*He sniffs at the mattress, frowning. Bacardi grins at him.*]

Bacardi: See?

[*Louise lets out a scream from the kitchen. They both rush out of the bedroom.*]

Source: Camera #9—Kitchen

[*Nico, Snout, Bacardi, and Titania all run in.*]

Nico: What's wrong?

Louise: The food! It's all gone!

Nico: What?

Louise: I came in here to get some Amalgamated Bran Lumps for breakfast, but there aren't any left! There were eleven bags yesterday, and now they've disappeared! Everything has!

Titania: [*opening cabinet doors*] Nothing in here, either.

250

Snout: [*opening the pantry*] No more Meteor Chowder! That supply was supposed to last our entire mission!

Nico: What about all the freeze-dried stuff?

[*Bacardi sticks her head into the freezer.*]

Bacardi: Nope. Gone and goodbye. Fine by me, that stuff was awful.

Titania: But it was still food, even by the loosest interpretation of the word. Where could it have gone?

Louise: Isn't it obvious? Clayton took it!

Titania: How is that obvious?

Louise: [*gestures around the room*] He's the only one not here. Duh.

Snout: Maybe he ate it all for himself!

Bacardi: Or maybe he flushed it down the toilet 'cause he's a douchebag!

Titania: Or maybe there's a perfectly good explanation that is none of those things.

Snout: But we're gonna miss breakfast!

Louise: We're gonna starve to death!

Bacardi: We're gonna have to kill and eat someone to survive!

[*All eyes, conspicuously and inconspicuously, drift to Snout.*]

Snout: [*frowning*] Oh, good gravy . . .

Titania: Time out, you guys. I don't think we need to turn to cannibalism just yet.

Nico: [*under his breath*] Famous last words.

Louise: Oh really? Do you have a better idea?

Titania: Yes. If we all calm down and think this through in a rational, composed manner—

Bacardi: [*brandishing her Slom bottle*] We need to find

Clayton and break this over his head and then stab him with the shards!

Titania: Off to a good start.

Source: Camera #3—Lünar Lounge

[*Everyone follows Bacardi as she barges into the Lünar Lounge, where Clayton is sitting on the puffy chair, plucking his eyebrows.*]

Bacardi: You there! I hereby accuse you of kidnapping all our food and jettisoning it off to Jupiter! You have the right to— ohmygod, *how* do you get your arches so perfect?

Clayton: [*demonstrating with the tweezers*] Little flick of the wrist. Just like that.

Bacardi: I can never get mine straight like that. You're, like, an eyebrow wizard.

Clayton: Thank you.

Bacardi: [*to Nico*] Where was I?

Nico: Jupiter.

Bacardi: Oh yeah! What'd you do with all the food?

Clayton: I flushed it down the toilet.

[*Everyone gawks at him.*]

Louise: You *what*?

Bacardi: I! TOLD! YOU! SO!

Nico: Why? Why would you do that?

Clayton: [*calmly resuming his plucking*] Because you deserved it.

Louise: Oh no, he lost his mind. He's got the space madness. Is it airborne yet? [*grabbing Nico and shaking him*] Maybe we all have it!

Clayton: I do not have the space madness because that is not a thing, you festering idiot. And even if it was, we aren't in space. But hey—you want to keep happily prancing around in the land of make-believe? Be my guest. We'll just let starvation prove one of us right. If the show is fake—and it *is*—DV8 will rescue us well before we're in any danger of dying. But if we're really in space, then by golly, I lose and you win! We all hurtle off into the deepest depths of the universe and suffer a slow, famished demise!

[*Dismay settles through the room.*]

Clayton: [*yawns and stretches dramatically*] Phew! All this sabotage has *really* tuckered me out. Think I'll go take a relaxing dip in what's left of the hot tub.

[*They watch him go. Seconds later, Clayton reappears in the hot-tub window, utilizing the bullet hole for something highly inappropriate.*]

Bacardi: [*advancing on him with the bottle*] I'll cut it off, I swear to God.

Titania: [*heading her off*] Guys, shhh. Do you hear that?

[*Everyone falls quiet and listens. A faint pounding noise is heard.*]

Item: Transcript of video recording
Source: Dashboard camera, DV8 Company Van
Time: 8:35 a.m.

[*IMAGE: The large steel wall of the soundstage. Matt is pounding on its door. Kaoru is standing next to him, arms crossed.*]

Matt: Let us in! We've been driving for hours and I really have to pee!

Kaoru: {I beg you to stop. These are the people who have been holding us against our will. They will not help us.}

Matt: [*pounding harder*] Hello! Is anyone in there?

[*The door finally opens.*]

NASAW Scientist: Oh hell. It's you.

Matt: Huh?

NASAW: I mean—hey, tough break, kiddo, getting eliminated and all. That must have been a real bummer.

Matt: Not really. I wanted to leave.

NASAW: Still, a mid-space rescue from an airlock—that must have been pretty cool, huh, sport?

Matt: Yeah, I guess. It was weird, though, because—I remember getting grabbed by the Enormous Robotic Arm and pulled into the airlock, but once the doors shut, there was a guy in there with a stun gun! Kinda like the one . . . in your hand . . .

NASAW: Don't move.

Matt: Oh God.

[*The NASAW scientist lunges at Matt. Matt ducks out of the way, causing the man to lose his balance. Kaoru, sensing an opportunity, grabs the scientist's arm and twists it around, causing him to stun himself. He falls in a heap to the ground. Matt and Kaoru look at each other.*]

Matt: Now what?

Kaoru: {Once again, I suggest we leave.}

Matt: No way, I'm not taking my chances with these psychopaths. We're outta here.

[*He stomps off toward the windowless van. Kaoru shakes her head and starts to follow him, but her attention is arrested by the exterior wall of the soundstage. She puts a hand to it, then backs up and looks at it from a distance. Her brow furrows as she walks out of the frame, no doubt wondering what could cause a massive, solid steel wall to bow inward to such a concave degree.*]

Item: Transcript of video recording—RAW, UNAIRED FOOTAGE
Source: Camera #3—Lünar Lounge
Time: 8:37 a.m.

[*The kids are still listening for more of the thumping noise.*]

Titania: It stopped.

Nico: What do you think it was?

Louise: Winnovian space barnacles, obviously. Can we get back to the matter at hand?

Snout: Yeah. What are we going to do about Clayton?

Louise: Isn't it obvious? We have to punish him.

Clayton: How are you going to do that? [*He has settled into the remaining foot of hot-tub water and is now listening to and conversing with and laughing at them through the bullet hole in the glass.*] Bore me to death?

Louise: There needs to be justice! We can't let him get away with this!

Titania: We can, because we have to. Stupid little fights will turn into big fights if we let them, and we need to keep our heads screwed on straight if we're going to get through this.

Clayton: Couldn't have said it better myself.

[*Snout gathers the others into a huddle and speaks low so that Clayton can't hear them.*]

Snout: But what if he tries something else? Something worse? We have to stop him before he gets a chance.

Nico: I agree. He's too unpredictable. He brought a gun, he doesn't care about our safety.

Louise: Or our food.

Bacardi: *And* he's a douchekazoo!

Nico: Exactly. Who knows what he'll try to pull next?

Titania: Guys, I get it. But what are we supposed to do? We're all *literally* in the same boat here. There's nothing we can . . .

[*She trails off, a devious smile pushing its way across her lips, and darts out of the room before anyone can stop her.*]

Source: Camera #5—Spa

[*Clayton is lying spread-eagle in the water, eyes closed, in a state so relaxed that when the spa door slams shut, his whole body jerks to attention.*]

Source: Camera #3—Lünar Lounge

[*A harsh sound rebounds from somewhere in the ship—a grating, unpleasant noise, like a chair being dragged across a floor.*]

Nico: What was that?

[*Clayton splashes across the hot tub and gets out to investigate. A second later, there is a series of pounds, followed by a series of curses.*]

Clayton: Hey! [*He comes back to the hot-tub window and bangs on it.*] The spa door is stuck!

Titania: [*returning to the lounge*] Oh, is it?

Clayton: You *know* it is. Let me out!

Titania: The thing is, I can't. With the high humidity in there, the wooden door got all warped and expanded. If it's wedged shut, there's not much we can do about it until we vent some of the moister air in here . . . which, I guess, since we're not in control of the ship, means we can't do anything about it at all until we get rescued.

[*With a look of horror, Clayton begins pounding on the glass.*]

Clayton: You slack-jawed Neanderthals! You oxygen-hogging compost heaps! Let me *out!*

[*Desperate, he head-butts the window, neatly knocking himself unconscious. He crumples into the shallow water, his head lolling about the edge of the tub.*]

Snout: Sweet, merciful quiet.

Titania: He won't be unconscious forever. We should use this time wisely. We need to figure out a plan.

Snout: But—wouldn't the plan depend on whether we're in space or not?

Titania: We're not.

Louise: Yes we are!

Titania: Louise, I'm sorry. I know this is hard for you. But we're not.

Louise: How do *you* know?

Titania: [*gesturing at the Windows Window*] The stars—

Louise: Are there because we're in space.

Titania: It's a screen saver, Louise. That's a computer screen.

Louise: [*stung*] No, it's not.

Titania: It is. We—

[*She looks at Nico, who winces.*]

Nico: Yeah. Tell her.

Titania: We—Nico and I—were looking out the Windows Window a while back, watching the stars go by, and we saw an error message.

Louise: An error message?

Titania: A pop-up. It said "Restart your computer to finish installing important updates." And then we saw a cursor fly across the screen and close the box, then it went back to the stars.

Nico: I'm sorry, Louise. I saw it too.

[*Louise looks at each cast member, then at the ground. Then back up at them again, close to tears, yet defiant.*]

Louise: *We floated yesterday.* You *can't* deny that. And what about those shwumpy noises? Those weren't from Earth, and you know it.

[*No one has an argument for this, each face a conflicting mess of doubt and confusion.*]

Titania: [*glaring at Clayton's limp form*] Clayton's right about one thing—if we're in space, we're screwed no matter what. So we might as well proceed as though we're still on Earth, since that's the only situation in which we have a fighting chance.

Nico: So what do we do?

Titania: I'd say we should start with the one thing Chazz told us *not* to do.

Nico: Mess with anything?

Titania: Yeah. Let's mess with *everything*.

Back in Los Angeles, DV8's attempts to contact NASAW are bearing no fruit. And Chazz's patience is wearing thin.

Item: Transcript of audio recording
Source: Chazz's cell phone
Time: 8:47 a.m.

Telecomm: Thank you for calling Telecomm customer service!

Chazz: Yeah, hi—

Telecomm: I'm excited and fully prepared to help you in any way I can. What is your name?

Chazz: Huh? Chazz. I'm in a hurry here, so—

Telecomm: Certainly! I'd be happy to help you explore solutions to your challenges today, Chazz. May I ask what—

Chazz: I'm trying to reach a certain phone number, and it keeps saying the line has been disconnected.

Telecomm: Certainly! I can go ahead and look that up for you. What is the number?

Chazz: (█████) ████-█████

Telecomm: Thank you, Chazz. I'll certainly be able to look that up for you. Please hold.

[*"I Will Wait" by Mumford & Sons plays. Four minutes pass.*]

Telecomm: It looks like this phone number has been disconnected.

Chazz: I already know that! What I want to know is *how* that number got permission to be disconnected, since *my* company is the one that purchased that phone line in the first place!

Telecomm: Certainly, I'd be happy to look into that for you, Chazz. If you'll hold for—

Chazz: No, don't put me on hold! You know what—forget about how it happened. Just *fix* it.

Telecomm: Certainly!

Chazz: Thank you.

Telecomm: I'd be happy to set up a new phone line for you—

Chazz: No, not a *new* phone line! I need you to restore *that* phone line!

Telecomm: Unfortunately, Chazz, I am unable to process that request at this time. Is there anything else I can help you with today?

Chazz: YOU CAN DRAG YOURSELF INTO A ROTTING SWAMPLAND TO DIE WHILE VULTURES PECK OFF YOUR

EYELIDS SO YOU CAN WATCH THEM SLURP UP YOUR
INTESTINES LIKE A BOWL OF SPAGHETTI.

Telecomm: I can certainly—

[*end of call*]

Back onboard the *Laika*, an hour has passed. The Spacetronauts
(minus Clayton) have pushed every button, pulled every lever,
flipped every switch, and cranked every dial on the ship.

Nothing has changed.

Item: Transcript of video recording—RAW, UNAIRED FOOTAGE
Source: Camera #4—Lünar Lounge
Time: 9:42 a.m.

[*Bacardi, having been pounding on the airlock for the better part of twenty minutes, has now taken to making direct appeals to her captors.*]

Bacardi: Let us out! I know you can hear us, nerds! I know you're making breakfast! I CAN SMELL BACON!

Titania: Hope it's not the Colonel.

Snout: Hey!

Bacardi: Could be. I haven't heard a single squeal since he waddled on out of here. Why was the pig the only one of us smart enough to make a run for it? [*She leans back against the airlock door and sinks to the floor.*] I give up. Real airlock or no, it's not opening.

Louise: [*scowling, upset*] I don't understand. Why aren't any of these instruments working?

Nico: Because this isn't a real spaceship.

Louise: Yes, it *is.*

[*She balls her hands into fists and stalks out of the room.*]

Titania: I hate to say that Clayton is right, but he is. About NASAW or DV8 being the ones controlling what the buttons do. I bet it's why the sprinklers didn't work. We hit that button while that earthquake-floating-shwump-thing was happening—maybe the powers that be were so busy dealing with whatever that was that they didn't notice us pushing the button, so they didn't trigger the sprinklers.

Snout: So now that they're not filming us anymore, they don't give a horse's patootie about what we tell the ship to do? They're gonna ignore us?

Nico: Sure. If we're not in space, then what's the point?

Bacardi: Hey guys?

[*They look at Bacardi. She is merely sitting with her back up against the airlock, but her hair is doing more than that—each strand is sticking straight out from her head, arching over her head like a rainbow. As though the airlock door were made up of balloons and she'd rubbed her head all over it, triggering a halo of static electricity.*]

Bacardi: You *sure* we're not in space?

It is at this point that the behavior of the internet must be addressed.

To say that *Waste of Space* captures the attention and imagination of the online world would be an understatement. It downright dominates. Rarely has a cultural phenomenon been so universally dissected and argued about and spoofed with such vim and vigor. The recipe is perfect: The cast members can't defend themselves. DV8 can't either; they're savvy enough to know that every word they say will be scrutinized to death, so they remain tight-lipped, not wanting to implicate themselves in anything they won't be smart enough to worm their way out of. The situation is mysterious enough to seize the wild imaginations of armchair detectives, who gleefully examine frame after frame, looking for clues as to what really happened. And the comedic ramifications can't be escaped either. GIFs, memes, clips, and quotes proliferate like virtual termites, burrowing into every pixelated nook and encrypted cranny.

Of course—because it is the internet—the dark side of humanity emerges as well. Cast members' families are tracked down; home addresses are distributed online. Innocent people are harassed, implicated, publicly shamed. Nico's brother is stalked by paparazzi. A small shrine of sci-fi paraphernalia and inflatable aliens materializes outside Louise's house. Crude words are spelled out in the crops of Snout's family farm. Difficulty is encountered in tracking down Titania's family, leading many to speculate and bellow that she applied for the show under a false name. Clayton's former nanny gives a tell-all interview, and Bacardi, the liquor company, files a defamation lawsuit against Bacardi, the person.

Countless think pieces are written about every topic under the solar-storming sun: the immorality of DV8 to conceive of such a show, the irresponsibility of the cast members' parents to allow them to participate in such a show, the irrelevance of think pieces at all because the show is so glaringly a scam. Just when it seems as though the online space will collapse under the weight of it all, a new outrage surfaces, and the spores of vitriol bloom and scatter once more.

And with the release of a minute-and-a-half-long video on the Fakefinders website, the media maelstrom—and Chazz Young's day—gets even worse.

[*person in Bigfoot mask facing the camera*]

Bigfoot: We're not going to bother to list *Waste of Space*'s egregious errors today. To continue to point out the obvious would be a waste of everyone's time and is, verily, beneath us.

And so this morning, we have only four words for you:

We told you so.

Oh, and three more:

WE HAVE PROOF.

[*CUT TO: Hibiscus, speaking into the camera*]

Hibiscus: Hello, sheeple. My name is Hibiscus, and I was a cast member on the reality television program *Waste of Space*. I was the first one to be eliminated—thank Goddess—and once I was released from that floating death prison, they made me sign a stack of nondisclosure agreements, but you know what? Chazz Young can't gag me anymore!

Everything about it was fake. The spacesuits were fake. The scientists were fake. The shuttle launch to the ship was fake. We felt some g-forces, true, but I think that's because they put us in a centrifuge, something that spun us around super fast but sent us nowhere.

The ship was a joke. We weren't allowed to touch any of the instruments, but as an experiment, I used my body to block some of the camera's sightlines and fiddle with some of the buttons. Guess what? They didn't do anything. We felt no atmospheric or pressure changes whatsoever. Everything on that ship was meticulously placed there for one reason: to get you to buy their products. It was one big commercial, driven by the corporate overlords who do all our thinking for us.

Wake up, America. Don't blindly follow everything our materialistic and celebrity-obsessed culture tells you. Don't believe Chazz Young. Don't listen to DV8.

Listen to *me*. I was there. I'm telling you the truth.

[*She produces her mandolin.*]

Waste of Space /

is a /

marketplace /

and a hoax and a blight /

on the human race!

Item: Transcript of video recording—RAW, UNAIRED FOOTAGE
Source: Camera #8—Bedroom
Time: 10:01 a.m.

[*Louise is on the large bed, once again sitting upright under a blanket. A flashlight wavers from within.*]

Source: Camera #5—Spa

[*Clayton is still passed out.*]

Source: Camera #3—Lünar Lounge

[*Nico, Titania, Snout, and Bacardi are sitting around, thinking. The static electricity has faded, but its effects have clearly unnerved the group.*]

Titania: What about air ducts?

Nico: What?

Titania: [*standing up*] Air ducts. We have a heating and air-conditioning system—we know that from when they cranked up the heat a few days ago. Which means there have to be air ducts somewhere.

Snout: I haven't seen any. Back when Colonel Bacon was stinking up the place, I looked around for somewhere to air him out—you know, diffuse the stench—but I couldn't find squat. Not one air vent in the ship, as far as I can reckon.

Titania: Not that we can see, at least. I bet they're blended into those instruments up there. [*She points at a complex web of instruments near the ceiling.*]

Nico: Maybe they figured that one of us would try to escape sooner or later, so they camouflaged them.

Titania: Which means we need to breach the walls some other way.

Bacardi: Ceiling's already breached.

Titania: Huh?

Bacardi: [*pointing up*] Clayton shot the ceiling, remember? Can't we make that hole bigger or something?

Nico: If the ceiling's made out of a thin enough material . . . maybe. That's actually a good idea.

Bacardi: Gee, thanks.

Titania: See what you can find to fit in the hole. Something we can use for leverage, like a crowbar.

[*The four of them look around. Bacardi wrenches a pool cue off the rack on the wall.*]

Bacardi: This'll work. [*She hands it to Snout.*] You're the tallest. You do the honors.

[*Snout clambers up onto the pool table, pokes the cue through the duct tape into the bullet hole, and jimmies it around while Nico, Titania, and Bacardi watch intently.*

Too intently. They're so focused on what he is doing that they fail to notice the wisps of vapor that have begun to seep into the Lünar Lounge.]

Snout: It's working! I can feel it widening! Shoot, it ain't thick at all—barely a piece of sheet metal—

[*Suddenly Snout drops where he stands, face-planting into the green felt of the pool table. Half a second later, the other three fall to the floor, out cold.*]

Item: Transcript of audio recording
Source: Chazz's cell phone
Time: 12:30 p.m.

Chazz: Hello?

Boris: Hey, Chazz. It's Boris.

Chazz: *Bor*— Jesus, what happened? You were supposed to get back to L.A. two hours ago!

Boris: Yeah, I ran into a few problems.

Chazz: Where are you?

Boris: A gas station in, uh . . . let me check the sign . . . Winslow. Arizona.

Chazz: Where the hell is that?

Boris: I'd say it's somewhere near Winslow, Arizona.

Chazz: Well, get back here! We need Matt and Kaoru to get their asses on *The Perky Paisley Show* tonight!

Boris: Yeah, that's gonna be an issue. The kids are gone.

Chazz: *What?*

Boris: They jumped me from the back of the van! Must have conked their heads together and woken up. I told you two at a time was a bad idea—

Chazz: You're not getting paid for your ideas. You're getting paid to transport sparkly-eyed space brats from point A to point B. And apparently you can't even do that!

Boris: Not from point C, I can't.

Chazz: *Why* are you stuck in Arizona?

Boris: They took the van.

Chazz: They *took* it? Where did they take it?

Boris: Now, how would I know a thing like that? I ain't in the van with them!

Chazz: Which direction did they go?

Boris: I don't know! Like I said, they knocked me out! Pushed me out of the van! Ran over my phone! Took my wallet!

[*pause*]

Boris: What do you want me to—

Chazz: Shh. I'm seething.

Boris: Yeah, but how am I gonna get home?

Chazz: Great question. I'm sure you'll figure something out.

Boris: You mean you're not gonna send someone for me?

Chazz: You're no longer an employee of DV8 Productions. So you are no longer my problem.

Boris: But—

Chazz: Good luck, buddy.

[*end of call*]

Item: Transcript of video recording—RAW, UNAIRED FOOTAGE
Source: Camera #4—Lünar Lounge
Time: 12:16 p.m.

[*Louise walks into the Lünar Lounge and sees the others passed out. She gasps and hurries to rouse them.*]

Louise: Hey! Guys, wake up! Titania, can you hear me?

[*She lightly slaps Titania in the face. Titania's eyes flutter. Louise moves on to the others until all four of them have come around, groggy and bruised from their falls, but otherwise intact.*]

Snout: Good gravy. What happened?

Titania: [*rubbing her eyes*] I think they drugged us.

Nico: My head is killing me.

Snout: My face hurts.

Bacardi: I kind of liked it?

[*Titania looks warily at the camera.*]

Titania: They must still be watching.

Nico: Who, though? DV8 or NASAW?

Titania: Either. Both. It doesn't matter. Someone is messing with us. And they don't want us to get out.

Louise: Of course they don't! They saved your life—that's the cold, deathly vacuum of space out there! You can't just punch a hole in the ceiling and *escape!*

[*Titania looks at the others with dread.*]

Titania: Guess not.

Item: Transcript of video recording
Source: Surveillance camera—IKEA, Store #863, Tempe, Arizona
Time: 12:18 p.m.

[*An IKEA employee approaches two kids sleeping in the bedroom section.*]

IKEA Employee: Excuse me. [*pokes the lump under the colorful Sömnig sheets*] Excuse me! These beds aren't for sleeping!

[*Matt groans, rolls over, and squints at her through the harsh lighting.*]

Matt: But we're so tired! We drove all night but then we were attacked by scientists so we had to drive back toward California but we don't have any money so we couldn't afford a hotel and we're just so hungry and *so tired!*

[*The employee signals to a nearby guard.*]

IKEA Employee: Security?

Kaoru: {Good job, foolish boy. Now we must run.}

[*She hops out of the bed. Matt reluctantly lopes after her.*

Together they dart through bins of pillows, knocking over Hampdåns and Jordröks in their wake to trip up the security guard, who follows in hot pursuit.]

Matt: [*peeling off to the right*] To the cafeteria! We can steal some meatballs!

Kaoru: [*grabbing his shirt and pulling him back*] {They will catch us. We must leave now.}

[*With a defeated groan, Matt obeys. They flee the store, run into the parking lot, and drive away in a purple windowless van before anyone can nab them.*]

Onboard the *Laika,* the Spacetronauts have retreated into individual corners to work through their anxieties in their own unique ways.

Item: Transcript of video recording
Source: Nico's camera
Battery charge: 28%
Time: 12:32 p.m.

[*IMAGE: The bedroom wall*]

Hi Mom. Hi Dad.

Battery's draining again.

So here's the situation. We have no food. We have no contact with the outside world. We're locked inside the ship. No banging or prying or button pushing has gotten us any closer to opening the airlock door. And even if we could open the door . . .

I don't know what we'd find out there. Something unnatural is going on. Some kind of test or experiment. The static electricity has gotten worse. Listen.

[*He rustles the bedsheets. The snap-crackle-pop of static electricity fills the air.*]

Whenever I touch a metal surface, I get a shock—like, a visible one, a tiny bolt of lightning. And the floating—*really* don't know what that was about.

Maybe it's psychological. Maybe they're trying to see how long a group of teenagers can be cooped up together until someone snaps and paints the walls with everyone's blood.

And up until today I thought it was relatively harmless—but then they gassed us. *We passed out.*

Why are they doing this?

The cameras are on, but I don't think DV8 is watching. There's no way to know if this footage is broadcasting. Everything we do and say—are we being watched by the world? Or by no one at all?

Which is worse?

Item: Transcript of video recording—RAW, UNAIRED FOOTAGE
Source: Camera #7—Confessional Closet
Time: 12:34 p.m.

Snout: I haven't used this thing much so far, but dang it, I've got some feelings. And they need to go somewhere, or—or I'm gonna pop!

I miss Colonel Bacon.

I know he was smelly and annoying and a mess and—heck, I guess I'm all of those things too. But he was the only friend I had up here, and now that he's gone, I feel way more alone than I ever did.

Although . . . I'm kinda glad he got out. And yeah, I'm worried about him—but you know what? I think he's okay. Our bond was deep and true, forged in the mud pits out back that Great-Aunt Ellie dug with her own eight fingers. If something bad had happened to him, I'd know about it. I'd feel it, somehow. Wherever he is, he's happy. A little scared, but happy.

[*He smiles to himself.*]

Yeah. Yeah, I reckon Colonel Bacon's doing juuust peachy.

Source: Camera #3—Lünar Lounge

[*Titania is sitting alone in the Lünar Lounge, mindlessly paging through the IKEA catalog. Clayton stirs, splashing water onto the glass of the hot-tub enclosure.*]

Clayton: [*through the bullet hole*] Where is everyone?

[*Titania looks up at him.*]

Titania: Around. Freaking out.

Clayton: Why? What'd I miss?

Titania: They drugged us. We were passed out almost as long as you.

Clayton: Heh. Karma's a bitch, huh?

[*Titania goes back to the catalog. Clayton pouts.*]

Clayton: So. What do you think those people are doing out there?

[*Titania flips a page.*]

Clayton: Come on, talk to me. You're one of the smart— you've got half a brain.

Titania: Thanks?

Clayton: I mean that you've known for a while we're not in space. And that it doesn't matter where we are—an underground bunker or the top of a mountain or Superman's goddamn Fortress of Solitude—whatever. What matters is that the NASAW scientists are right outside that door. They're *right outside*. They're the ones who have been swaying the ship, throwing rocks at us, setting things on fire. With the help of special-effects people, sure, but why do this? Why sign on with DV8? If they're serious scientists, they don't have time for this theme-park bullshit. So what's in it for them?

Titania: Maybe they have their own agenda.

Clayton: [*snorting*] They one hundred percent have their own agenda.

[*Titania frowns.*]

Titania: Do you know that for sure?

Clayton: No. But whatever they're doing, I bet they're almost done.

Titania: What do you mean?

Clayton: The rocking has stopped. Didn't you notice?

[*Titania puts down the catalog and takes a moment to assess the lack of movement.*]

Titania: Whoa. When did that happen?

Clayton: Probably while we were all unconscious. Plus, you're right, the static electricity's gotten stronger. They're either getting ready to wrap things up, or they're too busy with their own work to keep up the charade. Or both.

[*Titania studies him.*]

Titania: You got all that from one standstill?

Clayton: I get a lot of things from a lot of things.

[*Titania stands up. She takes a step toward him, narrowing her eyes.*]

Titania: Do you know something the rest of us don't?

[*Clayton beckons her forward, as if he's going to whisper something through the hole. Titania puts her ear up to the glass.*]

Clayton: LET ME OUT, BITCH!

[*He cackles maniacally while Titania calmly goes back to the* couch, sits down, and extends both of her middle fingers, holding the pose until well after Clayton stops laughing.]

Source: Camera #6—Bathroom

[*Louise is brushing her teeth. Bacardi walks by the bathroom, sees her, and ducks in.*]

Bacardi: What are you doing? It's not like we have any food to brush away.

Louise: [*with a mouthful of toothpaste*] Little trick from home—something about the mintyness of toothpaste suppresses the appetite. I have a big family, and sometimes there's not enough food to go around. This is a good way to trick your stomach into being full.

Bacardi: Oh. Interesting.

[*Louise spits her toothpaste into the sink, rinses, puts her toothbrush away, and turns to Bacardi.*]

Louise: What's going on with you? You seem different today. Like, sober.

Bacardi: And you're, like, blunt.

Louise: Well, sorry. But I don't know why you'd want to be drunk in the first place. Only the tiniest percentage of the tiniest percentage of humans have ever gotten a chance like this! Why would you want to be unconscious all the time? [*Bacardi starts to respond, but Louise talks over her.*] I don't get it. Both you and Clayton, wanting to come on this show just for attention, to become famous. Taking two spots that otherwise could have gone to any of the zillions of kids out there who wanted to come up here for the right reasons, because they love science and want to further their education and embark on a once-in-a-lifetime journey—

Bacardi: Oh, sweetie. I know you still think we're in space, and that's adorable, but here's the thing: even if this were real, it's for *entertainment*. It's *DV8*. You really expected a noble, scientific, educational venture from the people who brought you *Fornication Nation Vacation: On Location*?

Louise: But the NASAW scientists—

Bacardi: Are probably production assistants wearing lab coats that were left over from the *America's Got Plastic Surgeons!* costume bin.

[*Louise crosses her arms in a huff.*]

Louise: You sure know your DV8. Maybe you should spend less time watching television and more time educating yourself on the intricacies of the universe.

Bacardi: Oh, I know how to educate myself. It's simple math. Five hundred hours of DV8 reality programming plus the meticulous identification of the seven most common female cast-member archetypes divided by four to six frequently displayed personality traits times three years spent assimilating said traits plus two exquisite funbags equals a one hundred percent chance of being selected to join the cast of any given show of my choosing.

[*Louise blinks at her.*]

Louise: What are you, a spy or something? How—

Bacardi: HOLY SHIT WHAT IS THAT THING?!

Source: Camera #3—Lünar Lounge

[*Titania, still flipping off Clayton, comes to attention as Bacardi and Louise run into the lounge. Hearing the commotion, Snout and Nico run in from the Confessional Closet and the bedroom, respectively.*]

Bacardi: THERE'S A MONSTER IN THE TOILET!

Snout: A monster?

Clayton: I highly doubt there's a monster in our toilet. Unless Snout's been using it.

Bacardi: GO LOOK.

Source: Camera #6—Bathroom

[*Everyone but Clayton piles into the bathroom.*]

Nico: What *is* that?

Bacardi: IT'S A GODDAMN MONSTER!

Louise: It's a vergdorf! From the planet Yajifi!

Snout: Aw, heck. It's a Gila monster!

Bacardi: SEE? A MONSTER!

Snout: Oh, that's just a silly name. Nothin' but a big ole lizard!

[*Everyone flees the bathroom, Bacardi slamming the stall shut on the way out.*]

Source: Camera #3—Lünar Lounge

[*They run back to the lounge, where Clayton is struggling to ascertain what is going on.*]

Clayton: Did I hear you correctly? What is a "big ole lizard" doing in our toilet?

Snout: I reckon he crawled up the pipes . . .

Louise: *Or* he stowed away before we launched and has been hiding onboard all along! What other explanation is there?

[*They all give her skeptical looks.*]

Clayton: Snout, where do Gila monsters come from?

Snout: They're native to the Southwest. Arizona and New Mexico, I believe.

Clayton: [*to Louise*] Which is on Earth. I believe.

Snout: Oh, and they're highly venomous.

Bacardi: GODDAMMIT.

Source: Camera #6—Bathroom

[*Bacardi storms back into the toilet stall, shuts herself in with the Gila monster, and locks the door, which the group then bangs on.*]

Snout: Just leave it alone, and it won't hurt anyone! Don't kill it!

Bacardi: [*from inside*] I'm not killing it.

Snout: Then what are you doing?

[*no answer*]

Snout: [*to the rest*] What is she doing?

Titania: I don't know. But that stall is the only place on the ship that doesn't have a camera.

Item: Transcript of audio recording
Source: Chazz's cell phone
Time: 1:12 p.m.

DV8: Chazz?

Chazz: Talk to me.

DV8: We've, uh—we've got a problem.

Chazz: You *think*? Matt and Kaoru are MIA—and Hibiscus, that rotten little socialist—

DV8: No, a different problem. A major one. This is bad, Chazz.

Chazz: [*away from the phone*] Khloe! Kourtney's nipple is not a chew toy! [*into the phone*] Sorry. Go.

DV8: I'm from the team that got together and drove out to New Mexico, to Soundstage G-69. We put the address into the GPS, drove the eleven godforsaken hours through desert garbage land to get there, and—uh—

Chazz: And?

DV8: There's nothing there.

Chazz: What?

DV8: *There's nothing there.* I mean, Soundstage G-69 is there, but there's nothing in it. No spaceplane. No NASAW. No footprints or tire tracks leading up to the building—which we'd notice if they existed, since there's nothing but sand everywhere. There are padlocks on two of the three entrances; we went in through the unlocked one and found absolutely nothing. Just a big-ass room with grungy floors. Part of the ceiling is caved in. I don't think anyone's been there in years.

[*pause*]

DV8: Chazz? Are you there?

Chazz: Yeah. Yeah, I—I'm having a little trouble internalizing this information. [*heavier breathing*] But they have to be somewhere! Boris drove out there a bunch of times— *he* would know where it is! Ask him!

DV8: You fired Boris and left him to fend for himself in the Arizona desert.

[*Chazz swears loudly. Puggles bark.*]

Chazz: Find. Boris.

DV8: We left a message with his wife. Hopefully she'll get back to us soon, and hopefully he'll still be willing to help us.

Chazz: What about the ImmerseFX team? *They* must know where it is!

DV8: The ImmerseFX team is none too pleased with the manner in which their work has been portrayed, the misappropriation of their sizable investment in our show, the specificity of Hibiscus's remarks, or the way we have handled this situation. They are no longer returning our calls.

[*More swearing. More barking.*]

Chazz: So you found an empty soundstage and utterly failed your boss, your company, and your nation. What did you do next?

DV8: What else *could* we do? We got into the car, and now we're driving back to L.A.!

Chazz: Yeah, but—[*He emits a sort of panicked honk.*] But what do we do now?

DV8: We were hoping you would have the answer to that.

Chazz: How am I supposed to have the answer to that? I put my trust in *you*, my allegedly competent employees, to run a goddamn measly dumbass reality show, and you *lose* the cast and crew somewhere in the New Mexican desert? You *misplace* an entire show?

DV8: I—

Chazz: Find them!

[*end of call*]

After several failed attempts to lure Bacardi out, including the empty promise of more booze, most of the Spacetronauts give up on whatever she's doing in the bathroom stall and retreat to their separate corners.

The food situation is getting dire. They've missed only half a day's worth of meals, but hunger pains are being augmented by the swirling uncertainty, which mushrooms into a choking anxiety, all cascading into a domino effect of fear and ravenousness and hair-trigger anger and paranoia.

In short, they're freaking out.

Except for Titania.

Item: Transcript of video recording—RAW, UNAIRED FOOTAGE
Source: Camera #8—Bedroom
Time: 1:28 p.m.

[*Nico is sitting on his bed, biting his nails. Titania enters and sits next to him.*]

Titania: Are you scared?

Nico: Scared is my default setting, so yes. Aren't you?

[*Titania shrugs.*]

Nico: Are you kidding? How could you not be? [*He stops biting his nails and hugs his arms around his body.*] This is too messed up. I want to go home. I thought I wanted to run away, like you, but I was wrong. I don't belong here. I belong back in my shitty life, in my shitty Bronx apartment, with my shitty older brother. He's all I've got. That's all there is.

Titania: Don't say that. [*She tries to make eye contact with him.*] You have to keep going, Nico. Bad things happened to you. But you can't wallow in them forever. You can't go backwards. You have to keep moving. Keep exploring. Like sharks—if they stop moving, they die.

Nico: That's not me, though. I'm not like you. I don't want to spend my life searching for the next thing. At least back home I'll have my whole future ahead of me. At least there, I've got the chance to make it better. I can't do that from here.

[*Titania thinks this over. Her shoulders slump.*]

Titania: And I can't do it from anywhere *other* than here.

[*She runs a hand over the muscles in her neck.*]

Titania: What happened last night—it meant something.

I mean, it's what I was looking for all along, isn't it? Something to cut through the bullshit. Something strange, something mind-blowing. Something *real.*

Nico: Something dangerous.

Titania: But that's the thing—it *didn't* feel dangerous. Not to me. I don't—[*She balls her hands up in frustration.*] I don't know how to explain it.

Nico: You don't have to. Maybe we just felt different things. I believe you.

[*She opens her mouth but hesitates before she speaks.*]

Titania: Remember what I told you about where my sister— where I like to think she is?

What happened last night—

I don't know why, but it made me feel like that place could be real.

And I could go there.

And anything is possible.

That there is more to life than what we see. More to what we experience. More to who we are.

What happened last night made me feel more . . . *more.*

[*Barely a second passes before Nico leans in, as if he can't stop himself. The kiss lasts for a respectable amount of time, but when they part, he looks horrified.*]

Nico: I cannot believe I did that. I'm so sorry.

Titania: Why?

Nico: *Why?* You were talking about your dead sister—and I do *that*? What the hell is wrong with me?

[*Titania gives him a slight smile.*]

Titania: I think your "scared" setting isn't as default as you think.

Source: Camera #6—Bathroom

[*Snout pounds on the stall door.*]

Snout: Bacardi? Please don't hurt him. He didn't do anything to us. He's gotta be confused—

[*Bacardi opens the door and marches past him out of the bathroom.*]

Snout: Oh. Good.

[*He looks down into the toilet, where the Gila monster continues to soak, irked but unharmed.*]

Snout: Hey there, little fella.

[*The Gila monster hisses at him.*]

Snout: Point taken, bye!

[*He slams the stall door shut.*]

Source: Camera #7—Confessional Closet

[*Bacardi walks in, locks the door, and sits down. She removes her shirt and places it over the lens of the camera. Fifteen minutes pass, silent and dark.*]

Source: Camera #2—Flight Deck

[*Louise is by herself, fiddling with the instruments on the control panel. Clayton watches her from the hot tub.*]

Louise: [*pressing a button and speaking quietly into a device that she has decided is a microphone*] Lord Balway Galway? Can you read me? Please respond.

Clayton: [*through the bullet hole*] Hey.

[*Louise ignores him.*]

Clayton: What are you doing?

[*more ignoring*]

Clayton: Radioing your home planet?

[*She swivels around to face him.*]

Louise: Why do you have to be such a jerk all the time? Newsflash: we're not on TV anymore. So I don't know who you're trying to fool, but no one is that much of a dillweed all the time, to everyone around him, for no reason. I get it—every reality show needs a villain. More screen time, more attention. But now, when we're all alone and we might be in danger, there's no need to be so mean. I've never done anything to you, so I don't know what your problem is.

Clayton: You spout nonsense. You add noise and unnecessary confusion to each situation that arises. You insist on falling back into a fictitious world when the real one is the environment that requires your attention.

Louise: Well, according to you, the Ultimate Authority on What's Real, this environment is as fictitious as mine. And you know what? In a way, you're right. Nothing more artificial than a reality show.

Clayton: That's not the falseness to which I'm referring, and you know it. Do you realize how demented you sound? *We're not in space.* And the sooner you get that through your sci-fi-addled head—

Louise: [*snarling*] I'm *not* addled. Just because I choose to believe in something doesn't make me stupid. *You* don't believe in *anything.*

Clayton: I—

Louise: You know the only thing that's more pathetic than reality TV? The people who dedicate their lives to being cast on reality TV. Who measure their self-worth in terms of how much screen time and attention they get. You're not a person. You're an avatar. A username. Have you expressed a genuine thought since you got here? You're the fakest thing on this spaceship— and according to you, that's saying a lot, isn't it?

[*Clayton works his tongue around his mouth but says nothing. Louise watches him, then goes back to the control panel.*]

Louise: [*whispering into the microphone*] Lord Balway Galway? I know you're very busy. And I know you don't know who I am . . . yet. But I want to join you on your mission. I just need more time—but we're out of food, and I don't know how much longer we can last. If there's anything you can do—please. Help us.

[*With a pneumatic hiss, the airlock door opens to reveal an artfully arranged pile of fresh fruit, vegetables, eggs, rice, cheese, canned goods, and dozens of other staples—more than enough for six people to survive for at least another two months.*

Snout, Bacardi, Nico, and Titania come running into the lounge. Their mouths fall open.]

Snout: What the heck?

Bacardi: Where'd all this come from?

Louise: [*overjoyed*] Lord Balway Galway sent it! [*gleefully turning to Clayton*] See? *Now* who's spouting nonsense?

Clayton: *Obviously* NASAW was listening in on your insane ramblings and triggered it to open at exactly the right time, thereby brainwashing you even more than they already have—

Louise: Oh, so now this is all NASAW's doing? Like it's all part of some big conspiracy? Do you realize how demented you sound?

Clayton: *I'm! Not! The demented one!*

Louise: [*sweetly*] Then why are you the one who's yelling?

[*Clayton submerges his head in the hot tub and screams into the water.*]

DV8 schedules a press conference for 2:00 p.m. Never the type to pass up an opportunity for cross-promotion, the producers let

Perky Paisley host the media circus, essentially turning it into a breaking-news midday edition of her late-night show.

Item: Transcript of video broadcast
Source: *DV8 Breaking News*
Time: 2:00 p.m.

[*Perky stands at a podium behind a spray of microphones, looking delighted with herself.*]

Perky: Thank you for coming, ladies and gentlemen of the media. My guests for the press conference today are the two—that's right, two!—most recent exiles ousted in the double elimination this week on the reality phenomenon *Waste of Space*. Please give a perkilicious welcome to Matt and Kaoru!

[*Applause turns to confusion as Chazz Young steps out onto the stage, gives a confident wave to the camera, and stands next to Perky.*]

Perky: [*smoothing her hair*] Um, hi, Chazz.

Chazz: Hi, Perky.

Perky: What are you doing here? Not that it isn't always a pleasure to see you, but . . . where are Matt and Kaoru?

Chazz: [*adopting a serious tone*] Here's the deal, Perky. They wanted to be here. They really did. But we couldn't let that happen right now. I know DV8 has been tight-lipped about everything since our episode last night, but we have our reasons.

Perky: I don't blame you! There are a lot of rumors flying around, especially now that Hibiscus has released that video. A lot of people are questioning whether the Spacetronauts are really in space at all.

Chazz: Yes, I'm glad you brought this up. This is an urgent matter, and I want the whole world to hear what I have to say about it.

Perky: The floor is yours.

[*She steps aside, giving Chazz the full podium. The camera zooms in tight on his face.*]

Chazz: America, the *Laika is* still in space. It always has been. We *have* lost contact with the ship, but our control room is hard at work trying to reestablish communication. So if any of you out there feel the need to disparage our brave young American heroes by claiming they're not in space or never have been in space, you take a long, hard look at yourself and ask yourself: Do I love America? Or do I hate America?

Perky: [*poking her head into the frame*] I *love* America.

Chazz: So do I, Perky. So do I. As for Hibiscus's outrageous claim, I'll just say this: Our beloved Spacetronauts are under a lot of stress. It's natural for the claustrophobia and isolation of being in space to take its toll one way or another. Plus, solar radiation has been known to cause brief spells of paranoia and hallucinations, which is why Hibiscus seems confused about her time onboard the *Laika*. Also, Hibiscus does a lot of drugs, so there's that, too.

[*Perky shimmies back onto the podium.*]

Perky: Got it. Thank you for clearing that up, Chazz.

Chazz: Of course . . . [*He frowns.*] It could also be something else.

Perky: [*putting a hand on his shoulder*] Chazz? What is it?

Chazz: I wasn't going to bring this up, but so many people are asking about the mental state of our beloved Spacetronauts . . . and our loyal viewers *do* have the right to know, I suppose . . .

Perky: The right to know what?

[*Chazz heaves a melodramatic sigh.*]

Chazz: Matt and Kaoru have been quarantined.

Perky: Quarantined? Why? Are they sick?

Chazz: Yes. They've come down with a bad case of the space pox.

Perky: The what?

Chazz: It's a very rare disease that afflicts only those who have passed through the outer limits of the groposphere and back. Skippy LaRue got it when he returned from the Apollo 19 mission, and since Matt and Kaoru are now showing symptoms, we feel that it would be best—for their safety and for ours—to isolate them in a medical facility for the time being.

Note: The Apollo 19 mission never happened; it was canceled in 1970. Also, there are no astronauts, past or present, named Skippy LaRue. Also, there is no such thing as a groposphere.

Perky: Oh my God. That sounds serious.

Chazz: It's incredibly serious.

Perky: Is it fatal?

Chazz: Not as far as we can tell. Both of them are in good spirits—they want to thank their legions of fans for their support, and they have no hard feelings about being voted out. It was an honor just to be sent up there in the first place, they said.

Perky: Wow. So brave.

Chazz: Also—and this is critical—they made it clear that there should be no attempt to contact them in any way. No need to search area hospitals. They would *love* to appear on camera to deliver their thanks in person and let everyone know they're okay and verify their existence BUT their appearance is, frankly, too grotesque for television. The festering sores are . . . well, they're hard to look at. For now, they're perfectly happy in their hermetically sealed bubbles and would like to use this time to rest, recover, and reflect on how amazing and life-changing and stellar their time onboard the *Laika* was.

Perky: Wow. So, so much courage.

Chazz: And so, so much festering.

Perky: But they'll be okay, right?

Chazz: Yes, Matt and Kaoru are on track to make a full recovery. [*He frowns.*] Except . . .

Perky: [*putting a hand on his shoulder*] Chazz? What is it?

Chazz: I didn't want to bring this up, but I suppose it's the sort of thing that has to be addressed publicly. I've been hearing a bunch of nasty rumors about certain people—sick, cruel people—dressing up like Matt and Kaoru and trying to pass themselves off as the real thing. Spreading lies about the show, about DV8, trying to cause a panic—all to get attention and cash in on this tragedy. It's despicable.

Perky: Hell yeah it is! Who would do such a thing?

Chazz: Your guess is as good as mine, Perky. Details are fuzzy, but so far most reports seem to be originating in the Southwest—though that could change as the vileness spreads.

Perky: Is there anything we can do? I'm sure my viewers would be willing to help.

Chazz: I can't stress this enough: Matt and Kaoru are alive and well and in the care of the best physicians in the country. To allow rumors to the contrary flies in the face of every shred of bravery and courage they have displayed up to this point. If any of you out there spot someone posing as either one of them—*no matter how good their disguises may appear* *to be*—please contact DV8 right away. Email, social media, our website—whatever channel is fastest for you. Help us in bringing Matt and Kaoru to bloody, vengeful justice.

Perky: You mean Matt and Kaoru's *impostors.*

Chazz: [*after blinking at her for a few seconds, then smiling into the camera*] Yes. Of course.

◼◀ ••••••••••••••• **OFF–AIR** •••••••••••••••••

Item: Transcript of video recording—RAW, UNAIRED FOOTAGE
Source: Camera #1—Airlock
Time: 2:05 p.m.

[*The Spacetronauts (minus Clayton) warily make their way into the airlock.*]

Nico: What . . . the . . . hell?

Snout: Good gravy, look at all the food! [*He picks up a carton and lets out a whoop.*] Real eggs!

Louise: [*giddy*] Lord Balway Galway saved us!

Bacardi: [*holding a butternut squash and frowning*] What are we supposed to do with this?

Snout: What you want to do with that is cut it in half, pop it in the oven—if we had an oven—and roast it until it gets all creamy and scrumptious inside.

Bacardi: I thought you only made omelets. You can make other things?

Snout: Sure, I can throw some stuff together.

Bacardi: Great! I'll have a lasagna.

Snout: But—

Bacardi: I'll have. A lasagna.

[*Snout, looking a little scared, grabs some supplies and*

hurries off toward the kitchen. [Snout, looking a little scared, grabs some supplies and hurries off toward the kitchen. Nico and Titania drag the rest of the food into the lounge.]

Source: Camera #3—Lünar Lounge

[*Louise selects a package of hot dogs and heads over to Clayton with a smirk.*]

Louise: Here you go. [*She opens the package and sticks a hot dog through the hole in the glass.*] A wiener for a wiener.

Clayton: It's frozen. How am I supposed to eat this?

Louise: Defrost it in your tepid bathwater. Yum!

Clayton: [*straining to see into the airlock*] What else is there?

Louise: Oh, *loads* of good stuff.

Clayton: [*pouting*] I need food too.

Louise: You should have thought of that before you did what you did. Now the rest of us get a feast and you get whatever fits through this hole!

[*Louise flits away, leaving Clayton to dejectedly suck on the hot dog as if it were a Popsicle. Meanwhile, Nico selects a banana from the pile, and Titania looks accusingly at the airlock door.*]

Nico: Convenient, isn't it?

Titania: That the exact problem that needed solving was so easily solved at the exact right time? Yes. Yes, it is.

Nico: Is it the exact right time, though? Don't you think it's weird that they'd wait until we were desperate? Why would they do that?

Titania: To mess with our heads.

Nico: Exactly. [*He peels the banana.*] Add another point for psychological testing—

Snout: Stop!

[*Just as Nico moves in for a bite of his banana, Snout runs in from the kitchen and bats it out of his hands.*]

Snout: [*panting*] The eggs are off.

Nico: Huh?

Snout: The eggs! [*He catches his breath.*] Don't know exactly what's wrong with 'em, but I've handled about a million eggs in my lifetime, and these ones just aren't right.

Titania: What are you saying? The food has been tampered with?

Snout: I wouldn't put it past them. Would you?

Titania: No. [*She speaks slowly, thinking out loud.*] DV8's not trying to kill us—if they were, we'd be dead already. But maybe it's like you said, maybe they're using us like lab rats in a psychological experiment, testing us and watching us to see how we'll react to certain situations.

Nico: Or—[*His face darkens as he makes the realization.*] Or maybe NASAW's hijacked the reins away from DV8. What if they're completely in control now? Maybe we're the nuisances distracting them from their sciencing, whatever it is, and every time we get close to escaping, they knock us back a few pegs. Like they did with the gas.

Titania: And if they incapacitated us once before, they could do it again. [*She knocks a box of Pop-Tarts out of Louise's hands.*] Don't eat the food, Louise.

Louise: Why not?

Titania: Because it might make us sick.

Louise: But Lord Balway Galway sent it!

Titania: He—[*She stops herself, knowing that logic won't get her anywhere, and rephrases.*] He may have sent it—but he would have had no way of knowing whether NASAW . . . sabotaged it . . . while he wasn't looking. Right?

Louise: I . . . I guess not.

Titania: And neither do we. So until we know for sure, we can't eat any of it.

Bacardi: Are you *kidding* me? I'm *starving*!

Titania: Look, I'm hungry too. But we can't trust them.

Bacardi: But—lasagna!

Titania: Think about it: they've gassed us, thrown us around the ship, and set us on fire—why *wouldn't* they mess with our food? And why else would they wait until we're desperate, then suddenly present a cornucopia that's vastly better than the glop we've been eating for three weeks? They *want* us to eat it, because they *want* to stop us from trying to escape.

[*Clayton lets out a laugh.*]

Clayton: There you go again, buying into the paranoia.

[*They watch as he smacks at his fingers.*]

Louise: Did you eat that whole hot dog?

Clayton: Sure did.

Nico: But . . . what if it's poisoned?

Clayton: It's not. But by all means, carry on with your hunger strike. If the rest of you die of starvation because you refused to eat perfectly edible food, I'm going to laugh my *ass* off at your funerals.

[*Everyone looks back at Titania.*]

Snout: So do we eat it? Or not?

[*Titania bites her lip.*]

Item: Online article

Source: ViralLoad

Time: 3:01 p.m.

What is going on with our space buddies???

It's been fifteen hours since the Shwump heard round the

world, and man, are the conspiracy theories flying. We all saw those Spacetronauts floating, with our very own eyes—but then Hibiscus came out and stated that everything is a hoax—and now the prevailing theory is that it's one big psychological experiment? HAVE WE ALL TAKEN CRAZY PILLS?

If we have, DV8 isn't telling. Other than that bizarre, staged press conference, Chazz Young's pillowy lips have been sealed up tight. Matt and Kaoru are allegedly in the hospital getting treated for some unnamed malady (Chazz called it "space pox"), but there is no hospital in the Los Angeles area with any record of having treated them.

Not that America needs a reason to keep watching. *Waste of Space* fever is still gripping the country and hasn't shown any signs of dying down. If anything, it's intensified. It's difficult to go without spotting someone in a KISS MY ASTRONAUT T-shirt. Banners and graffiti screaming "Bring Home the Bacon" are a testament to the fandom of the *Laika*'s beloved pet pig, whose whereabouts are also still unknown.

The longer we speculate, the hungrier we get.

THE SUSPENSE IS TERRIBLE

I HOPE IT WILL LAST

Item: Transcript of video recording
Source: Security camera—A-X Conoco gas station, Socorro, NM
Time: 4:30 p.m.

Clerk: Can I help you?

Matt: I hope so. We—it's hard to know where to start. I think we were, like, kidnapped? And then we escaped and we've been driving in circles around half the Southwest and maybe Mexico and we got chased out of an IKEA and ran out of food and money and now we're here?

Clerk: I don't understand.

Matt: I know. I'm trying to explain a situation that's not explainable. We were on this show—

Kaoru: {Do not tell him about the show.}

Matt: —and we were voted out, so we were pulled into the airlock and tasered, and then we woke up in the back of the windowless van, and—

Clerk: Look, kid, I don't want to get involved. Why don't you call for help and leave me out of this?

Matt: Because we don't have a phone. We ran over the driver's phone when we escaped.

Kaoru: {We need to leave.}

Matt: Hey, can we use yours? We've been driving for a while and she doesn't want to take a chance but I think it's time. We can't keep driving forever.

Kaoru: {Come on, foolish boy. Get back in the car.}

Clerk: Phone isn't for customer use. There's a pay phone out back.

Matt: But we're out of money. Can I borrow a quarter?

Clerk: Sorry, no can do.

Matt: Come on, man. This is an emergency.

Clerk: You bet it is!

[*The clerk pulls out his cell phone, snaps a photo of Matt and Kaoru, and grins.*]

Matt: [*frozen, confused*] What was that?

Clerk: [*tapping at his phone*] Just sent a photo of you two off to DV8. They're gonna fry you dry!

Matt: What does that mean?

Clerk: It means you make me wanna puke, son. Capitalizing on other people's misfortunes, passing yourselves off as those two poor sick kids. How dare you?

Matt: Oh God. Look, sir, this is all a misunderstanding—

Clerk: That's what they said you'd say. But a superfan like me knows better! [*He rips open his employee vest to reveal a BRING HOME THE BACON T-shirt underneath.*] Catchphrase forever!

[*Kaoru swiftly delivers a punch to the man's face, then runs to a shelf and gathers several bags of junk food into her arms. After a second of bewildered hesitation, Matt follows suit and yanks some bottled drinks out of the refrigerator. By the time the clerk has recovered enough to dial 911, they're back in the purple windowless van, peeling out of the parking lot in a cloud of dust.*]

After more quibbling over the food and the resulting decision to shove it all in the pantry, the Spacetronauts go their separate ways again, frustrated by indecisiveness and the increasing static electricity.

Item: Transcript of video recording—RAW, UNAIRED FOOTAGE

Source: Camera #9—Kitchen
Time: 4:05 p.m.

[*Louise is delivering a speech to her reflection in the pantry door.*]

Louise: And furthermore, once I am welcomed onboard the *Interstellar Venture V*, I plan to make an impression right from the start. I know the standard thing to say is that we come in peace, but I feel like that's a little trite these days— plus, Lord Balway Galway has always had an appreciation for bold statements. So I've come up with something snazzier: BOW BEFORE YOUR FUTURE QUEEN, FOR HER BEAUTY IS UNSURPASSED AND HER VENGEANCE SWIFT AND TERRIBLE—

Source: Camera #6—Bathroom

[*Bacardi is in the shower stall, but no water is running. When she emerges, she is fully clothed and tucking something into her bra.*]

Source: Camera #8—Bedroom

[*Titania is on her knees, looking underneath a bunk bed when Nico peeks his head in. Seeing her on the floor, he tries to leave without being noticed, but fails.*]

Titania: Nico?

Nico: Oh, hey. What are you doing?

Titania: Trying to find a morsel of food. Like, a cracker. A mint.

Nico: And?

Titania: No luck.

Nico: Ah.

[*He shifts uncomfortably.*]

Titania: What's wrong? Besides the given.

Nico: I'm starting to feel weird about . . . what I did. With my mouth. And your mouth.

Titania: You'll note that I didn't stop you.

Nico: Yeah, but—do you even like me? Or is this more of a we're-stranded-on-a-desert-island-so-this-guy-is-good-enough situation?

Titania: Does it matter?

Nico: Uh, yeah.

[*Titania gets to her feet, brushing dust off her pants.*]

Titania: I don't know. I didn't come here thinking about any of that. All I could think about was getting away. Then when Chazz told us there was money involved, all I could think about was using that money to get even farther away. But now we're trapped here and antigravity is happening and you're . . . [*gesturing erratically at him*] you, and things have gotten all complicated.

Nico: Oh.

[*pause*]

Nico: So do you like me or not?

Titania: I like you. And if we were having this conversation at our lockers after third period and not in a fake spaceship commandeered by unbalanced, evil pirate scientists, I'd probably be hoping you would ask me to prom. Or—wait, what am I saying—I'd probably ask *you* to prom. Actually, to be honest, I never really saw myself as a person who would go to prom in the first place—

Nico: You're stalling.

[*Titania gives him a sad smile.*]

Titania: What I mean is—if we were anywhere else—

Nico: But we're not.

Titania: So I can't.

[*She looks down at the floor.*]

Titania: I took this giant leap into the unknown by coming here, and depending on what comes next, I need to be able to . . . keep leaping. You know what I mean?

Nico: Yeah.

Titania: But Nico?

Nico: Yeah?

Titania: I do like you.

[*Nico returns her smile.*]

Item: Transcript of video recording
Source: Nico's camera
Battery charge: 20%
Time: 4:37 p.m.

[*IMAGE: The bedroom ceiling. Nico has chosen to point his camera at Camera #8, its unblinking eye eerily staring back at him.*]

When I was in sixth grade, I made friends with this girl at my school who had leukemia. She sat next to me in art class and introduced herself—like I didn't already know who she was. Everyone did. She was bald, she missed school all the time, we were always being told to keep her in our thoughts. And here she was, this famous figure, talking to me.

Didn't take long for me to develop a crush on her. And she could tell, could see it happening, the way I got tongue-tied when I talked to her. She never told me to go away, but she never seemed to want to be friends either, always keeping me at an arm's length. When I finally got the courage to ask her to come over after school one day, she gave me this real sad, judgy look. Condescending, almost. Like she was saying, "Poor boy. You really shouldn't grow so attached."

298

That was the last time we talked. I didn't understand why she'd acted that way, but when she died that summer, I finally got it.

It's the same with Titania.

It's like her bags are already packed and she's just waiting for the green light to leave.

Item: Transcript of audio recording
Source: Chazz's cell phone
Time: 5:10 p.m.

DV8: Chazz?

Chazz: Where are you?

DV8: Two hundred miles from Los Angeles. We should be back at the office in about three hours.

Chazz: And do you have good news for me? Or more bad news?

DV8: Both.

Chazz: Christ on a cracker.

DV8: So we've been on the phone for as much of the trip as we could get cell phone service, and—and I think we've found them. For real this time.

[*Chazz exhales theatrically for several seconds.*]

Chazz: That *is* good news.

DV8: Actually, that's the bad news.

Chazz: What? Why?

DV8: It's kind of a funny story.

Chazz: Is it?

DV8: Well, no. See, we couldn't understand how Soundstage G-69 could possibly be empty, with no sign of any recent activity. After all, we have footage of the scientists setting it up—we asked for regular progress reports during pre-production, and ImmerseFX sent us a bunch of short videos that couldn't have been faked. So we rewatched them, and everything checks out—there's the ship, there are ImmerseFX team members installing special effects, there's the onboard furniture. All housed within a space that looks like Soundstage G-69—except the roof isn't caved in and it's not as grungy.

Chazz: So?

DV8: So we had everyone back at the office comb through our correspondence with NASAW. Remember: *we* allocated Soundstage G-69 for NASAW's use. And in all their emails to us, that's how they referred to it too—except for one. In a single email out of several dozen, they wrote "Soundstage G-96."

Chazz: So? It's a typo.

DV8: That's what we thought. But to be safe, we checked it out, and it turns out there really *is* a Soundstage G-96. About ninety miles away from Soundstage G-69.

Chazz: So? That doesn't mean they're there, either.

DV8: But they are! That's the good news! We tracked the coordinates of your satellite phone calls to Jamarkus, and they're consistent with the supposed location of Soundstage G-96!

Chazz: Let me get this straight. This all sprang from one little typo?

DV8: No, Chazz, don't you get it? It *wasn't* a typo. NASAW slipped up—that one email was where they made their mistake and tipped their hand. *We* allocated Soundstage G-69 for their use, but *they* went behind our backs and used Soundstage G-96 *instead*. They deliberately misled us so we wouldn't be able to find them, pretending as though they were in Soundstage G-69 all along.

[*noise of something being angrily flung at the wall*]

Chazz: Goddammit!

[*There is a pause, the only sound that of Chazz breathing angrily.*]

DV8: There's one more thing.

Chazz: What?

DV8: We found Boris. He hitchhiked to the Albuquerque airport and booked a flight—

Chazz: Tell him to cancel it. I need him to come with me.

DV8: ... What? We were planning to send out another team first thing tomorrow—

Chazz: No, screw that. Your first team accomplished precisely jack shit. I'm going on my own this time. Just me and Boris. And a modest film crew. And a few actors. And ...

DV8: And who?

Chazz: Silence! It'll be a surprise. Drama.

DV8: But they're supposed to be in space. And you, as everyone knows, are not in space. What's it going to look like when you show up at the door of their ship? You're going to blow the lid off the whole thing!

[*Chazz laughs.*]

Chazz: Have faith, my friend. Set up another press conference—I need to get in front of some cameras ASAP. And call—no, forget it. I'll call him myself.

DV8: Who?

[*end of call*]

■◄ • • • • • • • • • • • • • • • • • **ON-AIR** • • • • • • • • • • • • • • • • • • •

Item: Transcript of video broadcast
Source: *DV8 Breaking News*
Time: 5:30 p.m.

[*There is no sign of Perky this time. At 5:30 p.m. on the dot, Chazz breathlessly takes the podium, a slightly crazed look in his eye.*]

Chazz: 'Sup, America. I'll keep this brief—me and the tireless team at DV8 have got a long night ahead of us. I have a series of announcements I'd like to make, and following these announcements I will not be taking any questions. Ready?

We have reestablished contact with the *Laika*.

We have its coordinates.

The Spacetronauts are safe.

However, the ship is no longer under DV8's control.

We have reason to believe that the *Laika* has been hijacked by an unknown space criminal—*or* criminals. We do not know why they did this, we don't know how they did this, and, frankly, we don't care to know. America doesn't negotiate with space terrorists.

[*He pauses, perhaps to allow viewers to applaud at their screens.*]

But we do know this: We're going to go up there.

We're going to stop them.

And we're going to bring our brave Spacetronauts home, space safe and space sound.

Catchphrase forever!

📹 ◀ • • • • • • • • • • • • • • • • • • **OFF-AIR** •

Item: Transcript of video recording—RAW, UNAIRED FOOTAGE
Source: Camera #3—Lünar Lounge
Time: 5:41 p.m.

[*Clayton is listlessly swirling the water of the hot tub. Snout enters.*]

Snout: Bacardi's still giving me the runaround! Can't figure what the heck that girl is up to. [*He frowns.*] Sure hope she's not drinking again. [*He squints through the window.*] How you doing in there, Clayton?

[*Clayton puts his wrinkled fingertips to the glass.*]

Clayton: Pretty pruny, lardass.

Snout: Good gravy. I was just being polite.

Clayton: Be useful instead and give me some more food.

Snout: Sorry. 'Fraid I can't do that.

[*Clayton makes a crude gesture.*]

Snout: You know, Clayton, you can catch more flies with honey than with vinegar.

Clayton: What's that supposed to mean?

Snout: If you're nicer to people, they'll be more likely to help you out, and maybe not lock you in a room in the first place.

Clayton: They'll also be more likely to walk all over you.

Snout: Now, why would they do that?

Clayton: You can stop right there, Doughboy. There isn't a thing on Earth or in space that we have in common, so there's no need for us to have A Moment. Do I really need to say it again? *I didn't come here to make friends.*

Snout: Well, heck. Then what *did* you come here to do?

[*Clayton gives him a perfected isn't-it-obvious look.*]

Clayton: Get famous.

Snout: Is that all?

Clayton: Yeah. I want attention, pure and simple. I don't see why I need a deeper reason than that.

Snout: Well, shoot. You just came right out and said it, huh.

Clayton: I see no need to sugarcoat. My parents never paid attention to me. I was raised by a series of nannies, each of whom I drove away, each trailing more tears than the last. Chazz certainly did his best to ignore me, but I finally found a weakness in him to exploit. And here I am. Or here I was. You assclowns sure did shit the bed on this particular opportunity, but I'm not worried. I'll find another way to get myself out there.

Snout: You think so?

Clayton: Course I will. This is only the beginning of my reign of terror. A year from now you'll be sick of seeing me, but I won't go away. I'll feed off it, crave more, and the cycle of fame will continue. You'll think, "Surely the Clayton fad should have ended by now," but oh no, it won't end. It'll never end. It'll just keep going and going and going.

[*Snout studies him, then lets out a whoop.*]

Snout: I think you're whistling a big ole pile of Dixie, my friend. I might not be able to tell if a spaceship is real or not, but I've got about twelve years' worth of Iowa State Farm Swine Calling competitions under my belt, and I know bluster when I hear it. I think there's far more to you than you're lettin' on.

[*Clayton holds his gaze.*]

Clayton: All right, fine. You want to know why I'm really here?

Snout: Yessir! I'm all ears!

Clayton: [*practically snarling*] I want to win.

Snout: Well, of course you do. We all do. Who wouldn't want to win a million dollars?

[*Clayton lets out a laugh.*]

Clayton: You think I'm doing all this for a measly six figures? That shit is pocket change to me. I don't care about the money.

Snout: What do you care about, then?

Clayton: [*His face darkens.*] Glory. Infamy. [*then quieter, more to himself*] Respect.

[*Snout watches him, then shakes his head.*]

Snout: I'm sorry, friend, but I'm afraid I still don't understand.

Clayton: There's a lot more than money at stake here. You just need to know where to look—

[*Clayton gasps as he grabs his stomach. His face turns red.*]

Snout: Clayton? You all right?

Clayton: [*wincing*] My—stomach.

Snout: Oh my . . . the food *was* bad!

Clayton: Don't be stupid. It's probably the bacteria in this diseased cesspool that you won't let me out of—ow!

[*He doubles over as another stab of pain attacks.*]

Snout: Do you need me to—

Clayton: Unless you're going to say "unstick the door," then no. I don't want a goddamn thing from you. Leave me alone.

Snout: But should I—

Clayton: OW!

[*The rest come running in.*]

Bacardi: What happened?

Snout: He's sick.

Clayton: I'm not sick. I—[*He cringes again, letting out a long string of obscenities.*]

Louise: [*elated*] He *is* sick!

[*Titania steps up to the glass.*]

Titania: What's wrong, pool boy?

Clayton: Nothing. Leave me alone.

Snout: It's the food! I knew it!

Nico: So—what? They really are trying to kill us?

Clayton: I'm not dying!

Bacardi: How do you know? Maybe you are! Maybe we all are! Maybe we're getting radiated to death and WE WON'T KNOW IT TILL WE'RE DEAD!

[*Bacardi storms up to the flight deck. She dramatically throws herself into the swivel chair, puts her elbows on the control panel, and sinks her head into her arms. The rest rush over to console her.*]

Titania: Hey. It's okay.

Snout: Aw, Bacardi, don't cry.

Bacardi: [*whispering*] I'm not crying.

[*She squirms in the seat, reaching into her space bra and fiddling with something in her hand. Suddenly she sits up straight and holds a cell phone at arm's length.*]

Bacardi: Everyone smile!

[*She takes a selfie of the group.*]

Bacardi: There! *Yes!*

Titania: What are you doing?

Bacardi: [*giving the phone a few more taps*] Getting us rescued.

Clayton: How do you plan on doing that, Queen Lushface?

Bacardi: Queen Lushface smuggled a rooted cell phone onboard and is using it to call for help. Does King Pervert know how to do that?

[*Bewilderment settles over the room.*]

Titania: You've had a cell phone this whole time?

Bacardi: Yep.

Nico: That you hid in your space bra?

Bacardi: In a special hidden compartment in my space bra, yep.

Louise: But a cell phone would be useless in space. There's no signal, no WiFi. You can't call anyone or connect to the internet.

Bacardi: Unless you know how to make the internet your bitch, like I do. Never met an online security system I can't crack.

Louise: Wait. You're a *nerd?*

Bacardi: [*smirking at her*] Told you we weren't so different.

[*The others stare at Bacardi in utter stupefaction—except for Louise, whose confusion quickly shifts to scorn. She narrows her eyes and, quietly for once, leaves the room.*]

Bacardi: Unfortunately for us, NASAW knows what they're doing. Wherever we're being held is an impenetrable bunker or something; there's no cell phone signal, no bars, no reception, no internet—with the exception of NASAW's internal WiFi network. It's a strong signal—right outside the ship, I think—but they've got some high-level security I've never seen before. I've been trying to break into it all day.

Titania: And . . .

Bacardi: And I finally figured it out. Cracked their password, logged on to the network, and posted a photo online. Of course, the owner of the WiFi network saw what I was doing just now and shut it down, but that's okay. All I needed was a few seconds of connectivity.

Clayton: And *that's* what you did with it? Posted a *photo*?

Bacardi: A photo with a geotag.

[*They take a moment to absorb this.*]

Titania: So . . . our GPS coordinates are out there now for whoever wants to find them?

Bacardi: Not whoever. I encrypted the post, so it'll only be detectable to a certain number of my friends in the dark corners of the internet. If any of our theories are correct—if we're somewhere in the Southwest, if we're being experimented on, if we're the newest exhibit in a lizard zoo—they'll come looking for us. They won't be able to help themselves.

[*The others continue to stare at her, astonished.*]

Clayton: [*with a furious pound on the glass*] Why did you wait until *now* to do this?

Bacardi: There wasn't a poisonous reptile in our toilet until now.

Snout: Venomous, actually. Common misconception. See, poisonous means that the animal delivers its toxin indirectly, like through skin glands, but venomous means it has to deliver it by sinking its teeth into the victim—

Titania: But why *did* you wait until today? Why not days ago, when bullets started flying?

Bacardi: [*ticking off the reasons on her fingers*] One: Hacking other people's passwords isn't looked upon kindly by the government. Not exactly a smart move for me to broadcast illegal activities while we were still on national television. Two: I had one shot at this. I needed to do it while there wasn't anything abnormal going on. This ship has been one big question mark since everything that went down last night. The static, the gas—we don't know what those scientists are doing, what forces they're working with. We seem to be in a relatively stable state at the moment—and if their latest attack is a Gila monster, there's nothing staticky or magnety about that—so now felt like the best time to try.

Clayton: Or maybe it's because you're finally sober.

[*Bacardi gives him an amused look.*]

Bacardi: I was never drunk in the first place, you rat-faced hobgoblin. You think I'd voluntarily consume brain-scrambling substances aboard a spaceship-slash-reality show, the very model of a situation when I need to keep my wits about me? And with creepers like *you* onboard? How stupid do you think I am?

[*The amount of awe filling the room is as voluminous as the knockout gas.*]

Titania: Damn, Bacardi. You really *could* be a spy.

[*Bacardi looks dead into the lens of Camera #2.*]

Bacardi: Hear that, CIA?

Item: Transcript of video recording
Source: Fakefinders
Time: 6:02 p.m.

[*person in Bigfoot mask facing the camera*]

Bigfoot: Greetings, sheeple.

The space race is on.

The Fakestronauts are somewhere on this planet.

And we have zeroed in on their location.

If DV8 isn't going to come clean about their whereabouts, it's time to take matters into our own hands.

We are a group of technologically capable truth seekers. We will be the ones to find them and expose Chazz Young's lies to the world.

It's time to *literally* find the fake.

From here on out, a state of restless anticipation settles through the ship. Now that Bacardi has sent a distress signal of sorts, the kids are trapped in a limbo of ambiguity—half expecting to be rescued, half expecting another crisis. It's no wonder that impatience gives way to volatility.

Item: Transcript of video recording—RAW, UNAIRED FOOTAGE
Source: Camera #8—Bedroom
Time: 6:29 p.m.

[*Louise is sitting under her blanket again, the glow of a flashlight shining through the fabric. Snout knocks on the doorway.*]

Snout: Louise? You all right?

[*She whips the blanket off her head.*]

Louise: What do you want?

Snout: Just checkin' in on you. You snuck off—

Louise: [*grunting*] The things I've put up with on this ship. The dealings with you Earthlings. As if any of you are worthy enough to be in the presence of Lord Balway Galway.

[*Snout enters the room and sits on the big bed, across from Louise.*]

Snout: Who is this Lord Galway anyway?

Louise: The bravest, dashingest, most amazing Gavinjian ever to walk the Yacanite ice floes of Kafaldhia.

[*Snout frowns.*]

Snout: Louise, have you ever had a boyfriend?

Louise: No. Have you ever had a girlfriend?

Snout: No. So I may not be the most qualified one to be giving love advice. But if I ever did court myself a lady, I'd want it to be someone my own age. And maybe also . . . my own species?

Louise: What's your point?

Snout: Just that you may want to try dating someone from school before you move on to more, um, advanced relationships. And that—well, heck, maybe my tractor wasn't stolen by aliens. Maybe it was just Klepto Joe, up to his ole tricks again. Maybe there aren't any aliens at all?

Louise: Don't patronize me. You don't understand what's happening here, and you never will.

[*Snout rubs his chin.*]

Snout: You know, Louise, I had a real favorite book back when I was a kid. Changed the course of my life, I reckon. I read it every day. And soon enough, I started to believe that I was in it! I would picture myself saying the words, and I would act out the scenes. Heck, that story became more real to me than real life!

Louise: Does *this* story have a point?

Snout: Sure does! I'm just saying, maybe there's a chance that you love your space books and space movies and space TV shows so much that sometimes you think they're real. And there's nothing wrong with that! Imagination's a wonderful thing! I'd give anything to believe I was still back there on a boat, or with a goat, or on a plane, or on a—

Louise: Wait a sec. Are you talking about *Green Eggs and Ham*?

Snout: You know it?

[*Louise massages her temples.*]

Louise: Are we about done here?

Snout: Oh, sure, sorry. You in a rush or something?

Louise: If you *must* know, I've had an important revelation. The bounty that Lord Balway Galway bestowed upon us—that was a sign. A sign that the day of reckoning is at hand. A sign that I have proven myself worthy. A sign that he is finally ready to welcome me to his crew as I commence my duties as chief plasma deck engineer onboard *Interstellar Venture V.*

[*Louise beams. Snout frowns.*]

Louise: Wish I could say I'll miss you all, but, you know. I won't.

Snout: Well, uh—I wish you the best, Louise. I'm sorry I didn't get to know you better.

Louise: [*scoffs*] Nothing to know.

Snout: Oh, now, that can't be. I bet you're a real nice girl when you're not under the scary pressure of being in space.

Louise: Oh, do you think so? [*She begins to squeeze the blanket through her fingers.*] You think I've got a better, more colorful personality squished way down deep inside that I haven't gotten the chance to show yet?

Snout: Yeah!

Louise: Sorry. Don't have it. Colorful personalities are impossible to develop when you're the seventh of twelve children and ten hours a day are spent being homeschooled by your wacko parents who'd happily plop every one of their children in a boat and send them down a river if that's what Our Almighty Father told them to do.

Snout: Oh, dear.

Louise: [*squeezing the blanket so hard her knuckles have turned white*] Not much room to become "fun" and "quirky" and "camera-ready" when you're taught from birth that any one of those traits plus a million others will send you straight to a fiery, unforgiving hell. That having an imagination is wicked and wrong. That even looking up at the stars and wondering if they got there by any means other than Our Almighty Father's almighty hand is grounds for an exorcism.

Snout: I—

Louise: Which is *why* I've accepted a position onboard the *Venture*. Lucky for me, this stupid TV show coincided perfectly with its pass through Earth's orbit. Now all I need to do is hitch a ride as they go by, and it's off to a new life! New planets! New everything!

[*Snout gets up. He heads out into the hallway toward the bathroom before turning on his heel and sticking his head back through the bedroom doorway.*]

Snout: Louise, have you ever heard of cabin fever? It's when you go a little nuts from being cooped up inside for too long.

Louise: I don't have cabin fever. [*pulling the blanket back over herself*] I have a destiny.

[*Snout leaves the room, shaking his head.*]

Source: Camera #3—Lünar Lounge

[*Clayton is curled into a ball and shivering in his sleep, causing gentle waves of water to ripple up against the glass. Nico and Titania are sitting together on the couch. Surprisingly, there seems to be very little tension between them; both seem to be comfortably settling into the friend zone.*]

Nico: Do you think we'll all stay in touch after this is over?

Titania: All of us? I doubt it.

Nico: Oh? No girly sleepovers at Louise's house in your future?

Titania: Yeah, that'll happen when you and Clayton join the same frat.

[*Nico snickers.*]

Nico: What about us?

Titania: What about us?

Nico: I know we live on opposite sides of the country, but—

Titania: *I* don't live anywhere anymore.

Nico: Oh. Right. Well, if you need a place to stay, you can crash on my couch.

Titania: Thanks. I might take you up on that.

Nico: But we'll still talk, right? Or text? Or something?

Titania: Sure. How could we not?

Nico: [*relieved*] Good. I just don't want us to . . .

Titania: Drift apart? [*with a smile*] We won't. Promise.

[*Bacardi enters, frowning.*]

Nico: What's up?

Bacardi: [*holding up her phone*] I've been sitting in the Confessional Closet for the last half hour, trying to get back online. Nothing's working, but I'm picking up on some bizarre interference in that room—and only in that room.

Titania: Hmm.

Bacardi: I'm guessing it has something to do with whatever the psycho scientists out there are doing, but I need more height. Can someone come hold the stool while I stand on it, maybe wheel me around? I don't trust that rickety-ass thing.

Nico: Sure.

[*He gets up from the couch, gives Titania a wave, and follows Bacardi back to the Confessional Closet. Titania watches him go, smiling slightly.*]

[*After a minute or so, Clayton taps on the glass.*]

Clayton: [*weakly*] Titania? [*He puts his finger through the hole.*] Can you get me some water?

[*Titania ignores him. Clayton sinks dejectedly back into the disgusting tub.*]

Clayton: I don't deserve this.

Titania: Seems to me it's exactly what you deserve.

[*Clayton sighs.*]

Clayton: Okay, maybe it is. But I'm not as much of a dick as I've led everyone to believe.

[*Titania raises her eyebrow at him.*]

Clayton: Okay, maybe I am. But I'm not, like, a monster.

Titania: Could have fooled me.

Clayton: Oh, give me a break. I've only been gunning after you so hard because you're my biggest threat out here.

Titania: Threat to what? This isn't a competition anymore. What could any of us possibly have to gain now?

[*Clayton watches her. He runs his finger up and down his jawline, as if debating whether to speak up or hold his tongue.*]

[*Finally, with some hesitation:*]

Clayton: Do you remember what NASAW stands for?

Titania: The . . . National Association for the Study of Astronomy and Weightlessness, right?

Clayton: Uh-huh. But do you know what it *really* stands for?

[*He tips his eyebrow conspiratorially. Titania sits up.*]

Titania: What do you mean? You think it stands for something else?

[*He cracks his neck.*]

Clayton: I have a guess.

Titania: You have a . . . guess.

Clayton: Like I said—my parents hold a lot of sway at the Smithsonian. Once I heard what this show was all about—and that NASAW was involved—I made some very secret calls to some very smart people to find out all I could about what was going to be happening here.

Titania: Right. If you sweet-talked them like you sweet-talked all of us, I'm sure they were *real* forthcoming.

Clayton: All part of the game, sweetheart. When intimidation and feather-ruffling is what's called for, that's what I deliver. But when there are answers I want, it's just as easy for me to turn on the charm.

Titania: And what did you charm these very smart people into giving you?

Clayton: Dead ends, mostly. A whisper here, an insinuation there. So I dug deeper. Scraped up a few more clues. But this went deep—real deep. Even with the charisma cranked way up, I couldn't get anyone to blab. So I was forced to turn to less credible sources, people way out on the fringes of the scientific community. And eventually, a fuzzy picture began to emerge.

Titania: And are you going to tell me what it is, or do I have to sit through another hour of this?

[*Clayton beckons for her to put her ear up next to the hole.*]

Titania: Right. Like I'm going to fall for that again.

[*He adopts a dead-serious expression.*]

Clayton: I am not messing with you anymore, Titania. I swear.

[*She studies him. Then, warily, she puts her ear to the glass.*

His whispers are so soft that even the highly sensitive microphones can't pick up what he's saying.

But it's enough to transform Titania's face.

Her eyes widen.

Her jaws go slack.

And a fire starts to burn in her eyes, slowly growing from a spark to an inferno.]

Item: Transcript of video recording
Source: Surveillance camera—Visitor Center, the Karl G.
Jansky Very Large Array, New Mexico
Time: 6:30 p.m.

[*Matt is banging on the glass façade while Kaoru watches, her arms crossed. A security guard opens the door.*]

Matt: Finally!

Security Guard: Sorry, kids, but the Visitor Center is closed. It'll open tomorrow at 8:30 a.m.—

Matt: I need to talk to a scientist! A real one!

Security Guard: Uh—what?

Matt: Someone who can help us without calling the police!

Security Guard: The police? What's—

Matt: *This is a science emergency!*

Security Guard: Okay, okay—calm down. Come on inside. I think the director's still here, she usually stays late.

Matt: Thank you!

Kaoru: {We are making yet another mistake.}

Item: Transcript of video recording—RAW, UNAIRED FOOTAGE
Source: Camera #3—Lünar Lounge
Time: 6:32 p.m.

[*Titania backs away from the glass. When she speaks, her voice is raspy, intense.*]

Titania: I don't believe you.

Clayton: Believe me or don't. But you *are* one of the smart ones. You know something unprecedented is happening. And I'm ninety-nine percent sure that's what it is.

Titania: Why haven't you told anyone?

Clayton: Same reason you're not going to tell anyone: because I wanted to keep it all for myself. I wanted the glory, even if—

Titania: Even if you wouldn't be around to see it? You, the most desperate-for-attention wannabe on television?

Clayton: [*chagrined*] Yes. But at this point it's clear that if anyone's going down with this ship, it's going to be me. So you might be the only one who has a fighting chance. [*He looks around the ship, paranoid.*] Do you hear that?

[*They keep still.*]

Titania: [*frowning*] That hum?

Clayton: Yeah. It's new. Or maybe it's been there all along, too faint for us to notice, and it's just now getting stronger. Which means things are escalating. It's almost time.

[*Titania swallows.*]

Clayton: If it can't be me, it should be you. All you have to do is find a way out of here.

[*They hold each other's gazes. Slowly, as if approaching a dangerous animal, Titania picks up a Slom bottle from the bar, raises it to the hole in the glass, and pours some water through. Clayton slurps it up.*]

Clayton: Thanks.

[*Nico walks in, then stops short once he spots the two of them.*]

Nico: Am I . . . interrupting something?

Titania: Nope.

[*Titania caps the bottle and slams it onto the bar. Nico jumps at the noise.*]

Nico: [*puzzled*] O . . . kay.

[*Clayton turns away from the window and curls up as if he's going to sleep. Nico sits on the couch and pats the cushion, but Titania doesn't join him.*]

Nico: There *is* some interference in the Confessional Closet, but we couldn't figure out what it is.

Titania: [*pacing*] Oh really?

Nico: Yeah, it seemed to be coming from—are you okay?

Titania: Yeah. Why?

Nico: You seem . . . not okay.

Titania: We're trapped in a fucking prison. Of course I'm not okay.

Nico: Yeah, but—come here. Sit down.

[*She does, but on the other end of the couch from him this time. She crosses her legs, her foot on the floor bouncing up and down.*]

[*There is an awkwardness.*]

Nico: I was thinking—not to be too pushy about it, but if you *did* come to live in New York, there's a lot of theater and Broadway and stuff there—maybe you could build sets or something, you know? Put your woodcarving skills to work?

Titania: Right.

[*Nico studies her. She is staring straight ahead and biting at a hangnail.*]

Nico: Are you *sure* you're okay? You're acting weird.

Titania: I'm fine.

Nico: [*eyeing Clayton*] Is it him? What did he do this time?

Titania: *Nothing.*

Nico: It's just—five minutes ago you were—and now you're . . .

[*another uncomfortable pause*]

Nico: Anyway . . . I asked Bacardi if she thinks we'll all keep in touch after this. She said that if we want to escape with our sanity intact, we'll have to.

Titania: Mmm.

Nico: Like, because this is such a life-wrenching thing we've all been through, it'll be hard to explain it to other people when we get home. She said we'll probably want to keep talking to the ones who were here, who'll understand what it was like, you know?

Titania: Yeah. [*distracted*] I guess.

Nico: I don't know if I'd talk to *everyone*—I don't think I could hold a conversation with Hibiscus without wanting to jump in front of a train—but at least you and I are definites.

Titania: Yeah, um—[*She scratches her head. When she talks, it is as if she's talking to herself, not registering his presence.*] I don't know. I don't know if that's a good idea.

[*Nico frowns.*]

Nico: What do you mean?

Titania: Maybe it's better to make a clean break. Keep moving forward. Don't look back.

Nico: But you said—

Titania: I know what I said, but—[*She gets up and paces around again, her movements manic.*] I changed my mind. When this is done, I want it to be done. No baggage. No leftovers.

[*Nico is crestfallen.*]

Nico: Oh.

[*She stops pacing. She looks at the flight deck, then in the direction of the hallway.*]

Titania: I'm going to go hang out in the closet. I need to rest, or think, or . . . something. Be alone.

Nico: Okay.

[*She leaves. Nico stands up but doesn't follow her. Instead he crosses to the hot-tub window and puts his hands flat on the glass. His voice is tight.*]

Nico: [*to Clayton's huddled form*] What did you do to her?

[*Clayton, asleep or not, doesn't answer.*]

Item: Transcript of audio recording
Source: Voice recorder app—phone of Dr. Carla Emmy
Time: 6:52 p.m.

Dr. Carla Emmy: We are now recording. Repeat what you just told me.

Matt: What part?

Dr. Emmy: All of it. From your escape to when you got here.

Matt: After we woke up in the van and knocked out the driver, we drove back in the direction we came from. After about six hours we arrived at the soundstage. One of the scientists came out to talk to us, but it turns out he wanted to attack us instead, so we fought back and then escaped.

Kaoru: {The foolish boy was of little help.}

Matt: Since we didn't have a phone or GPS or anything, we just started driving, not knowing where we were going, stopping only to get gas with the cash we grabbed out of the driver's wallet. We got to Arizona and slept in an IKEA for a few hours, then got on the road again. I think we doubled back by accident. I kept wanting to call someone for help, but every time I tried to access a phone, Kaoru stopped me. But it turns out she was right, because when we tried to ask for help at a gas station and get our bearings and figure out a plan from there, it turns out that we're kind of, like, fugitives? I guess DV8 told everyone that we were in the hospital and that anyone else claiming to be us is *not* us, so now the whole world is looking for us and wants to rip out our throats for some reason?

Kaoru: {Fortunately, I have kept a clear head through all of this.}

Matt: So we panicked, grabbed a bunch of food and drinks, escaped from the convenience-store lunatic, and got back on the road—but we still didn't know where we were going, and we couldn't ask for help anymore, not unless we wanted to get attacked again.

Kaoru: {The situation is less than ideal.}

Matt: Basically we've been driving blind, taking random turns and highways, going in circles, over every inch of—what state are we in?

Dr. Emmy: New Mexico.

Matt: So finally, after miles and miles of nothing but flat scrubby land in all directions, we saw these satellite dishes. And we thought, oh no, scientists! Those are the people who got us into all this trouble in the first place! But then we thought, hey, maybe they're good scientists instead of bad scientists, and we're down to five bucks and we can't buy any more gas so it's not like we're going to get any farther, so we decided to take a chance and hope that you'd be able to help us and not turn us over to Chazz Young for him to make space dust out of us!

Dr. Emmy: Have you had anything to drink since yesterday that wasn't soda?

Matt: Nope!

Dr. Emmy: Let's pause for a minute to get you both some water.

[*The recording cuts out, then cuts back in.*]

Dr. Emmy: All right. We've calmed down and taken a few cleansing breaths. Are we ready to continue?

Matt: Yes. Wait, can you tell me something? What is this place? All those huge satellite dishes—

Dr. Emmy: Twenty-seven of them, to be exact. And they're not satellite dishes, they're radio telescopes. We use them to observe radio omissions, black holes, pulsars, quasars, and lots of other things in deep space. This observatory is called the Very Large Array.

Matt: Oh. Couldn't come up with a snazzier name for it?

Dr. Emmy: We're scientists, not poets.

Matt: One more thing: Can I ask who you are? No offense, but we've gotten jacked around a lot lately and I'm not sure which adults I should be trusting anymore.

Dr. Emmy: Certainly. I'm the director of the National Radio Astronomy Observatory. And if that's not enough to convince you, behold the "very large array" of degrees displayed on the wall behind me. [*chuckles*]

[*pause*]

Dr. Emmy: That was a joke.

[*pause*]

Matt: So if you're an astronomer—then you must have detected the explosion last night! The one we all felt on the *Laika*!

Dr. Emmy: I'm afraid I don't know what you're talking about.

Kaoru: {He is wasting your time, Doctor. He still thinks we were in space. We were never in space.}

Matt: When we were in space!

Dr. Emmy: *You* were in space?

Matt: Yes! That's the reality show I'm talking about, *Waste of Space*. Don't you watch it?

Dr. Emmy: I don't own a television.

Matt: But it's online, too. Jeez, lady, how can you not be watching it? You're an astronomer!

Dr. Emmy: The folly and frivolity of entertainment on Earth will forever pale in comparison to the majesty and mystery of the universe—

Matt: Yeah, sure, sure—but still, if you're watching the skies, you must have noticed the explosion.

Dr. Emmy: I'm sorry. There have been no extra-orbital explosions over the past week. Nor the past month.

Matt: Then . . . dang. I don't get it.

Dr. Emmy: Who are these "bad scientists" you referred to earlier?

Matt: I don't know. I think they were from NASAW.

Dr. Emmy: NASA? But—

Matt: No, NASAW. With a *W* on the end.

Dr. Emmy: Huh. [*pause*] I've never heard of them.

Item: Transcript of video recording
Source: Nico's camera
Battery charge: 12%
Time: 7:11 p.m.

[*Nico is lying on his bed, pointing his camera at the ceiling.*]

Hi Mom. Hi Dad.

We're playing the waiting game. Bacardi pinged our location, and all we can do is hope someone in the outside world noticed it.

I can't talk for long—the others will be back in a minute. Bacardi and Louise are in the bathroom, brushing their teeth.

Snout is checking on the Gila monster. We think it's around bedtime, but we can't tell. We've lost all sense of time.

We're tired and starving.

We're running out of water.

And Titania . . .

[*He heaves a shuddering sigh. There is a quiver in his voice.*]

Something broke her.

Item: Transcript of video recording—RAW, UNAIRED FOOTAGE
Source: Camera #7—Confessional Closet
Time: 7:11 p.m.

[*Titania is staring unblinkingly into the camera.*]

Titania: Keep moving.

Keep exploring.

Keep moving.

Keep exploring.

I have to get out of here.

I have to get out of here.

I have to get out of here.

[*This repeats for five minutes and thirty-nine seconds.*]

Item: Transcript of audio recording
Source: Aero Albuquerque Charter Service
Time: 7:58 p.m.

[*A message plays: "This call may be recorded for quality assurance."*]

Dispatcher: Aero Albuquerque. How may I help you?

NASAW: I need a helicopter. This is for the DV8 account.

Dispatcher: All right. Let me pull up your location . . .

NASAW: No, no—the location on file isn't accurate. We're actually at ███████ north, ███████ west.

Dispatcher: All right. And how soon do you need it?

NASAW: In—hold on a sec.

[muffled voices off-mike]

NASAW: *[away from the phone]* Yeah, *I know* it's ahead of schedule. But that brat with her geotag—people will be coming for us now. DV8, too. We're almost out of—

[unintelligible speech in background]

NASAW: *[away from phone]* Because the timing is too unpredictable! *Something* we did yesterday worked—but nothing we've tried yet *today* has worked, and we don't even know for sure that it's something we *can* replicate.

[unintelligible speech in background]

NASAW: *[away from phone]* I don't want to hear it. If we can open it up by midnight, great; if not, we're done. Either way, we gotta get out of here.

[unintelligible speech in background]

NASAW: *[away from phone]* Too bad. Team A, keep trying; Team B, start wiping the hard drives. We're at T minus four hours. *Go!*

[back into the phone]

NASAW: Sorry about that. How we coming on that helicopter?

Dispatcher: When do you need it?

NASAW: As soon as humanly possible.

[end of call]

Item: Transcript of video recording—RAW, UNAIRED FOOTAGE

[*Bacardi, Nico, Snout, and Louise are in bed, though the lights haven't gone out. Having gone nearly a full day without food, their energy is zapped. Louise is hiding under her blanket again.*]

[*Suddenly Titania bursts in, a new degree of urgency in her voice.*]

Titania: What about the lights?

[*The others mumble a "huh?"*]

Titania: [*pointing at the ceiling*] There are light bulbs screwed into sockets up there. Maybe we can intentionally blow a fuse and knock the power out. And if we knock the power out, maybe we can manually open up the airlock!

Nico: How do we do that?

Titania: I don't know. Break the bulb and stick a fork in the wires or something?

Nico: That sounds dangerous.

Titania: What's the worst that could happen? A fire?

Nico: It's—

Titania: They gas us? They poison us?

Nico: That's not—

Titania: What more can they do to us? They can keep smacking us down and we can keep crawling back to life, but not eating—and I can't stress this enough—*not eating* is something we *cannot* survive.

Nico: I know, but sticking a fork into an electric socket sounds a little . . . desperate?

Titania: We *are* desperate!

Snout: Titania, are you okay? You sound . . .

[*Snout trails off. The video recording doesn't show much, but* judging by the looks on the cast members' faces and the way their bodies tense up, something odd is happening. During this period there is a low-frequency rumble in the background. It lasts for about five seconds, then appears to let up; the kids relax and look around at one another. Then Bacardi gasps.]

Bacardi: Titania, your nose. It's bleeding.

[*Titania's hand flies to her face. When she pulls it away, it's red. She looks back at Bacardi.*]

Titania: [*pointing a bloody finger*] So is yours.

Nico: Mine too.

Snout: And mine! Louise, what about you?

Louise: [*muffled, beneath her blanket*] If my nose *were* bleeding, it would have nothing to do with NASAW and everything to do with the interstellar microwave radiation beacon that Lord Balway Galway is dispatching.

[*They all look miserably at one another's bloody faces.*]

Snout: Radiation, huh?

Item: Transcript of audio recording
Source: Chazz's cell phone
Time: 9:02 p.m.

DV8: Chazz, where are you?

Chazz: Taxiing to the runway. Had to sneak onto the airstrip so those Fakefinder pricks wouldn't see us—they were spying on my private jet, can you believe it?

DV8: Chazz—

Chazz: Assholes. Anyway, we're on our way. Should touch down in Albuquerque in a couple hours. I'll grab Boris, then head to the soundstage.

DV8: Chazz! Listen to me. We were looking back through all those NASAW files, and we found something . . . bizarre.

Chazz: Save it. I don't have space in my brain for anything extraneous right now. I need to focus on storming the shit out of those scientists.

DV8: I really think you should hold off on that until you see this, Chazz. NASAW isn't who you think they are. The acronym doesn't even stand for—

Chazz: I don't care who they are or what they stand for. They kidnapped my show and are *this* close to making a mockery of everything I've worked for, and the only way I can stop it is if I can do what I need to do without shit-for-brain producers calling me every five seconds to whine about pointless bullshit garbage!

DV8: But—

Chazz: We're about to take off. I have to go into airplane mode. I'll call again when I get there. Later hater!

DV8: But Chazz—

Chazz: LATER. HATER.

[*end of call*]

Item: Transcript of video recording—RAW, UNAIRED FOOTAGE
Source: Camera #8—Bedroom
Time: 9:04 p.m.

[*The lights are still on. The noses are still bleeding.*]

[*Bacardi exhales.*]

Bacardi: We're gonna die here.

Snout: Aw, come on. No, we're not. You sent out our location!

Bacardi: Yeah, but who knows if anyone is paying attention? And what if the scientists decide to snuff us before help arrives?

Snout: You can't think like that.

Bacardi: [*snorts*] You wouldn't say that if you knew who this ship is named after.

Nico: Who, *Laika*? Chazz said a famous astronaut or something, but I've never heard of him.

Bacardi: Not him. Her.

Nico: How do you know that?

Bacardi: Because she was Russian. Like me.

Snout: I thought you were from Brooklyn.

Bacardi: I am. Brighton Beach, Brooklyn. Where my parents moved after the collapse of the Soviet Union, along with a gazillion other immigrants.

Snout: And y'all know who Laika is?

Bacardi: Yes. She was the first ever to be launched into orbit.

Nico: So how is that a bad thing?

[*Bacardi's voice tightens.*]

Bacardi: Because Laika was a *dog.* She was owned by the Soviet space program. In 1957 they stuffed her into Sputnik 2 and launched her into space to determine whether or not human cosmonauts would be able to survive the trip.

Snout: [*quietly*] Did she? Survive?

Bacardi: She made it into orbit. But she died only a few hours later.

Snout: Oh, dear. Poor Laika.

Nico: Yeah, but . . . but that was in the early days of space exploration. Accidents like that were bound to happen.

Bacardi: It wasn't an accident. It was a one-way ticket.

Nico: What do you mean?

Bacardi: They knew she wasn't coming back. The technology to return to Earth didn't exist yet. Even if she'd survived the initial phase, her oxygen supply was limited and her food was laced with poison.

Nico: Jesus.

[*Bacardi looks at her blood-soaked pillow.*]

Bacardi: They sent her up there to die. And now they're doing the same thing to us.

Item: Transcript of audio recording
Source: Voice recorder app—phone of Dr. Carla Emmy
Time: 10:16 p.m.

[sound of a door opening and shutting]

Dr. Emmy: Sorry to keep you waiting, kids.

Matt: No problem. So when is someone coming to get us?

Dr. Emmy: Well . . . I've got a confession to make. I hope you'll forgive me.

Kaoru: {She is not speaking in a promising tone.}

Dr. Emmy: I wasn't making phone calls. I haven't let anyone know you arrived. I haven't notified DV8 or your families.

Matt: What? Why?

Dr. Emmy: Because of what you said earlier about the explosions. You see, our job here is to monitor the skies; the goings-on of the immediate vicinity on Earth don't concern us. But out of curiosity, I checked our records from the past few days, zeroing in on the time frame that you suggested. And what I found was . . . intriguing.

Matt: How so?

Dr. Emmy: Forgive me if this explanation is obtuse; I don't normally interact with people outside the scientific sphere, so it's sometimes difficult for me to switch in and out of technical-speak. But the plain English version is: something highly irregular is going on in a supposedly empty patch of desert roughly ninety miles from here.

Matt: Irregular in what way?

Dr. Emmy: Irregular in that certain unbreakable laws of physics are being broken.

Matt: That sounds bad.

Dr. Emmy: Bad? Not necessarily. Intriguing? Absolutely.

Kaoru: {It sounds like she is not concerned about our safety.}

Dr. Emmy: It is as though someone is trying to accomplish something impossible by . . . let's see . . . how to explain this? I shall use a metaphor. It is as though someone is trying to start a theoretically impossible fire by sparking every tool in a scientist's arsenal—radiation, static charges, electromagnetic induction—to see if anything catches.

Matt: But what does this have to do with us? Why haven't you called for help?

Kaoru: {It sounds like she wants something from us.}

Dr. Emmy: I'd like to keep this under wraps until we figure out what's going on over there. From what you've told me, I believe these aberrations are occurring at the exact location from which you escaped. I'd like to head out there myself to take a look, and I'd like you two to accompany me.

Matt: But we just escaped from there! Now you're going to bring us back?

Dr. Emmy: If you are in fact the only witnesses who laid eyes on this location, then I would like you to be able to confirm it firsthand. What do you say?

Matt: I don't know . . .

Dr. Emmy: I understand your hesitation. But this could be something extraordinary. You could help make one of the biggest scientific discoveries of the century, or of any century! Don't you want to be a part of that?

Kaoru: {Tell her we are not willing to cooperate, foolish boy.}

Matt: We'll do it!

Back on the *Laika,* the lights are still on. The kids are exhausted, but unable to sleep. Scared, strung-out, and disoriented, they can't even tell what time it is or how many hours they've been awake. Before long, the bedroom is mostly abandoned, the kids listlessly drifting around the ship like ghosts.

Item: Transcript of video recording—RAW, UNAIRED FOOTAGE
Source: Camera #3—Lünar Lounge
Time: 10:47 p.m.

[*Clayton is shivering uncontrollably. Bacardi is sitting on the couch, watching him.*]

Bacardi: You look terrible.

Clayton: Thanks. I feel terrible.

Bacardi: Sorry you're sick. And sorry we locked you in there.

Clayton: No, you're not.

[*Bacardi shrugs.*]

Clayton: So it was all an act, huh? Even when it came to our . . . liaisons?

Bacardi: Not entirely. We're healthy teenagers with healthy teenage needs, are we not? We enjoyed ourselves. Our actions were mutually beneficial. I don't see what's wrong with any of that.

Clayton: What's wrong is that you lied.

Bacardi: I didn't hear you complaining in the throes of passion . . . short as they were.

Clayton: Whoa. Uncalled for.

Bacardi: You sound a little pissed, Clayton.

Clayton: Well, I feel a little used, Bacardi.

Bacardi: *You* feel used? *I* was supposedly drunk. Which makes some of the stuff *you* did supposedly illegal.

Clayton: Okay, let's drop it—

Bacardi: You're a pig, Clayton. And you've treated a lot of girls like trash. But maybe you'll think a bit harder about your actions next time, because maybe the next girl won't be as forgiving as I am.

Clayton: Oh, you forgive me? Thanks *so* much.

Bacardi: Don't get mad just because someone beat you at your own game.

Clayton: I'm not mad. I'm impressed.

Bacardi: [*with a glance at his nether regions*] I can see that.

Clayton: Damn right you can. Care to grant a dying boy one last wish?

Bacardi: You're not dying. But I'll tell you what. [*She walks up to the window, her chest pressing against the glass.*] I'm easy to find online. Hit me up once we're back home and maybe— *maybe*—I'll grant you a second or two of my precious, invaluable time.

[*Clayton is seized with another stomach pain. Grabbing his belly, he screws up his face and lets out a whimper.*]

Bacardi: [*with disgust*] But, you know. Probably not.

[*She leaves the room. Clayton is left alone, trembling, listening to the ceaseless hum.*]

Source: Camera #8—Bedroom

[*Louise is still under the covers, flashlight still flashing.*]

Source: Camera #6—Bathroom

[*Nico enters. He finds Snout looking at the closed door of the toilet stall.*]

Nico: What are you doing?

Snout: Trying to screw up the courage to go in there and take a leak on that poor Gila monster. Reckon he won't like it. [*Seeing Nico's distraught face, he frowns.*] What's wrong?

Nico: Titania locked herself in the Confessional Closet again. She won't let me in.

Snout: Cripes.

Nico: Something's wrong with her. She got real weird real fast.

Snout: What happened, exactly?

Nico: I don't know! We were talking in the lounge earlier, and then I left the room for, like, five minutes, and when I came back, she started acting like she'd snorted a bucket of cocaine. Did you see her eyes, darting all over the place?

Snout: Yeah. Maybe she's gone stir-crazy.

Nico: Maybe. But I don't know what to do.

Snout: Me neither.

[*He looks at the toilet stall.*]

Snout: Oh, heck, I can't hold it any longer.

[*He opens the door, walks in, and looks in the toilet. Then whips his head around the small space.*]

Snout: Uh-oh.

Source: Camera #7—Confessional Closet

[*Titania is peering into the camera. Her eyes are bloodshot.*]

Titania: Everything is quiet now, but not in a good way. In the way that things were quiet then. Afterward. When the beeping stopped.

It's a tense quiet. A "what now?" quiet.

So quiet you can finally hear the hum of the Earth, that fixed vibration underneath it all.

A steady, repetitious drone.

Keep-moving, keep-moving, keep-moving.

Two windowless vans are steadily making their way toward Soundstage G-96. One contains Chazz, Boris, and a small film crew; the other contains a small squad of armed men—and a familiar face.

Item: Transcript of video recording, with phone audio—
RAW, UNAIRED FOOTAGE
Source: DV8 remote film crew
Time: 11:21 p.m.

[*The camera operator is in the cargo area of the van, aiming the shot at the road. Chazz is driving; Boris is in the passenger's seat. Chazz keeps taking angry glimpses at the side mirror.*]

Chazz: [*shouting into his cell phone, which is on speaker*] Can't you drive any faster? Keep up!

SWAT Team Member #3: [*on phone*] Sir, I'm going to have to ask you to stop calling me. You just focus on your driving and I'll do the same.

Chazz: I'm in the van directly in front of you and we're the only ones on this road and it's eleven something at night. It's not exactly a deathtrap.

SWAT Team Member #3: [*on phone*] Still, sir.

Chazz: I think you're failing to grasp the urgency of this predicament. This is a hostage situation. Those rotten scientists have hijacked the show and are keeping those kids against my will! I mean—their will! We're losing precious time!

SWAT Team Member #3: [*on phone*] Sir, I'd like to point out that *you* hired *us*.

Chazz: And I'm starting to regret it! I could have chosen any SWAT team in the world, but I chose you! I expect a little more professionalism!

[*pause*]

SWAT Team Member #3: [*on phone*] Sir, are you expressing displeasure with SWAT Team Member #3's performance? Or are you expressing displeasure with *my* performance *as* SWAT Team Member #3?

Chazz: Oh, Jesus. Dude, I picked all your head shots out of our database because you were the beefiest actors we had on call. This has nothing to do with talent and everything to do with having an army of threatening-looking guys to storm the ship.

SWAT Team Member #3: [*on phone*] Okay, sir. Sorry. Just checking.

Chazz: Dammit, now we'll have to edit all this out. Can you just do the job you're getting paid to do and stay in character? Let's just get there, goddammit!

SWAT Team Member #3: [*on phone*] Yes, sir. I'll—

[*There is a commotion on the other end, as though the phone is changing hands. A new voice comes on the line.*]

Jamarkus: [*on phone*] Chazz, are these real guns?

Chazz: I told you not to play with those until we get there. Put SWAT Team Member #3 back on the phone.

Jamarkus: [*on phone*] We're bringing real guns?

Chazz: The ammunition isn't real. They're marking cartridges typically used for military training. I got a great deal years ago, and I've been waiting for the right time to use them. That time has come.

Jamarkus: [*on phone*] These can still cause serious damage, Chazz. Especially in the untrained hands of, oh, I don't know, actors on loan from the Noble Shakespeare Company.

SWAT Team Member #3: [*on phone, in background*] I know stage combat!

Chazz: See? They're professionals.

Jamarkus: [*on phone*] But—

Chazz: Enough questions, Jamarkus. Just do as you're told and you'll be rewarded handsomely. This'll all be over before you know it.

Jamarkus: [*on phone*] But this was never part of the bargain! Doing the show, hawking the products, making ImmerseFX look amazing—that was *all* I agreed to. You can't say you're going to pay my tuition and then refuse to do it until I meet more of your demands. That's extortion!

Chazz: Oh, cry me a river. In less than an hour you're going to get to storm a spaceship like something out of goddamn *Cosmic Crusades*. Wait until MIT sees *that*.

Jamarkus: [*on phone*] Could I at least try calling the satellite phone to warn them—

Chazz: Absolutely not. Any advance warning will ruin the reality. Just stick to the plan, all right? GOD.

[*He ends the call.*]

Boris: Hard to find good help these days, huh, Chazz?

Chazz: I don't want to hear it, Boris. I said I was sorry. I was emotional and confused and under a hell of a lot of stress.

Boris: Why do you need me, anyway? I coulda just given you directions to the place.

Chazz: I've got one more job for you.
Boris: You always do. The usual?
[*Chazz nods, then gives him a wink.*]
Chazz: Better dead than look bad.

By this point in time, the *Waste of Space* debacle has captured the involvement of five distinct parties whose paths have irrevocably begun to converge. The first is, of course, the cast onboard the *Laika*. The second is NASAW, the scientists who have severed all communications but are still operational inside Soundstage G-96. The third is Chazz Young and his crew. The fourth is Dr. Emmy, Matt, and Kaoru, now en route to Soundstage G-96. And the fifth consists of the Fakefinders who think they have zeroed in on the cast's location, thanks to Bacardi's online post—a ragtag, nebulous group of internet truth seekers with nothing but a thirst for validation and a Friday night to kill.

(What they don't realize is that, due to the conditions under which Bacardi's transmission was sent, the coordinates were scrambled. The Fakefinders are heading into the New Mexican desert, to be sure—but are aiming for a patch of empty land thirty miles west of the actual soundstage.)

It is also imperative to note that no legitimate authorities have been contacted. Viewers of the show are torn, believing that either a) the cast is in trouble but DV8 has the situation completely under control, or b) the cast is still participating in a television production, this has all been part of the plan, and, boy, is it entertaining.

Item: Transcript of video recording—RAW, UNAIRED FOOTAGE
Source: Camera #3—Lünar Lounge
Time: 11:52 p.m.

[*Everyone (minus Titania) has migrated to the lounge. Toes are tapping, nails are being bitten, sweat is flowing. Cabin fever has set in hard and is nearing a breaking point.*]

Bacardi: It's gotta be past midnight. Maybe later.

Snout: Why won't they turn the lights out?

Nico: Like we'd be able to sleep if they did.

Louise: Maybe it's because—

Clayton: No. Do not speak, Louise. Your delusions are the last thing we need right now.

Bacardi: Actually, the last thing we need right now is a venomous lizard loose in the ship. But that's what we've got.

Snout: It's dangerous for Titania to be in that closet alone—the Gila monster could find its way in. Why isn't she out here with us?

Nico: I don't know. [*glares at Clayton*] Do you?

Clayton: [*innocently*] Your guess is as good as mine.

Nico: [*taking a step toward the glass*] Is it?

Snout: [*pulling him back*] Maybe you should go check on her again.

Nico: Yeah. Okay.

Source: Camera #7—Confessional Closet

[*It's difficult to assess Titania's mental state at this juncture; she appears to be vacillating rapidly between alertness and hysteria.*]

Titania: Keep moving, keep exploring. That's why I made

the canoe. That's why I came on this show. I had to move forward.

I've tried to make it up to you.

I've tried to fix things that can't be fixed.

I've tried to make you look at me the way you used to: like a daughter. Instead of the daughter that killed your other daughter.

I've tried to forgive myself.

I've tried to move on.

But I've failed. On all accounts, I've failed.

That's why I came onto this show.

I know you can't stand the sight of me, and I know you'll never forgive me.

I don't want you to. I don't expect you to.

So I removed myself from the equation.

But this isn't what I expected. I'm more trapped than I ever was.

I failed again.

[*She balls her hands into fists and begins to pound on the walls.*]

I just wanted a new place.

[*pound*]

I just wanted to go somewhere quiet.

[*pound*]

I just—

[*She stops. Looks at the panel that her left hand was thumping. Sticks her fingers into the crevices between the panels—and lifts.*]

[*There is a knock on the door.*]

Nico: [*muffled voice outside*] Titania? Please let me in.

[*Distracted, she unlocks the door. Nico steps in.*]

Nico: *Finally.* What—[*He stops short, seeing her bent over the wall.*] What are you doing?

[*Titania turns around to face him, revealing the satellite phone in her hand.*]

Titania: [*with disbelief*] This was in the wall.

Nico: Oh my God. [*His eyes bulge.*] You think it's what caused the interference Bacardi was noticing?

Titania: I don't—

[*The phone's display lights up; it's ringing.*]

Nico: Whoa.

Titania: What do I do?

Nico: Answer it!

[*She pushes a button and holds the phone between their ears.*]

Titania: Hello?

[*The voice on the other end is loud and clear.*]

Jamarkus: Titania? It's Jamarkus. Put me on speaker.

[*Though flustered, she does.*]

Titania: Jamarkus, where are you?

Nico: And how did you know about this phone?

Titania: And what—

Jamarkus: I'm calling to warn you. In about ten minutes, a SWAT team and I are going to raid the ship. You need to—

Chazz: [*in background*] What are you doing over there, Jamarkus?

[*Muffled noise, then nothing.*]

Item: Transcript of video recording—RAW, UNAIRED FOOTAGE
Source: DV8 remote film crew
Time: 11:58 p.m.

[*DV8's camera is haphazardly pointed at Jamarkus, standing*] *in a patch of desert brush. The image is unfocused; the film crew hasn't begun to shoot in earnest, but the camera is recording. Audio is recording as well. Chazz is offscreen.*]

Chazz: What are you doing over there, Jamarkus?

[*Jamarkus covers the phone with his hand.*]

Jamarkus: Adjusting my helmet cam.

Chazz: We're done setting up. You ready to go?

Jamarkus: Yep, just about.

[*Jamarkus keeps his eyes fixed on Chazz while surreptitiously slipping the phone up his sleeve, leaving enough room for the mouthpiece end to stick out.*]

Source: Camera #7—Confessional Closet

[*Jamarkus is no longer speaking directly to them, but he hasn't ended the call. Nico and Titania are still huddled around the satellite phone, listening in.*]

Chazz: [*on the phone*] SWAT team, are we good to go?

Jamarkus: [*on the phone*] Yep.

Chazz: [*on the phone*] Crew, good to go?

DV8 Producer: [*on the phone*] Yep.

Chazz: [*on the phone*] Control room, good to go?

[*Pause. They are likely confirming via an earpiece.*]

Chazz: [*on the phone*] Good. Everyone's accounted for. We're going live in one minute to coincide with the start of *The Perky Paisley Show,* so be ready.

[*Ambient noise follows, with no more clear voices—but the call persists. Nico starts to leave the closet.*]

Nico: We have to let the others hear this.

Titania: No. Wait. Stay for a few more seconds.

Nico: Why?

Titania: Because *SWAT team.* SWAT teams have guns.

Nico: What are you talking about? This is a good thing! They're coming to get us!

Titania: *Chazz* is coming to get us. Has that man done or said a single thing to us that wasn't a lie, a misdirection, or some twisted, wrong version of the truth? He can call this a "rescue operation" all he wants. But that's not what it's going to turn into.

Nico: Yeah, but even Chazz Young isn't evil enough to shoot a bunch of innocent kids, is he?

[*Titania raises an eyebrow.*]

Nico: You don't really think this is it, do you?

[*Titania chooses her next words carefully.*]

Titania: If it is, I want you to know that you mattered to me. Through all of this. I didn't come here to make friends, or throw anyone under the bus, or go big, or go home—but I did make a friend, and it was you.

[*Note: This excerpt is taken from footage recorded at a later date.*]

Item: Transcript of video recording
Source: Nico's camera
Battery charge: 100%
Date: March 1, 2016

Nico: I grabbed her hand just then. I couldn't help it. Not in an I-love-you way—though I probably did love her—but in a you-are-not-alone way. A we-are-both-alive-at-the-same-time-and-here-is-the-proof way.

Item: Transcript of video recording—RAW, UNAIRED FOOTAGE
Source: Camera #7—Confessional Closet

Date: February 19, 2016

Time: 11:59 p.m.

[*Chazz's voice comes through clear on the satellite phone again.*]

Chazz: [*on the phone*] Ten seconds, people. Places.

[*Nico heads out the door.*]

Nico: Come on.

Titania: Right behind you.

■◁ • • • • • • • • • • • • • • ▐ **ON–AIR** ▌ • • • • • • • • • • • • • • • • • •

Item: Transcript of video broadcast

Source: *DV8 Breaking News*—aired live on DV8, DV8.com, and the DV8 app

Date: February 20, 2016

Time: 12:00 midnight

[*ON-AIR GRAPHIC:* **DV8 Breaking news**]

[*IMAGE: Chazz is standing somewhere outdoors. Darkness has fallen; a harsh spotlight is aimed at his face, making his hair practically fluorescent. It is not plainly apparent that he is in the desert, and nothing can be seen behind him but more darkness. As far as viewers know, he could be anywhere.*]

Chazz: And we are *live*, America! Apologies to those of you tuning in for *The Perky Paisley Show*—we'll throw over to her if we have time left, but for right now I'm *thrilled* to report an electrifying new development in the *Waste of Space* saga. Here's the situation: Our specially trained Space SWAT Team—led by fan favorite Jamarkus!—just blasted off from our classified launch site as part of a daring rescue mission. In eight and a half minutes this elite squadron of galactic specialists

346

will reach orbiting altitude, dock with the *Laika,* and liberate our intrepid explorers from whatever undoubtedly harrowing situation their journey has become. Join us right now for a very special *Breaking News Edition of Waste of Space,* brought to you by *Soupernova Soups,* as we make history once again. See you in eight and a half minutes! Catchphrase forever!

◼️◀ · · · · · · · · · · · · · · · **OFF–AIR** · · · · · · · · · · · · · · · · · · ·

Item: Transcript of video recording—RAW, UNAIRED FOOTAGE
Source: Camera #3—Lünar Lounge
Time: 12:01 a.m.

[*Bacardi, Snout, Louise, and Clayton huddle around the bullet hole in the glass while Nico holds up the satellite phone for everyone to listen, as Jamarkus has kept the line open.*]

Chazz: [*on the phone*] Annnnd . . . we're out. All right, attention, everyone! We've been staying out of the soundstage's range in case NASAW tries to pick up on our signals, but the time has come to move in. Once we're close enough, we might even be able to establish an uplink with the cameras inside the ship so we can see what's happening in real time. Just to be safe, though, we are going dark until it's officially go time— in exactly eight minutes, when I give the signal to storm the building. Radio silence starts . . . now!

Jamarkus: [*whispering into the phone*] I'll do my best to keep you safe. Good luck.

[*The connection is severed. The kids look at one another, incredulous.*]

Bacardi: Storm the building? That sounds bad.

Clayton: Who cares? They're coming! Finally this waking nightmare will come to the bitter end it deserves!

Louise: But we're not done here yet!

Clayton: Oh yes we are. Didn't you hear him? He said *building*.

[*Louise puts her hands over her ears.*]

Louise: No. No, he didn't.

Clayton: And soundstage.

Louise: [*shaking her head*] No, no . . .

Clayton: Which means we're on *Earth*.

Louise: [*hands over her ears*] No! It's not time! It's *not fair!* [*She flees the room.*]

Source: Camera #8—Bedroom

[*Louise storms into the bedroom. She reaches under her blanket and pulls out her backpack, along with the item she's been using her flashlight to tinker with all along.*]

Louise: [*whispering to herself*] They're ruining *everything*. [*She leaves the bedroom.*]

Source: Camera #3—Lünar Lounge

[*Louise enters the Lünar Lounge.*]

Louise: Look, guys, I've tried to be patient. I've tried to be nice. But certain events have forced my hand.

[*She presents a bulky, plastic-looking green device with a digital clock display, several colored wires, and a triangular antenna sticking out of it.*]

Nico: What's that?

Louise: An FTL drive. I made it.

Clayton: Looks like Nerf made it.

Louise: Shut up!

[*She hits a button on the device. It begins to emit a steady beep, its antenna swiveling merrily as the digital display counts up.*]

Snout: What are you doing?

Louise: I've set our coordinates for the *Interstellar Venture V.* In exactly five minutes, this bad boy will finish charging and blast us across millions of light-years into the ninety-seventh quadrant, where I will finally prove my worth to Lord Balway Galway by hand-delivering him five Earth-human slaves!

[*They gawk at her.*]

Nico: Um. What?

Louise: Nine would have been better. My plan to jam the I QUIT™ button was working perfectly until those stupid eliminations kicked in. [*She tosses her hair.*] No matter. I think he'll still be happy with just you five.

Clayton: As usual, Louise, you are positively overflowing with—

Louise: Shut up! [*grinning*] It's already charging. Ten percent. Won't be long now. Once we reach our destination, the *Venture* will dock with our ship. *They'll* override the airlock, *I'll* escape, and then, as my first act as chief plasma deck engineer in service of Lord Balway Galway, I'll turn *you* awful people into a beautiful gift of captivity!

Clayton: Well, she cracked. For real this time.

[*Louise's grin widens.*]

Louise: Thirty percent.

Item: Transcript of video recording
Source: Dashboard camera, removed from DV8 company van, now in Dr. Emmy's car
Time: 12:03 p.m.

[*IMAGE: Night. Headlights on the road. Camera picks up audio of conversation in car.*]

Dr. Emmy: Is it recording?

Matt: I think so.

Dr. Emmy: Does any of this landscape look familiar?

Matt: Yeah, it does.

Dr. Emmy: Good. Then we're on the right track.

Matt: But promise you won't, like, abandon us there or anything. We already escaped once, I don't want to have to do it again.

Dr. Emmy: I won't. Please take your feet off my dashboard.

Matt: Sorry.

Dr. Emmy: You all right back there, Kaoru?

Kaoru: {I feel as though I have been driving through the desert for weeks.}

Dr. Emmy: Good. Shouldn't be long now. The building should be right about . . .

[*A hush descends.*]

Matt: Oh God. Why are there so many people?

Kaoru: {I see Chazz Young's frosted tips.}

Matt: There's a camera crew and—oh God, a SWAT team! They have guns!

Dr. Emmy: Oh my goodness.

Matt: We have to go stop them!

Dr. Emmy: I—I don't think that's a good idea. Statistically speaking, adding ourselves to the mix will only increase the likelihood of fatalities.

Matt: But our friends are in there! Innocent kids! We have to do something!

Kaoru: {Maybe we should call the police.}

Dr. Emmy: Let me park around back, near those shrubs.

It's not much cover, but it'll have to do. Then I'll . . . I'll sneak around the front. You kids stay in the car.

Matt: Are you sure? You shouldn't have to go in on your own.

Dr. Emmy: I am the adult here. And I am somewhat responsible for you kids. So yes, it has to be me.

Kaoru: {It seems the police are not being called.}

Item: Transcript of video recording—RAW, UNAIRED FOOTAGE
Source: Camera #7—Confessional Closet
Time: 12:05 a.m.

[*Titania sinks down onto the leather stool, defeated. The look she gives the camera is the haunted, desperate look of someone who knows they've lost, the fire all but gone from her eyes.*]

Titania: They're coming.

It's over.

Dammit—

BOOM

[*The same noise that sounded the day before reverberates through the ship.*

Titania stands up.

The fire is back.]

Item: Transcript of video recording—RAW, UNAIRED FOOTAGE
Source: Jamarkus's helmet camera
Time: 12:06 a.m.

[*IMAGE: The shot jolts with Jamarkus's footsteps as he walks toward the soundstage.*]

Jamarkus: Whoa. Did you guys hear that?

Chazz: [*on Jamarkus's radio*] Don't worry about it. Proceed as normal. Do we have eyes inside the ship yet?

DV8 producer: [*on radio*] Yes, uplink to Camera #3 confirmed—that's all we've been able to get so far.

Chazz: [*on radio*] Fine. It'll have to do.

DV8 producer: [*on radio*] Uh, Chazz? Louise is threatening everyone with a . . . a toy or something.

Chazz: [*on radio*] Her personal item? It's a hunk of plastic. The girl's nuts. That's why we cast her.

DV8 producer: [*on radio*] So should we . . .

Chazz: [*on radio*] Proceed as normal.

[*IMAGE: The large steel door of Soundstage G-96. A battering ram swings into the lower part of the frame, building momentum.*]

Jamarkus: Is the camera working, Chazz?

Chazz: [*on radio*] Yes, I can see everything you see.

Jamarkus: Then we're ready to move in.

Chazz: [*on radio*] Excellent. On my signal.

[*pause*]

Chazz: [*on radio*] Go!

[*The battering ram makes contact with the door and dents it substantially. With a few more blows, the door buckles. The shot bounces and jolts as the SWAT team moves into the soundstage.*]

Jamarkus: Everyone freeze!

[*Half a dozen NASAW scientists are gathered around computers set up along the walls. They appear to be mid-celebration, judging by their jubilant expressions—which slide right off their faces the second they see the SWAT team. Wide-eyed, they put their hands in the air.*]

Chazz: [*on radio*] SWAT team, secure them!

Jamarkus: SWAT team, secure them!

[*Jamarkus's helmet camera sweeps around the soundstage, capturing the action as the SWAT team members fan out and restrain the NASAW scientists. Pushed off to an unused corner is the staging-room set, in which the Spacetronauts first got into their spacesuits, plus the remains of a disassembled steel contraption with parts from an airplane cabin.*

Then Jamarkus looks at the ship.]

Jamarkus: Oh my God.

[*At the center of the soundstage is a colossal blocky structure completely shrouded in black fabric, all sitting atop a mechanical apparatus similar to a large-scale motion simulator ride. The far wall behind it is glowing brightly, but from Jamarkus's vantage point, the source of the light is blocked by the ship.*]

Jamarkus: Chazz, something's back there—I can't see what it is—

[*There is a creaking noise. The camera pans back to the busted-in door. Dr. Emmy has snuck inside and flattened herself against the wall, taking in everything with an overwhelmed stare.*]

Jamarkus: Who are you?

Chazz: [*on radio*] Who is she?

Jamarkus: Chazz, what do I do?

Chazz: [*on radio*] I have no idea who that is. Tell her you've got everything under control and to stay where she is.

Jamarkus: We've got everything under control, ma'am. Stay where you are or . . . or I'll shoot!

Chazz: [*on radio*] *Don't* say you're going to—forget it. Keep going!

Item: Transcript of video recording—RAW, UNAIRED FOOTAGE

Source: Camera #3—Lünar Lounge

Time: 12:07 a.m.

[*When the cast hears the Shwump, they panic—then rejoice at the sound of the battering ram.*]

Nico: Did you hear that?

Bacardi: They're coming! Chazz is coming!

Louise: [*fretting about the FTL drive*] No no no! It's only at sixty percent!

Clayton: Oof, tough break. Lord Balway Galway is going to be so disappointed in you.

[*Louise scowls.*]

Item: Transcript of video recording—RAW, UNAIRED FOOTAGE

Source: Jamarkus's helmet camera

Time: 12:07 a.m.

Chazz: [*on radio*] Jamarkus, there should be an entrance to the ship somewhere.

Jamarkus: Okay, but—there's something going on here, Chazz. One of the scientists is all suited up for something—my ears are popping—there's that freaky glow—

Chazz: [*on radio*] Proceed as planned. Get one of the nerds to open the outer airlock door, then go inside and wait for further instructions.

Jamarkus: But—

Chazz: [*on radio*] Do it!

Jamarkus: [*to the closest NASAW scientist*] Open the airlock.

NASAW: But—

Jamarkus: Do it!

[*The scientist hurries to a computer and taps a few keys. The outer airlock door slides open, and Jamarkus leads the SWAT team into position.*]

Jamarkus: Ready, Chazz.

Chazz: [*on radio*] Excellent. Keep the camera trained on the inner airlock door. Going live in three, two . . .

◼️◀️ · · · · · · · · · · · · · · · · ▮ **ON–AIR** ▮ ·

Item: Transcript of video broadcast
Source: *DV8 Breaking News: Waste of Space Edition*, brought to you by Soupernova Soups
Time: 12:08 a.m.

[*Chazz is now standing outdoors with his back to Soundstage G-96's wall. As the wall has no identifying features, once again, he could be anywhere.*]

Chazz: Welcome back, America! It *literally* could not get any more electrifying than this. Jamarkus and SWAT team, what is your status?

Source: Jamarkus's helmet camera

[*IMAGE: Jamarkus is inside the airlock, his helmet camera pointed at the door.*]

Jamarkus: We have successfully docked with the *Laika* and breached the outer airlock door. We are now in position, ready to breach the inner airlock door upon your signal.

Chazz: [*voiceover*] All right, team. It's go time.

Jamarkus: [*pounding on airlock door*] Attention, Spacetronauts! Prepare to be boarded!

DV8 Producer: [*on radio*] Wait! We have a situation here!

Chazz: [*voiceover*] Uh, hold up, Jamarkus. Hold up, America.

[*CUT TO: Stock footage of the* Laika *floating in space*]

▇◀ · · · · · · · · · · · · · · OFF–AIR · · · · · · · · · · · · · · · · · ·

Item: Transcript of video recording—RAW, UNAIRED FOOTAGE
Source: Camera #3—Lünar Lounge
Time: 12:08 a.m.

[*Jamarkus has just banged on the airlock door. Jubilant at the sound of his voice, Nico, Bacardi, and Snout move toward the door, but Louise grabs her backpack, darts out in front of them, and blocks their path.*]

Louise: Okay, new plan.

[*She reaches into her backpack and pulls out Clayton's gun. Everyone flinches and screams, their voices rising and bouncing off the tight walls.*]

Clayton: Fuck.

Louise: Everyone be quiet. And listen. [*with increasingly berserk eyes*] Here's what's going to happen. You're all going to stay perfectly still. You will make no attempt to contact those on the outside. You will make no attempt to facilitate this rescue operation. We are going to stay here until the FTL drive finishes charging so we can blast off to Lord Balway Galway so he can take you all prisoner.

Clayton: Then we're gonna be here for a long-ass time—

Louise: Shut up! [*She aims the gun at him.*]

Nico: Louise. Put the gun down.

Bacardi: [*snorts*] She probably doesn't know how to use it.

Louise: [*with a laugh*] I grew up in rural Idaho. [*She cocks the gun and aims it at Bacardi.*] I sure as heck know how to use it.

Bacardi: But the SWAT team's already here, Louise. They're right outside that door! They're *going* to rescue us. We're *going* to get off the ship.

Louise: Not if you're dead.

Snout: What? That don't make no sense!

Louise: Sure, it does. If you try to escape, I'll shoot.

Snout: But why? You can't give us to Lord Balway Galway if we're dead!

Louise: Actually, I can. All he cares about is conquest. As long as no assets fall into the hands of his enemies, it doesn't matter to him whether his trophies are dead or alive. So either way, I come out on top.

[*The others let that sink in. Then they all begin yelling at once.*]

Clayton: You can't just shoot us!

Nico: Please don't do this, Louise.

Snout: All we wanna do is go home!

Bacardi: And not die!

[*Louise calmly sits on the puffy Püffi chair, keeping the gun trained on the others.*]

Louise: Then you better not leave this ship.

Item: Transcript of video recording—RAW, UNAIRED FOOTAGE
Source: Remote DV8 film crew
Time: 12:09 a.m.

Chazz: [*whispering to offscreen producer*] What's wrong?

DV8 producer: [*offscreen*] Louise pulled Clayton's gun.

Chazz: *What?*

DV8 producer: She's saying that if anyone comes in, she'll start shooting. The SWAT team needs to stand down.

Chazz: No way! They're already in the airlock!

DV8 producer: But they're not a real SWAT team! They don't have real ammo!

Chazz: Maybe they'll scare her into surrendering—

DV8 producer: No, Chazz. This is getting out of control. You need to stop this.

Chazz: Yeah. I suppose I could stop it.

[*pause*]

Chazz: Or I could film it.

Item: Transcript of video recording—RAW, UNAIRED FOOTAGE

Source: Camera #7—Confessional Closet

Time: 12:09 a.m.

[*Titania is seeking an exit strategy, looking like a caged animal as her frantic eyes dart around the room. She puts her hands into the satellite phone's hidden compartment, digging into the crevice, pawing desperately.*]

Titania: Keep moving. Keep exploring.

Source: Camera #3—Lünar Lounge

Time: 12:10 a.m.

[*Louise is perched on the puffy Püffi chair, aiming the gun at Bacardi, Nico, and Snout. Clayton is doubled over in pain. All four of them watch her, wary, while she recites the Gavinjian Pledge of Allegiance.*]

Louise: . . . to the interstellar banner of the United Galactic Federation of Gavinjia . . .

Nico: [*whispering to the others*] Why isn't the SWAT team coming in? They're not going to let her shoot us, are they?

Bacardi: They will if it's good television.

Snout: Cripes.

Bacardi: [*inhales sharply*] Look.

[*She nods her head toward the hallway. The Gila monster is waddling into the room, looking peeved.*]

Snout: [*studying the Gila monster*] I have an idea. You two step aside.

Bacardi: I hate to break this to you, Snout, but gun beats Gila monster. Every time.

Snout: All due respect, ma'am, but I've been wrestling hogs since before I could walk. I know what I'm doing.

Nico: But if it's venomous—

Snout: I'm not gonna hurt her.

Bacardi: Who? Louise or the lizard?

Snout: Both. Neither.

Louise: . . . and to the republic—that word doesn't mean the same thing to the Gavinjians as it does to us, but there isn't an equivalent, so I'm using it here for simplicity—for which the tentacled vegetation stands—

[*Snout dives at the floor, scoops up the Gila monster in his arms, and charges at Louise. Perplexed, the Gila monster opens its mouth wide in a furious hiss. Snout plunges its teeth into the puffy Püffi chair, which starts to deflate with staggering speed. Louise, caught in the folds of the collapsing fur and fabric, flails about, distracted. Bacardi leaps forward, wrestles the gun out of Louise's hand, and points it at her head.*]

Bacardi: Stand up!

[*Louise stands up. She is red-faced, furious, snarling.*]

Louise: You're *really* going to regret that.

Bacardi: I regret that the puffy chair is ruined. I do not regret disarming you, and I guarantee I never will.

[*Louise stands there, huffing and growing ever angrier until, quietly, she begins to cry. For a moment, there is no sound but that of her sniffling. When she speaks, it is barely picked up by the microphones.*]

Louise: All I wanted was a different life.

[*Bacardi lowers the gun slightly.*]

Bacardi: Honey, that's all any of us wanted.

Source: Camera #7—Confessional Closet
Time: 12:11 a.m.

[*Finding nothing inside the satellite phone compartment, Titania withdraws her hands—then, compelled by an idea, feels around again. Using the edge she'd exposed by removing the soundproof panel, she pries another panel out of place.*

And another.]

Source: Camera #4—Lünar Lounge
Time: 12:11 a.m.

[*Bacardi crosses to the airlock door and knocks on it.*]

Bacardi: All clear, Jamarkus! Come on in! [*to Nico*] Go get Titania.

Source: Camera #7—Confessional Closet
Time: 12:11 a.m.

[*Nico appears in the doorway of the Confessional Closet with a giant smile.*

It fades when he sees what's inside: a pile of wooden soundproofing tiles on the floor, and a cavernous hole in the wall.]

Nico: Titania?

[*Warily he removes his GoPro from his pocket, turns it on, and aims the lens at the hole.*]

Item: Transcript of video recording
Source: Nico's camera
Battery charge: 5%
Time: 12:11 a.m.

[*Shaky footage as Nico's leg enters the frame, kicking into the empty void.*]

Nico: Guys! There's a passage!

[*more shaky footage as he stoops to fit inside the cavity, holding the camera as upright as he can—then, darkness as he creeps inside.*]

Item: Transcript of video recording—RAW, UNAIRED FOOTAGE
Source: Camera #4—Lünar Lounge
Time: 12:11 a.m.

[*Offscreen, Nico yells, "There's a passage!" Eyes flock to the hallway. Taking swift advantage of the diversion, Louise grabs the gun back from Bacardi.*]

Bacardi: Shit.

Louise: [*fully unglued now*] Did he say passage?

[*She storms out of the lounge, gun steadily aimed forward.*]

🎥 • • • • • • • • • • • • • • • **ON-AIR** • • • • • •

Item: Transcript of video broadcast *ce Edition,*
Source: *DV8 Breaking News: Waste*
brought to you by *Soupernova Sou*

Time: 12:12 a.m.

    Chazz: Welcome back, America! We now go live to Jamarkus and the Space SWAT Team, about to enter the *Laika!*

Source: Jamarkus's Helmet Cam

    [*The airlock door opens. Snout and Bacardi are just inside, terrified.*]

    Jamarkus: Get into the airlock!

    [*They do as he says. Jamarkus pushes past them into the Lünar Lounge and sees Clayton banging on the glass.*]

    Clayton: I'm trapped! Get me out of here!

    Jamarkus: Chazz?

    Chazz: [*voiceover*] Do it!

    [*Clayton ducks out of the way as Jamarkus fires a few shots into the glass, which shatters.*]

    Jamarkus: [*helping Clayton out of the hot tub*] Where are the rest?

    Clayton: I don't know. A passage or something. [*pointing at the floor*] Watch out for the Gila monster.

    Jamarkus: [*hopping over it*] What the—!

OFF-AIR

    Item: T▊ript of video recording
    Source: ▊ camera
    Battery c▊ 4%
    Time: 12:1▊

    [IMAGE: ▊arkness. Nico is attempting to narrate what's happer▊t his speech is halting and breathless, *and he is periodically interrupted by the swishing noise of drapery.*]

Nico: I think I'm—I'm between the exterior wall of the ship and some kind of heavy fabric—I can't see anything—

[*There is a muffled commotion behind Nico; Louise has entered the cloth-cloaked passage and is hot on his heels. But Nico doesn't seem to pay her much attention, focused as he is on moving forward.*]

Nico: [*in a whisper*] Titania? Are you in here?

📹 ◀ · · · · · · · · · · · · **ON-AIR** · · · · · · · · · · · · · · · ·

Item: Transcript of video broadcast
Source: *DV8 Breaking News: Waste of Space Edition,* brought to you by *Soupernova Soups*
Time: 12:12 a.m.

[*Shaky footage as Jamarkus makes his way through the Lünar Lounge, down the hall, and into the Confessional Closet. The camera pauses on the pile of panels on the floor, then pans up to the dark hole of the passage.*]

[*There is half a second of silence as everyone realizes what he's looking at: an escape tunnel.*]

Chazz: [*on radio, to DV8 producer*] Cut away. Cut away!

[*CUT TO: Stock footage of the* Laika *floating in space*]

📹 ◀ · · · · · · · · · · · · · **OFF-AIR** · · · · · · · · · · · · · · · ·

Item: Transcript of video recording—RAW, UNAIRED FOOTAGE
Source: Jamarkus's helmet camera

Jamarkus: What do I do?

Chazz: [*on radio*] Follow them!

[*The screen goes dark as Jamarkus enters the hole; rustling noises are heard as he progresses through the passage.*]

[*Shots are fired up ahead of him.*]

Chazz: [*on radio*] Were those gunshots?

Jamarkus: I think so—

[*There is another **BOOM***

*and a **SSSHHHWWUUUUMMMP***

*and a **FLLLLRRRRRRRRRRX***

and a **WWWWWHHHHHHSSSSSSK**]

[*All cameras stop recording.*]

Item: Transcript of video recording—RAW, UNAIRED FOOTAGE
Source: Jamarkus's helmet camera
Time: 12:13 a.m.

[*When the camera turns back on, the image is still one of darkness; Jamarkus is still in the tunnel.*]

Chazz: [*on radio*] Show me what's happening! Turn on your night vision!

[*The darkness gives way to a night-vision image. Up ahead is Louise, cast in a neon green light. She looks back at Jamarkus, her eyes hot white spots.*]

Jamarkus: [*yelling at Louise*] Give me the gun!

Louise: [*raising her empty hands*] I dropped it!

Jamarkus: Then get back into the ship!

[*Louise obeys, scrambling past him out of the shot. He keeps moving forward, picking up her dropped gun on the way. He finds Nico half hanging out of a gap in the fabric tunnel, light streaming in through the aperture. Jamarkus grabs Nico's leg and drags him inside. Before the cloth slides back into place and the light fades away, Nico can be seen going limp, clutching his camera to his chest.*]

Chazz: [*on radio*] Jamarkus—status?

Jamarkus: Nico is secure.

Chazz: [*on radio*] What about the cameras?

DV8 Producer: [*on radio*] Coming back online now.

Chazz: [*on radio*] Back to Camera #3!

———————————————————

Item: Transcript of video broadcast
Source: *DV8 Breaking News: Waste of Space Edition*, brought to you by Soupernova Soups
Time: 12:13 a.m.
Source: Camera #3—Lünar Lounge

[*Jamarkus walks in from the hallway with Nico thrown over his shoulder. He takes him through the Lünar Lounge and toward the airlock, where Snout, Bacardi, Clayton, and Louise are waiting.*]

Jamarkus: Chazz, what are your orders?

Chazz: [*voiceover*] Get them out of there!

Jamarkus: What about Titania?

[*Jamarkus looks at Nico. His face is pale, his expression blank.*]

Jamarkus: Chazz?

[*pause*]

Chazz: [*voiceover*] Leave her.

Jamarkus: Roger that. Departing *Laika* now. Over and out.

[*He pulls Nico into the airlock. The inner door closes.*]

Item: Transcript of video recording—RAW, UNAIRED FOOTAGE
Source: Camera #1—Airlock
Time: 12:14 a.m.

[*The five remaining Spacetronauts, plus Jamarkus, are now sealed alone in the airlock. They look at Nico.*]

Snout: What happened to Titania?

[*Nico ignores him; he's looking down at his GoPro.*]

Nico: [*quietly*] One percent left.

Bacardi: Louise? What happened?

Louise: [*bitterly, without looking at any of them*] I shot the gun in her direction, through the opening in the curtain. But I didn't see what was out there.

Snout: Nico, what about you? Did you record anything?

[*Nico looks up at them. He opens his mouth to tell them, hesitates, and lies instead.*]

Nico: No. [*He lowers the camera.*] Battery died.

[*The outer airlock door opens.*]

Item: Transcript of video recording—RAW, UNAIRED FOOTAGE
Source: Jamarkus's helmet camera
Time: 12:14 a.m.

[*The six Spacetronauts walk out into the soundstage. Members of the SWAT team are waiting for them, looking bewildered.*]

Jamarkus: What happened? Where are the scientists?

SWAT Team Member #3: When that shwumpy noise happened—it was really loud and scary, so we sort of lost our grips on them and they sort of . . . got away.

Jamarkus: Got *away*? Where is there to go?

Item: Transcript of video recording
Source: Dashboard camera, in Dr. Emmy's car
Time: 12:14 a.m.

[*IMAGE: An idling helicopter, sitting outside the soundstage. A figure clad in a white lab coat and clutching a laptop dives into the cabin, helped inside by more lab-coated figures who had previously boarded. Once all of them are secure, the helicopter departs.]*

Item: Transcript of video recording—RAW, UNAIRED FOOTAGE
Source: Jamarkus's helmet camera
Time: 12:15 a.m.

[*Jamarkus continues to sweep his camera around the soundstage. The woman who entered is still cowering against the wall. The SWAT team is looking at the area that had previously been glowing but no longer is. Nico joins them. All of NASAW's laptops are gone. Suddenly a high-pitched squeal echoes off the barren steel of the soundstage.*]

Snout: Colonel Bacon!

[*The pig trots over to Snout, who sweeps him into a fierce embrace. Louise folds her arms and stares at the floor. Nico turns his GoPro back on and watches the footage he just shot, while Bacardi picks up a pencil from one of the desks.*]

Bacardi: [*reading the pencil's inscription*] Property of NASAW, the—

[*She stops short. Clayton, shivering and sweating, takes a step forward to look, but doubles over in pain.*]

Clayton: The what?

[*Bacardi swallows.*]

Bacardi: The National Association for the Search for Atmospheric Wormholes.

Item: Transcript of video recording
Source: Nico's camera

Battery charge: 1%
Time: 12:12 a.m.

[Out of the darkness, a faint glow of light. Nico crawls toward the end of the tunnel and maneuvers his camera through the panel opening.

For one frame—

For one-thirtieth of a second—

There are five scientists standing in a large, open soundstage.

All of them are looking at the soundstage wall.

At the massive, impossible thing set into the soundstage wall.

At the circle of light, glowing brilliantly, blindingly, brighter than the sun.

And the girl walking into it.]

[Video cuts to static.]

PART FOUR

FOUR

POST-PRODUCTION

Item: Online article
Source: ViralLoad
Date: February 19, 2016

I am literally speechless.

I've been staring at my computer screen for hours, trying to process what happened.

Because what happened was complete . . . and utter . . . GREATNESS.

Part of me thinks we've been wrong about Chazz Young this entire time. We've always thought of him as shallow and Hollywood and unpredictable and ridiculous, but with occasional bursts of genius. Now, though, I think he's ALL genius.

I mean, that ending! How many run-of-the-mill reality shows can you think of that ended with a Gila monster, a SWAT team raid, and a missing person?

And who among us MILLIONS AND MILLIONS OF VIEWERS would have thought, as we were glued to it LIVE, that everyone would survive and land safely back on Earth?

Certainly not me.

But that's what happened.

Chazz Young ----------------------->

YOU'RE A GODDAMNED

...IG

Item: Transcript of video recording
Source: *The Perky Paisley Show*
Date: February 22, 2016

Perky: America, I'm not going to waste any time this evening—we want to get straight to our guests. Everyone please give a warm, back-to-Earth welcome to Chazz Young, Clayton Young, Aliya "Bacardi" Kolesnikova, Jamarkus Curbeam, Louise Evans, James "Snout" Whitson, and of course, Colonel Bacon!

[*The cast members emerge from behind a curtain. All dressed up, they wave to the audience and make their way toward the six director's chairs that have replaced the lip couch. They each take their seats. Colonel Bacon, wearing a bow tie, plops down in front of Perky's desk. The audience laughs.*]

Perky: I think I speak for all of America when I say that *Waste Space* was, by far, one of the most pioneering, innovative, and groundbreaking events in television history. Do we all agree?

[*The audience goes wild.*]

Chazz: Thank you, Perky. I'm quite proud of it myself.

Perky: How did you pull it off, Chazz?

Chazz: Well, I can't take all the credit. At least a small percentage must go to our intrepit explorers.

Perky: Of course, our beloved Spacetronauts! We are overjoyed to have you all back on Earth, safe and sound. Guys, what were you thinking during that last insane day?

374

[*Through their enormous smiles, each cast member glances warily at Chazz before speaking. Chazz's smile doesn't falter for a second.*]

Snout: I was scared out of my muffin! But I had a feeling good old Chazz would come and rescue us.

Bacardi: Never doubted it for a second.

Perky: Of course! None of us did! And Louise—you sure had us worried there for a minute, waving around that phony gun!

Louise: [*giggles*] I know. Sorry. I—[*looks at Chazz*] it turns out I was coming down with a bad case of the space pox, just like Matt and Kaoru. But my symptoms manifested as a type of space-induced psychosis, which explains why I was so out of my head.

Perky: Explains it perfectly! Clayton, I understand you were felled by the pox too—a far more severe case, in fact. That was so amazing, what you did—quarantining yourself in the hot-tub room to keep the others from getting infected! What sacrifice! You're a hero!

Clayton: Thanks, Perky. I just did what I had to do.

Perky: What were you thinking when you made that impossible choice?

Clayton: I guess I decided that I didn't want to die hundreds of miles above my home planet for nothing. That I owed it to my fellow Spacetronauts to get them back to Earth alive, even if I didn't make it out myself.

[*huge round of applause*]

Perky: Amazing. You're all so amazing. And how's Colonel Bacon doing?

Snout: Real good, Perky, thanks for asking! Poor thing somehow burrowed into the innards of the spaceship, found the sewage container, and was happily eating the Meteor Chowder that Clayton flushed down the toilet!

[*The audience lets out a collective "awww."*]

Snout: Look at him! He's tickled pink to be back!

[*The audience chants, "Brought Home the Bacon, Brought Home the Bacon!"*]

Perky: Well, I don't want to keep you heroes too long—I understand you're all heading back home to your families tomorrow for some much-needed rest and recuperation. But before you go, I'd like to know: What does the future hold for each of you? Clayton?

Clayton: I'm glad you asked, Perk. The super-generous people at DV8 have offered me my own reality dating show. We start filming in a few weeks, and I couldn't be more pumped. Be on the lookout for the premiere of *Matin' with Clayton*, coming this fall, only to DV8!

[*applause*]

Perky: Wouldn't miss it! Snout, what about you?

Snout: Oh, me and Colonel Bacon are going straight home to our farm—which will stay in our family's possession for generations to come, thanks to a super-generous donation from DV8!

[*applause*]

Perky: Yee-haw! And you, Bacardi?

Bacardi: I could tell you, Perky, but then I'd have to kill you.

[*laughter*]

Perky: Aw, come on! How about a hint?

Bacardi: Let's just say that the super-generous folks at DV8 may or may not have managed to pull a few strings, and that I may or may not have snagged a cybersecurity internship with a certain governmental agency.

[*Audience ooohs.*]

Perky: That sounds so cool, whatever it is.

Bacardi: Only my dream job. Hope they let me wear my space bra!

[*She yanks her shirt up to display her bra to the crowd, which goes wild.*]

Perky: And Jamarkus, I understand your next steps are also academic in nature?

Jamarkus: That's right, Perky. I'll be attending MIT next fall with a full scholarship, thanks to the super-generous folks at DV8.

Perky: Fantastic. And last but never least—Louise? What's next for you?

Louise: [*practically bursting*] I'VE BEEN GIVEN A ROLE IN THE NEXT *COSMIC CRUSADES* MOVIE!

Perky: Unbelievable! Sounds like we've got happy endings all around, huh Chazz?

Chazz: That's exactly right. [*He makes brief eye contact with each of the Spacetronauts.*] And we hope it'll stay that way.

[*They smile harder.*]

Perky: Now, unfortunately, we're missing a few familiar faces here. Can you give us some updates on those who weren't able to be with us this evening? How are Matt and Kaoru?

Chazz: I'm pleased to report that both Matt and Kaoru have made full recoveries from their brushes with illness. Kaoru has already returned home to Japan, and Matt—well, Matt, if you'll recall, was always a bit high-strung—

Perky: He sure was!

Chazz: So we all decided—the DV8 staff and Matt—that it might be best for him to head to an all-expenses-paid stay at the world-famous Esalen coastal retreat in Big Sur, California. Hot springs, massages, yoga, burritos—everything the dear boy will need to make a full recovery.

Perky: Aw, that's so sweet of you!

Chazz: It is.

Perky: And where's Nico?

Chazz: Nico has returned home to New York.

Perky: And? No scholarships for him? No extraordinary new opportunities?

Chazz: [*shifting in his seat*] This is somewhat awkward to talk about, Perky, but as I'm sure many of you have heard, it turns out that Nico actually *forged* his guardian's signature on the release form, making his appearance on *Waste of Space* all kinds of illegal.

Perky: What?!

Chazz: Yeah, he's practically a felon. We did our due diligence, of course, but there's only so much you can do to prevent fame-hungry exhibitionists from crashing the party. If people have it in their heads that they're going to lie, cheat, and bully their way onto reality shows, they're going to find a way to do it.

Perky: Wow.

Chazz: So Nico, for all intents and purposes, is no longer considered a cast member of *Waste of Space.* We'd strike him from the record if we could, but that's impossible to do when you've got such a *monster* hit on your hands!

[*wild applause*]

Perky: Great! So Nico's dead to us. And lastly, the million-dollar question: *Where* is Titania?

[*Chazz theatrically pulls at his collar.*]

Chazz: In order to explain what happened to Titania, I'm afraid I'm going to have to pull back the curtain a bit, take you behind the scenes and into the secrets of the production of *Waste of Space*. Spoiler alert!

[*The audience laughs.*]

Chazz: We'd originally planned, a few more weeks down the road, to reveal that there was in fact an escape pod onboard the *Laika,* and that the first Spacetronaut to find it would be able to race home to claim a huge prize. But since the show got cut short, we never got a chance to offer the opportunity to our Spacetronauts. Titania, however—enterprising young lady that she is—sniffed it out on her own and successfully left the *Laika* only minutes before Jamarkus and the Space SWAT Team arrived!

Perky: Oh my God. So where is she now?

Chazz: I'm afraid that's another sad story, Perky. Turns out that Titania *also* forged her parents' signatures, but for a very different reason. She was a runaway. Her family didn't know she was going to be on the show. Titania wasn't even her real name.

Perky: You're kidding.

Chazz: Nope. In fact, DV8 enlisted the help of Hibiscus and the good folks at Fakefinders to find her, and I'm proud to report that . . . they did!

[*The audience gasps.*]

Chazz: However, out of respect for her privacy, we've decided not to release any statements regarding her current whereabouts. She does not want to be found by her family or anyone else, and we plan to honor that.

Perky: That is extraordinarily noble of you, Chazz. [*looking into the camera*] Titania, wherever you are, we wish you the best of luck.

[*polite applause*]

Perky: I think that about wraps it up! Thank you so much, all of you, for talking with us, for your bravery in times of interstellar strife, and for your service to this country. And Chazz, thank you for bringing this exquisite, unforgettable show to life. How can I ever repay you?

Chazz: I can think of a few ways.

Perky: Until next time, folks—say it with me, everyone— Catchphrase Forever!

━━━━━ ··················· **OFF-AIR** ··················

Item: Fire Incident Report
Source: http://inciweb.nwcg.gov/
Date: March 3, 2016

Incident Type: Wildfire

Cause: Lightning

Date of Origin: February 20, 2016

Time of Origin: 12:20 a.m

Time of Report: 1:56 a.m.

Location: 90 miles southwest of Socorro, NM

Incident Description: Remnants of large abandoned building. Possible warehouse. Fire 95 percent extinguished at time of discovery. Remains of some electrical equipment, a bit of charred Styrofoam, and a battering ram. Some tire tracks and footprints around perimeter, but no human remains found.

Item: Transcript of audio recording
Source: Dr. Carla Emmy interview
Date: March 6, 2016

Dr. Emmy: Hello?

Intern: Hi, is this Dr. ███████?

Dr. Emmy: It is.

Intern: Great, it's nice to put a face to the email. And don't worry, I'll be changing your name for the official report. Do you mind if I record this phone call, solely for the purposes of transcription?

Dr. Emmy: Go right ahead.

Intern: Thank you. So I'd like to jump right in, if I could?

Dr. Emmy: Certainly.

Intern: I'm going to skip over the details of your interactions with Matt and Kaoru—those meetings seem fairly straightforward. Although I did wonder—why would you record those in the first place?

Dr. Emmy: Old habits, I'm afraid. I've always tended to get carried away during brainstorming and research sessions, so I long ago got in the habit of recording conversations with my colleagues so that I can go back and listen to them later, to catch anything I may have missed or forgotten.

Intern: Got it. So what I mostly want to talk about is what you saw in the soundstage that night. As far as I can tell, you are the only independent witness to the events that occurred inside that building. Everyone else was either an employee of DV8—none of whom will talk to me—or a member of NASAW— who have all disappeared. So you can imagine how significant your account is.

Dr. Emmy: On condition of anonymity, of course.

Intern: Yes, of course. I first have a few follow-up questions about the timeline you emailed me. Thank you for outlining the events so precisely, by the way.

Dr. Emmy: Again, old habits die hard. As soon as I was able, I wrote down the events in the order in which they occurred, in bullet-point format.

Intern: Yes. Very scientific.

Item: Email

To: ███████████████████████████████

From: ███████████████████████████████

Date: March 4, 2016

- I parked on the eastern side of the building, about two hundred feet away.

- After instructing Matt and Kaoru to stay in the car, I approached the building and began to circle it. As I got closer, I could hear a strange hum, followed by a loud, booming noise.

- Along the north-facing wall was a man with brightly colored hair and a small crew filming him, so I chose to walk around to the south.

- As I rounded the southwest corner, I observed that the west-facing wall had bowed inward, as if sucked in by a suction cup.

- I entered through the only door, in the northwest corner. It had been broken in by a battering ram, which lay on the floor. Inside was an enormous structure covered by a black curtain, and several desks and laptops against the walls of the building. SWAT team members were restraining several people wearing lab coats.

- A young man in a SWAT team uniform briefly questioned me, then instructed me to stay out of the way. As he was carrying a rather large rifle, I was inclined to obey. I stayed put against the northern wall and witnessed the rest of the events from there. The young man then entered the structure.

- A large, glowing circle was growing rapidly across the surface of the western wall of the building. Because of my acute angle, I could not see what, if anything, was inside it.

- A girl, roughly eighteen years of age, emerged from a slit in the black curtain. Once she fully exited the structure, she proceeded to walk across the floor toward the west-facing wall, while the men and women in lab coats screamed for her to stop. A boy, also roughly eighteen years of age, then appeared in the curtain's opening. He held a camera in his hand and filmed the scene as it unfolded.

- The girl continued walking toward the wall. Just as she was about to meet it, another loud noise sounded, and a bright, blinding light flashed. I was forced to avert my eyes. When the light subsided, the glowing circle in the wall remained, but the girl was gone—and a live pig had appeared.

- The scientists broke out into raucous shouting—some seemed pleased, while others were horrified. The SWAT team, disoriented by the light and noise, lowered their guns. The pig ran around the room, squealing.

- Another girl, roughly fourteen years of age, appeared in the curtain's slit. She shoved the boy aside, aimed a gun at the glowing circle, and fired several shots at it.

- The circle began to shrink at a steady rate. Within five seconds it closed completely and disappeared.

- Taking advantage of the SWAT team's bewilderment, the people in lab coats broke free from their captors, swept their laptops off the desks, gathered up the rest of their equipment, and fled the building.

- Both the boy and the younger girl disappeared back into the curtain's folds. About a minute later, they, along with four other teenagers, emerged from the boxy structure. The SWAT team hurried them out of the warehouse door, leaving me as the last person inside the building.

- When I exited the building, I saw the SWAT team pushing the children into a pair of windowless vans, and a helicopter receding into the distance. The vans drove away.

- When I returned to the car, Matt and Kaoru were no longer there.

- As I drove off, I noticed a shifty-looking man lingering around the perimeter of the building.

Item: Transcript of audio recording
Source: Dr. Carla Emmy interview [continued]

Intern: That man was Boris, one of DV8's contracted employees. I believe he set fire to the building shortly thereafter, on Chazz's orders. So any evidence we could have hoped to recover has been destroyed.

Dr. Emmy: That's quite a pity.

Intern: Agreed. Though it's also a blessing, in a way—not long after he set the fire, a group of loosely aligned people called the Fakefinders arrived on-site. Have you heard of them?

Dr. Emmy: I heard them mentioned on the news. They're the ones who called the fire department, correct?

Intern: Yes, and let's be thankful that's all they did. I can't imagine what kind of new lies and rumors would have been spread if any of that evidence had fallen into their hands.

Dr. Emmy: Indeed.

Intern: And you do know by now that crew members from DV8 found Matt and Kaoru, correct? Apparently Matt had decided to get out of the van and poke around, Kaoru went after him, and then DV8 took them along with the others when they left?

Dr. Emmy: Yes, I heard something to that effect. I hope they're all right.

Intern: Oh, I'm sure they've been rewarded handsomely. Chazz Young takes excellent care of his witnesses.

[*pause*]

Intern: Doctor, what do you think really happened that night? What do you think that glowing circle was?

[*Dr. Emmy clears her throat.*]

Dr. Emmy: I'd prefer not to venture a guess, if you don't mind.

Intern: Why not?

Dr. Emmy: Because what I think doesn't matter if there's no proof to back it up.

Intern: Is that why you prefer to remain anonymous in this investigation?

Dr. Emmy: Yes. The things I saw that day—I can't prove them. Science is rooted in proof. I am a well-respected scholar in my field, and making claims such as these—it wouldn't look good for me, is all.

Intern: But you maintain that these events did in fact happen.

Dr. Emmy: Yes. And to be fully honest . . . there are a few more points that should be on that list that aren't. But as a woman of science, I just couldn't bring myself to type them.

Intern: Can you tell me what they are?

[*pause*]

Dr. Emmy: Earlier in the account I mentioned that the west-facing wall had bowed inward.

Intern: Right.

Dr. Emmy: When I left the building, after everything had transpired and I was the only one left—aside from the shifty man, who I didn't notice until later, as I was driving away—I made sure to walk past the west-facing wall once again. And . . .

Intern: Yes?

Dr. Emmy: It was no longer concave at that point.

Intern: I see.

Dr. Emmy: And there were no bullet holes in it. Of course, the absence of bullet holes does not automatically indicate a— a portal of some kind. It's possible that the gun was firing blanks—

Intern: Though we have reason to believe that it wasn't, as it previously shot two holes inside the ship.

Dr. Emmy: I see.

Intern: Anything else?

Dr. Emmy: Well, good heavens, where did that pig come from? It made such a racket; if it had been there before the flash of light, I would have noticed it. But it appeared so suddenly, as if out of thin . . .

[*She trails off.*]

There is . . . one last thing. As I said earlier, I found plenty of footprints in the sand around the other three walls of the building. And—

[*pause*]

This is the one that keeps me up at night.

[*pause*]

I will swear to my dying day that I watched that girl walk through that wall. But there wasn't . . .

[She sighs.]

There wasn't a single footprint on the other side.

_____

Only one piece of evidence remains to be parsed: the last minute of footage that Nico recorded with his personal camera.

When the windowless vans returned to Los Angeles, Chazz Young released all the Spacetronauts—except for Nico. Nico, he interrogated for several hours. That interview, regrettably for Nico and fortunately for DV8, was not recorded.

When DV8 finally let him go, Nico headed straight for the media—but DV8 got there first, preemptively releasing the news that Nico had applied to the show under false pretenses, and that any statements he would try to make on the matter should be considered too libelous and inflammatory to confirm as true.

From that point on, Nico refused to talk to DV8, the media, or anyone else—not about the show, not about the other cast members, and not about the contents of his recording. He was not willing to cooperate with any of DV8's requests and did not accept any of DV8's super-generous offers.

And so they disowned him, dragged his name through the mud, and threw him under the bus.

_____

Item: Transcript of audio recording
Source: Nico interview
Date: June 30, 2016

    Intern: Do you mind if I record this?

Nico: Kind of. It's nothing personal. I'm just more careful about that stuff now.

Intern: Understandable. Tell you what—if you're uncomfortable with anything that's said, I'll delete the recording once we're done chatting. Promise. You can watch me do it.

Nico: Okay.

Intern: So I wanted to start by asking—

Nico: Hang on. You look familiar. Were you—do you work for DV8?

Intern: I did. But I don't anymore.

Nico: You gave me a bottle of water right before they taped the promo interviews, when I was all nervous and sweaty.

Intern: [*uneasy laugh*] Yes, that was me. I was hoping you didn't remember.

Nico: It's okay. You were only doing your job. I remember you because you seemed nice. You didn't seem like anyone else at DV8.

Intern: Thank you. You have no idea how much of a compliment that is.

Nico: Weren't you also the one who convinced them to let me bring my camera onboard?

Intern: Yes.

Nico: Thanks for that.

Intern: You're welcome. And thank *you* for agreeing to talk to me. None of the other cast members would.

Nico: That doesn't surprise me.

Intern: It didn't surprise me, either. The deals that Chazz struck with them must have encompassed the harshest nondisclosure agreements DV8's lawyers could devise.

[*pause*]

Intern: You must be pissed about that.

Nico: I'm not, actually. I don't resent them at all. We went through hell out there, all in the name of entertainment and product placement and ratings—seems the least DV8 could do is give them everything they ever wanted.

Intern: *You* didn't take any deals.

Nico: I already got what I wanted.

Intern: Must have taken some serious balls to reject Chazz like that.

Nico: I guess.

Intern: What about Hibiscus? You know that part was untrue, right? Chazz never recruited her or the Fakefinders to track Titania down. The opposite, in fact—he gave them an enormous sum of money *not* to look for her, and to keep their mouths shut.

Nico: Yeah, I know.

Intern: That doesn't bother you either?

Nico: No.

Intern: [*letting out a noise of disbelief*] I gotta say, Nico—you're a saint.

Nico: Nah. I just think the other cast members are good people, more or less.

Intern: Less, in the case of Clayton.

Nico: But even Clayton was in search of something bigger than himself. Louise too. Who would have guessed she'd be right about underground organizations developing wormholes? I mean, except for the lizard-people thing.

Intern: [*laughing*] Technically, we can't rule that out, since we still can't find any traces of NASAW's existence. They wiped themselves clean. They've got a lot to answer for too.

Nico: I'm not mad at them, either. Louise, Clayton,

NASAW—none of them were the enemy. DV8 was the enemy. Chazz Young was the enemy. They're the ones I'm mad at. The rest—I'm happy for them. Honestly.

[*pause*]

Intern: How are you doing, Nico?

Nico: I'm okay.

Intern: Really, though? It just seems like it'd be such a tough transition back to civilian life.

Nico: [*small laugh*] Once the hype finally died down, things got better. The world moved on, and so did I. Things are better at home, even. I worked hard to make sure of that. So yes, really. I really am okay.

Intern: That's remarkable, given what you've been through.

Nico: I guess it gave me a new perspective on things.

Intern: Oh?

Nico: Yeah. As awful as it was, and how it ended, and what happened to—[*He breaks off, then clears his throat.*] It was still a thing that I decided to do. I did it on my own, I powered through, and I came out the other side. I hadn't ever—

That was a big deal for me. I was always so scared of everything. Now, not so much. Now, I feel more . . .

More.

[*pause*]

But . . . I'm scared about this. What you're proposing, this book idea. No one's going to believe me.

Intern: I do. And I'm going to make the rest of the world believe too.

Nico: How? All the evidence is gone. Everything burned up in the fire.

Intern: Everything did burn up in the fire. Except for the server, the one that stored all the video files recorded on the ship—before *and* after the signal loss.

Nico: What?

Intern: Remember: Chazz Young is an exceedingly insecure, exceedingly paranoid man, with backup plans and bargaining chips always at the ready. He'd never give up all that footage, not when he could use it as leverage at some point in the future.

Nico: [*incredulous*] Chazz took the server?

Intern: Boris took the server. Chazz instructed him to retrieve it before setting the fire, as his final assignment as an employee of DV8. Boris didn't take too well to getting fired again, and three months later the server arrived at my house, along with a few personal dashboard camera video files and a note that said, "Chazz thinks it's better to be dead than look bad. So make him look *real* bad."

Nico: Wow.

Intern: Which, it turns out, isn't hard to do when you're dealing with a guy who records all his cell phone conversations and takes no precautions to protect them from hackers. All I had to do was call in a favor to Bacardi, and, long story short, I'm now in the possession of every conversation Chazz had on that phone. Add that to the couple of videos Titania recorded on her own cell—which we confiscated and never gave back—and I've got everything I need. Everything but the very last piece of the puzzle.

[*pause*]

Intern: I know this is a lot to ask, but . . . let me see what's on your camera, Nico. Let me watch the footage you shot onboard the *Laika*. Combined with the other evidence I've been compiling over the past four months, it should be enough to convince the skeptics that what happened that day was real.

[*Nico swallows.*]

Nico: How do I know I can trust you?

Intern: Because I'm scared too. And I bet Titania was scared when she did what she did.

The truth is, Nico: everyone is scared of everything. All the time. But we do what we have to do anyway. And what you and I have to do is tell the world about what she did.

[*pause*]

[*rustling noises as Nico reaches into his bag*]

Nico: Okay. Take it. Everything's on there. From my audition to the . . . end.

Intern: Thank you, Nico. I hope—

[*pause*]

Intern: I hope you really did get what you wanted.

[*He thinks about this.*]

Nico: She was all about escape, you know? For her, it was forward. But for me, it was back. Back home, to make things better. So, yeah. I got what I wanted.

Intern: Do you think she did?

Nico: I know she did.

[*pause*]

Intern: Maybe she'll come back. Like Colonel Bacon.

Nico: Yeah. Maybe.

[*background noise as he starts to leave—then a sudden backtracking of steps*]

Nico: Wait—there's another message to my Mom and Dad on there that I recorded after everything, when I got back home to New York. Don't use that. It's too weird, and private, and . . .

[*pause*]

You know what? Never mind. Use that too, if you want.

Intern: You sure?

Nico: Yeah. [*with a small laugh*] Catchphrase forever.

As of this writing, Maddie "Titania" Pearce has been missing for 144 days. Despite several attempts to find her, no trace has been found. She has not made any attempts at communication, with her family or anyone else. Her case is listed as active by the National Center for Missing & Exploited Children. In public matters, DV8 has maintained the position that Chazz Young stated on *The Perky Paisley Show,* that Titania absconded in an escape pod. In legal matters, the official stance of DV8 is that in the confusion of the SWAT team raid, she simply ran away.

It is my opinion that she did not.

I now leave it to you to decide for yourself.

Item: Transcript of video recording
Source: Nico's camera
Battery charge: 100%
Date: March 1, 2016

[*Nico is looking directly into the camera.*]

Hi Mom. Hi Dad.

I'm home.

A lot happened since my last video to you, right before the nosebleeds. Too much to describe. I'll do it someday, I promise.

Long story short, she's gone.

[*He exhales.*]

Part of me wishes I'd said, out loud, how much she meant to me. But the other part of me knows I didn't have to.

She told *me*, though. Right before the end, the last time we were both in the Confessional Closet together. When it seemed like she had given up. She told me that I mattered to her.

I grabbed her hand just then. I couldn't help it. Not in an I-love-you way—though I probably did love her—but in a you-are-not-alone way. A we-are-both-alive-at-the-same-time-and-here-is-the-proof way.

It was my favorite part. Out of everything.

So I think she knew.

[*He takes a deep breath.*]

The last time I saw her—the footage doesn't do it justice. That split second of video, right before it cuts out—it's *bad*. The light is too bright. The image is blown out. All you can make out is her figure walking into a circle of white light.

Even though we were all looking at the same thing, I don't think anyone saw what I saw, except for her. What we both saw on the other side of that wall.

And even when Chazz was grilling me about what happened, even though I told him where she went—I haven't told anyone about what else I saw. It feels wrong to. Like I'm betraying her trust.

But on the other hand, I can't let her be remembered like that. A runaway, a missing person. A liar, a coward. Especially when none of it's true.

Maybe one day I'll tell the rest of the world. But I don't think they'll believe me. So for now, you're the only ones who get to know what I saw.

What I saw was:

Blue.

A whole planet of it.

Blue snow blanketing the ground.

Blue flakes falling from the sky.

Blue above, blue below.

A gentle wind blowing through the trees.

A little girl in the distance.

And quiet.

Pure, still, absolute quiet.

I hope she's happy there.

I hope you are too.